Désirée Meyler

Forget Tomorrow

St. Martin's Press, New York

FOR RICHARD HAMERSLEY

Copyright © 1981 by Désirée Meyler
For information, write: St. Martin's Press,
175 Fifth Avenue, New York, N.Y. 10010
Manufactured in the United States of America

Library of Congress Cataloging in Publication Data

Meyler, Désirée.
  Forget tomorrow.

  1. Title.
PR6063.E86F6   1982   823'.914   81-14595
ISBN 0-312-29894-3   AACR2

First published in Great Britain by Macdonald/Futura Publishers Ltd.

Forget to-morrow !
Weep nothing : only lay
In silent sorrow
Thine head my way :
Let us forget to-morrow
This one day !

Ernest Dowson (*Verses,* 1896)

PROLOGUE

Through the thin wall Hester could hear her stepmother in bed with the lodger. She rolled over in her bed and stuffed her ears. Night after night when her father was out at the Black Bull, Sal would be in with the lodger. 'Just taking him his supper,' she would say airily as she passed Hester's door. But Hester knew that they made love: the walls were so *thin.*

She was only fourteen, but there had been precious little shelter in her life since her mother died two years ago and her father had married Sal Ribbans. She and her mother, Nancy Kelsey, had known Sal by sight for she was one of the herring-gutters on the fish pier – one of the band of tough, rowdy women whose clogs stood ankle deep in fish entrails and heads, who kept up a lively conversation all day by a series of shouts. They were there in all weathers, their faces red with the salt air, their toughened hands moving so fast among the fish that you couldn't see them.

Sal had been one of the liveliest of them, a gipsy beauty not much older than Hester herself, who seemed to have the most raucous tongue of them all and could hold her own among the fishermen, of whom Hester's father was one. Sometimes when she and her mother had passed them, Sal had called out, winking knowingly as she did so. Her mother had always said, 'Don't look at them,' holding her remnants of respectability round her like a cloak.

Then she had died and Will Kelsey had wasted very little time in marrying Sal and bringing her to live in the row of cottages overlooking the harbour. He had been a handsome fellow once, poor Will, before the drink got him. There was still an air of the buccaneer about him when Sal married him; but it had soon faded and she had begun to turn her attention elsewhere. The lodger was not really a lodger at all, Hester knew. It was easy to fool her father nowadays when he was always befuddled, and Sal did so blithely and recklessly. When Will fell in at the door, Sal would nip downstairs and drag him onto the couch in the little front room. Then she would go back upstairs to hand-some Ben Warley, mate of the *Coral Maid*.

Hester unstuffed her ears and relit her candle. She won-dered what time it was. They were quiet next door now, so she reopened her book and was soon lost to the world. The new lending library up in the town had opened up fresh vistas for Hester and, at the moment, she was shedding tears over *The Mill on the Floss*. Sometimes she read until the candle guttered, and still her father hadn't come home. Then she would lie awake and worry, knowing a sweet relief when at last she heard his stumbling footsteps.

She raised her head now and listened intently. He was coming. Or was it someone else? The footsteps weren't stumbling tonight, but quiet and purposeful. No, it was probably only Mr Ross from three doors away. She returned to her book.

The next thing she knew was a terrible cry from the room next door. 'No, Will, no!' Sal was screaming now.

Hester jumped out of bed. It *had* been Father then – but so quietly that she hadn't heard him mount the stairs. And he was there – in the lodger's room where Sal had been for the last hour. . . .

Someone was shouting in a choking voice and Sal was shrieking: 'Let him go, you varmint. . . . '

Hester ran out onto the tiny landing and saw the horrify-ing shadows dipping and swaying in the lodger's room. Sal burst out of the room naked, her face distorted, yelling at the top of her voice: 'Get the police – get the police. . . . '

10

But Hester was rooted to the spot, watching her powerfully-built father beat the much smaller lodger with his bare hands — hands that now possessed the power of a maniac. There was a last choking cry then the man lay quite still. He was naked too, Hester saw as she crouched on the landing unable to move. It was only when Sal shrieked again, 'No, Will, no!' that she came to life, for her father was now advancing on the girl as she tried to retreat, beseeching him, cajoling, her voice ragged and thin. 'No, Will, don't do it . . . . I beg you, Will . . . he made me do it . . . Will. . . . '

The big powerful hands were closing on her olive-skinned throat, choking the life out of her. Hester sprang at her father, trying to pull him away, beating at him with her hands — but to no avail. He hardly noticed her.

Then suddenly he stopped. He straightened, looking down on his weeping child with eyes that hardly saw her. He was panting hoarsely like an animal, his whole body heaving. He flung away Hester's hands, turned and lumbered down the stairs and out into the night, leaving her with the lodger and Sal, both naked, both dead.

PART ONE
Hester Kelsey

CHAPTER ONE

It was market day at Sewerston. February: a bitter cold day in Queen Victoria's golden jubilee year. Already the little shops were displaying loyal messages. Large posters in garish colours depicted Her Majesty looking severe under a queen-empress's crown. Red, white and blue favours were already for sale at Willy Hoggarth's newsagent's shop: trust Willy to be first on the market, his rivals noted sourly.

Hard flecks of snow were settling on the canvas awnings of the market stalls congregated on the cobbled square. Wrapped up to their noses, the stallholders shivered and blew on their raw hands, stamping their feet and losing patience with the few sluggish customers who wandered about. A hurdy-gurdy was playing on one corner, and a group of children who had been bowling their hoops, had gathered round.

'Come on, lady, a fine cabbage for the pot!' they yelled, holding up the largest they could find. 'How about a fine big swede to fill your man's belly? Only a penny.'

The tinker selling pots and pans was making the biggest noise of the lot. He roared and ranted, rattling the goods enticingly while he reduced them by the minute. All to no avail. People were too cold to linger and hurried past. Very little money changed hands that day.

The farmers, arriving in their best clothes, had disappeared into the warmth of the Black Bull or the Rising Sun Inn. Their wagons were drawn up on the fringe of the market and children tumbled in and out of them; while the farmers' wives went along to the Sewerston Emporium to buy lengths of gingham and calico for dresses to meet the spring when it came. Up here in North Yorkshire that wouldn't be until late in April. Nevertheless, with Christmas well behind them now, it was pleasant to look forward hopefully to warmer weather. The saddler's shop was also full, and one or two farmers were having their hair cut at Ogwyn's the barber's.

Outside Newlands, the Farm Produce Centre as it was rather grandly called, hung a whole range of meat, poultry and rabbits. Mr Newlands prided himself on having the custom of all the big houses in the area and carriages were to be seen stopping outside his shop every day. In his white coat, blue-and-white apron and straw hat, Mr Newlands himself emerged to bow and scrape before the quality, advising and taking orders from Lady Prickard, Mrs Cates and the Honourable Mrs Winfield-Woods. The market was quite beneath Mr Newland's notice, although the stalls were nearly up to his door. None of *his* customers would visit the stalls selling belly pork, chitterlings and pigs' trotters.

Mr Beddows, the fishmonger across the square, was in the same class as Mr Newlands: the carriage trade was entirely theirs and that was where the money was.

On the days of Sewerston Fair (twice a year, in spring and autumn) the shops closed their doors, for not only horses, cattle and sheep thronged the streets; but also their drovers and bands of gipsies with horses to sell. Sewerston Fair was a day to make a solid tradesman shudder.

Into the noise and clatter of the square now came a little procession: two men, one in front and one behind, pushing the parish bier on which rested a cheap coffin. No brass handles or plates shone from the poor deal box. No flowers softened it. Four black-garbed people walked behind – all women. A tall thin female wrapped in a shabby cloak and wearing a purple velvet bonnet led the procession. She held her head proudly, even disdainfully, her eyes deliberately

16

unseeing. The square might have been empty for all the notice she took of onlookers.

Men doffed their caps and drew aside, silence falling over them. A funeral was a funeral, whether the coffin travelled in a glass coach pulled by plumed horses or not. Besides, it was the way many of them would travel up to the new town cemetery themselves.

And then a word began to be whispered from mouth to mouth.

'It's the murderer....'

'Murderer!'

'It's him, Will Kelsey....'

'*Murderer.*'

They said the word with relish. It was only twenty years since the last public execution had taken place. Although Will Kelsey's crime had gone unindicted because he had killed himself, there was a feeling of excitement, that a crime had been committed here in Sewerston, where nothing much had happened for years.

The woman in the purple bonnet stalked on, her head held high. But the three who followed her were obviously and painfully startled and frightened by the wave of animosity sweeping the square. Two of them looked sufficiently like the woman walking ahead for the onlookers to see they were sisters. Grey-haired and white faced, with that peculiar pallor of people who seldom went out, they scurried in the wake of their sister; looking as miserable as if they, and not the man in the coffin, had committed Sewerston's worst crime for years. They dragged the slight figure of a young girl between them. She was nearly as tall as the women although not yet fifteen. She wore a black woollen cap and a jacket that had once been navy blue, but was now worn to antique-green. A limp blue skirt emerged from under the jacket and hung crookedly over her stout boots, too stout and heavy for her slim legs. She was dressed like a child and yet was nearly a woman. Two dark plaits sticking out from under the cap framed a small wedge-shaped face. She kept her eyes resolutely down, too frightened to look at the people who were now hissing her father's body on its last journey. Her teeth were biting her lower lip and she was doing her best not to cry. Hester Kelsey could hear the ugly words they were hurling after the coffin and fear was making her feel weak. Were those rough-looking men going to attack them? Oh, why hadn't the aunts taken another route to the cemetery even if it were longer? It had something to do with Aunt Agatha refusing to pay the undertaker's men more money. To Hester it was one more example of the misery of not having any money. The rich could ride past in a closed carriage and not be exposed to the insults of the mob. Some day, she told herself grimly, some day I'm going to be rich too. It's not worth living if you aren't rich.

Particles of ice stung their faces, but Hester hardly felt them. The pace of the procession was slower now and the men were breathing hard, as they began to go up the incline on the further side of the square. The word 'Murderer!' still followed them, and it was only some hidden depth of self-control that kept the terrified tears from rolling down her face. Aunt Martha was already snuffling like a small frightened animal and Aunt Mary kept repeating over and over under her breath: 'I told Agatha how it would be . . . I told her. . . . ' But Agatha Kelsey stalked ahead of them, unmoved by the mob.

At last they were out of the square and climbing the hill to the cemetery. A tall man about to cross the road paused to allow the small procession to pass. He was very well-dressed in a Chesterfield coat of finest black facecloth and a silk top hat. His hands were covered by dogskin gloves and he carried an ebony cane.

Sir Joseph Prickard had once been the owner of a fishing vessel and had taken it to the fishing grounds himself. Now, newly created a baronet, he owned a fleet of deep-sea trawlers and passenger-carrying vessels. In local parlance he had 'done well for himself'. He was a ruddy-faced man with a protruding lower lip and a large thrusting nose. With his grey side whiskers there was still an air of the sea about him. His red skin was made up of a series of tiny broken blood vessels and his small clear blue eyes were as alert and far-seeing as they had ever been.

As he waited impatiently, taking off his tall hat automatically, he glanced at the women trudging up the hill behind the pauper's coffin.

Hester raised her eyes and saw this imposing figure regarding them with benevolent curiosity. She wondered who he was and tried not to stare at his splendid clothes. He couldn't be the Prince of Wales, could he? For she had heard *he* was very grand. But she knew the prince had a beard, for she had seen a drawing of him in a newspaper. Yet this man was also very grand in his way although he hadn't got a beard. She looked him full in the face as she passed.

Sir Joseph's eyes had sharpened. Embarrassed recognition crossed his face as he recognized the three Miss Kelseys. Then he met the girl's eyes and felt a sharp stab. Just as if something had stung him, he thought, as he jerked his head after them. For those eyes had belonged to his half-sister, Nancy; they were clear and turquoise in colour with a strange outer ring of dark blue to them. Highly unusual eyes. Rare eyes one couldn't forget. That girl must be Nancy's child.

The leading figure in the procession had seen him and, without a sign, had continued up the hill. But the girl had done an unaccountable thing: she had turned to stare again, and had been called to order by the women on either side.

Prickard stared after them, flooded by a swift tide of memory. He realized at last what the sullen murmur of voices had been uttering. *Murderer.* So that deal box was taking Will Kelsey to his last resting place. Well, he had hated the fellow for years for taking Nancy and ruining her life. Could he hate him now? He didn't think so. Pity was uppermost in Prickard's mind as he stared after his brother-in-law's funeral. The man had ended his life in the harbour. So that was the child. A tall slim girl on the edge of womanhood whom he had never seen before. Nancy's girl. Well, well. He took out a fine linen handkerchief and blew his nose. Life was queer and no mistake, he told himself. Then, replacing his hat, he crossed the road with his head in the air, elbowing people out of his path, until he reached the sedate green door of his solicitor's office.

'Here comes Sir Joe,' one of the clerks hissed, bobbing his head below the frosted glass of the window. Into this window were traced the words ALFRED BRACEGIRDLE SOLICITOR AND COMMISSIONER FOR OATHS. 'Walking like the furies was after him,' went on the clerk, taking another peep. 'And he's . . . ow, Mr Jordan, that hurt!'

'You mind your own business, young Boothroyd,' the chief clerk told him, relinquishing his ear, 'and nip upstairs and tell the governor Sir Joseph's here – none of your Sir Joe's, mind. You've no respect, you young'uns. And blow your nose. There's a drip on the end.' Mr Jordan smoothed his own hair and ran an exploratory hand over the straggling beard that covered his small face. Sir Joseph Prickard with his piercing eyes and blunt uncompromising manner had this effect on underlings; they were apt to flutter nervously in his presence. Now Bracegirdle's chief clerk, having run his hands over himself and found a fly button undone, was bowing in their richest client.

'Good morning, Sir Joseph. An inclement one if I may say so. May I take your coat, sir?'

'You may not. This place is as cold as a morgue,' Sir Joseph was looking round with distaste. The fire in the iron grate was only a heap of slag from which a small tail of brown smoke issued. 'Why don't you keep a decent fire going, eh? Coal's cheap enough.'

'There's a nice fire in Mr Bracegirdle's room, sir,' the clerk assured him. 'Boothroyd has gone upstairs to inform Mr Bracegirdle of your presence here below, so perhaps you would just step this way, sir? Thank you, sir, allow me.'

Obsequiously, he bowed their client out. The stairs were narrow, covered in worn oilcloth and ill-lit. What scroungers these dam' solicitors are, Prickard thought as he followed the anxious chief clerk. Top fees. All profit. No coal downstairs, no light on the stairs. Moneygrubbers.

Mr Bracegirdle, pale and clean-shaven, rose to greet his important client and friend. 'Joe! Delighted to see you, my dear fellow. Come and sit by the fire. That will be all, Jordan.'

'How much do you pay that fellow?'

'Who? Jordan? My dear Joe, what a question! As if I could possibly remember off-hand! But he's doing well – very well, I should say. And they've nothing to spend it on, you know. Nothing to keep up like you and me. He's got a nice little house behind the harbour – I own it and he pays me rent. I own all that lot behind your house, you know. Bought the last parcel of land only last year.'

'I should know.' Prickard's voice was dry. 'You pipped me to the post.'

'I did?' The solicitor raised pale brows. 'My dear fellow, I'm sorry to hear that. I assure you I had no idea.'

Prickard smiled, saying no more. But as he looked round the office, he thought what a complete contrast it presented to the one inhabited by the clerks below. Four clerks meant there was much business, yet they sat in an unheated room, coughing and sneezing over their ledgers, while icy air poured through the ill-fitting windows. Remembering the light and warmth in his own shipping office, Prickard felt a renewal of contempt for this mean man who was getting rich on the hardships of others. Misers always irritated Joseph Prickard. A generous man himself, he knew that cheeseparing didn't spell success, although it was obvious that Bracegirdle thought it did. His room was warm and comfortable, with a brisk fire and two red leather chairs drawn up before it.

Bracegirdle motioned him to one of the chairs. 'Would you like one of the clerks to make some tea?' He paused with a hand on the bell.

'Not for me, thank you. I'm lunching with Lord Abbotsbury at the County Club in half an hour.'

'Indeed?' Fingertips together, Alfred Bracegirdle digested this snippet. Now what was brewing there? he wondered. Joe

21

Prickard was getting too many irons in the fire all at once. Bracegirdle was one of the few who knew that the Prickard Line was going into the Liverpool-to-Boston route any day now. So, half-smiling, his eyes narrowed, Mr Bracegirdle hung on his client's words.

'He wants to put my name forward for High Sheriff next time.' Prickard threw down the words casually and enjoyed the chagrin in the other's eyes. He deduced that the solicitor had had an eye on that honour in the distant future. 'So I've decided to buy myself a place in the country. I'd like to go over my list of stocks and shares. I shall sell certain ones to cover the sale. The Harbour House should fetch a good sum too.'

'Where were you thinking of moving? I hear Bempton House is for sale. . . . '

'Oh, I don't think that would suit my needs at all. I had something larger in mind – Stanhope.'

Ambition, long dormant in the solicitor, now flared up like a Roman candle. 'But you must know I intended buying that place myself, Joe. Edith's father died in November and I can now contemplate a move. If I had known it was on the market. . . . '

'Alfred, don't let's fool ourselves. You couldn't buy Stanhope in a month of Sundays, let alone keep it up. You're not in the right income bracket, my dear fellow. Now if you'd like to make an offer for my house I might consider it. It would be a vast improvement on Norton Terrace – quite a rise in the world for you. I know how much Edith's father left – quite good for a small draper, but nowhere near the price being asked for Stanhope. I'm stretching myself a little to buy it. However it's a risk worth taking with the Atlantic route to start next month.' Prickard had spoken dryly and rather cruelly, but Bracegirdle's social ambitions (which stemmed from his wife) always irritated him. 'I'll not horse-deal with you. We'll get in reliable agents to fix a price – it won't be a fancy one, I promise you. You've been working like a beaver to buy up all those piffling properties behind the harbour and the gamble hasn't come off, I'm afraid. You knew I needed to expand in my business and thought of the land behind the Harbour House. But I found all the land I needed the other side of town and I'm afraid you've been landed with a lot of small houses with leaking roofs. They don't bring in much in the way of rents, do they?' He gave a sudden roar of laughter at the discomfiture on the other's face. 'Let that be a lesson to you, lad! Don't use your knowledge of clients' affairs to feather your own nest. It seldom works.'

Mr Bracegirdle restrained harsh words with difficulty. Inspecting his nails, he smiled in a chilly manner. Now it was his turn for a dig. 'Maybe you are right. By the way, did you see poor Will Kelsey's funeral passing through the square? A pauper's funeral – a man with rich relations.'

Prickard chose to misunderstand him. 'I don't think those poor old sisters have a penny, you know. They own that tiny millinery shop and the property's mortgaged, no doubt. Not one of yours, Alfred?'

Bracegirdle shook his head. 'What a tragic end he had. Married your sister, didn't he?'

'My half-sister ran away from home and married against her mother's will. Her father – my father he was too – was dead by that time, not that it would have had any effect on her. She was determined to marry handsome Will Kelsey.' Prickard gave a heavy sigh, for the memory was sore within him. 'She was only seventeen. A child. He wasn't doing too badly then, with his own boat. But there was already something unstable about him. Women, drink, fisticuffs with other fishermen. I knew he would never amount to a row of beans.'

'You ought to have brought her home.' Mr Bracegirdle allowed a modicum of reproach to filter into his voice; not enough to antagonize, but just enough to stir regret in Joe Prickard's heart, for the fellow was too cocksure.

He was shaking his head sombrely, his eyes fixed on a point above the solicitor's head. 'It was too late. She was two

23

months pregnant. My stepmother went to see her occasionally, but I never saw her again.'

'Poor young woman. She needed help by all accounts. When Kelsey became an alcoholic there wasn't a man who would sail with him.'

'She knew where I lived. She could have come back any time but she had too much pride,' Prickard said in a low voice.

Pride. They had both possessed more than a fair share of that. 'I'll never speak to you again, Joe!' she had cried and she never had. And he had deliberately cut her out of his life. She had made her own bed, now let her lie on it, he had told his stepmother time and time again. Yet he had doted for years on this very much younger little half-sister, he remembered. She would have been only thirty-two or three now if she had lived; but she had died after a long illness two years ago. She had kept the illness a secret even from her mother, and when the end was near he was abroad. The first bitter news reached him in Aberdeen where he had gone on business. *Nancy is dead*, his stepmother had written and he had wept, sitting in that hotel bedroom in Aberdeen.

A few months later Kelsey had married a trollop, a young herring-gutter, a wild-looking beauty whom all the men knew as 'a dam' good sort' with all that meant. It had seemed to Joe Prickard an insult to Nancy, that her husband should marry a woman of that kind. Then, only ten days ago, Kelsey had come home to find her in bed with another man and his child asleep in her room. He had killed the man first, using his demonic strength, then strangled the screaming woman in front of his daughter; silencing her lying tongue for ever.

And all the time his own girl had watched, her hands to her mouth, terror rooting her to the spot.

Prickard had read an account of the double murder in the local paper, and been sickened to see his own sister's name mentioned. It had been just as well the poor wretch had ended his life in the black, greasy water of the harbour. He had saved a great deal of trouble all round by so doing.

Of course there had been an inquest and young Hester

Kelsey, the only witness, had given her faltering evidence. But her name had meant little to him; she was just the child who had caused his sister to marry Kelsey in the first place. He had felt he hated her – Kelsey's daughter, he had thought with loathing. And then today he had seen her, seen those eyes that were Nancy's again. My God, but life was queer.

He came out of his reverie to find Bracegirdle's eyes fixed calculatingly on him. 'What ought I to do about the child?' he asked abruptly. It was his nature to go to the heart of the matter. It was too late to help Nancy, but there was the child. There was much he could do for her; after all she was an orphan now.

Bracegirdle sighed to himself. It seemed that there was no way he could make Joe Prickard feel ashamed of the past or of his relations. He had no false snobberies, and perhaps that was why he had succeeded in the way he had. Even this unsavoury business about his brother-in-law hadn't had the effect it would have had on many men. 'You could offer to bring her up, couldn't you? The Miss Kelseys haven't much money – Will had a pauper's funeral.'

Prickard shrugged. 'Agatha Kelsey wouldn't put her hand in her pocket for that fellow and I don't blame her. But I'm sure you're right – they'll have barely enough to live on themselves. A girl like that will need clothing and feeding.'

'Or putting out to work herself.'

Prickard nodded slowly. 'They might put her in a shop or send her into service.' Nancy would have hated that, he thought sadly. The girl was little more than a child and her eyes had held quick intelligence. He heaved himself out of his chair, thrust out a hand. 'Well, I'm glad we've had this talk. It's cleared my mind. I'll see to things right away. She could take my name, be like my own daughter.'

Bracegirdle took the proffered hand and then walked to the door. 'But your wife, Joe? Would she care for the idea? You have a boy of your own, after all.'

'Ellen will do what I want as she always does,' Prickard said with assurance. 'As for Wilfred, it will do him good to have a sister at last. He's getting to be a spoilt lad.'

Alfred Bracegirdle sucked in his cheeks dubiously. 'They're a bit old to start being "brother" and "sister", Joe. Could be trouble there.'

But Prickard only laughed. 'Oh, rubbish, man. Wilfred's very immature for his age and the girl's a mere child. Well, we'll take a look at my shares another day. I must go. Abbotsbury doesn't like being kept waiting.' And with a nod he went down the stairs, his heavy footsteps making the rather shaky edifice echo.

Bracegirdle shut the door and stood deep in thought. His client's visit had given him much to think about. It was all very well for Joe Prickard, he had enough money to sail through every difficulty. Stanhope Manor. High Sheriff perhaps next year. The Atlantic route for the Prickard Line next month – those were the things people would associate him with and not this morning's pauper's funeral, the orphan girl who walked behind in rags and was his niece, the double murder and then the suicide. It could have ruined a lesser man, the solicitor thought moodily.

Snow was falling in earnest now. It had partly obliterated the sign over the bow window of *A. and M. Kelsey, Milliners*. The M was Mary. Poor Martha was too ham-handed to be of much use in the shop, so true to her name, she was the cook and housekeeper and seemed contented in her role.

Agatha fumbled in the dolly bag that hung from her thin arm and eventually retrieved the key to the shop. The other three shivered unhappily on the top step and Mary said for the hundredth time: 'I wish we could build on a porch. This wind comes straight off the sea.'

Agatha's look was meant to wither such inanity. 'Wipe your feet,' she told the girl sharply. 'If you're going to live here, you'd best learn our ways. I hope your fire's not out Martha, for I've never felt more in need of a cup of tea in my life.'

'No, I made sure by building it up before we left,' Martha

assured her. 'It ought to be nice and red by now.' She had a very homely Yorkshire voice and Hester had decided that if there was any warmth and friendliness it lay with this aunt.

'Shall I help you, Aunt Martha?' she asked, as they all paused in the narrow passage.

Agatha, undoing the strings of the purple bonnet, swung round, her long face sardonic. 'Oh, so you've found your voice, have you? I was beginning to wonder if you had one. No, you'll not help your aunt Martha as I want to speak to you and there's no time like the present.' She led the way into the square room behind the shop.

It had heavily-decorated wallpaper that made it even more claustrophobic and Hester went in and looked round rather fearfully. One tall window overlooked the yard and had Nottingham lace curtains across it. A glass door leading into the shop was shrouded in a similar pair. An iron stove in the corner emitted quite a lot of warmth as Mary Kelsey rattled it into life. Two of the walls were covered in shelves, where the stuff of their trade was stored in white boxes. Most of the room was filled with a mahogany table covered in green baize on which were laid sharp scissors, an iron, velvet pads, shapers, curling tongs for feathers, boxes of pins and threads, spools of ribbon. A half-finished hat stood on a stand and Hester bent over it, her eyes gleaming with interest. But Agatha's hand came down and pulled her away. 'Don't you dare touch anything in this room, girl.'

'Oh, no, Aunt. I was only looking. It's such a funny hat — like a cake in ribbons.'

'Don't talk nonsense and sit there,' Agatha directed, pointing to a horsehair sofa under the window. 'There's a lot that you and me need to clear up between us. First of all, I'm the head of this establishment and what I say is final. Understood?'

Hester, her eyes wide with surprise, shook her head.

'Good gracious, girl, don't you understand plain English?'

'But I shan't be living here, Aunt Agatha. I live down in the harbour and after we've had tea I'm going back there.'

'Rubbish, you're not setting foot in that hovel again. If there's a stick of furniture worth selling then it can go to the sale room, but it's my belief that the whole lot wants burning. As for living there, you can think again. From this day on, your home is here and it's on our charity that you'll be living. Martha, is that tea ready?'

'Coming, Agatha.' The door was pushed open and Aunt Martha and her loaded tray lumbered in. The girl's eyes didn't brighten at the sight of the plates of sandwiches, sausage rolls and 'funeral cake' from the bakery. She had not eaten all day and turned her head away, aware of an aching anxiety and fear. It would kill her to live here in this horrible old house that smelt damp, with these three aunts whom she barely knew; for they had had no dealings with her father. Especially Aunt Agatha. There was something steely about Agatha that struck terror into the girl's heart. She thought with longing of the easy-going Sal, her father's wife, who had let her do what she liked all day, and of the father who gave her a rollicking affection when he wasn't too drunk. She swallowed nervously and said, no, she didn't want any tea, thank you. Her head was beginning to ache now and she felt sick. The scenes of the last ten days were flashing across her brain like a permanent nightmare. She could see the expression on poor Sal's face as her father's huge hands closed on her throat, the look of disbelief, her last cry of 'Will, don't. . . . ' choked off for ever, and her own screams going on and on.

'Did you hear what I said? You're not deaf, are you? Then take this cup of tea and don't be silly. Pass the sausage rolls, Mary.'

'No, I couldn't. . . . '

'Do as you're told.' Agatha, who had never had a child, was in her glory with this young thing; frail and timid as a rabbit, sitting on the sofa and shaking beneath her glance. 'We don't stand any nonsense in this house. You don't want to get sent to bed, do you?'

Hester shook her head, the cup shaking in her hands. Forc-

28

ing back the tears, she attempted to drink the tea. It was scalding and burned her mouth. Horrified, she put it down, attempted to bite into the hard shiny crust of a sausage roll and failed. Huge tears began to roll down her cheeks.

'Leave her, sister,' Martha said, hastily filling Agatha's plate again. 'She'll come round. It's strange for her here just yet.'

'She'd better,' Agatha said direfully, 'or I'll have something to say before long.'

If only they would let her go! Let her creep off to some dark hole and cry it out! But, no. They had held her prisoner since that morning, when they had fetched her from a neighbour's to attend her father's funeral. There had been policemen in her life for a week and the aunts, holding her between them as if afraid she might escape, seemed to her to be policemen too. Soon they would begin to question her and she would have to find answers. But her head ached so that she felt she couldn't begin to understand their questions.

'There's no money for you to learn a trade,' Aunt Agatha was saying. 'But I can find you plenty to do.'

'She can help me in the house, sister,' Martha suggested but Mary, who had been quietly eating a large meal, suddenly observed, 'We've needed someone for a long time to take out the orders. Hester would be good at that.'

Hester looked up and scrubbed the tears away. 'Yes, I could do that,' she agreed with animation.

Agatha's eyes narrowed. 'We shall see,' she said. 'I'll have to think about it. She can't take the orders out in those rags. We would have to find her a jacket and that means more expense.'

'Oh, I don't know, Agatha; the secondhand stall in the market is very good. I'll take her along next week. Martha can knit her a new cap . . . then there's her boots. . . . ' All three aunts bent their heads to stare at what were quite obviously boys' boots on their niece's feet.

'Boots!' Agatha groaned. 'That means all of ten shillings for boots. She's going to be nothing but expense from beginning to end.' She began to do hasty sums on a pad. 'I hope you appreciate what we're doing for you,' she told Hester. 'After your father's disgraced us, too. I'll never forgive Will, never. Us with a business to run, too. In a place like this everyone knows everyone's business and there was no use trying to hide he was our brother. Well, he's buried now and I don't want him mentioned again . . . nor the whole disgusting business. Do you understand?'

Hester nodded wearily. 'Yes, Aunt Agatha.'

Mary nodded approvingly. At least she had good manners, she whispered to her sisters. Nancy Kelsey had taught her well. 'Can you read? Read and write? It would be a help if you could.'

Hester stared. 'Of course I can. Mother taught me every day until . . . until. . . . ' Her voice trailed away.

'Can you do simple sums?'

'Well, I can but I'm not very good. Mother used to say I didn't try hard enough.'

Mary looked triumphantly at the other two. 'It's my belief that Hester will be very useful to us. You know you've never liked the paper work, Agatha, Martha's worse than useless and spelling's not my strong point.' Comfortably full of rich funeral cake, Mary beamed round the circle.

'Take the tray away, Martha.' Agatha flapped her hand in dismissal. 'Before we start making all these grand plans we'll have to see how madam here shapes. Now listen to me Hester, every morning you'll get up as soon as we waken you. Then you'll come down here and tidy this room. The flat iron has to be heated on the stove over there, so first you'll see to that. You'll rake out the ashes and make a fresh fire. Then you'll wash the tiles round it and the four outside steps. Then you'll wash your hands and lay out – carefully mind – the contents of this box. Like this. The pads here, the stand there. . . . ' On and on, relentless as a stream went Agatha's voice and Hester murmured assent now and again. But she was too bewildered to take much in.

The other sisters listened with growing interest, as the most disliked early morning tasks were taken off their shoulders and given to their niece to perform. They looked on with admiration. How clever of Agatha to see how useful the girl could be in return for her keep.

'I hope you appreciate what we're doing for you,' she said once more.

'Yes, Aunt Agatha. Thank you.'

The dark day grew even darker, but no one made a move to light the brass oil lamp in the centre of the work table. Hester wondered if the aunts had forgotten to do so. Their disembodied voices continued to come from the dark corners of the room, but no one brought light to the proceedings. She was to learn that this was part of the sisters' way of life. They always downed tools as evening drew on in the winter. They called it 'saving an hour', which was another way of saying that they had saved some precious oil. When it was nearly pitch black and Hester was almost asleep, Mary lit a spill at the stove and the ceremony of lighting the lamp was gone through. Supper was eaten in the basement kitchen. Here was real warmth, the smell of home baked bread, a settle and a rocking chair before the big black stove, a scrubbed oak table and a dresser. Out of the oven came potatoes baked in their jackets into which one plunged a lump of butter and a piece of cheese. A jug of cocoa was set on the table and the sisters ate in silence. They never spoke at the table she was to learn. Just a terse prayer from Agatha and then silence except for the sounds of eating.

There was no sink, only a tap in the wall and a bucket under it to catch the drips. Water out of the iron kettle was poured into a bowl and Martha washed the dishes and set them on end on a tin tray. Hester dried them carefully and Mary walked to and fro putting them away. Agatha sat and rocked in the chair, her eyes going from one to the other. But she said nothing although Hester could feel her watching. The house had no bathroom and the privy was a small odorous shed in the yard.

31

Presently Mary lit a small lamp. 'It's time you were in bed, Hester. Say goodnight to your aunts.'

Dutifully she kissed them, shuddering a little at the whiskery dryness that was Aunt Agatha's cheek.

As they climbed up through the narrow slice of house there seemed to be three storeys not counting the basement. Mary showed her the unoccupied bedrooms on each floor. 'We take in boarders come the summer. We three sleep in that big room over there.' She held the lamp high, so that Hester could see the cold rooms with the polished linoleum floors and the iron bedsteads with striped mattresses rolled back at each foot.

Hester looked, beginning to shiver with cold and apprehension. Where in this cold and gloomy house was she going to sleep herself? Not with Aunt Agatha, she prayed hastily.

But no, they were mounting yet another staircase. 'We've prepared the attic for you,' Aunt Mary said, leading the way into the darkness. 'We shan't hear if you make a noise, Agatha thought.'

There was a queer smell up here. The girl sniffed delicately like a young dog – she knew that scent. It must be apples and onions they had stored here. Perhaps there would be rats to eat them too, she thought with aversion.

The room that was to be hers was very small and clean. It was under the eaves, lit only by a skylight through which the wind now whined. The bed was hard and lumpy, no better than the bed at home, she realized with disappointment. The sheets were rough and smelled of a long dampness. There was a piece of towel tacked behind the deal washstand; so that the walls could not be splashed. There was a cake of yellow soap for her use and a big jug of cold water for her to wash in. Beneath the wash-stand was a large chamberpot.

'Now we don't want to hear another sound from you until tomorrow morning.'

'No, Aunt Mary.'

'Martha will ring a bell on the landing at a quarter to seven tomorrow. You'll get up as soon as you hear it.'

'Yes, Aunt, I understand.'

Leaving half an inch of candle burning in a brass candle-stick Mary left, taking the lamp with her.

Hester stood and shivered on the icy linoleum. Above her head, the wind whined terrifyingly through the skylight. There was no window. She could feel it whistling through the slates and thin covering of plaster. Between the roof and the walls was a long gap, through which a few flakes of snow were now blown. She could plainly hear the roar of the sea coming up over the rooftops.

A terrible feeling of desolation enveloped her. At home they had been warm at least and had had enough to eat when Father sold his catch and brought back the money, before he spent it all in the Black Bull. Her bedroom had been above the road and there had been cheerful sounds of whistling and rough voices calling to one another. You never felt lonely down at the harbour. And when her mother was there they had . . . but the tears that had threatened for so long now overflowed and she cried noisily. The aunts wouldn't hear her, Aunt Mary had said so, so she cried with abandon and it did her good. Mopping her eyes with an arm, she began to climb out of her skirt.

Her small parcel of possessions had been left on the bed and, with icy fingers, she began to untie the string. The calico nightgown her mother had made her was now much too small, but it was all she had. The rest of her clothes had come to her a few weeks ago from the Sailors' Mission ladies. They had often come to the rescue since her mother died, and she had grown out of the few things that she had owned then. The calico drawers – no flounces and with a linen button on either side of the waistband – had been the result of the Sailors' Mission sewing bee. She looked at everything with loathing, the coarse cotton chafed wherever it touched her skin; everything was so ugly.

There was an eerie sound on the roof that made her jump. It must be a loose slate she told herself firmly. The candle gutted and went out. She stood very still, feeling panic rising

3   33

in her throat. She had meant to look in every dark corner before getting into bed. There were some queer shapes in the corner over there. . . . A shudder went through her and she leaped into bed – a stunning blow on the head reminding her too late of the curve in the roof. She lay under the thin blankets and shivered from cold and dread. Everything was so strange and uncomfortable at the aunts' house – all except the kitchen. If she could stay with Aunt Martha in the kitchen she could be happy, she felt.

She must have fallen asleep eventually, because the next thing she remembered was waking with a start. Her heart raced as she lay very still and listened. She felt that someone had been in the room, had been leaning over her to stare at her. She sat up, defensively pulling the bedclothes round her and said shakily, 'W-Who's there?'

There was no answer. As she listened, she heard the stairs creak as if someone was creeping down them, back to the empty storey below, or even further, to the aunts' room.

She didn't sleep again for hours, and when the bell went her eyes were heavy and her head ached.

When he emerged from his luncheon with Lord Abbotsbury at the County Club Prickard – who only drove about the small town in his carriage when accompanied by his wife – walked thoughtfully home. As he walked, his hands behind his back swung the silver-topped cane to and fro, to and fro, like the echo of his deep thoughts.

He was thinking again of his half-sister's child. Even during luncheon she had come into his mind. He knew he would have to do something about her. Those Kelsey women were in a poor way. They couldn't do much for the girl. They would probably make use of her; make her an unpaid skivvy.

His route took him back across the market square again. The light was failing fast this afternoon and already the tar-soaked flares were being lit. The stalls were doing a slightly brisker trade now, and the noise of hucksters and the shrill cries of children bowling their hoops round the square filled the air. But he was aware of none of it and presently he turned out of the square and began to descend towards the harbour and the sea. The wind blew hard up Chaundler's Street and he had to hold on to his hat. But his steady sailor's tread, feet planted well apart, didn't falter; although it was with some relief that he turned aside down a narrow lane which came out on a steep hill. At the top of this was his home, the Harbour House as it was known.

He turned in under a wide arch in a stone wall and looked at his property rather regretfully. It would be a wrench to leave here for Stanhope Manor, even though it would be a step up in the eyes of the world. They had lived here all their married life.

Three sides of a cobbled courtyard were bounded by the stone house, stables and coach house. The house had been built in the days of the Regent for the harbour master. Stiff Nottingham lace curtains, exactly equal in the way they were hung, garnished the staring windows. Snowy steps led up to a green front door with its brass knocker in the shape of an anchor. Joseph Prickard mounted them, turned the huge door handle and entered his home.

Agnes, the elderly parlour-maid, was hurrying across the hall to open the door for her master, having seen him from the stillroom window. She was a stout grey-haired body, who panted as she bobbed a curtsey. 'There, I'm just too late, sir, as usual,' she lamented, taking his hat from him and stroking its silk appreciatively. Having been with Prickard during his rise to fortune and a respected place in the county, she took a proprietary interest in the outer trappings of his wealth. There had been many times when she had threatened to give her notice in, finding her mistress impossible to please; but Prickard had refused to countenance it and had promised to look after her in her old age. Between them was a very good understanding and Agnes leaned forward now and muttered, 'The mistress is up in her room with one of them dratted headaches.'

Prickard nodded, but inwardly he sighed. Oh, Ellen, Ellen, one of your headaches again, he thought. He had diagnosed these long ago as boredom. She missed the boy whom he had insisted on sending away to one of the newer public schools, St. Peter's College at Radley. She had cried for a week with Wilfred's going. She had never cried when he went to sea, Prickard remembered resentfully. But the boy, their only child, loomed large in her life. Their sex life had been non-existent for years and he had long ago found comfort elsewhere. Instead of sex, she ate rich food in large quantities and was now a fat woman with frequent headaches and stomach upsets. To the world they were a happily-married couple and she enjoyed being Lady Prickard. But his room was on the other side of the landing and he came and went as he liked.

The swiftness of his rise in the world had taken her by surprise. They had been comfortably off for years, living in the Harbour House with Agnes as maid-of-all-work. He had sailed confidently through the trade depression of the last ten years by keeping his head, being cautious and never borrowing. When the crash came, caused in part by several bad harvests and the importing of foreign meat, he had been able to weather the storm and turn his boats back to fishing again. Many businesses like his had foundered when the money got tight. Four years ago he had started to expand a little. Then stopped. Then a further expansion while things were still cheap. Now it was literally full steam ahead: next month his ships would be setting out for the first time on the Liverpool-Boston route, carrying both passengers and cargo. He fully intended sailing on that first voyage himself, and was as excited as a schoolboy at the prospect. His new ship had been called *Golden Jubilee* and was the very latest steam model.

He rapped on his wife's door. 'Ellen?'

The room was in darkness.

'Is that you, Joe?' asked a faint voice from the direction of the bed.

36

'Yes, my dear, I've just got in. I'm sorry to hear you have a headache, but I daresay it's the best place to be on a day like this.' He strode across to the window and cautiously pulled back the heavy satin curtains a little, for the room was like a cave. Outside, darkness was falling like a veil across the sea. He watched the grey heaving water with nostalgic affection – at Stanhope they would be miles from the sea.

The figure in the bed was struggling into a sitting position. She wore a white cambric nightgown, much goffered and buttoned to the neck. A matching cambric cap with blue ribbons tied under her three chins. She looked like an ancient baby, he thought with distaste, wondering how on earth he had ever come to be physically in love with this woman. So much so at first, that he couldn't wait to get home at nights to take her to bed. He almost laughed aloud at the memory. The madness of young lusty love, he thought with a weary cynicism that had become second nature nowadays. He had gone thin with wanting Ellen Braintree, daughter of the local piano teacher, who had thought herself so much above a poor skipper of a sailing vessel. Now she lived in the luxury he provided and was a lazy peevish woman who only showed her best side to her sixteen-year-old son.

'I'm sorry you've got one of your heads, m'dear.'

She put a hand to it, blinking in the light that came from the window. 'It came on just after breakfast this morning. So I decided to stay in bed today.'

He visualized the breakfast one of the maids would have carted upstairs. The cream and butter, the eggs and ham and toast, a large pot of strong tea: enough for two or three people and she would eat everything herself. He stared at her – poor Ellen, she had become a glutton.

Now she was yawning and saying peevishly: 'Why doesn't Agnes bring me tea? I fancy a little toast. Where have you been, Joe?'

'I was lunching with Abbotsbury at the County Club. I told you yesterday.'

37

'Did you? My head's been so bad that I can't remember a thing. What's the time?'

'About four. Ellen, I want to talk to you. . . .

'*Four!* Then ring at once for Agnes. . . . '

'My dear, can I have a word with you before you do that?' He leaned over and lit the lamp by the bed, turning the wick down when she made a peevish movement. 'That's better.'

She drew a cashmere shawl over her shoulders. The fire had gone dull and needed mending, she noticed. She hoped he wasn't going to be too long in what he had to say – good heavens, was it about the bills? Well they were high but he could afford it. Then those clothes she had bought in Harrogate for the Mayor's reception had cost a great deal. She had also bought three bonnets there. She really couldn't be expected to wear Agatha Kelsey's bonnets on important occasions. She opened her mouth to defend herself but he spoke before her.

'I saw a funeral today. Kelsey's.'

'Oh?' she said blankly. She knew his bitter feelings about the fisherman who had captivated his adored half-sister, and she knew that they had nothing to do with the Kelsey family as such. The Kelseys had been respectable people for years; they had come down the social scale rapidly and had ended with Will killing that slut he had taken as a second wife. But everyone was sorry for the three sisters, who were careful quiet people.

'I saw his girl. Nancy's daughter. Ellen, we must bring her to live with us.'

She stiffened with shock. 'The Kelsey child? Impossible! Why, those people from the harbour are a terribly rough lot. And we've Wilfred to think of – yes, Wilfred,' she babbled, leaning forward in the bed. 'Joe, what about Wilfred? He's becoming such a little gentleman that we can't possibly expose him to the influence of the harbour people. Depend on it, that girl won't be fit company for our boy. Her language will be filthy . . . '

38

'Stop it,' he said, suppressed anger in his voice. 'If Wilfred finds himself too exclusive to mix with ordinary people then he'd better leave school at once.'

'You'd never do such a thing!' she gasped.

'Ellen, you must know me by now surely? I won't have a snob for a son. And you're forgetting that this is Nancy's child we're talking about. Nancy's only been dead two years – that's not long enough for the child to have deteriorated too much. I was wrong not to do something about her before, but I don't suppose Kelsey would have taken any help from me. It will do Wilfred all the good in the world to have another child in the house. He's getting spoilt. We should have had another child ourselves, Ellen.'

'You know I'm not strong!' Ellen retorted. 'Mother always wondered how I managed to have our Wilfred. It nearly killed me, remember? If you men knew what we women have to go through.' She was launched on her favourite theme of unsubtle bullying, reproaching him for giving her a child in the first place. So often did she resort to this weapon that it had ceased to have any effect, and he now brushed her aside impatiently.

'I saw the child in passing. She's tall but looks a child still; although she must be about thirteen or so.'

'She's older than that,' Ellen said tartly. 'Almost a woman.'

'She's too thin, of course, pale and thin. Needs feeding up. She has Nancy's eyes,' he added half to himself. 'Extraordinary to see those eyes again.' A feeling of warm pride went through him as he remembered Nancy's daughter; there had been nothing coarse about the girl. She had just looked poverty-stricken.

'Pity you didn't think of her years ago,' Ellen said spitefully. Anger made her want to turn that screw again. 'You never saw her again – well! you couldn't have cared much for your half-sister! Goodness knows, your step-mother pleaded with you often enough. But you were too stubborn to give way.'

'I know I was. I regret it bitterly now.' He took a turn about the room, his uneasy mind making him restless. 'I made up my mind to cut her out of my life and that was that. I was a damn sight harder in those days. I don't know how I could have done it . . . I loved her dearly. But when I heard she was having his child. . . . ' He stopped pacing and stared out of the window. My God, but he had wanted to kill Kelsey then! Nancy, his little sister who was almost young enough to be his daughter. Nancy who had looked to him for everything after his father died. New dancing slippers, a silk shawl, a bonnet – she could coax anything out of him. He had adored her for her prettiness, her wheedling ways and her high spirits. And then had come Kelsey, a man he employed on his own boat. A rascal with black curly hair and a lot of muscle. He had ruined her life had Kelsey, and Joseph had wanted to kill him with his bare hands. Instead he had washed his hands of her.

Ellen watched his back, her eyes smouldering resentfully. He had been much too fond of the girl, she told herself, much fonder than he had been of *her*. Now she could have her own back at last. 'Joe, I'm not strong enough to take that girl of Nancy's on.'

He turned round slowly and faced her. 'There's nothing wrong with you, Ellen. You're simply indolent.'

'Doctor Dent says it's my heart – I'm not at all strong but you'll never admit it, Joe.' She began to cry, reaching for a handkerchief on the side table.

God, what a mess she looks, he thought with cruel distaste. Raising his voice angrily, he found himself shouting that he wasn't surprised her heart was giving trouble as she never took any exercise and ate too much. But his anger was directed against himself really. His beloved sister had died in abject poverty because of his stubborn refusal to do anything for her. The only way he could repay this awful debt was by bringing up the child as his own. Hang Ellen and her refined objections. This time she would have to obey him.

Her eyes watched him resentfully over the handkerchief she was applying to them. What had got into Joe all of a sudden? Kelsey had been dead for over a week, but he hadn't hurried round to see the child or to enquire what was to become of her. It was seeing the girl this morning – yes, that was what had done it. She was frightened of him in this mood. She was aware that he let her have her own way most of the time because he no longer cared. It was all the more alarming when he turned on her like this.

'I've bought Stanhope Manor,' he said with an abrupt change of subject.

'Oh, Joe!' she said rapturously, her tears drying. 'That's wonderful news.'

'We'll have plenty of room there. You'll need more servants. We can employ a governess.'

Her joy faded as she saw the way his mind was moving. So he really meant what he said about adopting that girl.

'We can afford the best of everything now, Ellen – provided this government keeps income tax down to sixpence in the pound.' It had been a relief to him, as to many big business men, when Gladstone was defeated over the Home Rule for Ireland bill and a Conservative government under Lord Salisbury came to power. It looked as if the future was rosy now and long may the old queen stay on the throne. They were over the depression and the order was 'full steam ahead' for trade. 'There are boom years ahead and we can afford to branch out a bit.'

Branch out a bit. Was that what he called buying Stanhope, one of the best estates in the North Riding and empty since old Lord Garvin had gone bankrupt? There had been no heir to succeed him and when the old man died the title became extinct. And they were to live there now and some day Wilfred would succeed to the baronetcy and his son after him. Ellen's spirits bounded upward despite the dismal news about the Kelsey girl.

'My name is to be one of the three put up for High Sheriff next year. Abbotsbury is very keen.' It was nice to be able to call him *Abbotsbury*, when not long ago he had called him *my lord* and had stood cap in hand before him.

'You've done well, Joe, I'll say that, and you've been honest about it unlike some I could name. I'll have to think about the girl. I can't promise anything.'

He raised his eyebrows in secret amusement, for he knew that she realized the matter was entirely in his hands and she would have to do what he said. But it would be better if she welcomed Nancy's girl; for he wanted the child to be happy and have the best of everything. A governess, a pony to ride, new clothes – a whole new background, so that she would never have to think of the past.

He called on the Miss Kelseys a few days later.

It was Mary who saw the carriage outside the shop and cried, 'Look, sister, a gentleman's carriage. Now who can it be? It's not Mrs Cates – ' Then she saw the man who was getting out and speaking to his coachman. Oh, mercy, it was Sir Joseph Prickard, Sewerston's most successful son. Now what would he be wanting? Lady Prickard seldom bought from them now. Hastily, she tidied her hair with trembling hands and prepared a cautious smile of welcome.

Agatha, she saw with some surprise, wasn't agitating herself at all. Unmoved, she continued to arrange bonnets on stands for a window display of the new spring collection. 'Go through to the work room, Mary, and leave this to me. And see that Hester is employed in the kitchen. She can peel the potatoes. Whatever you do, don't tell her Sir Joseph is here – not that he will mean much to her, I daresay. Do as I say, Mary.' Mary was gaping a little, it really looked as if Agatha had *expected* this call. And as for Hester – surely Sir Joseph hadn't come about her?

'Go on, you fool, do as I say – quickly.' Smoothing her dress, seeing that her cameo brooch was in position at her throat, Miss Kelsey faced the door, a frosty smile touching her lips. She knew how to deal with Joe Prickard, she would punch where it hurt most. He had written her a formal note telling her he would call 'unless inconvenient' to discuss the future of his step-niece, Hester Kelsey.

The idea that the great Sir Joseph Prickard would want anything to do with the daughter of a man who had provided a nine-days wonder in the town had not occurred to her. When it did, she found she disliked the idea very much. Hester, this wretched little girl whose will she was determined to bend to hers, Hester would be the foster child of the richest man in the area. She would wear fine clothes and ride in a carriage. The idea was loathsome to Agatha Kelsey. What had Hester done to deserve such a thing? While they, the three Kelsey women, would continue to scratch a living making bonnets for the local tradesmen's wives. No, it didn't bear thinking about.

'Good morning, Sir Joseph. This is an unexpected pleasure.'

Prickard looked closely at the thin woman with the watchful eyes. She was totally unlike the handsome brother who had captured Nancy's fancy, he realized. 'Unexpected, Miss Kelsey? Did you not get my letter?'

Her eyes met his, daring him to bring in a note of intimacy. And suddenly, he knew he wasn't going to succeed in his mission; this woman had made up her mind already.

He looked round for a chair. 'Could we talk somewhere?'

She motioned him into the work room. 'Will you take a glass of Madeira?' Madeira and biscuits were kept here for favoured customers. One bottle usually lasted for months, but now she wanted to show this man that the niceties of life were within her reach.

'Thank you, no. I never drink in the mornings. I've come about Hester Kelsey, Miss Kelsey. My niece.'

She inclined her head. 'My niece too. Her father was my brother whereas her mother was only your half-sister, Sir Joseph, with whom you had had nothing to do for years. Hardly the same relationship.'

43

'I disapproved of the marriage,' Prickard said stiffly. 'She was much too young. But – for we mustn't mince words, Miss Kelsey – she was pregnant, a foolish silly child who didn't know what she was doing.'

'And your object in coming here today?'

Well, there was something to be said for this gaunt female, he thought; unlike most women she came straight to the point. So he would do the same. 'I want to adopt her.'

She was silent, feeling for words. But anger was warm inside her. So she had been right. He wanted to take Hester and raise her above her aunts, make a fine lady out of her. 'The answer must be no. Will would never have approved.'

This so took his breath away that he could think of nothing in return for a few moments. He leaned back in his chair, staring at her, wondering what her true feelings could be. A warped woman by the sound of her – warped and dangerous. Could she truly care for her niece's welfare? He knew that the Kelseys had no money and lived frugally on what the hat shop brought in. What could they do for Hester? He asked her that abruptly.

'Do? We shall feed and clothe her and in return she will help us in the house and shop. I intend to teach her the millinery trade so that she can take over from us some day. She has quite a bright future, I believe, and in many ways is a lucky girl.' She smiled again, that smile that held no warmth. 'Frankly, Sir Joseph, I'm very much surprised by your offer. I understood that you wished to have nothing to do with my brother's family.'

'That is true. I very much regret it now. I acted wrongly and harshly but I felt bitter at the time. If my sister hadn't died so prematurely, I have no doubt we should have been on friendly terms once more.'

'So you want to salve your conscience by adopting the girl? Really, Sir Joseph!'

He stared back wlth dislike. It appeared that her chief feeling was a desire to thwart him, to pay him back for ignoring them all in the past. Perhaps it was natural; she was using the only weapon she had at hand: the girl.

'Would you consider taking money for her welfare? I could put a monthly sum in your name.'

'Quite out of the question.' She rose, led the way to the door.

'Can I see the little girl?' He would like above everything to look into those eyes that were Nancy's – to look and remember.

'No.'

Bowing frostily, he went out and the shop bell rang a knell over him.

From the basement window of the kitchen that was level with the street, Hester saw the strange gentleman's legs descending the stone steps. She wondered who he was; not many gentlemen called at the shop. What shining boots he had! The feet paused on the pavement and she craned her neck to see his face.

'Hester! Look sharp with those potatoes. The dinner will never be ready at the pace you're doing them,' Martha called.

She drew her head back. There had been something about those long legs in the checked trousers that seemed to be familiar. But how could they be! She didn't know any fine gentlemen.

It was only in bed that night that it came to her – it must have been that tall man who had stared at her the day of her father's funeral.

CHAPTER TWO

By the middle of March, Hester had fallen into the ways of Number 8 Pride Street. She hated her room as much as ever and would still wake in the middle of the night, convinced that someone evil bent over her. The creaking attic stairs sounded horribly like stealthy feet. Then there were all those empty rooms downstairs . . . The thought of these frightened her so much that she always ran past them on her way to bed. The bleak little room was becoming a refuge to her. She now knew every moan of the wind through the empty spaces in the roof, every creak of the scrubbed boards.

After helping Martha about the house, she would be sent out to deliver the accounts or a bonnet in a box. This meant blessed freedom for an hour and she would run, stretching her young limbs with pleasure, the white bonnet boxes bumping against her thighs. On the corner of the square, groups of little boys would be playing marbles and their excited squeals would turn to shouts of rage as Hester ran heedlessly through them, the bonnet boxes bowling them into the gutter. If Agatha Kelsey could have seen her precious creations being shaken up in their boxes on the way to important customers, her easily aroused rage would have exploded.

Watching her pack these bonnets was enthralling to Hester. Her aunt folded snowy tissue into delicate folds until she had built a nest into which the bonnet nestled like a vivid-hued bird. The harsh colours of the velvets and taffetas she used were horrible, Hester thought. Brick red velvet, a royal purple velvet (very popular just now), puce and bright green were the colours chosen by the local ladies. A bonnet from Miss Kelsey's was an event in their lives and was nearly always for a special occasion. So it had to be a colour that was showy, that would shout out its newness and the fact that Mr Hoggarth and Mr Newlands could afford to send their wives to Miss Kelsey.

On this mild spring day, Hester was carrying a particularly hideous creation to the big house on the hill above the town. Mrs Weston was a rich widow and could afford to go to the milliner at Harrogate, but the train journey was too much for her now that she was old. But a bonnet for the Queen's Jubilee she must have so she and her companion, Miss Dicker, had come down to Pride Street in the barouche and chosen three: an expensive one for the celebrations and two plainer ones for every day. An excellent order, Agatha had purred.

The expensive one was now in the box Hester was so recklessly swinging, as she ran up the street and into the square. She was looking quite neat in a cap knitted by Martha, a secondhand jacket from the stall in the market (brown fustian which was warm but not beautiful) and her old blue skirt that had been washed and pressed. Thick black woollen stockings clothed her slim legs and she had new boots that shone like glass and were her especial pride at the moment. But her face was still thin and pale and she was often hungry, for food was not plentiful in Pride Street.

As she charged into the square, Tommy Hoggarth hailed her. He was a freckled youth, weighed down by the delivery satchel his father had just loaded on to him. They had been at the National School together and Tommy, who had had a soft spot for Hester, had washed her slate for her with his better sponge.

'Hey, Hes, which way tha going?'

'Oop t'hill to big house. Westons.' When with her own age group, Hester slid easily into the vernacular. It was the way they had talked at school but when she returned home, Nancy would pull her up sharply. Thus she possessed two languages and could slide from one to the other with ease.

'I'll walk wi' yer.'

Hester paused, irritated by Tommy's devotion. She much preferred to wander alone, singing to herself, pausing to inspect something that caught her eye. With Tommy trailing along, begging her to wait while he delivered *Yorkshire Posts* at houses on the hill, the expedition would be spoiled.

'*Tommy!*' roared his irate father, coming to the door of the newsagents. 'Get along there, will you? I want you back here to mind the shop in an hour. As for you, Hester Kelsey, get along with you before I tell on you to Miss Kelsey. And not the same way as my lad, *if* you please.'

'I'm sure I don't know the way your lad's going, Mr Hoggarth, but *I'm* going up the hill on business,' Hester retorted cheekily. As the newsagent turned away, she pulled her tongue out which made Tommy choke with laughter. They hurried across the square together and parted after he had given her a bull's eye to stuff in her cheek.

Hester felt a proprietary interest in the bonnet she was carrying up to Hill House. For the last week or two, she had been allowed to join Agatha and Mary in sewing bonnets. She made neat stitches and, with her young eyes, was a fast worker. She could sew on ribbons, place a feather and finish very expertly now. But more than that, she had picked up the art of constructing a bonnet: the slicing into the material with the big shears, the fixing of the interfacing with gum, the tacking and stitching of the silk lining. So she had had a hand in the fashioning of Mrs Weston's Jubilee bonnet – but what a hideous purple it was! Mrs Weston was a white-haired old lady with a wizened face; Hester had seen at the first fitting that the large purple bonnet did not suit her at all. However it was very expensive velvet, and Agatha needed' to sell it to someone rich and Mrs Weston was certainly that.

The house stood at the top of the hill on its own, down a

drive bordered with laurels. Hester paused at the gate to straighten her cap and then marched up the drive holding the box before her like a crown.

A butler opened the door, took one look at her and said severely, 'Tradesman's entrance *if* you please.' The door shut in her face and she looked round for another way into this imposing building. The notice TRADESMEN ONLY was over an arch in the wall. Going through it, she found herself in another world, a small hive buzzing with activity. The milkman's cart was in the yard and the milkman was conducting a flirtation with a pretty housemaid. A bootboy was cleaning shoes inside an outhouse, and two dogs tied to a kennel were barking a greeting.

The housemaid snatched the bonnet box and hastily said, 'You better wait. I'll see Mr Johnson about this.' She threw a last inviting look over her shoulder at the milkman who reluctantly began to turn his cart. The bootboy stared at Hester and Hester stared back. There was a delicious smell of cooking coming from the kitchen and her stomach rumbled emptily. A fat woman in a print dress and large white apron came out to look at her too.

'You look a very thin bairn,' she observed. 'What would you say to a nice hot bap and butter?'

Hester knew the answer to that one. 'Yes, please.'

'Come in then, come in.'

The kitchen was warm and clean, the hot bread delicious. Watched by the cook she ate two in quick succession. 'My, but you're starving, child,' the cook said.

'I'm growing,' Hester explained. 'I'm always hungry now.' And so she was. The meals eaten in the basement kitchen were so very small that they hardly made any difference to her constantly empty stomach.

The housemaid returned. ' 'Ere, she wants to see you in t'drawing room – wipe your feet.' She delivered Hester to the butler who, walking slowly ahead of her, ushered her into a room that was more like Aladdin's Cave than a drawing room, it seemed so crowded and rich.

In the dim light Hester looked round, blinking. She could smell expensive furniture and hangings, see heavily framed pictures on the dark red walls. There was hardly a foot of wall that wasn't covered with pictures and tapestry. The tables – and there were many – were crowded with treasures and she looked and looked; gaping at the glass and silver and brass that was everywhere. The mantelpiece was clothed in Berlin woolwork of many colours. In the centre was a clock under a glass dome and this was flanked by china ornaments; the whole reflected in a huge mirror that nearly reached the ceiling. A bright fire sparkled in the grate and two pug dogs barked threateningly at the intruder.

Hester released her held breath in a huge gasp and a voice laughed. 'Well, child, have you looked your fill?' and there was old Mrs Weston smiling and nodding at her in a friendly fashion. She was almost engulfed in a large arm-chair and opposite her in a smaller chair sat her companion.

Hester bobbed hasty curtseys, blushing. Mrs Weston had caught her staring, so now she looked at her boots.

'Haven't you ever been inside a room like this?'

'Oh, no, mum, never.'

'Do you like it?'

'It must be just like a palace!' Hester said, her eyes now on the conservatory that was filled with exotic flowers.

'Well, well, to you it may seem so but it's very ordinary, I assure you.' She looked down at the new bonnet that was on her knee. 'I had forgotten what a strong colour this was. Is it really the one I chose?'

'Oh, yes'm, it's the expensive one,' Hester explained. 'We have other colours, but not in so good a velvet.'

'Hmm.' The old lady twirled the bonnet in her hand. 'Really, Dicker,' she said reproachfully to the companion, 'why didn't you stop me being so foolish? This is hideous.' She looked up and caught the expression on Hester's face. 'There, you think so too! Tell me the truth, it is hideous, isn't it?'

Hester sighed. 'I never did like that purple, mum. It needs

50

a big, strong face under it. Someone like Mrs Newlands. She's got plenty of colour.'

'Mrs Newlands.' Mrs Weston looked thoughtful. 'Thank you, child, an honest opinion at last.'

'It would be much prettier in a soft blue, mum. A sort of greeny-blue. We have that velvet in, I know.'

Mrs Weston smiled up at the eager face before her. Greeny-blue was the colour of the child's eyes; she noticed they had a strange rim of darker blue to them. Extraordinary eyes. 'I can't possibly wear this bonnet Dicker. Write a note to Miss Kelsey and tell her I would like it in turquoise blue. Pack it in its box, child, and take it back to your aunt.' She searched in her reticule and suddenly produced a brand new shilling. 'A Jubilee year shilling,' she said. 'For you.'

Jubilee year or not, a shilling was a shilling and Hester took it joyfully. 'Oh, thank you, mum, thank you very much.' She looked at the coin sparkling on her palm; she had never possessed a shilling of her own before. Together with the three pennies stitched into her coat lining she was amassing a fortune! She had learned early in her first week as errand girl that Aunt Agatha regarded all tips as hers; so she had begun to slip coins into her boots and to sew them into the coat lining at nights.

She took her leave, carrying the box and Miss Dicker's note and sped down the drive, her heart as light as a feather. As she walked down the empty road she racked her brains to think of a safe place for the shilling. It would break her heart if Aunt Agatha purloined that as well. Just as she was passing a five-barred gate into a field of cows, the idea came to her. She would bury it under a hedge until she needed it.

As she jumped over the gate, the bonnet box fell out of her hand, the bonnet rolled out and lay on the grass. Oh, Aunt Agatha would kill her if she saw the precious bonnet lying on the grass in Farmer Berriman's field!

She gathered up box and bonnet and repacked them. Then, with a sharp stone, she tugged at a small square of turf, digging deep under it. Transferring the shilling and the three pennies to the hole was the work of seconds. When the turf had been replaced and carefully trodden down, the money was safely banked. No one, she thought exultantly, would ever suspect it was there. Her fortune lay warm in the earth and some day she would bring some more pennies to join it.

To her dismay, she found (as she hurried homewards) that there was a smear of mud on the box and, however hard she rubbed, nothing would remove it. Well, Aunt Agatha would probably never notice it, she thought blithely. For her mood was a blithe one now.

Reading the note from Mrs Weston, Agatha Kelsey exploded with anger. 'She wants to change the bonnet – well, that woman has a nerve! It was made expressly for her – I sat up two nights fashioning it – just look at this, Mary. Now she wants it in turquoise velvet, if you please. We haven't such a colour,' and she flung the bonnet back into the box.

'Oh, but we have, Aunt Agatha. It's that lovely greeny-blue over there . . . I told Mrs Weston about it. . . . '

A stinging blow hit Hester on the side of her face and she staggered, her hand going to her head. Agatha's face was working with rage. 'I'll teach you to interfere in my business! *You* told her indeed! Very well, miss, so be it. I'll cut out the new bonnet in turquoise velvet and you shall stay up and sew it. And you'll not get a bite of supper either – Martha will see to that. No, not another word. Now be off and get your dinner and make the most of it; for you'll not get another bite until this is finished.' She was about to remove box and bonnet when she gave a sudden scream. 'What's this? Where have you been with this box? It's got *cow-dung* on it. That settles it. No dinner either. You'll not eat again in this house until that bonnet is finished and ready for Mrs Weston.' Suddenly, she brought her face low to Hester's. 'I'll teach you to play games with my bonnets,

52

you little bitch!' she snarled and shook her until Hester's head rang.

It was the first time she had seen Agatha in a rage and she was terrified. Even Mary had shrunk back murmuring 'Nay, sister, you'll hurt the girl,' but she was too cowed by Agatha to say more. She was uneasily aware that Agatha possessed the same manic temperament as their brother Will, only without the excuse of drink.

Agatha's rage was a tight distorting mask on her face and she breathed hard. Words poured out of her. 'You little slut! I don't know why we've given you a home here. . . .' and she pushed Hester so that she stumbled against the table. 'I could kill you . . . kill you. . . .'

'Sister, sister. . . .'

But now the rage was over. Panting, Agatha Kelsey had sunk on a chair, her eyes mere pinpoints, her mouth a thin line. 'I should never have taken you in,' she said. 'Never. You're worthless.'

Three hours later, Hester was still working on the new bonnet. She had had to force back her tears because it would have spoiled the velvet and now, apart from hunger, she felt better. Indeed she hummed under her breath and thought of the bright shilling buried in the soil of Berriman's field.

Downstairs it was tea time and Martha was pleading for her niece. 'She's young and growing, Agatha. She'll work better for a cup of tea and a muffin.'

'Not a thing shall pass her lips,' Agatha decreed, her own mouth full, 'until that bonnet's finished.'

Martha looked at Mary. Both women were aware that Agatha was enjoying herself. There was a gleam in her eyes, a satisfied look on her face. She loved power; it was as heady as wine to her. Besides, she had discovered some hidden exultation in hitting and frightening her niece. It had filled a need in her life.

There was no saving hour tonight. The lamp was brought in and Hester bent lower over her work. She was very hungry and she ached all over. Thinking of that warm bap and yellow butter at Hill House, she felt water run into her mouth. And as she got hungrier she also grew colder; until her feet were lumps of ice and her head ached.

Presently, lamplight passed her door. They were going to bed.

The bonnet was almost finished and she was pleased to see that it was a bonnet fit for Mrs Weston's head. It was trimmed with picot-edged ribbon and was very pretty – no, dignified and pretty, Hester corrected herself. It had a lightness about it that was unlike Agatha's solid touch and Mrs Weston was to notice this and eagerly ask Miss Kelsey to make her another bonnet like that lovely Jubilee one she made in 1887. But she was never to have another bonnet like it, and she wore it until the velvet faded.

Hester yawned and rubbed her eyes. She felt light headed and dizzy from lack of food. Perhaps if she crept down to the kitchen, she would find something to eat. Aunt Martha might have left her some cold pudding or something. But the door to the basement was firmly locked.

Disconsolately, she wandered back into the workroom and looked round. It was then she remembered the bottle of Madeira that was kept in the cupboard with clean glasses, the whole set on a small black lacquer tray to be offered to favoured customers. Eagerly, she drew the bottle out and poured herself a glass. It looked lovely, she thought fleetingly, as she tipped it to her lips. It was indeed a delicious new experience . . . like . . . like a warm flame creeping along her veins. And here was another find – a small japanned box containing sweet biscuits, the biscuits that were always offered with the Madeira. She crunched them enjoyably with her strong teeth, beginning to take courage again. Without a pause, she refilled her glass. She really did feel better now – much better if a little lightheaded.

She was singing softly to herself when she at last put the

new bonnet into its nest of tissue paper and closed the lid. She turned the lamp down as she had been taught and, carrying it before her, went up the first flight of stairs. The aunts' door was firmly closed. She paused, contemplating it, thinking of them full of supper snoring in their beds. Mischievously smiling, she banged on their door. 'Good-night, Aunt Agatha, the bonnet's finished!' Bang-bang. 'Good-night, Aunt Mary. Good-night, Aunt Martha!' She finished with a pair of bangs on the brown paint that threatened to split the door in two. There were sounds from inside. Agitated, muffled voices. Singing at the top of her voice, she continued on her way to bed.

She reached the top and sat down abruptly, for her heart seemed to be throbbing in her head and there were suddenly two lamps in her hand. She crawled the rest of the way to her bedroom. A noise on the landing below failed to attract her interest as she dazedly began to climb out of her skirt; so when Agatha burst into the room it came as a total surprise and Hester could only stare at her.

Agatha's face was working with fury and she was babbling incoherently through gums innocent of teeth. She looked a fearsome sight in her long flannel nightgown with a nightcap over one eye and her sparse grey hair on her shoulders. Hester, clad only in cambric drawers and a bust bodice, could only gape at the sight.

'My patience is at an end!' mouthed Agatha and brought her hand up. She was holding a pliant cane with which she swished the air above Hester's head. 'Bend over, you're going to get the thrashing of your life.'

Hester was almost as tall as her aunt. She didn't move, her eyes blinking in surprise. So Agatha brought the cane down with a resounding whine on her shoulders.

'Oh!' She recoiled with pain and then leapt forward and easily wrenched the stick from her aunt. With a swift movement she broke it across her knee and threw it into a corner. 'Don't ever do that again! I'm not a child any more. If you dare touch me again – hit me as you did this morning, I'll hit you back!' They were both breathing hard, standing close to each other. 'So don't you dare!' Hester repeated.

For a moment Agatha seemed to lose all power of movement. Her mouth opened and then closed again. Then she said, 'You'll pay for this, you young madam! Just like your murdering father all over again. I'll have the police on you first thing tomorrow morning.'

'Aunt Agatha, you're a fool,' Hester said. 'Now I want to go to bed. I've made you a new bonnet. I've apologized for what I did. But you're never going to beat me – never. No one is.' Pushing her aunt out, she shut the door firmly. Listening, she heard the creak of the stairs; first one flight, then another. Then a door shutting a long way off. Smiling, Hester threw off the rest of her clothes and collapsed on her bed. That night she slept dreamlessly.

She knew as soon as she woke next morning that her head ached abominably. Moving it, she groaned. Oh, how sick she felt! But she mustn't let the aunts guess this, she told herself grimly, splashing cold water over herself. So this was what Madeira did to one. How could grown-up people bear it?

She saw, as she entered the kitchen, that they were all frightened of her. They stared furtively as she slipped into her place and attacked her porridge hungrily. As she ate, she began to feel better and when Martha put an egg before her, she hid her amazement and said, 'Thank you, I am hungry,' very cheerfully. 'The bonnet's finished, Aunt Agatha, shall I take it up to Mrs Weston this morning?'

Very much on her dignity, Agatha inclined her head. She had drawn her chin well into her neck and there was a bilious look on her face. The girl is mad, of course, she had told the frightened sisters. Ought to be certified and sent to the County Asylum. After all, look what Will did. Like father, like daughter.

'She's very upset,' Mary said when Agatha had gone up to the workroom. 'You behaved very badly last night, Hester,

56

and frightened us very much. You're only fourteen and your aunt is only concerned in training you. . . . '

'I was fifteen last week.' Hester scraped the last vestige of egg out of its shell. 'I had a birthday but none of you noticed. No one is going to beat me now. I'm too big. And if Aunt Agatha stops my meals again, I'll go into service. The girls at Mrs Weston's seem to have a nice time. Their kitchen smelt of lovely bread and stews.'

'Oh, Hester, no. You're *our niece.* It wouldn't do at all for you to go into service – not in the town anyway.'

'I'm sorry, Aunt Martha, because I like you and Aunt Mary. But I don't like Aunt Agatha and no one can force me.' And Hester smiled cheerfully at her aunts before going up to join Miss Kelsey in the workroom.

As Prickard's cab turned into Seaview Terrace, excited anticipation began to filter through his veins. Here in this quiet Liverpool suburb he owned another house where he kept his mistress. Pressure of work over on the other side of the country had kept them apart for two weeks. He had had to visit the shipbuilding yards on the Tyne, as well as completing the sale of the Harbour House. They were expecting to be able to move in to Stanhope some time in May; but there was much to be done to the house because it had been standing empty for years. Ellen was in the throes of choosing carpets and curtains and spending his money like water. Joseph Prickard liked his women to be happy so long as it was at his hands.

Paying off the cabby, he opened the gate and walked up the red-tiled path to the little house. Emmy O'Neill had found the house. 'It's just what I want!' she had begged. 'Oh, Joseph, isn't it beautiful?' It had coloured glass in the windows and doors and any amount of nooks and gables. Inside, she had made a cosy nest of cushioned chairs, soft beds and heavy velvet curtains. Everything wore a frill and pictures and ornaments covered every available space. There was dim candlelight, flowers and plants and Emmy's rose perfume everywhere. While most ladies favoured a little lavender water, Emmy used an intoxicating essence of red roses.

Emmy knew how to treat a man, Prickard thought with satisfaction as he rang the bell. He possessed a key of course, but he was a courteous man and, after two weeks, felt he should give her a minute or two to tidy her hair or change her dress. 'Well, Polly, your mistress at home?' he asked the little maid-of-all-work as she took his hat and gloves.

Polly's red cheeks seemed to be redder than usual. 'Yes, sir, but – well, I better tell missis you're here, sir.'

He looked at her quizzically. 'Your mistress quite well? Then don't bother to announce me – I'll run up myself.' For now he was here, her scent in his nostrils, he could hardly wait to take her in his arms.

'Oh, but, sir – the missis – ' Polly called after him.

He ran lightly up the stairs to the small living room. 'Well, Emmy, my girl, here I am at last.'

The room was dim, lit only by flickering firelight. A small tea table was drawn up to the fire and its snowy lace cloth was laden with silver and fine china. A small stand held sandwiches, iced lemon cake and plum cake. A muffin dish was in the grate. The pair of canaries in their cage by the window fluttered in alarm at the invasion; as did the two people who had been sitting very close together on the sofa.

'Joe! Why, Joe, I wasn't expecting you!' Emmy sprang up to greet him. 'Mr Wortle and I were just having a cup of tea.'

Prickard bent to kiss her on the cheek, raising his brows at the elaborate tea table. If this was 'just having a cup of tea'!

Mrs O'Neill was small and plump, just as he liked his women. Red hair framed a wide-cheeked face with small eyes set too close together. A long upper lip and freckles made sure that Emmy O'Neill, widow of a sea captain and

58

just forty years of age, wasn't considered pretty. But fascination and an easy manner she had in abundance.

'Had we not better have a lamp brought in, m'dear?'

'Oh, yes, of course. I'll ring for Polly. She must have forgotten it. May I present Mr Daniel Wortle, Joe? Daniel, this is my friend, Sir Joseph Prickard.'

The two men bowed, seeing each other only dimly in the firelight. But Prickard noticed that Wortle had a broad Lancashire voice. Where on earth had Emmy found him? The bitch, he thought. So this is what she gets up to in my absence. I'll have a word to say to this. 'You were just leaving, Mr Wortle? Don't let me detain you.'

Wortle looked helplessly at Mrs O'Neill. His teacup was still full. 'Well, think on what I've just been talking about, lass, and thank 'ee for the tea.' He bowed stiffly in Prickard's direction and then his heavy footsteps went down the stairs.

'I'll get Polly to make fresh tea.'

'Not for me – *lass*.' He cut a broad finger of rich plum cake and ate it standing. 'Quite a tea, m'dear. Muffins and jam, sandwiches – potted meat, of course? – lemon cake, my word you were doing him well, Emmy. Who was the gentleman?'

She had had time to think. 'A friend of mother's. She asked him to call.'

'Oh? And what was it he wanted you to *think on* about?'

'He wants to take me to the music hall,' she said sulkily.

'That's very nice of mother's friend. I hope you told him you couldn't go?'

Pouting, she drew him down to the sofa beside her. 'Now, Joe, don't be like that. Why shouldn't I go to the music hall occasionally? It's dull here on my own. You can't expect me to live for weeks on end on my own, never seeing anyone but Polly – why, it isn't natural.'

'I've only been gone two weeks, m'dear. And where is the gentleman's wife? Or has it become usual for gentlemen to call on ladies who are alone and sit in the dark *on the same sofa*. I'm not a fool, Emmy, although you seem to think I am. He's got designs on you, my girl. It was in every line of his face.'

She flounced from him, angry colour covering her freckles. 'I tell you he's only a friend of mother's. I've known him for years. I like him, so there!'

He had gripped her plump little wrist and twisted her to face him. 'Now listen to me, my girl. This is my house. That's my food you're giving him. Every stitch on your back I own, madam. You belong to me as much as if we were married!'

'That's where you're wrong! Daniel says you've no legal rights over me. . . . ' She stopped, a scared look crossing her face as she saw his face tighten ominously.

'So you've been consulting that red-faced oaf, have you? He thinks of taking you over, does he? I warn you, Emmy, you can't play fun and games with me. That fellow Wortle will have to pay up if he wants you. A thousand pounds it cost to set you up in this house, and another five hundred a year to keep you in the manner you're not accustomed to. It's been four years, hasn't it? Has he got three thousand pounds? That's my price for selling you.' His voice was icy with contempt and she began to cry.

'I knew it would end like this! You've no respect for me, Joe. All you think of is the money. I wish I had it so that I could throw it back in your face!'

'I treat you with the contempt you deserve. Do you think I don't know the tricks you get up to when I'm away?' This was a long shot, but by the expression on her startled face it had reached its target. 'You're a whore!' he shouted suddenly, jealousy getting the better of his control. His feelings alarmed him. Was he *in love* with the baggage?

She leapt up, screaming abuse at him, hysteria mounting until she had collapsed in a heap. Polly grabbed the sal volatile, while Prickard clumsily tried to unfasten her tight clothes.

'We'd best get her on to her bed, sir,' Polly gasped. 'Gi'

us a hand, will ye? Eh, poor mistress, she's got 'em bad this time.'

'Undress her, Polly,' he ordered and went back to pace the sitting room floor, anger still bright in him. She was two-timing him, the whore! The whore!

It gave him the utmost satisfaction to mouth that word. Under her very proper manner that's all she was, wasn't she? Why, look how she behaved in bed! Ellen had never behaved so. Ellen was too much of a lady to behave in an abandoned manner. She had just lain there and suffered his attentions while Emmy positively *enjoyed* their physical relationship.

He had totally – if temporarily – forgotten that that was the very reason he had set Mrs O'Neill up in this little house in the first place. She gave him the physical satisfaction that years of living with Ellen had denied him. She was voluptuous and encouraging, and he had looked forward to his nights with her as if he was half his real age. She had made him feel young again. Satisfied at last, he could be indulgent and undemanding with Ellen.

'She wants to see you, sir.'

Emmy was propped up by lace-edged pillows, wearing only a silk negligee through which her pink flesh peeped invitingly. His senses leapt as they always did at the sight of that body.

'Joe . . . ' Her voice was low. 'Oh, Joe, I'm so upset! Don't leave me, Joe.' The easy tears flowed again.

'No man likes to be made a cuckold –'

'But we're not married!' Emmy wailed. 'If we were I'd never receive gentleman visitors alone – never! But how can I go on year after year only seeing you occasionally? I've got no position in society. I'm just a woman on her own and men take advantage of me. . . . ' Her voice choked and she plied her handkerchief to her eyes.

She needs to be taught a lesson, he told himself sternly. He would return to town at once. Nevertheless he sat down on the bed and took her limp hand. 'How can we get married,

Emmy? I have a wife already. You knew that at the beginning.'

'Why can't you divorce and marry me?'

'Emmy! You must be mad! Do you want to ruin me? I should be kicked out of every club, every organization I belong to! Have you taken leave of your senses, woman?'

'But you don't love her. You've told me so often. Yet she's Lady Prickard and I'm nobody!'

Ah, so that was it. It was the title she hankered after. Poor little Emmy, poor little woman, what a child she was! Melting rapidly, he gathered her in his arms. She smelled of roses, he thought dizzily. 'It's not possible, dear, much as I would wish it.' He kissed her tenderly and she clung to him, hiccuping a little.

Without another word he rose and locked the door.

Lying back on her pillows, she watched him as he clumsily and hastily removed the apparel of a gentleman of business. The frock coat, black trousers and waistcoat were hung on a chair, and now he stood in his flannel shirt struggling with the cuff links. When he was at last in his long woollen pants and vest, she wanted to giggle. If he only could see himself as she saw him now, she thought. With an air of abandon he stripped and at last looked like an ordinary male, vulnerable and ageing.

She flung back the bed clothes with a little squeal of pleasure. 'Oh, Joe!'

He had much to thank Emmy for, he thought as he eagerly found her plump body. Ellen had never greeted him with a scream of delight. Yes, he would have to make it up to Emmy somehow. He had been too stern with her. Perhaps a new set of sables would fit the bill.

The whole town had been invited to a public meeting in the drill hall 'to discuss the Jubilee celebrations' as the bills posted round the town had announced.

The drill hall was the biggest public building Sewerston

boasted, and it was packed to capacity on the night of March 15. Agatha and Mary Kelsey were there and found themselves standing uncomfortably at the back; elbow to elbow with the ragged citizens from the harbour who traditionally crowded that space in the hall.

In the centre of the platform sat Lord Abbotsbury as chairman of the proceedings. He was accompanied by his wife and surrounded by the various people of importance who traditionally held sway in the forefront of town government. Prickard and his wife were there, the town clerk, the vicar and his wife, the methodist minister, the doctor. They sat and looked down on lesser mortals, confident of their position in society.

Lord Abbotsbury was a slightly deaf old man, with a soft voice that made the ragged clan at the back shout, 'Speak up, gov'ner!' This was to Lady Abbotsbury's intense annoyance and she would raise her lorgnette to quell the mob; but the mob, being freeborn Yorkshiremen, had no intention of being quelled by this glassy stare and continued to riot noisily.

'Can't you see a free seat anywhere else?' Mary asked her sister, holding a handkerchief to her nose for the freeborn Yorkshiremen had a strong smell.

'Can't you see it's packed to the door? Do be quiet, Mary.' Agatha was made of stronger stuff than her sister. Besides, she was consumed with curiosity to discover the town's plans for the Jubilee. And after many emotional references to 'our revered and beloved sovereign' Lord Abbotsbury proceeded to reveal them. A subscription list was to be opened and the proceeds would be used to finance a day of celebration in the town square.

'Hurrah!' shouted the rabble who scented free beer.

There would be a free tea and games –

'And of course a service in the church first,' interposed the vicar quickly.

'What was that, my dear fellow? A service? Well, naturally,' Lord Abbotsbury said severely.

At this point someone jumped up to suggest that a triumphal arch be erected over the square, this to consist of yew and roses. Two minutes later, someone else suggested a local girl should be chosen as the town's Jubilee Queen.

It was at this point that Mr Newlands, owner of the Farm Produce Centre, rose and suggested that, as his was far and away the biggest butcher's shop in the area, he would like to be asked to supply all the meat and ham required.

'That's very handsome of you,' his lordship said warmly, and the butcher's wife pinched her husband angrily, 'Great fool! We can't afford to do that!'

'Nay, Lizzie, I didn't mean *give*.'

'Best keep thy mouth shut,' his wife advised, seething.

Now the minister had got to his feet. Clean-shaven, with pince-nez flashing at his audience, he launched into a tirade against the demon Drink. He did hope his lordship did not mean to suggest that liquor would be consumed that day. . . .

'Aw, put a sock in't it!' shouted old Hawke, who had once been the coxswain of the lifeboat. 'T'ould lady wouldn't say no to a drop herself, I reckons.'

'That she wouldn't,' agreed the back row, nodding at each other. 'The queen would *want* us to enjoy ourselves.'

Old Hawke spat on the sawdusted floor. He had been born in George IV's reign when, as he now informed his neighbours, folks knew how to enjoy themselves.

Walking home across the square afterwards, Agatha said with satisfaction, 'Well, I'm going to be busy. Did you see how many stopped me to say they would be needing bonnets for the day? It's a good thing I've taught Hester to make bonnets. She's picked it up fast, I will say that. . . . '

'Sister, don't you think it would be nice for Hester to enter the competition for Jubilee Queen?'

Agatha stopped dead and peered incredulously at her sister in the light cast by a street lamp. 'Mary, I sometimes wonder at you. The girl's flighty enough without putting ideas in her head. I'd never get a day's work out of her if she got hold of that idea. Mind, now. You're not to say a word about it.'

It was Tommy Hoggarth who told Hester that a Jubilee Queen was to be chosen. His father's shop was distributing the pamphlets and he smuggled one to her. Propping themselves against a wall, they devoured the smudgily-printed paper.

'See, it says between twelve and sixteen years of age.'

'To sing and recite before an audience at the Drill Hall on April 10.'

Hester's eyes sparkled. Sometimes she had delicious dreams: she was standing on a stage – a vast stage that was all dazzling lights, mirrors and red brocade curtains . . . and she was in its centre, singing before an enraptured audience. She wore pale green – a rustling taffeta dress that made people gasp – and her voice soared up into the gilded roof and exploded in a myriad stars –

'Hes.' Tommy was plucking her sleeve impatiently. 'Can you sing?'

'Anyone can sing,' Hester retorted scornfully. 'I know lots of songs Sal taught me. But I haven't got a best dress though – only this,' and she looked down at the faded blue skirt and fustian jacket.

'You better leave off your cap and fluff your hair out,' advised her impresario. 'You'll knock 'em cold, Hes. You're the prettiest girl in Sewerston,' he added shyly.

'Me?' Hester gave a little skip of excitement. 'Oh, Tommy, really?'

'Course you are. Everyone thinks so – even Ma. She said the other day that you were too pretty for your own good.'

Hester considered this gravely. No one had ever told her she was pretty before; but Tommy had always been sweet on her since school, so his judgement couldn't really be trusted.

'Come on, you got to fill in this form,' Tommy urged. 'You do it. You write good, Hes, always did at school. And I've pinched a pencil out of the shop.'

They pressed the document against a flat piece of wall and Hester licked the pencil. 'It says here: *Must be signed by parent.*'

'Just put *orphan*,' Tommy advised.

'Aren't we to take the child with us, sister?' Mary asked on the night of the concert to choose the Jubilee Queen. 'She'll be very disappointed. It is for young people, you know.'

'Certainly not,' Agatha said coldly, answering the first question and ignoring the rest. She was pulling on her gloves with deliberation.

'But she doesn't get much enjoyment. . . . '

'I'm not concerned with Hester's enjoyment. Isn't it enough that she has a roof over her head? Besides, she has nothing fit to wear. I'm certainly not going to be seen with a ragamuffin,' Agatha added, stalking to the door and wrenching it open. 'Now, are you coming or not?'

Mary still hesitated. It seemed unnecessarily hard to leave Hester at home with Martha, but years of obeying Agatha made her follow her sister.

Down in the kitchen, they were washing up the tea dishes. Martha cocked her head. 'There, they've gone. Go and get my boots and we'll slip in at the back. Agatha will never see us.'

Hester was overjoyed for she had planned to make her escape via the privy in the yard. But if Martha was going to take her – She skipped upstairs to fetch her aunt's outdoor boots and presently, rather breathless, they had slipped into the back row among the noisy element from the harbour. Children who were bare-footed and ragged, carrying their baby brothers and sisters in their arms, children on crutches; all enjoying themselves to the full. They kept up a ribald commentary on the proceedings as the daughters of the tradesmen sidled on to the stage and warbled of lost children, early graves and snowdrops.

'Put a sock in it, luv!' they advised Miss Alice Beddows,

whose ditty became more tearful with every stanza. When Miss Cissie Newlands announced that her heart was pleasure filled, dancing with the daffodils, and her voice broke on a top note, the harbour mob rocked and stamped with glee.

'Aunt Martha, I shan't be a moment,' Hester whispered in the unsuspecting Martha's ear and before her aunt had taken this in, she had skipped on to the stage and given her name to Miss Mimms from the National School, who was acting as mistress of ceremonies.

'Where's your music, Hester?'

'There's no music,' Hester assured her confidently and stepped forward to hear her name announced.

Martha buried her face in her handkerchief and perspired with fright. Oh, what would Agatha say? There she was sitting near the front . . .

Agatha had half-risen in her seat and was opening her mouth to order her niece off the stage, but Mary pulled her down.

'For pity's sake, sister, don't make an exhibition of yourself!'

'But look at those terrible clothes! What will people think?'

Mary looked at her sister. 'Yes, it's about time we did something about that,' she said reproachfully. 'The only child performing in rags. Well, I hope we can live this down.'

'I'm going out.'

'Sit still, sister!'

In her imagination, Hester was wearing a dress of floating silk. There were rows and rows of pearls round her swanlike neck. Her hair had changed colour and was molten gold and the whole audience had risen to throw red roses at her feet.

'This is Hester Kelsey,' announced Miss Mimms.

Joseph Prickard, suddenly remembering his duties as a member of the selection committee, was arriving late. Making his way down to the front row to join the Abbotsburys, he heard the name being announced and stopped to

67

look up at the stage. It was the child. Nancy's girl. The child with Nancy's eyes and colouring. A wisp of a girl, much too thin and in shabby faded garments – surprising tears suddenly blurred his vision. What would Nancy think if she saw her child now? My God, but he was going to do something about this!

The shabby young figure stood with legs slightly braced, her hands on her hips, and began to belt out the song she had heard many a time from her young stepmother's lips. Sal would sing it as she threw a piece of fish in the pan to fry for Will Kelsey's supper:

> *A little old woman her living she got*
> *By selling hot codlings hot, hot, hot;*
> *And this little old woman who codlings sold*
> *Though her codlings were hot, she felt herself cold,*
> *So to keep herself warm she thought it no sin*
> *To fetch for herself a quarten of gin –*

There was a screech from Agatha Kelsey who had leapt up in her seat. 'Hester! Come down at once! *At once*, I say!' But her voice was drowned by a roar from the harbour children who knew Grimaldi's ditty well.

> *Ri tol iddy iddy, ri tol iddy iddy ri tol lay!*

They stamped and clapped and awaited the second verse.

But Prickard had now reached his seat and, standing in front of the stage, offered Hester his hands so that she might jump down.

'I'm afraid you'll have to come down, Hester. You see, as my niece you aren't allowed to compete. I'm afraid I'm on the selection committee. It's a pity when you were doing so well but there it is – rules are rules.' He smiled at her reassuringly as he firmly lifted her down.

Hester had recognized the tall man at once as the man who had stared so hard at her on the day of her father's funeral. But how could she be his niece? Suspicious, disappointed at the sudden end to what she believed to be a

68

winning song, she backed away from him. But he grasped her firmly and led her to a seat next to his own. 'Come, Hester, sit here next to Lady Abbotsbury.'

The Abbotsburys, who believed that Sir Joseph's niece was dressed in ragged clothes to fit the song (and what a relief after such a parade of stilted children in ugly velvet and satin!) leaned towards her. 'That was most amusing, my dear, but your uncle is quite right. Never mind!' Lady Abbotsbury patted her knee and turned her attention to the stage once more.

Captured by the firm hand on her arm, Hester sat with a thunderous frown on her face watching Lizzie Umpleby, daughter of the Sewerston draper, being chosen as the Jubilee Queen. It had been decided in whispers among the committee that Umpleby was the parent best fitted to provide his daughter with a special dress for the day. The girl was pretty enough and docile too. An excellent choice, they congratulated each other over Hester's head.

Then it was over and they were singing God Save the Queen. Hester thought it time she slipped away but down came that firm hand on her arm again.

'Where are your aunts? I would like to speak to them.'

Hester didn't know it yet, but that night was to be a memorable one for her. That night she became a member of Joseph Prickard's family. But Agatha knew it. She could see it in his face as he advanced on her. This time she was to give in without a struggle.

CHAPTER THREE

'So I'm going to live with them,' Hester said. 'Is there any more pie?'

Tommy shook his head silently. Her news had taken him horribly by surprise. He felt sick with disappointment. She was going away to live at a grand place called Stanhope and he would never see her again.

'Your mother makes a lovely pie,' Hester sighed. Wetting a forefinger, she thriftily mopped up every crumb still remaining inside a copy of the *Yorkshire Post*. Every day, Tommy had been bringing her something to eat from his mother's larder. It had begun after the concert when his mother had exclaimed, 'That girl's starving! Just look at her colour!' Startled by the pity in her voice, Tommy had looked closer at the familiar face of his friend. It was then that he had started smuggling food to her, clumsily wrapped in a newspaper he was on his way to deliver.

Today they were sitting on the seawall at the bottom of Chaundler Street. She had just given him her news. Her aunts had only told her last night, although it was more than a week since the concert. She was very frightened at the prospect.

'Uncle Joe – that's what I have to call him – is going to America soon and I'm going to Stanhope then. They used to live down there,' and she pointed at the Harbour House.

'Oh, those people. I know the boy who lives there. Don't think much of him,' Tommy added scornfully. 'He's a bit like a girl – curls and things.'

'He's my cousin Wilfred,' Hester said gloomily. 'I shall hate it there. I know I shall. There's servants and things. Aunt Agatha told me. She says a ragamuffin like me will never learn to live with them.' There was real terror in Hester's face for a moment. Servants. Dinner at night. Polite folk. Agatha Kelsey had kept up a perfect litany all through supper, taking a malicious pleasure in the fear that Hester hadn't been able to hide.

She told Tommy all this, pouring out all her fears just to hear him dismiss them one after the other. He was good at this. 'Go on, Hes! You're not a ninny. You'll soon learn.' He paused, thinking wistfully that Hester would probably learn all too fast and would forget him quite soon in her new life. 'Will I see you afterwards, Hes?' He couldn't resist asking this question. Hester, he knew, hadn't an inkling that she was his first love. There was a pain in the pit of his stomach at the thought of losing her.

'Of course you will. We'll be at the Jubilee celebrations for one thing. Uncle Joe's on the committee and that's why I can't be the Jubilee queen,' Hester added, her face darkening at the thought of Lizzie Umpleby queening it over them all on June 21. Lizzie Umpleby was often spotty, even though her dresses were nice. Then her mind swung to something else and her face lit up. 'Uncle Joe wrote to me this morning. The first letter I've ever had. He says he's having a room papered specially for me. What d'you think of that?' She jigged suddenly with excitement and Tommy tried to smile. He wanted to be glad for her. He knew he ought to be glad for her. Those old aunts had nearly starved poor Hes to death – but somehow his face felt stiff.

'I've got to go,' he remembered suddenly. 'Pa gets mad if I'm late for tea.'

'What is it tonight, Tommy?' Hester asked greedily. Tonight's high tea at the Hoggarths would provide her with tomorrow's treat.

'Cold beef and one of Ma's pies.'

Hester's eyes lit up. 'I'll meet you here at the same time tomorrow,' she said briskly. 'Perhaps it will be jam pie?'

They were all seated round the table behind the shop where Willy Hoggarth sold newspapers and fancy goods. Mrs Hoggarth was seated behind the Britannia ware teapot, Mr Hoggarth behind the cold beef over which he was wielding the knife and steel sharpener. Matty, the younger boy, sat with his back to the fire with an empty chair beside him. The chair at the head of the table was held by Grandfather Hoggarth who, although retired, still owned the shop and the house, and would do so until his dying day.

'Now I've told t'lad once and for all he'll get no tea if he's late again,' Willy Hoggarth pronounced. 'There's got to be discipline in this house. You spoil t'lad, Dorrie.'

Mrs Hoggarth went on placidly pouring out the tea. She had heard this reproach too often before.

'I know where our Tommy is,' Matty began and felt a pinch from his mother. She was shaking her head at him.

'Where is he?' his father was saying. 'Best tell me, lad.'

'Oot wi' a lass, that's where he is,' Granpa Hoggarth chuckled. 'Like I was and you was, Willy lad, at t'same age.'

Mrs Hoggarth was handing cups of tea round the table. 'He's called in at t'library for me,' she said calmly. She had known for the past two weeks that Tommy was carrying food to the half-starved Kelsey girl; so every night she had put out inviting slices of pie and plum cake on a convenient larder shelf and every morning they had disappeared. If Willy got to hear of it, it would be bad for his blood pressure, she told herself. There was abundant food in the Hoggarth house and she couldn't bear to think of any child going hungry. She looked round her table now, loaded for high tea which was the main meal of their day. There were slices of underdone beef, half a ham, pickled cabbage and potatoes in their jackets, a jar of pickled onions, a pie and a couple of homemade cakes, a large round of Wensleydale cheese and a huge pot of tea to wash it all down. There was a pint of cream, a slab of yellow farm butter and a few hard-boiled eggs to fill any corners left in Tommy.

She sighed to herself as she put sugar in her tea. She knew only too well that there was hunger and sickness in the town, especially down in the harbour cottages. Here there were children crippled by rickets and TB, children who begged at her side door for a crust of bread, children not as old as Matty who carried a younger child in their skinny little arms and had another one clinging to their ragged petticoats. Dorrie Hoggarth sometimes wished that she could feed them all. The only thing she was able to do was to smuggle bread and soup and a pair of Matty's out-grown boots to the harbour cottages – knowing it was never enough. Hester Kelsey had been different, Dorrie remembered. She had never starved when her mother was alive because Nancy had taken in sewing, doing alterations for the local draper's shop. Dorrie Hoggarth, who had liked and respected her, wasn't going to see her child starve in the hands of those old skinflints, her aunts. Not that they could be all that badly off with their thriving business, she thought indignantly. What wouldn't she like to say to them!

They had reached their second cups of tea when the door opened and Tommy came in, taking his cap off and slicking his hair down.

Willy Hoggarth pushed his chair back. 'Well, m'lad, what have you to say for yourself? It's disgraceful coming in at this time. . . .'

'Where's tha' bin, lad?' Grandpa asked, cutting off his long-winded son. 'Walking some lass I'll wager. Eh, young blood – there's nowt like it. Come every spring and sure as fate there's some lass in trouble. . . .'

'*Granpa.*' Mrs Hoggarth's voice was sounding a warning for Matty, she saw, was all ears. 'Let me fill your cup again. Did you get me that book I wanted out of the Free Library, Tommy? I'm sorry it made you late for your tea. I clean forgot I'd asked you to get it. Just wash in't scullery and

73

your father will cut you some nice slices of beef.'

Tommy came back from the scullery rather sheepishly. 'I'm sorry, Ma – it was because I wanted . . .'

She pressed his foot under the table, hoping that she wasn't pressing Granpa's by mistake. 'Now, not another word. It was my fault. It's quite a walk from the library and it looks as if Miss Fraser hadn't kept me that book after all. Never mind, I'll look in myself next week.'

He read the message in her eyes and smiled at her. Good old Ma, she always helped a fellow out of a hole if she could. He ate hungrily, putting the pickled onions whole into his mouth until his mother caught him. Swallowing a mouthful of beef he suddenly said, 'I'm going into t'army.'

There was an intake of breath round the Hoggarth tea table.

Tommy repeated it. 'I'm going into t'army. I've joined up.'

'I've never heard such nonsense!' his father exploded. 'Mother, did you hear that? Going into t'army, he says, as cool as you please. And how old are you? Nay, don't interrupt – I know your age only too well. You've no business to be off joining t'army without a word to me. I'm your father and what I says goes in this house. That shop out there – that my old father worked his fingers to the bone for all these years – that shop is going to be Hoggarth and Sons very soon now. I need you here in t'business, not out in Africa fighting fuzzie-wuzzies like t'Prince Imperial.'

Tommy's jaw had set stubbornly. 'I've been round to t'recruiting sergeant at Drill Hall. I've taken the Queen's shilling.'

'*What!*' screamed his father. 'You bloody young fool!'

'Willy!' remonstrated Dorrie Hoggarth. She hid her trembling hands in her aproned lap. Not Tommy – her first-born – her favourite child. It was something she had always dreaded, this day that would take Tommy away from her. There had been a restlessness about the boy lately and she had begun to fear that he wouldn't stay home much longer.

74

He was seventeen. Almost an adult. The army meant India. India swallowed the best of England's youth, took all the beautiful young men from those who loved them and sent them out to serve the Queen-Empress in that God-forsaken continent on the other side of the world. They came home hard-bitten, dried up and changed – if they came home at all. Hot tears trembled under her lids and, to hide them, she snatched Granpa's cup and refilled it once more, much to the old gentleman's astonishment.

'Nay, Dorrie, nay, I'll be running all night,' he protested. Holding her mouth very firm she said not a word. It was right that he should go. She mustn't try to keep him by her side much longer. It was the tragedy of having sons that they became men so soon and left you, she thought. Matty, thank God was still a child. There had been a daughter once, between the two boys, but she had died very young. When Matty went in a few years, she and Willy would become old people.

Old grandfather was looking from one to the other. No one was listening to him so, like a spoilt child who was being ignored, he spilt his full cup of tea all over himself and squeaked that he was burned to death! It had the effect of creating a diversion while Mrs Hoggarth fetched a cloth and mopped the old man. 'Now, Father, you're all right,' she admonished. 'It's not even through your clothes.'

'What made you do it, lad?' Willy asked his son. 'You've ruined all my plans for the future and you've broken your mother's heart, but I don't suppose you care.'

Tommy's eyes met his mother's. She shook her head, forcing a smile. 'We'll miss you, Tommy, but you're right to do what you want. You're not a child any more. You've got a head on your shoulders and you'll see summat of the world – eh, but I envy you that! We can't keep him at Sewerston for ever, Father. It wouldn't be right.'

The boy's face was clearing. He smiled gratefully at his mother. She was making it easy for him. He knew that he could never bring himself to tell them why he had joined up. That it was because Hester was leaving the town for good, that he would never see her again and that his heart was broken. The thought of Sewerston without her burned in him like a pain. He loved her, but they were both too young. All he could think of was going away and forgetting her in a new life for himself.

It was on a dull grey day at the beginning of May that Agnes came to fetch Hester. The rain had stopped, but a cool wind blew in from the sea.

Hester had been up since six, cleaning her room and packing her few possessions. She stood at the door, dressed in her hat and jacket and looked round the little room for the last time. She had spent three months there and now knew every crack in the plaster intimately. It had become her refuge, and she was surprised to find that she felt affection for the shabby little attic.

She went downstairs to the workroom and sat with her brown paper parcel on her lap. The aunts were already at work, feverishly fulfilling orders for Jubilee hats and bonnets. They were going to miss Hester's help for she had become a neat-fingered bonnet maker.

'If you've got nothing better to do than sit like a fine lady,' snapped Agatha, 'you can go and help Martha in the kitchen.'

So down to the basement she went and began to peel potatoes for the dinner she wouldn't be eating here herself. She was sick with apprehension, her mouth dry with fear. It was a tremendous step she was taking this morning; sometimes she wished she hadn't agreed to go. At least she knew the worst here – but what of Stanhope and her relations who lived there?

Of the three aunts, only Martha had remained kind where her sisters had become resentful and bitter at the change in Hester's fortunes. Martha was glad the girl was going to a good home, much as she would have been if Hester had been a puppy she was sending out into the world. Beyond that, she hadn't a thought; the barley stew was occupying the whole of her mind. Barley stew was the Kelseys' great standby on lean days.

When the carriage arrived at eleven o'clock, Hester hadn't heard it and had to be summoned upstairs. Her stomach dropped. The moment had come. She kissed Martha affectionately. 'I'll come back and see you some day soon.'

'Look after yourself, dear.' Martha watched the thin black-stockinged legs flying upstairs to the new life. We did nothing for her − nothing, she thought with brief regret, before turning back to her work and forgetting all about her. The impact Hester had made on the lives of the three old maids was infinitesimal.

Agnes came up the steps into the shop and found Miss Kelsey waiting with hands folded in front of her and a forbidding expression on her face.

'I've come for Miss Hester, mum,' Agnes announced, bobbing a curtsey. Eh, what a tarmagent this old 'un looked! 'If she's ready we'd like to start at once. Coachman doesn't want t'keep horses waiting after our long drive.'

'*Miss* Hester is ready for you,' Agatha said sarcastically and gestured behind her.

Agnes saw a tall thin young girl framed in the doorway. 'Well, I never,' she said under her breath. Was this ragged young thing Sir Joseph's niece? Honest indignation burned in her. The child looked ill and tired, an over-anxious expression on her face. It looked as if Sir Joseph had come to the girl's rescue only in the nick of time or this old besom would have killed her off. 'Good morning, miss, I'm Agnes, Lady Prickard's personal maid.' For Agnes had been promoted to that favoured position after the move to Stanhope. She beamed at the girl. 'I've come to take you home.'

Hester looked gratefully at the plump rosy-cheeked woman who had come to fetch her. She wore a black bonnet and short cape and looked so clean and smiling that Hester felt a smile bursting out of her in response. A wave of sympathy and liking went between the two in those first few moments of meeting – it was to last a lifetime.

Dutifully, she kissed her aunts and then opened the shop door with an alacrity that Agnes didn't understand. The carriage, a lovely dark green one, Hester noted gleefully, had its door open and waiting. The coachman in a dark green livery, glanced over his shoulder and touched his hat.

'Good morning!' Hester called stepping into the carriage and her new life without a backward glance.

Sir Joseph was still in America, Agnes told her as they started, but he would be home in a fortnight's time. They were crossing the cobbled square now and Hester looked hopefully out of the window; it would be nice to see someone she knew and to bow graciously to them as she passed in the carriage. Yes, there was Tommy waiting on the corner to see her go! She pulled down the window, leaned out and yelled, 'Yahoo, Tommy! Goodbye!'

The boy saw her, saw the grin that covered her face and an answering smile lit up his face. Taking off his cap, he waved it above his head and ran along beside the carriage. 'Goodbye, Hes, good luck!'

'My friend Tommy,' Hester explained unnecessarily as she sank back on to the seat once more. 'He brought me something to eat from his mother's larder every day. His mother makes a very nice sort of pie – it melts in your mouth,' Hester said wistfully. She was going to miss those pies of Mrs Hoggarth's, she told herself.

Agnes looked sharply at her charge. 'D'you mean to tell me you haven't bin getting enough to eat? Well, that's disgraceful!'

'Well, no, but it's because I have a large appetite – because I'm growing,' Hester said hastily. 'I had *enough* but I could always do with more – except Aunt Martha's porridge,' and she shuddered at the recollection.

'If Sir Joseph knew of this. . . . '

'Oh, please don't tell him! It doesn't matter any more, does it?'

'You're right. It's all best forgotten', and she patted her charge's hand comfortingly.

'What am I to call you?' Hester asked presently.

'Agnes.'

'Mrs Agnes?'

'Bless you, no! Just Agnes. And I call you Miss Hester because you're Sir Joseph's niece.'

'Is – is he very grand?'

'Not a bit. He's a real kind gentleman. So's Lady Prickard,' she added hastily. 'Kind, I mean. And I'll be looking after you myself. I was parlourmaid for years, but I'm Lady Prickard's personal maid now. I look after her hair and clothes and suchlike. It's easier work than the other and I'm not getting any younger. The master asked me specially to look after you.' She beamed happily at her new responsibility. *Don't bother your mistress about the girl*, Sir Joseph had said and it was as if he had winked at her. She had understood at once.

It was a long time since anyone had 'looked after' Hester, and she wondered uneasily how she would take to it again. The last two years had made her very independent. 'I can look after myself very well,' she said earnestly. 'I'm fifteen now.'

But Agnes only smiled and shook her head silently. It gave Hester the uneasy feeling that she was going to be looked after with a vengeance.

As the carriage bowled along the country roads, Hester began to ply Agnes with questions about Stanhope. But 'You'd best wait and see,' was all Agnes would say.

They had left the town behind long ago now and were travelling across the hills above the sea, going northwards all the time. The busy sea-lanes of the German Ocean were dotted with sailing ships carrying coal, bricks and slate from Aberdeen to London, from Portland to Newcastle. Next time she saw it, Hester thought, it would be as a visitor. It would feel odd, for she had lived within sight and sound of the sea all her life.

Suddenly, the carriage wheeled sharply westwards across moorland and peat bogs. They descended a hill and when they crested the next one it was to find another type of country, a pleasant agricultural land with clumps of trees and red-roofed farmhouses.

Hester darted from side to side in the carriage calling out breathlessly, 'Oh, Agnes, look!' at every turn in the road. For one who had never been outside Sewerston the scenery was a revelation. It was early May and new leaves of tender green clothed the trees. They were every colour from pale to dark green and in the forests the larch was yellow. Hawthorn frothed over the roadside hedges and the smell of damp vegetation wafted powerfully through the window that Hester had pulled down.

Agnes loathed fresh air as Hester was now to discover. 'Mercy, we'll catch our death!' she protested, as she firmly put up the window once more. 'Now come and sit down, Miss Hester, before you wear us both out.'

So Hester leaned back against the padded leather interior of the carriage and stared ahead, all sorts of scenes passing through her head.

Agnes watched her. My, but she was going to be a real beauty some day when they'd got her fattened up, she told herself. Those eyes. Such a colour! And that skin. Agnes regarded her new charge with the greatest satisfaction. She reckoned the years ahead would be full of excitement now they had added this young thing to the household. Wilfred was a nice enough lad when his mother stopped fussing him and making him think about himself; but it would be a deal more fun watching this girl grow into womanhood. She chuckled happily to herself and began to suck another peppermint, for the carriage always made her queasy.

Hester was beginning to feel queasy herself as the miles passed. It had nothing to do with the swaying carriage. A thousand misgivings had taken the place of her earlier excitement. She glanced across at Agnes, longing to ask for her reassurance, but the woman had fallen into a doze. So for

80

another quarter of an hour Hester tried to keep still. Then Agnes sat up and announced, 'Reckon we must be nearly home now.'

Then she stared at the girl, a troubled and thoughtful look on her face. How was she to get her into the house without the servants seeing her? Those new servants were proper snobs. They'd seen service in some grand houses – like that Mr Wiston who had been with a marquis and never let you forget it. But her charge was a ragged little object – nicely spoken and all that, but she looked a harbour child. Sir Joseph's niece. Bless the man, he hadn't given the matter a second thought. But it wouldn't do for the servants to see her. It would be a really bad start and that Agnes was determined to avoid. 'Will you mind if I suggest something, Miss Hester? I'd like to put this carriage rug round your shoulders and take you straight to your room.'

Hester looked ruefully at herself. 'I am shabby, aren't I? But Aunt Ellen will have to see me soon, Agnes. I haven't anything else to wear.'

'I wasn't thinking of your aunt. It's the new servants. So we'll wrap you up in this and say you've caught a chill – and that's only a white lie,' Agnes added hastily. It wouldn't surprise her if the girl had more than a chill wrong with her; there wasn't a smudge of colour in her cheeks.

'What is Aunt Ellen like?'

'A very nice lady,' Agnes said firmly. But she was remembering: *I suppose you have to go for that girl today, Agnes? What a nuisance! Just when I need the carriage myself.* 'Oh, look, Miss Hester, there's Stanhope!'

Hester craned her head sideways. 'Oh, Agnes, are those the gates?' A high stone wall, then a thick band of trees and now a pair of iron gates. A woman came out of a cottage beside the gates and opened them, calling out something to the coachman, as he carefully wheeled the horses into the drive.

'That's Mrs Irwin – quite a nice woman,' Agnes conceded.

6   81

'Bin here years of course – since the old lord lived here. She calls me Mrs Bentley, but I never was married.'

The horses were now trotting down a long winding drive, bordered first by elms and limes and then by rhododendrons in flower. Rooks were calling from the top branches of the trees and a flock of pigeons suddenly rose with a clatter of wings and wheeled against the sky. A black horse, looking over the park railings, whinnied and began to keep up with his companions between the carriage shafts. Then suddenly they were round the last bend and there was Stanhope, for over three hundred years the seat of the Earls of Girvan and now the home of that very new baronet, Sir Joseph Prickard.

A long white house seeming to rise from the halfmoon of grass in front of it came into Hester's view and she heard herself gasp aloud. All those windows and chimneys – it was vast!

That the Prickards were still in the throes of moving was evident, because a veritable army of builders and painters and gardeners were still at work on its exterior. Some were perched on the roof replacing tiles. Some were painting windows. A broken conservatory was being removed piecemeal from one side of the house, and a man and a boy were cutting the grass with scythes. They all paused to stare as the carriage drew up. Then the front door opened as if by magic and a large fat butler emerged and stood waiting on the top step to receive Miss Hester Kelsey.

'That's Mr Wiston,' Agnes whispered, arranging the rug round Hester's shoulders. 'Just say good afternoon to him, miss.'

Wiston looked as if he and not Uncle Joe owned Stanhope, Hester thought with awe. He was bowing slightly, looking in some surprise at the huddled figure being steered past him by Agnes. 'Shall I take the rug, Miss Bentley?'

'No, thank you, Mr Wiston. Miss Hester's got a chill. I'm going to put her straight to bed.'

'The young lady certainly doesn't look well, Miss Bentley.'

Agnes was nodding at the coachman. 'Thanks, coachman, a very nice ride. Most enjoyable.'

Waterman touched his hat with his whip and the carriage moved away. Pressing Hester's shoulders warningly, Agnes hurried her past Wiston and across the huge echoing hall covered in black and white tiles just like a chessboard, Hester thought, twisting her head this way and that and wishing Agnes wouldn't hurry so. They went up an un-carpeted oak staircase to the wide landing that was almost a gallery. Here was an expanse of green carpet and dark green papered walls rising up into the centre of the house. Then they went up again (this time the stairs were narrower and covered in Turkey carpet) and turned down a corridor into what Agnes called the west wing.

'Your room's got a lovely view,' she promised and threw open a door. Hester walked into a high-ceilinged room smelling of fresh paint and beeswax. She trod on a thick carpet covered with red roses as big as cabbages. There were roses all over the walls too; pink and fat with ferns and ivy twined through them. Very lifelike Hester thought, marvel-ling. There were two big mahogany wardrobes, a chest of drawers covered with a lace cloth, a dressing table with a lot more drawers and white crocheted mats, a high bed hung in white dimity and a marble-topped washstand across one corner.

Hester stared round almost fearfully. It was so big! She had no possessions to put in all those drawers and cupboards.

'Come and look out here,' Agnes invited her from the window. 'There! What d'you think to that?'

There was a lovely view across a lake to some woods and rising hills. Hester looked and shuddered with delight. She had seen nothing like it in her life. It was all more beautiful than she believed possible.

'Then through here is the old schoolroom.' Agnes opened another door. 'Sir Joseph thought it would make you a nice sitting room. It's just as it was in the last Lord Girvan's youth. He and his sister took their lessons here, no doubt. See these old desks?'

One could see children had lived here. There was a fire-guard, a deep leather Chesterfield sofa, some basket chairs and a shabby table. Hester began to feel more at home. 'It's lovely, Agnes. Can I really use it?'

'It's yours, Miss Hester,' Agnes said, returning to the bedroom. 'You can change things round just as you please. Now, I want you to get undressed and take a bath. Melia will bring it in for you.' Agnes knelt and lit the fire. 'That will warm the room for your bath.'

'It's a funny time to take a bath,' Hester objected. She wanted to go downstairs and run about in the garden exploring. 'Must I have a bath now?'

'Yes, miss, now. And after that into bed with you.'

'Bed? But I'm not really ill!'

'No, I daresay not. But you haven't a stitch to wear, Miss Hester, and you'll just have to give me time to get something for you. There's a good dressmaker in the village – she's been making print dresses for the maids – so you'll just have to stay in bed until we've thought of something for you. There's a bolt or two of pretty stuff put away in the press – I'll have to see.' Agnes was in her element organizing Hester, and going to the wall she tugged a handle. 'That's a bell, miss, you ring it if you want anything. I've rung for Melia to bring in your bath.'

A plump girl in a print dress appeared after a knock on the door. She looked flurried. 'Oh, Miss Bentley, m'lady's bin a-ringing and a-ringing for you. Won't have anything to do with me and Lizzie – it's you she wants urgent.' She glanced at Hester, smiling and bobbing a curtsey as she babbled. 'Oh, Miss Bentley, you'd better go at once. . . . '

'Dear me, Melia, you haven't the sense of a sparrow. Why didn't you tell m'lady I was unpacking Miss here? Now stop chattering and fetch in the bath and hot water. Miss Hester's not well and is going to bed.'

A large white towel was laid on the carpet in front of the

sparkling fire. Then a hip bath was brought in and put in the exact centre. Then Melia and another girl in a print dress ran to and fro with copper cans of hot water which they emptied into the bath. A screen was put up and Hester was invited to undress. The two girls left and Agnes prepared to depart. 'I shall be back in a few minutes to wash your hair in the basin,' she promised.

A hot bath in front of the fire was a luxury unknown at 8 Pride Street. Washing bit by bit in cold water had been the daily routine. But when her mother was alive, they had bathed in turn before the fire Hester remembered, as she tested the water with a finger. Remembering her mother, she choked suddenly. Oh, if only her mother had been alive to come with her to Stanhope, how happy she would have been!

'It's silly to cry,' Hester told herself, concentrating hard on the big tablet of pink soap that stood in a dish shaped like a shell. What lovely thick towels – three of them. She cast her clothes off and got into the bath. It was blissfully deep and hot and the soap smelled of geranium and not roses. Soaping herself vigorously she began to sing.

Agnes came back. Hester could hear her on the other side of the screen. 'What's in this parcel, may I ask?'

'My nighties, my spare chemise and my drawers.'

There was a rustle of paper. 'Tch! You'll surely not get into these any more, Miss Hester. They're not big enough.'

'They're terribly tight,' Hester agreed, soaping her face and spluttering. 'It's my bosom, you see. I've suddenly grown bosoms. . . . '

'Hsh. Young ladies mustn't talk so! Just say yes, they are a little tight for me, Agnes. . . . '

'They're very tight!' Hester protested. She had better not tell Agnes that recently she had been forced to sleep in her skin. . . .

'They're nowt but rags,' Agnes said bluntly. 'I'm surprised at your aunts – I am really. Now get dried, miss, for I'm going to wash your hair in this basin. I've got some nice

85

rainwater for rinsing it.' And wash it she did, vigorously, as if consumed with a religious ardour to wash the last smell of 8 Pride Street out of Hester's hair. And as she washed she muttered under her breath, her mind busy. Presently, Hester was kneeling in front of the fire wrapped in a large white towel; while Agnes brushed the silky dark hair into a cloud. 'Now, we'll tie it back with this ribbon and you can put on this nightdress; it's an old one of Lady Prickard's, one she used when she was young.'

Hester regarded it with delight. It was white lawn, very fine with drawn thread work and baby ribbon. 'Oh, it's much too beautiful to wear in bed!'

Agnes snorted. 'A pretty sight you'd look wearing it anywhere else! Now into bed with you.'

The bed felt like thistledown when Hester bounced on it experimentally. She rolled over and stretched. 'Ooh, I do feel tired. I was up so early you see.' She also felt hungry but forbore to say so. Perhaps Agnes would tell her that that was another thing young ladies didn't say. Over the top of the sheet, her eyes followed the bustling figure of her benefactor. It was due to Uncle Joe that she was here; but it was Agnes who was the first person to care for her, to scold and order her about, the first person since her mother had died. Yes, for Agnes she would always have a special feeling.

'Melia will bring you your luncheon shortly,' Agnes said. 'You eat every scrap and then go to sleep – you look worn-out, child.'

'Could I have some window open? Just a little? It's very warm in here now.'

Agnes looked horrified. 'After your bath? D'you want to catch your death? And don't gossip with Melia, Miss Hester. She's a gabby girl – as curious as a cat and she's got as long a tongue.'

Melia was soon upstairs with the tray which she arranged carefully on the new arrival's lap, stealing many glances as she did so. My word, she thought, she's a beauty. Too thin though. Wonder how old she is.

The two girls smiled at each other.

'Feeling better, miss? You looked proper poorly when you arrived.'

'Yes, much better, thank you.' She was trying not to eye the food too avidly. It smelled so good when Melia removed the silver covers: soup with cream in it, salmon poached in caper sauce with a small mound of creamed potatoes, treacle tart. There was also a jug of lemon barley water. Waiting only until the door had shut again, Hester fell on the food with squeaks of delight. She ate every scrap, finishing with a warm roll and butter. Her stomach, so little used to food, felt tight and uncomfortable. Long before Melia returned for the tray she had fallen asleep with her mouth open.

'Well, there's not much wrong with you,' Melia muttered as she examined the dishes scraped clean of food.

Agnes waited until her mistress had finished luncheon before mentioning Hester again. She had told her that Hester had arrived and had been put to bed as she was tired. She had left it at that and Ellen, who was completely uninterested, had asked no questions.

It was Ellen's habit to go up to her bedroom after her meal and 'have a rest'. As she had done nothing more strenuous than a little embroidery, this was a misnomer for a re-charging of the batteries after overeating. For Ellen loved food. The pounds of butter and the quarts of cream she consumed shone from her smooth, oily skin. A small-boned woman who had once boasted an eighteen-inch waist, she was now like a small mountain of flesh. Agnes came up as usual to divest her of her garments, and to wrap her in the shabby pink wrapper she preferred to her smarter *robe de nuit* which she donned when the doctor called. Having drawn down the blinds and comfortably settled her mistress, Agnes folded her hands across her stomach and fired her first shot.

'Well, I've bin an' fetched her, m'lady. She's a very nice young lady but it's to my way of thinking that maybe there's something wrong. She's that thin. . . .'

'You mean Hester Kelsey?' Ellen peevishly shifted her head on the pillow.

'Yes, m'lady. Looks very sickly. Might be TB. She's that thin – why you could put your hand round her waist! I was wondering . . . ' She stopped for Ellen was sitting bolt upright, a look of horror on her fat face.

'TB! You mean tuberculosis? We can't have her here. She must go away – go to a hospital – we can't have that disease in the house. There's Wilfred to consider – I knew it was a mistake. I said so from the first!'

'M'lady, I didn't say she had got it. It's just that those harbour children are full of it and it would be best for the doctor to see her. Will you send for the doctor from the village? His lady called on Tuesday if you remember, mum.'

'Yes, Doctor Mayne is his name. Is she coughing?'

'Oh, no, mum. But she looks sickly. She needs feeding up and plenty of rest I'd say. But we ought to have the doctor to be on the safe side.'

Ellen nodded. She wanted to meet Doctor Mayne for herself. Mrs Mayne, an agreeable little woman, had told her the doctor was extremely interested in heart disease. She felt certain that Doctor Dent at Sewerston had never understood her case – he had been quite off-hand at times. Yes, she would ask Doctor Mayne to call and prescribe for her; he could see Hester afterwards. She closed her eyes and flapped her hand at Agnes. 'Send for him,' she said.

But when she woke an hour later, the uneasy thought of the girl had returned. Could she be really sick? Perhaps have TB? It was too bad of Joe to go off to America on the maiden voyage of *Golden Jubilee* and leave all the responsibility for *his* niece on her shoulders. Well, if it was lungs, the girl would have to go.

She rang for Agnes to help her dress, choosing a plum-coloured tea gown when she heard the doctor had sent word

88

that he would call at five o'clock. When Agnes suggested that Ellen should go and see the girl before going down for tea, she refused. 'Let everything be done for her that's needed but don't bother me.'

'She has no clothes fit to be seen in, m'lady. They were in rags and I burned 'em,' Agnes said with satisfaction. 'You'll need to send an order to Umpleby's – it'd be quicker than writing to Harrogate. Coachman could go over and wait to collect the parcel. She needs everything and she can't get up until she gets 'em.'

Ellen stared, her round face blank with surprise. 'Nothing at all of her own?'

'Not a stitch, mum. Not even a pair of stockings.'

'Well, I never heard of such a thing! It's too bad that I have to be bothered.' Grumbling she sat at her desk and, with a nib that scratched, penned an order at Agnes's instructions.

'I should ask for a selection suitable for a fifteen-year-old girl. Bust bodices, chemises and drawers,' Agnes directed and Ellen meekly wrote it down. 'Then, mum, I was thinking. . . .'

'You can stop thinking. I've done all I'm going to do.'

'But she must have a skirt and bodice, mum. There's a nice little dressmaker in the village called Miss Ward. She could run something up for Miss Hester in no time if you gave the word. . . .'

It occurred to Ellen, as she penned the second note, that Agnes Bentley was thoroughly enjoying herself. Well, she had never wanted the girl in the first place and she might have known there would be all this bother. All very well for Joe – men never had to trouble themselves with details like stockings and drawers for impoverished nieces. 'Get her all she needs,' Joe had said and had then gone off to America.

'Will you come and see Miss Hester, m'lady?'

'I suppose I must.'

Together they went up the stairs and into the west wing. In the corridor, two young women were hanging curtains

89

at the long windows. They bobbed curtseys as Lady Prickard passed. Green brocade, she thought angrily, when she had *told* Joe that she wanted dark red with velvet tassels. He simply hadn't taken any notice and had chosen everything as he wanted it himself. It was too bad. He never listened to her at all now.

As Agnes opened the door, Ellen found herself face-to-face with a young edition of Nancy Prickard, Joe's dead half-sister. Those eyes. That white skin. A wave of surprised colour swept over Ellen's face and neck. The girl was the image of her mother.

But here Ellen was wrong. Hester was not really like her mother except for those unusual eyes. She was taller and thinner; her dark hair was her father's for Nancy's had been fair. Their features were not alike. But so strong was the general impression that she looked like Nancy, that most people who had known the dead woman saw the inherited look at once.

'Aunt Ellen?' Hester sat up in bed and smiled her wide smile.

Now that she was here, Ellen was at a loss for words. 'How – how are you, Hester?'

'I'm very well, thank you. I've been asleep,' and she laughed. 'Asleep in the middle of the day! This is a lovely room, Aunt Ellen. Thank you for everything.'

Ellen looked round in surprise. She had barely seen this room. It seemed very ordinary to her, filled as it was with the old stuff from the Harbour House. 'I'm glad you like it,' she said lamely. 'Now, Doctor Mayne will be coming to see you shortly because Agnes doesn't think you're very well.'

Hester looked reproachfully at Agnes. 'I'm not really ill, Aunt Ellen. It's just that I have no clothes to wear and Agnes says I must stay here until she finds some for me.'

Ellen's eyes were suddenly on the nightdress Hester was wearing. 'Where did she get that?' she asked Agnes sharply. 'It is mine – one of my trousseau nightgowns. You had no business to give it to her! She must take it off at once, do

90

you hear? *At once.*' One plump hand had gone to her quivering mouth and she stamped her foot with anger. How dared Agnes? Her lovely nightgown that she had embroidered herself all one winter. She had worn the gown on the first night of her honeymoon and Joe had said . . . had said. . . . She turned away, a terrible and hungry regret filling her. She had been a young slim girl once and very much in love. What had happened? 'She must take it off at once,' she mumbled and left the room.

Hester looked down at the nightgown. 'Oh, Agnes, she's angry. I didn't know it was Aunt Ellen's.' But Aunt Ellen was so fat. Could she ever have worn this lovely fairytale garment?

'She's got no use for it any more,' Agnes said, folding her lips in a long line of suppressed anger. 'It wouldn't go over her shoulders and she knows it. Never you mind, love. I'll get you one of Melia's.' She hurried after her mistress. 'What d'you suggest, m'lady? Shall I borrow from one of the young servants for your niece? It'll look mighty queer. . . .'

'I don't care what you do!' Ellen burst out. 'You shouldn't have done such a thing. It's wrong of you.' She went down the stairs holding tightly to the bannister. To see that girl so like Nancy in *her* nightgown. She was unable to unravel her thoughts; they were too mixed-up. She had known how devoted Joe had been to his young half-sister, had known and been bitterly jealous. She had considered it a strange relationship and had regarded it with a secret loathing. And she had often accused him of being fonder of Nancy than he was of his wife. 'She should never have come here,' she said aloud, and now she was thinking of Hester.

Doctor Mayne arrived promptly at five o'clock, very pleased to have got the call to the manor. He had rather feared that the Prickards would still retain the services of old Doctor Dent at Sewerston, but it now looked as if Polly's call on Lady Prickard on Tuesday was bearing fruit. As he drove his smart dogcart up the drive, he congratulated himself on being firm with his young wife. The silly little thing was a prey to the most absurd fears about her social duties and had asked him not to 'make her call on Lady Prickard. She felt that she wouldn't know how to do it properly and begged dearest James to forgive her . . . ' but he had been firm. Kind but firm. To please him she had gone docilely up the long drive, left her cards, stayed the prescribed fifteen minutes and had returned home quite flushed with success. Doctor Mayne smiled fondly under his beard. Firmness. That's all that women needed.

He was somewhat disconcerted to be passed from the butler to a grey-haired woman in a black sateen dress and white apron. So they had called him in for one of the servants –

'Lady Prickard wishes you to examine her niece, Miss Kelsey, sir,' Agnes said, bobbing a curtsey. 'She came to live here today and m'lady's a little uneasy about her health. She wondered if you would test her lungs, sir. You know what that consumption does to young ladies and she's that thin.'

'Indeed, I do. Lady Prickard is perfectly right,' Doctor Mayne agreed as he followed the woman upstairs and looked round him with unconcealed interest. My word, they had made a good job of the old place! Very fine. Very rich.

Twenty minutes later he was bowing over Lady Prickard's hand in the drawing-room. 'Delighted to make your acquaintance, m'am. My wife has called, I believe? Now let me put your mind at rest with regard to your niece. Her lungs are clear I'm glad to say. She is however extremely thin – too thin for good health. Where has she been living? Abroad with her family perhaps? India takes a toll of young growing people. . . . '

'She has been living in Sewerston with her father's sisters.'

Doctor Mayne raised his brows. 'Well, Lady Prickard, the young lady is very anaemic – I suspect her blood is very weak. She needs plenty of rest and good food and one of my efficacious tonics. She's thoroughly debilitated. One of my lads shall bring over the medicine this evening. Rest in bed for a few days will be no bad thing. Never fear, m'am, we shall take good care of her,' Doctor Mayne added with a pleased smile. 'Let nature do the rest. Sleep and food – I may say that raw meat sandwiches would be a useful addition to her diet – and fresh air when she feels strong enough to take it. These declines are often puzzling, but I flatter myself I know how to deal with them.'

Ellen had waited with increasing irritation as his voice rumbled on. What a talker the man was, she thought as she opened her mouth and waited for a gap to enter the conversation. She listened only in part to his diagnosis and recommendations. Let Agnes take care of the girl, she thought indifferently. 'Doctor Mayne, I have a serious complaint of the heart and would value your opinion. Doctor Dent at Sewerston never did understand me. I am sure you will.'

Their eyes met. Doctor Mayne smiled expansively. 'Ah, yes, the *heart* – a very tricky organ with a multitude of symptoms. Now, dear lady, tell me what troubles you. I am in no hurry – no hurry at all.'

Tommy Hoggarth approached 8 Pride Street with some trepidation which he attempted to conceal beneath a brave manner. He was going to be a soldier wasn't he? Then there was no need to be afraid of that old dragon, Miss Kelsey. Proper tartar she was, everyone said. Look at the way she had treated poor Hes.

He looked down fondly at the letter in his hand. He'd made a good job of it, using the paper and envelope he had purloined from his father's shop. Ink he had found on the mantelshelf above Granpa's chair. Carrying everything up to his room, he had found his old penholder from schooldays, cleaned the rust off the nib by sucking it and then composed his letter to Hester. In it he had explained that by going into the army he hoped to make fame and fortune

in some war somewhere. Would she write to him sometimes? If she addressed her letter care of his mother, it
would be sent on to the barracks. He hadn't heard yet where
they were being sent – those five Sewerston boys who had
taken the Queen's shilling. Some said down south, London
way perhaps. He hoped she was enjoying her new life and
that her uncle was kind to her. As for him, he would never
forget her and he remained hers truly, Tommy.

Truly. Yes, it had the right sound to it. He would never
love another girl.

Snatching off his cap, he mounted the steps and opened
the shop door with some diffidence. He had never been in a
ladies' hat shop before. He looked round with interest and
some amusement. That was a funny one. . . .

'Well?'

He whirled round and met the basilisk stare of the eldest
Miss Kelsey, the dragon one. 'Please, miss, please, Miss
Kelsey, I've got something for Hester. A letter.'

She took it. 'Who is it from?'

He stammered, 'Me, m'am.'

Her eyes rose from the envelope and bored into him. 'She
doesn't live here any more.'

'No, but I thought you could put her address on it and I
would post it. It has a stamp on it . . . see. . . . '

'I shall have to look it up and I haven't the time now.
You had better leave it with me and I'll see to it later.'

But he hung on to the envelope. 'I'd better come back
later. . . . '

With a flick of the wrist she obtained possession of the
envelope once more. Moving away she said, 'You can leave
it with me, good morning.'

Walking away from the shop he cursed himself for being
such a fool. He didn't trust her. Hes had told him what she
was like.

In the workroom, Agatha was slitting open the envelope,
rapidly reading the contents of the letter. A sardonic grin

94

flitted across her face. Little fools. The world was full of them.

She walked across to the stove, opened its top and thrust the letter and envelope inside. She dusted her hands in a satisfied manner. Well, she had quite a nice appetite for dinner so she had better close the shop.

CHAPTER FOUR

It was almost five weeks to the day when Joseph Prickard travelled home and was met at the junction by his carriage.

'Well, John, how are things at Stanhope?' he asked the young footman who was seeing to the luggage.

'Everything's fine, sir,' the boy answered shyly.

Joseph nodded and strolled out to speak to Waterman who, like Agnes, had been with him at the Harbour House. The man doffed his billycock hat, holding the reins of the restless horses with his left hand. 'They don't like the sound of those steam engines,' Joseph said by way of greeting. Master and man eyed one another. 'All well at home?'

'Ay, master, all well, God be praised.' Waterman had a slow deep voice and steady eyes and was a lay preacher at the methodist chapels in the district. Joseph had heard that his sermons (with their promise of hellfire) were famous in methodist circles and could well believe it. He occupied a neat cottage behind the stableyard at Stanhope and had brought up three boys who feared him. The youngest had just started as garden boy a few weeks ago.

'How is Michael shaping?' Joseph asked, as he waited for John to put the luggage in the boot.

'A bit slow, Stead says, but he'll learn, sir. His only fault is youth,' said Waterman with a glimmer of a smile. 'The wife and I appreciate your taking him on, sir. There's wild company and temptation outside the home. We like to keep our lads with us.'

Joseph shook his head wonderingly. How did Waterman

hope to keep three healthy boys – one of them almost a man – tied to his coat tails all their lives? Some day they would defy him and would break away. That was human and right.

Leaning back in the carriage he became lost in thought, a little smile on his clean-shaven face. His thoughts were with Emmy O'Neill whom he had left that morning. Four days of Emmy had left him surfeited and in high humour with the world. He had been hungry for her after more than four weeks away. She had guessed this and when he had reached the villa on Monday evening she had been waiting for him in bed, naked and inviting. What a woman! There was no one like her, he thought gratefully. A wife would have jibbed at the games he liked to play – a wife would find them ridiculous at his age. But not Emmy. Emmy's squeals of mounting desire still echoed in his head, bringing that smile to his face. Thank God for Emmy, he told himself devoutly. And then firmly put her out of his mind.

The trip had been a huge success – no doubt about that. The *Golden Jubilee*'s maiden voyage had not broken any record, but there had been no mishaps, and her engines had turned as sweetly as their designer had promised they would. He had been fêted in New York and Boston and had made many new friends. It was while the ship was being turned round that he had made the trip to New York for a few days on a sight-seeing excursion. The shops had amazed him and he had spent freely. He could see Emmy now (there she was, back in his thoughts!) sitting up in bed looking towsled, opening the many presents he had brought her. The hat with ostrich feathers, the little silver clock and heart-shaped locket, the fine linen handkerchiefs, the embroidered petticoat (worked by Swiss nuns, they assured him and he had chuckled, seeing the petticoat on that baggage, Emmy!).

Until suddenly, she had stopped, her eyes had narrowed and she had demanded, 'What have you brought *her*?'

He knew she meant Ellen. Exasperated, he had bent and kissed her breast. 'A feather boa. Grey and very expensive.'

7   97

It amused him to see the rage in her expressive face. 'Come now, Emmy, you wouldn't want me to forget her, would you?'

'Yes, I would. I want to be first, Joe.'

'But you are . . . you are. . . .'

'I must always be first with you, Joe, always.'

He sighed, wearying of the same old jealous argument. She hated the very thought of Ellen. And only a little later, she had suddenly demanded: 'Why don't you take me to New York, Joe? Your next trip? I'm sick and tired of being cooped up here while you're gallivanting in America. I mean to come next time,' and she had nodded her head emphatically.

'I shan't be going again for a long time,' he lied.

What she asked was quite impossible. He couldn't take her about with him. Did she want to ruin him? It was Ellen whom he must persuade to accompany him on his next trip. For America had got into his veins, and he knew he must go back soon. Ellen would have to accompany him and meet his directors who would also be bringing their wives. They had vaguely mentioned the autumn – it would be one of the last trips of the year. He would give a reception on board and Ellen must be at his side. In a year or so, when Wilfred left Radley, he would take him too. But Emmy never.

They were turning in at the gates. His heart gave a great leap of gladness. All his. As far as the eye could see. He leaned out as if he would drink it all in better by being able to touch the overhanging branches that made the drive a dark cave. Then they were out in the open again and the May blossom was in full flower, the grass high. A squirrel leapt across the road and landed on the park fence. There were the horses deep in lush grass just raising their heads to watch the carriage pass. All his, his heart sang. Yes, he had done remarkably well to achieve this lovely place. And he was still making money fast. If this government stayed in office ten years, he would be a millionaire. There was nothing to stop him reaching the very pinnacle of success –

nothing that hard grind and an astute mind couldn't achieve.

Now the house was in view. He let his breath out in a renewal of satisfaction. It looked so lovely in the sunlight, all the panes of the long windows glinting. The broken stonework had been mended so cunningly that one could scarcely see the joins.

His butler had come out on to the steps. He was home.

'Has my niece arrived yet?' he asked Wiston as they went into the hall.

'She's been here more than two weeks, sir. It's very nice to have some young life about the house while Master Wilfred's away. And a very nice young lady she is, sir. Very popular with the staff.'

So Hester was here at last. He had foiled those aunts. He suddenly felt as gleeful as a boy. 'And her ladyship?'

'She is in the drawing-room, sir. I have just served tea.'

Prickard went up the stairs two at a time and Wiston watched him indulgently. Must be very fond of her ladyship, he thought sentimentally, as he turned back to give John a piece of his mind for not being faster with the luggage.

Prickard opened the drawing-room door quietly and looked round eagerly. Ellen appeared to be alone. She was sitting near a window, the tea table at her side glinting with silver, its starched lace cloth throwing off a white light. She was in the shadow of the halfdrawn curtains herself, her head bent, busily eating. She had to swallow hastily when she caught sight of him.

'Why, Joe, I never heard you arrive!'

Good God, she was fatter than ever! he thought with dismay. Almost grotesque, her fine looks quite gone.

'Yes, my dear, here I am.' He bent over her and kissed her forehead. She was dabbing at her mouth with a linen napkin, choking a little in her haste. But even as he greeted her, one plump hand was stretching out for more hot teacake dripping with yellow butter . . . She behaves as if she's famished, he thought with irritation. Nothing must interrupt the important ritual of eating.

'Have you had a pleasant voyage?'

'Capital. Everything went like clockwork. Ellen, I would like you to come with me next time – in the autumn perhaps.'

'I? Oh no, I dislike the sea,' she answered indifferently, pouring tea for him. 'Do try these muffins, Joe; they are remarkably good. I really feel I must have one more.'

Why was her gluttony such an irritant? he wondered. Was it because he remembered her as a thin girl and he couldn't reconcile that image with this fat woman?

'How are you liking the house?'

'It's a great responsibility,' she said complainingly and swallowed her tea fast. 'Such a big place and all these servants to look after. . . . '

'My dear, they are supposed to be looking after *you*.' He looked approvingly round the room. Yes, it was just as he had hoped it would look when that pale green watered silk had been put on the walls. He would have to buy some fine pictures – perhaps something by that fellow Landseer the Queen was so fond of – for the walls looked bare with those pale water colours and only a mirror or two to cover their surfaces. His spirits rose as he thought of the hours of pleasure he would have in going round the sale rooms, looking for pictures in decent heavy frames. He liked big still life pictures himself. Yes, it all looked very nice and smelled freshly of paint and wax polish. 'But where is our niece? Where is Hester? I understand she has arrived here. Why isn't she at tea with us?'

She wiped her lips and looked at him sideways. It suddenly occurred to him that she was nervous. He looked at her sharply, but now she was avoiding his eyes. 'She is upstairs in her room.'

'Then please ring for her to come down.'

'She didn't want tea.'

'Silly child. She must learn to do what we want, Ellen. I want her to have easy manners and she won't learn staying up in her room.' He went across to a table and took up several parcels. 'For you, my dear. From America.'

100

'Oh, Joe!' Her full cheeks flushed with pleasure. At last she forgot the tea table and was concentrating on his presents: several pairs of beautiful doeskin gloves in white and grey came out of the first box. Some had tiny buttons at the wrist; some came halfway up the arm. She concealed her dismay, knowing they would never go over her arms. 'Joe, they're so elegant!' A grey box with a name in silver next caught her attention: among its bed of tissue paper lay a grey feather boa, its feathers the finest and fluffiest she had ever seen. It would be perfect with her new Jubilee outfit for June 21. Smaller boxes contained silver trinkets for her reticule, a pair of amber and gold eardrops and a tiny enamel box for her pills. Tears came into her eyes; how generous he was. She got up to kiss him, but he had moved away.

'I'll go up and fetch Hester down. Is she shy?'

'Not in the least,' Ellen retorted. 'That's the trouble. If you must know, I've sent her up to her room and she's to stay there until I send for her.'

He turned and looked alertly into her face: so she was not fond of the girl. He could see it in her eyes, in the pout of her lips.

'Isn't she a little old for that sort of punishment? What can she have done to merit this?'

Ellen's lips were now folding righteously. 'She was making eyes at the butler during luncheon. I caught her at it.'

Prickard stared at her. Then he threw back his head and roared with laughter. 'My dear Ellen, you can't be serious! Making eyes at the butler! Why, Wiston's a grandfather! I have it on the best authority that he has seven grandchildren, some Hester's own age. Surely you are joking?'

'I am not then!' Ellen always disliked being corrected. 'I knew she'd be a handful. I told you not to adopt her, didn't I? Those harbour brats are far too mature for their age. She will be a terrible trouble to us when Willy comes home in the summer. . . . '

'Nonsense! It's absurd! You must have taken leave of your senses. I'm going straight upstairs to fetch her down.'

She stared miserably at the closed door. He was angry with her when it ought to be Hester; for it was she who was to blame. And she had felt quite close to him a few minutes ago . . . She *knew* it had been a mistake to take in that child of Nancy's. She got up heavily and went across to the bell in the wall; the tea was cold and more must be brought. Then she went back to the table and cut herself a wedge of plum cake.

He had hoped she would accept the girl, he told himself as with long strides he mounted the stairs and went along the corridor to the old playroom. He had hoped that some maternal spring in her would be touched, that she would be delighted to have the girl as her daughter. But it seemed he had been wrong; all her maternal feelings were poured on to Wilfred. The boy was becoming a milksop, Prickard told himself wrathfully, just because Ellen sheltered him too much – or he supposed it must be that. At his son's age he had gone to sea. Do Wilfred all the good in the world if he had to rough it a bit. Ellen had never punished the boy as she was punishing Hester. It was because she was resentful of the girl for being Nancy's child. She had never loved Nancy, because she was jealous of his feelings for his half-sister. He sighed. There were going to be difficulties.

The schoolroom door was ajar. He peeped round it.

She had her back to him. The window was open at the bottom and she was kneeling on the windowseat, her arms on the sill. She was looking out on the park that stretched to the lake and the trees and singing under her breath.

'Hester.'

She jumped, banging her head on the window. Rubbing it with one hand, she came towards him smiling ruefully. 'You gave me a shock! I'm so glad you're back, Uncle Joe.'

He bent to kiss her, then held her away from him, studying her face. In the two weeks she had been at Stanhope there had been a change. He remembered a grey-faced waif

102

with lank hair; this girl was beginning to look like a healthy person again. He felt an enormous satisfaction at having done the right thing. There was warmth under the skin, a fullness to the cheeks and a sheen to the dark hair that had been absent before. Then he looked into her eyes searchingly, he could always tell a person by their eyes . . . and Hester's passed the test. He nodded to himself.

'You're looking very well, my dear child. Much better than when I last saw you.' But what a dreadful dress she was wearing!

Joseph Prickard, who knew a great deal about women's clothes (Ellen would have been surprised how much he knew and noticed) classed his niece's dress as 'orphanage garb'. It was obviously one she had brought with her; perhaps it was her best so he mustn't criticize it. Ellen must order new dresses at once. He couldn't have the girl going round looking like a poor relation. The skirt and bodice were a dull brown (a colour that Hester would never look well in) and, with its starched white collar, it was reminiscent of an institutional uniform. It was also badly-made. Well, all that would be seen to in time. He had thought he had urged Ellen to clothe the girl when she came – she must have forgotten.

Now he dipped one hand in his pocket and brought out a tiny square box; it was black, tied with gold string with the name *Tiffany* across its centre. 'For you. From New York.'

A flush of excitement lighted her face and she bent over the little box, as eager as a squirrel with a nut. As she opened it she said, 'Oh!' and then stood looking at the gift in complete silence. It was a slim gold watch on a long slender chain.

'It goes round your neck like this – ' he looped it over her hair – 'and fits into your waistband pocket here. But I see you haven't a pocket. Never mind, you'll be having new dresses soon and you can have all the pockets you want.'

'It's beautiful. Beautiful . . . ' A watch of her own, a golden watch that had her initials on the back, the H and the K intricately woven into a tracery of flowers. Tears stung

103

her eyes and she continued to bend her head so that her uncle shouldn't see them. His kindness was almost unnerving her. She didn't know how to deal with it.

'Hester, look at me.' He was patting her shoulder. 'It's only a watch, you silly child! No need to cry. You know, your mother was very different in her reaction,' he went on, giving her time. 'Whenever I came home from a trip she would meet me at the door crying, "What have you got for me, Joe?" Into my pockets she would go, turn everything out and almost cry with disappointment because there was nothing there. You see, I would have hidden it in my hat or behind a plant as I came in. I was always able to fool her,' he added, smiling to himself as he remembered.

'Like the pearls,' Hester nodded. 'The pearls you gave her when she was seventeen.'

He jerked his head up. Those pearls (pretty pink seed pearls) were the last thing he ever gave Nancy. By the time her next birthday came round she had run away with Kelsey. 'Those pearls would suit you, Hester. Have you got them now?'

She shook her head. 'Mother had to sell them. But I saw her wear them sometimes before they went.' She was looking up at him gravely. 'How can I thank you for this? A watch of my own,' and she sighed deeply with satisfaction.

'Hester, are you very fond of that dress? It's really very ugly and doesn't suit you. I would like you to get rid of it.'

'But it's new, Uncle Joe! Wouldn't it be a great waste? Miss Ward from the village made it. Agnes told her how.'

So Ellen had been too lazy even to supervise the girl's dress, he thought irritably. He led her to the door. 'Shall we go down for tea?'

She had drawn back, looking instantly confused and distressed. 'Aunt Ellen told me to stay up here until she sent for me.'

'What happened, Hester? At luncheon, I mean.'

'I don't know how to manage all those knives and forks

at dinner and luncheon,' she said in a low voice. 'At home we never had so many.'

He saw he was getting to the truth at last. 'But did something happen to annoy your aunt? Tell me, child.'

'Aunt Ellen told you she sent me out of the room?'

'Yes. But why? And how does Wiston come into it?'

'Mr Wiston's been very kind to me, you know. He watches out to see I don't make silly mistakes. If I don't use the right knife or fork – and, Uncle Joe, there are a terrible lot, aren't there? – he sort of looks at me. Like this.' She screwed her face up with a look that was so like Wiston's when he wanted to be wise that Joseph had to smother a chuckle: narrowed eyes, a shaking head and wobbling cheeks, all depicting cautious disapproval. 'Today Aunt Ellen caught us. He was trying to tell me not to use my pudding spoon for the soup. Usually Aunt Ellen doesn't look up, but today she wanted more bread and she saw what I was doing.'

'And what was that, Hester?'

Hester narrowed one eye. Yes, it was a wink all right, Joseph conceded and laughter shook him again.

'Uncle Joe, I'll never learn,' Hester wailed. 'All those spoons and forks – how can you ever know which to use?'

'I promise you I'll teach you myself, then you'll never have to worry about it again. Now come on down for tea, and if you spill it all over that dress I for one will be gratified.'

Ellen was still eating when they reached the drawing room.

'I've brought Hester down, my dear. Can you ring for fresh tea? Come, child,' and he drew up a chair.

Looking from one to the other, Ellen's eyes sharpened. When the tea came, Joseph said jokingly, 'Now let's see if you can spill that, Hester!'

Hester, who had eaten no luncheon, ate cucumber sandwiches with a will, trying hard to take only small nibbles. She drank some tea and only splashed a little into her saucer. She caught her aunt's eyes on her, but a sense of achievement was now filling her, and she exchanged a triumphant look with her uncle.

'You've done splendidly – far better than I did when I went to the Abbotsburys for the first time!' and he laughed again at the recollection. 'I knocked over a jug of m'lord's best claret . . . all over the tablecloth. Lady Abbotsbury smiled with the politest air imaginable. . . . '

'Joe, you didn't!' Ellen looked appalled. She took their rise in the world far more seriously than her husband.

'I did indeed and what was worse, I shook so much I could have knocked anything over – including Lady Abbotsbury herself!'

Hester's chuckles joined his for she had met Lady Abbotsbury who was a fairly solid woman.

But Ellen looked offended and stiff. If only Joe wasn't such a plain mannered man, she thought plaintively – ah, what she could do with the right man at her side!

After tea, Hester asked if she could take the large parcel her uncle had brought her up to the schoolroom. As she closed the door, Prickard took up a position on the hearthrug and with his hands under the tail of his coat said patiently, 'Now, Ellen, don't make things miserable for us here. I can see you haven't accepted Hester yet, but she is here for good, you know. She is now to all intents and purposes our daughter. I want the best for her. The best of everything possible. I shall educate her for one thing. She's bright and the right woman as governess will be the making of her. What is that appalling garment she is wearing? Made by the village dressmaker? It isn't good enough for my niece. Don't you understand? She's not the poor relation in this house. She's my flesh and blood.' His eyes, hard and unyielding, met his wife's. Hers dropped and there was a sulky pout to her mouth.

'I'm doing my best. She's difficult. I can't understand her.'

'If you're not prepared to dress the girl properly then I'll have to take her across to Liverpool on my next trip. I have a – friends who will be delighted to help.'

'But you know I'm not strong enough to traipse round shops with her! Doctor Mayne thinks my heart needs great care taken with it. I'm delicate. I've been delicate since Wilfred's birth.' She put her handkerchief to her eyes. 'Mother always said . . . '

He groaned silently. 'Very well, my dear, I'll take her across to Liverpool next week.' He tried to smile. 'Oh, come now, Ellen, this is my first evening at home after many weeks. Don't let's spoil it.' He took her hand and patted it.

But she was not to be won over too easily. 'Doctor Mayne says I could die at any time.'

'Not very clever of him,' Joseph said drily. 'So could we all.' It looked as if this Mayne fellow had found a sinecure, Joseph thought grimly. She was going to adopt ill-health as a pastime. 'My dear, doesn't he think you too fat? You have put on a great deal of weight in the past year or so. It cannot be good for you.'

'But, Joe, I hardly eat a *thing*. I am a little plumper I believe. What about the Queen? She's a great deal fatter than I am.'

Joseph grinned. 'The Queen is an exception to all the rules, my dear Ellen. A wonderful woman. Which reminds me, we must give a reception here the night before the official celebrations. It will be the true anniversary of her coronation, June the twentieth. We will have a buffet supper for about a hundred people, and we'll invite all those families who have called on us, as well as our Sewerston friends. I'll start making out a list at once,' Joseph said with relish, for he enjoyed entertaining.

Ellen's mouth had gone down at the corners. She hated it.

Hester went into raptures at the news she was to take a railway journey with her uncle. He was amused to find that she had never been in a train in her life, and had no other wish

107

than to sample this experience before she was much older.

From her aunt's wardrobe a cloak was produced, one that Ellen had worn in the days when she was slimmer. Ellen never threw away a thing even now that she was rich. 'It might come in,' she would murmur vaguely. So boxes and drawers and cupboards were packed with discarded clothes; all reeking of mothballs.

The cloak still smelled slightly on the day Hester set out for Liverpool. Agnes had shaken it and steamed it, but the nose-pricking smell of camphor still clung to it.

At Sewerston Junction they got into the Leeds train. Leeds! It was enormous! A black and smoky city filled with hurrying people who all seemed to have gathered in the station in order to jostle one another. She clutched Joseph's arm, terrified of losing him as they made their way to the Liverpool boat train. She held a gloved hand to her nose, for the glass-roofed station was filled with black coils of acrid smoke that was making her sneeze. Business men hurried past, catching trains to the woollen mill towns; there were whole families looking for seats in the boat train, children cried, porters shouted. Hester had never seen anything like it in her life, and she was thankful when the attentive conductor, who seemed to know her uncle, led them to a quiet first class compartment. A porter put their luggage on the rack and Sir Joseph joked with him as he pressed a coin in the man's hand. Everyone seemed to know him, Hester thought proudly; even the businessmen who put their heads round the door to exchange a few words.

She inspected their compartment with close attention: the buttoned fabric of the upholstery with a white lace antimacassar for each head, the small mirror on each wall flanked by framed photographs of Yorkshire pleased her. It would be just like travelling across England in a comfortable room, she told herself gleefully. The conductor had returned and was now taking Sir Joseph's order for luncheon baskets to be brought on board at Manchester.

The memory of that first railway journey remained with

her all her life – *the day I went to Liverpool with Uncle Joe*. How fast the train travelled! She felt dizzy at first and clung to the armrest, but Joseph assured her that the train wouldn't fall off the narrow rails; so at last she settled down to watch the passing scene outside the windows, too rapt to look at the book he had bought her.

And then they finally reached the other side of the country and saw the tall masts on Merseyside and the grand city of Liverpool, with its milder wetter air that caused the local voices to sound nasal.

They got into a cab. 'Where are we going to stay, Uncle Joe?'

He looked down with amusement at the happy face raised to his. How Hester enjoyed everything! It had done him good to be with her, to see everything through her un-sophisticated eyes. 'You are going to stay with a friend of mine. Her name is Mrs O'Neill and she's a widow. You'll like it with her, I promise you. It is she who is going to buy your clothes – look, Hester, isn't it a fine city? Booming,' he added with satisfaction, for this meant trade for his cargo-carrying vessels.

At last the cab turned down a tree-lined avenue in Crosby. It stopped before a little house with starched curtains at the window and a monkey puzzle tree in the front garden. It was exactly like a doll's house. Hester loved it at once and thought that whoever lived there must be the happiest people in the world.

Emmy was waiting for them upstairs in the dark little sitting room. She and Joseph greeted each other with a prim handshake as if they hadn't met for weeks. 'Well, Emmy, I've brought my niece to stay with you. Hester, this is Mrs O'Neill who is going to take you shopping for the next few days.'

Emmy nodded excitedly, her eyes shining at the prospect of spending Joe's money. She eyed Hester critically but not unkindly. A thin tall figure, immature but full of promise – yes, she thought she knew exactly how the girl should be dressed. Nothing too childlike. She was too tall for that and on the brink of womanhood.

'Leave her to me, Joe dear, and I promise you won't be disappointed,' she said, remembering too late that she must be circumspect in front of the girl. So she hurriedly caused a diversion by showing off her canaries to her visitor.

It was late and Joseph refused her invitation to dine. Hester stayed in the room while the two adults murmured to each other on the landing. She wondered why they looked at each other as if they were sharing a secret joke. And Mrs O'Neill called him Joe dear; now who would do that except Aunt Ellen? But she seemed a very nice person, Hester thought with relief, and in some ways reminded her of Sal, her dead stepmother. Sal had liked a joke and a romp – perhaps Mrs O'Neill did too. Her eyes certainly sparkled in the same way. Although much more genteel than Sal, Mrs O'Neill had the same raucous laugh and she did look as if she wanted to kick her legs in the air! Sal had often done so to make her father laugh and slap her on the bottom. Mrs O'Neill, for all her proper air, could out-kick Sal any day, Hester thought sagely.

The adults on the landing would have been startled had they known the quality of these thoughts; they considered they were being very discreet.

From the moment Emmy returned and took her cloak and showed her to her bedroom, Hester began to enjoy herself. In Stanhope with its many servants and daily problems of propriety cropping up, Hester had been tense. Here in Acacia Avenue, Crosby, the smell of supper rising from the kitchen, she felt more at home. They ate a simple meal off a table set in the window. There were pink slices of galantine of beef with pickled beetroot and crisp potato rissoles smelling delicately of onions. The meal was served on such pretty flowered plates that Hester had exclaimed over them. Mrs O'Neill said they had been wedding presents, and her face had grown so solemn that Hester wondered uneasily if Mr O'Neill had only recently died. But Mrs O'Neill was wearing bright red

110

taffeta, and she cheered up wonderfully after two glasses of port.

The canaries had gone to sleep and Hester herself was smothering yawns when Polly came up to take the tray down.

'You must go to bed, Hester, for we have to be up early tomorrow to do our shopping. Now, don't open your window, if you please. The smuts in Liverpool are a terrible trial and quite ruin the curtains.'

Lying in bed, Hester could hear the distant hoots of shipping on the great river. The mournful sounds touched a chord in her suddenly. At home, in the harbour cottage, she had been able to hear the hoots of the boats coming into the harbour. Her mother would look in on her on her way to bed. 'Is Father in yet?' 'Not yet. Go to sleep.' The words had been a benison and she had smiled and turned over. It was all over. She was in a new life. 'Then don't be such a silly little ninny,' she told herself fiercely and firmly shut her stinging eyes.

The shops in Liverpool were a bright fantasy; so big and glittering and overflowing with goods. Hester followed Emmy O'Neill round in a daze, her eyes stretched in amazement.

'Hurry, Hester! We've an appointment with Miss Trimmer in Corsets.' Gathering her skirt up, Emmy started up a wide staircase to a discreet department on the third floor.

Corsets. The dreaded word woke Hester from her dreamy examination of the fairytale kingdom she had just entered. 'But, Mrs O'Neill, I don't wear corsets. . . . '

'That was apparent from the moment I saw you.' Emmy paused to utter solemn words. 'Remember, Hester, a corset is absolutely essential for a girl your age. Why, your waist's quite big already!'

There was to be no escape. Miss Trimmer, the fitter, was a formidable woman with a look of despair and with several tape-measures round her neck. 'Well, madam, I don't know I'm sure,' she muttered as she prodded and measured. 'Miss

111

is very thin. No figure to mention. I shall have to pad her here and here – ' A pair of bony hands turned Hester round once more and the two women began to throw urgent words at each other.

'Whalebone?'

'I think steel would be best. . . .

'Covered in chamois?'

'Yes, to begin with. It's going to be uphill work, madam,' Miss Trimmer mouthed over Hester's head. 'It's been left so late, you see. I like to see my young ladies in whalebone by the time they're twelve. It can't do anything but good.'

'I can't breathe!' Hester wailed, when at last she stood in chemise and drawers and the dreaded corsets were laced on. 'It's like being in a steel cage . . . oh, it hurts. . . . '

'Now, Hester, be sensible.'

'I can't breathe!'

Miss Trimmer pulled once more – sharply. 'There, that will do to begin with.'

'You've cut me in half!' Hester could see how red her face had become. Her breath was coming in gasps.

'Quite a nice little figure to build on now,' Emmy observed with satisfaction.

Hester stared down at herself. Her small breasts had been pushed upwards by the shaped corset. Its steel 'bones' bit into her flesh. Hot agony gripped her and she felt dizzy. But the two women ignored her pleas. Miss Trimmer's assistant brought pads and these were sewn into the corset to give Hester hips, on which petticoats and then skirts were hung. A small bustle was then brought, and this proved to be another pad over which the godets of the skirt were hung. Bodices to match the skirts and broad belts of shiny leather were cinched round the now smaller waist.

A sense of doom filled Hester as she stood being turned into a woman. She knew she would never be able to run again.

For three whole days, Emmy O'Neill took Hester from

shop to shop buying clothes, until the pile of boxes in her room overflowed on to the landing.

'Uncle Joe's spending too much money on me,' she demurred at last.

'No man can spend too much money on a woman,' Emmy told her sharply. 'Never under rate yourself, Hester. Remember that now.'

Mrs O'Neill had taste and Joseph Prickard had money. Together they transformed the waif into a well-dressed girl who was going to be beautiful one day. Now she saw that clothes were not just to keep out the cold, but to enhance.

By the third day Hester had had enough. She became silent and limped. Emmy looked at her sharply. 'Do stand up, Hester. You're ruining my good work.'

'Are we going home now?'

'No. We're going to meet a friend of mine for tea . . . ah, there he is!'

Hester looked round quickly, half-expecting to see her uncle; for there had been the same note of purring excitement in Mrs O'Neill's voice as when she spoke to Sir Joseph. But the man advancing towards them was a thickset red-faced man with black side whiskers. He hastily took off his bowler and bowed as if he were not used to doing so.

'Mr Wortle!' Emmy was all smiles, nervously swinging the ends of her white feather boa as she greeted him.

'May I escort you for a cup of tea, Mrs O'Neill,' he asked, his small eyes darting in Hester's direction.

'Well, that would be very kind,' Emmy fluttered. 'Hester, come here, dear – this is Mr Daniel Wortle. Mr Wortle, Miss Kelsey, niece of Sir Joseph Prickard,' she added with emphasis.

Mr Wortle shook Hester heartily by the hand. 'Pleased to meet you.'

They strolled down the street, Hester behind the two adults who were talking absorbedly together. It was a particularly fine day and the city was busy with shoppers, but Mr Wortle seemed to know exactly where to take them. They went down a shady side street and into a tearoom that was dark and quiet, with potted plants filling the lace-curtained window. There were six marble-topped tables and one near the window was empty. Mr Wortle seated them and then summoned the waitress with a crisp ' 'Ere, miss.'

Mrs O'Neill was at her sparkling best. There was evidently something about Mr Wortle that was very agreeable to her. Hester thought him a dreadfully dull man. But Mrs O'Neill poured tea and gave him an inviting sidelong glance as she handed him his cup, and he in return beamed on her, his red face glistening with perspiration. Leaving Hester to do justice to the cherry cake and maids-of-honour, they conducted a low-voiced conversation that seemed satisfactory to both.

An hour later, Mr Wortle helped them into a cab with all their small packages (the bigger ones would be sent up that evening) and stood bowing and smiling and waving his bowler after them.

'A real gentleman,' Emmy said, smiling to herself. 'And he's very, very rich, you know. Wortle's Hair Tonic.'

'Oh,' Hester said blankly. She wondered if that was why he had such a thick head of hair for quite an old man. She said so aloud.

'Good gracious, he's only forty-three!' Emmy said indignantly.

The next day the shopping marathon was completed to Emmy's satisfaction. That evening, Sir Joseph was coming to take them to the music hall to see Dan Leno. Hester was in a fever of excitement at the prospect, and obediently dressed herself in the yellow spotted foulard Polly had laid out for her. Then she went into Emmy's room to have her sash tied and found her hostess having her hair dressed by the ubiquitous Polly, whose mouth was full of hairpins as she teazled and built up the coarse red hair into the style favoured by the Princess of Wales.

Emmy was also in a fever of excitement, bent on coaxing Joe to stay the night with her. He would be hard to persuade she knew because the girl was in the house, but . . . tush! . . .

the girl slept like the dead, and he could be away early before she came down.

'Now, Hester, I hope you haven't loosened the laces of your corset? How are you able to loll like that?'

Hester sat up quickly. 'Oh, no, Mrs O'Neill,' she lied quickly.

'Never, never do that,' Emmy said impressively. 'Your figure will be ruined overnight and then where will you be?' She sprayed herself lavishly with attar of roses and pronounced herself ready.

The doorbell rang sharply.

'Run, Polly. It's Sir Joseph. Tell him we will be down presently. Never be on time for a man,' she added to her pupil. 'It does them good to wait for us. Have you been to the lavatory, Hester? You're sure? There's nowhere at the hall, you know.' Then she was swimming down the stairs, and offering her hand to Joseph who was waiting in the hall, resplendent in a cloak and opera hat.

He looked up, saw Hester and a beam of delight lit up his lean face. 'My word, Hester, I'm proud of you! Emmy my dear, you've wrought a miracle!'

'Yes, haven't I?' Emmy agreed complacently. 'Now, come along, Hester, or we shall be late and I don't want to miss the first acts. They say the conjuror has to be seen to be believed.'

Hester realized she had seen the music hall before. It was the place of her dreams, the place where she herself stood on the stage and performed before a rapt audience. It was almost exactly as she had imagined it: red velvet, gold swagging and mirrors. There was a sense of excitement, of people out to enjoy themselves. And they had a box. A box that was nearly on the stage itself. She sat throughout the evening with her lips parted, her breath shallow, afraid of breaking the spell.

Through this dream went a procession of figures: a funny man called Dan Leno who made everyone sway with laughter, a fat woman who balanced three men on her hips and

115

neck, a girl in a large hat who sang roguish songs. 'Isn't it wonderful?' Hester whispered to Emmy.

Joseph's eyes strayed to his niece's face. Fifteen and still a child who could be entranced by life. How he envied her. But could it last? A heavy feeling of foreboding filled him. Perhaps she would be spoiled by her new life, become a creature of selfish whims always wanting her own way. All he wanted was to make up to her for her bad start in life as Will Kelsey's daughter. It would be terrible if instead he proved her evil genius.

'Your mouth didn't shut the whole evening, Hester,' he chuckled as they set off for home in the hired cab.

Hester, who was watching the traffic in the gaslit streets, threw a smile over her shoulder. 'Oh, Uncle Joe, it was wonderful! Thank you for taking me.' Dreamily, she pressed her nose to the window, thinking that Liverpool was the most magical place in the world and she was sorry to be leaving it tomorrow. In the reflection in the glass she was suddenly aware of something – *Uncle Joe and Mrs O'Neill were holding hands.* Embarrassed she turned her eyes away, biting her lip in a sudden collapse of her high spirits. *Uncle Joe and Mrs O'Neill. Sal and Bert Warley.* Fear flashed through her. What if Aunt Ellen got to know about it? More to create a diversion than for any other reason, she said quickly, 'Oh, look, Mrs O'Neill, isn't that the tearoom where Mr Wortle took us yesterday? They had the loveliest cakes you ever tasted, Uncle Joe!'

The adults were suddenly rigid. Silence reigned in the cab until Prickard said drily, 'Wortle, eh? I thought you hardly knew him, Emmy? A friend of your mother's, wasn't he?'

Mrs O'Neill was sitting up very straight, a ludicrously haughty expression on her peasant face. She said nothing.

'Being attentive, was he? Meeting you for tea?'

'It was pure chance. I beg you not to make an issue of it, Joseph.'

'Out of the mouths of babes and sucklings,' Joseph said sourly.

The little spy! The telltale! Emmy looked hotly in Hester's direction. After all I've done for her, she thought bitterly. I'll teach her to meddle in my affairs!

They reached the villa in silence. Joseph got out of the cab and escorted them up the path to the front door.

'Thank you very much, Uncle Joe. I did enjoy it.'

'Goodnight, my child. Be sure to be ready by eight-thirty tomorrow morning. We have a long journey before us. Goodnight, Emmy.' He replaced his hat and walked back to the waiting cab.

Emmy didn't reply. She stalked into the hall and banged the door behind them. Then she rounded on Hester, her eyes blazing, her voice rising in rage. 'You interfering little bitch! Your loose mouth looks as if butter wouldn't melt in it, but I know better. Talking about my friend to your uncle like that!' Her voice trembled upwards to a scream. 'Take that, you little varmint!'

If Emmy O'Neill had taken off all her clothes and danced naked in the hall, Hester could not have been more astounded. She put her hands up to her stinging cheeks and retreated hastily as if faced with a rabid dog, a friendly dog who had suddenly gone mad and started to bite. Her heart pounded with fright, and she looked round the hall as if wondering how to escape.

Emmy had now collapsed on the bottom stair and was screaming and crying and drumming her heels. Polly came running from the kitchen.

'Eh, dear, pore missis . . . it's the 'istericks again . . . all that tight lacing! 'Ere, miss, give us a 'and, do.' She was expertly unbuttoning Emmy's evening dress down the back, plunging her hand in and releasing the lacings on the corset. 'She's put on weight but won't have it,' she panted. 'She goes into 'istericks that easy these days . . . it's her age, pore dear.'

Emmy did nothing to help, screaming at the top of her

117

voice and drumming her heels on the floor. Her face was scarlet, her eyes staring, her careful coiffure in rags round her face.

Together, Hester and Polly heaved her up the stairs. She was a solidly-built woman and this was no light task. Once on the bed she lay like a huge fish thrown up by the tide; one leg twitched and she flapped a hand in the air. Polly whisked a feather out of her apron pocket and held it over the oil lamp. Blowing it out as it caught fire, she applied it to her mistress's nostrils.

'Does . . . does this often happen?'

'Once a month regular. If anything happens to put her out . . . woof! off she goes like a bit o' dry tinder.'

Moans came from the bed, but the screaming rage had subsided.

'Best go to bed, miss. I'll watch over her.' Polly was busy uncorking a bottle. 'She'll be as right as rain after a drop o' this,' she added with a wink.

Hester recognized the bottle as one her father was fond of resorting to when he couldn't go to the pub. The familiar smell reached her across the bed as Polly poured it down her mistress's throat. She went out on the landing and ruefully felt her face. She was suddenly glad to be returning to Stanhope next day.

'Agnes! Agnes!' Hester burst into her bedroom and danced round the servant who was unpacking for her. 'There! Now what d'you think of me?' and she twirled round in her new kid boots, delicately lifting the hem of her dress to expose six inches of petticoat. Then she put her hand to her chest with an expression of exaggerated agony. 'Oh, oh, that corset's killing me!'

'Give over,' Agnes advised, but her expression was pleased. 'You shouldn't jump about like that – it's not ladylike. But I will say someone's done a proper job of you. Very nice and tasteful.' Her knowing fingers felt the material of

118

the sailor suit Hester was wearing and she nodded. 'Very fine material that. Who was the lady what fitted you out? She knew what's what.'

Hester looked evasively away. 'Oh, someone Uncle Joe knew in Liverpool. A Mrs O'Neill.'

'She's got daughters of her own, that's plain to see. Now, Miss Hester, we want no more tomboy running about. You're quite a grown-up young lady. I've just been unpacking your new things so you can help me hang them up.'

'Shall I tell you something?' Hester's voice was muffled by the folds of the dress she was hanging. 'Two gentlemen on Leeds station stared at me and one said, "Well, there's a little beauty." '

'Miss Hester!' Agnes was horrified. 'You oughtn't to have listened to them! The cheek of it! It's a good thing Sir Joseph didn't hear them.'

'But why, Agnes? I was pleased.' She peeped in the mirror, a mischievous expression on her face. 'Am I pretty now, Agnes, am I?'

But Agnes refused to be drawn. She took the clothes and hung them herself, advising her charge that it was time to change into the foulard for dinner.

After dinner when Hester was sitting in the drawing room with her aunt, Ellen said curiously, 'And what was Mrs O'Neill like, Hester? I've never met her, you know.'

Hester felt a telltale blush mounting in her face, so she bent to retrieve a ball of wool for her aunt. 'Very kind. A – a nice old lady.'

Ellen took the wool. 'You forget I've seen your new wardrobe. An old lady didn't buy those dresses, Hester, although it's nice of you to try and pretend. Some day you'll be married yourself and you'll learn that gentlemen sometimes lead two lives. You must never let it trouble you. It doesn't trouble me.'

But this was not strictly true. Her uneasy suspicion that Joe had a woman in Liverpool made her afraid. Was this woman a real threat in her life? Would Joe leave her for this

Mrs O'Neill? Looking round on her home, Ellen wanted to scream with rage and anxiety. Instead she began very calmly to cast on another row of stitches, and Hester crept thankfully away to one of the windows. She wished her aunt would open the doors on to the terrace for it was a perfect night. They sat in silence, and when presently Joseph came in he said, 'What? Not yet in bed, Hester? Isn't it time she went up, my dear?'

Hester approached her aunt and kissed her shyly. She suddenly felt an overwhelming pity for the stout, dull woman, who seemed to have no attractive qualities; for she instinctively sensed her unhappiness.

Ellen barely responded, but she was flattered. Hester had never kissed her first before.

CHAPTER FIVE

Hester came out on to the terrace where grey urns held pink and white perlargoniums, and leaned over the balustrade with a glum expression on her face. She had on one of her new summer dresses, a pretty blue and white cotton trimmed with dark red braid, and on her head was a small chip straw boater. She looked nice – she looked pretty – and there was no one to notice her in her finery. How Tommy's eyes would bulge if he could see her now, she thought; but it would be a whole week before the Jubilee celebrations in Sewerston and she would see him again. A whole week with nothing to do. *Run away*, Aunt Ellen and Agnes kept saying to her, busy with preparations for the big reception Aunt Ellen was giving on June 20. It would be the eve of Jubilee Day and the first big party they would be giving. Everyone was coming, Aunt Ellen said exultantly. She had been stirred out of her usual apathy and really seemed to be enjoying herself. Hester had written down the bill of fare at her dictation. A hundred and fifty people were invited and they would between them eat several roast fowls, mayonnaises of salmon and lobster and trout, garnished tongues, ribs of lamb, collared eels, two decorated hams, some pigeon pies and as for the sweets – Hester's mouth watered at the sound of them. Charlotte Russe à la Vanille, Savoy cake, cheesecake, fruit pie, compôtes of fruit, bowls of strawberries in liqueur and hundreds of small, decorated pastries. There were also to be ices of every description and wine cup and ginger beer and lemonade. Hester had never heard anything like it in her life.

She sighed heavily. It was still a week away, the day was

perfect, the air full of birdsong and small white clouds barely moving in the sky. A huge yawn stretched her face. If only they wouldn't treat her as a child! She no longer felt a child – not since the day that man had said, 'What a little beauty!' Ever since then, she had been aware of herself as a woman. But there was no one to see her or appreciate her here at Stanhope and she wasn't allowed out by herself – that was the rub.

She stooped and took hold of the small basket of sketching things she had brought down from the schoolroom. In the other hand she carried the small canvas camping stool Wiston had found for her. She would go down to the lake and sketch.

A man, a boy, a grasscutter and a pony were cutting the lawns as she sauntered across them. A sweet smell of mown grass mingled with the scent of lime blossoms. She could feel the sun hot on her shoulders; she would have to find a really shady spot to sketch or it would be unendurable. She sauntered round the corner to the stableyard. Here it was already gay with red, white and blue bunting and a Union Jack hanging limply from the clock tower.

The stableyard had become one of her favourite places at Stanhope, full as it always was of bustle and horses and boys. If Ellen had known she would have been shocked – a stableyard was no place for a young girl. At that moment two boys were busy with buckets and brooms swilling down the cobblestones, another was sitting in the sun rubbing up harness and bits while the carriage horses, just brought up from the meadow, were standing patiently while they were groomed.

Hester stood and watched the boys busy with the body-brushes on the chestnut coats, growling 'Stan' still!' now and again. They took no notice of her. Waterman himself came out of the coach house and shouted, 'Anyone seen Aaron?' He looked disapprovingly as he touched his hat, for he shared Lady Prickard's views about young women in the stableyard. That dratted girl was forever walking through

the place upsetting t'lads, he thought gloomily. They pretended not to be watching her, but they were peeping at her
all t'same and thinking carnal thoughts. 'G'morning, miss?
Is there something you want?'

'I'm just going to see Mrs Waterman,' Hester smiled.

Mrs Waterman always made her welcome. The Watermans had three sons. Aaron, the eldest was very different
to his smaller brothers. He was a hefty fellow of eighteen,
red cheeked with black eyes and a fine set of whiskers. Hester
had noticed him at once. Of the other two she remembered
only that Ben had a squint and Michael's mouth hung open.
But Aaron was a fine-looking boy. He was head lad at the
stables now and could have found a good position in one
of the big houses in the North Riding, but Waterman
wouldn't let him leave home. The coachman ruled his family
with the Bible and the strap. The boys sullenly obeyed and
Aaron had long been planning to leave home – secretly and
at night. Only that morning there had been a terrible row
because Aaron had come in after hours the night before.
The coachman had threatened to take the strap to him –
only threatened however, because he knew that Aaron was
now big enough to turn on him. If he could have had a girl,
perhaps one of the maids up at the house, Aaron would have
been a different fellow. But Melia and Lizzie were walking
out with two of the other stable lads, and Aaron had to
resort to haunting the village at night and watching the girls
in their bedrooms. There was one girl – the postman's
daughter – a plain but buxom girl who always undressed
without drawing her curtains and Aaron, from a good spot
up a tree, was assured of a good view. He looked forward to
it, thought excitedly about it several times a day, and was
almost in love with plain Mary Hodgson at the post office.

When they had lived at Sewerston in a cottage behind
the Harbour House, Aaron had more than once felt the strap
because he had run with the local gang of boys. Here, there
was nothing and if Hester was bored, Aaron was as frus-
trated and as dangerous as a caged beast.

Peeping through the open cottage door, Hester saw that Mrs Waterman was busy preparing the midday dinner. Sunlight poked through a small window space and Mrs Waterman, bent over a wood stove, was perspiring. Wiping moisture off her face with an arm, she called out, 'Well, miss, you look a proper pitcher in that dress!'

'You really think so? It's one of my new ones.' Hester sat down and watched the coachman's wife rapidly peel onions and drop them in a steaming cauldron.

'Fits like a glove too. I had a dress like that once. When I was courting it was. My man said I looked a queen in it.'

Hester was astonished. Imagine holy old Waterman being stirred to say sweet things to his girl! 'I'm sure he still thinks you look like a queen.'

'Him? Go on with you. T'weren't Waterman who said such things to me. He couldn't twist his tongue round 'em. T'were when I was in Lincoln . . . I'm not from Yorkshire, y'know . . . I was in service. Nice house enough, but the master was always drunk. He'd come in from the hunting and hit the bottle hard. I had a sweetheart working in the house – ' Mrs Waterman paused and looked into the distance. 'Howell Evans. He was Welsh. Lovely skin he had . . . fresh-like and the blackest eyes you ever saw.' She turned and reached up for the saltbox, her face suddenly bitter. Howell had given her Aaron and then run off without marrying her. Waterman had done the handsome and married her, but he'd never let her forget her slip. Couldn't love Aaron at all and the boy knew it. She sighed, smiling at the girl who was watching her. 'Don't you trust pretty words, Miss Hester, they don't mean nothing. Sly beasts men. Only want one thing from you. . . . '

'Oh, Mrs Waterman, what?'

Mrs Waterman looked round before leaning across and whispering: 'Your body, miss.'

Hester's heart pounded with excitement. 'You mean . . . is that how babies come?'

The woman nodded, her face earnest. 'You watch out,

124

miss. You're just the sort to get taken in. A man can ruin a girl's life in two minutes.' Then she salted the stew with vigour and said, 'Good gracious, is that the time?' Hester took the hint and left. Her mind was in a ferment. She remembered when she was at the National School her mother had said, 'Never let a boy put his hands on you, Hester.' But Hester knew that that was not all. You didn't have a baby just because a man touched your skirt. If only Mrs Waterman hadn't seen it was half-past eleven she might have told her more. She remembered Mrs Waterman when they had all lived down at the harbour. She had always looked a harrassed woman as she hurried along the fish quay to buy bits of cod to make a meal. It was rumoured that Waterman thrashed her as well as the boys, something that Will Kelsey had never done to his wife.

And as Hester sauntered through the long rose walk that led down to the park, she was suddenly remembering other things. That her mother had always held herself aloof from the Watermans and people like them, had always hurried her past the Harbour House with her head turned the other way – not that the harbour cottages had been on the same side of the harbour but they had occasion to pass that way sometimes. She hadn't wanted to come across her grand step-brother; indeed she had never mentioned being related in any way to the people at the Harbour House. They had kept themselves very much to themselves, had been lonely and isolated and proud. Poor Mother! Hester thought. If only she and Uncle Joe had made friends again perhaps she wouldn't have died.

She put these sad memories behind her with resolution. It was a glorious morning and the lake was gleaming in the sun. It had become a favourite haunt of hers. In the centre was a tiny island, the home of coots and mallards. The rest of the park might be absolutely deserted and still but the lake was always full of life. One side was screened by what she called the rainbow garden, a bank of rhododendrons and azaleas of every colour. She made her way towards this now,

125

picking her way carefully across the oozing ground, for she was wearing white buckskin shoes.

She opened her little canvas stool and sat on it, watching the lake for a rise. She was rewarded quite soon by a cloud of mayfly rising from the water and a couple of big trout leaping up after them. But when the splash had died away there was silence. No birdsong here, but the gentle stirring of leaves above her head made a soft swishing sound as if someone crept near. She shivered and turned uneasily. There was no one there, and presently a family of ducks fussed past and absorbed her attention.

Preparing to take out her sketching block, she paused to take up some soil in her hands, crumbling it between her fingers. Stanhope soil. It all belonged to Uncle Joe but he couldn't love it as she did! Stanhope had crept into her blood; she never wanted to leave it again – never. She was beginning to love it with a fierce and possessive love; how lucky she was to have been permitted to live here. Did Wilfred, this unknown cousin, love it as she did? If he did, it would be a bond between them. She was already a little nervous of meeting Wilfred when they went to his school after the Jubilee celebrations. The school held a summer celebration of their own called a Gaudy. A twig cracked. Startled, she looked round but there was nothing. Nobody. She was alone here and could dream to her heart's content. . . .

'Good morning, miss.' Aaron Waterman suddenly loomed over her.

So there had been someone there all the time. Although he had startled her, she concealed it and smiled. 'Good morning. I've just been talking to your mother on the way down. Your father was calling for you.'

'Let him call.' He dropped on his haunches beside her without asking permission. Indeed, there was a freedom about his manner that quite surprised her. He was in his usual flannel shirt and leather waistcoat and breeches, hot though the day was. His florid face glistened with sweat and he had pushed his cap to the back of his curly head. He looked the same as usual, and yet there was this difference in his manner that sent a small dart of uncertainty into her heart.

There was a knowing smile on his face as he said, 'Seed you about the harbour 'fore you come here. Thought you were pretty then.' He edged closer, his eyes avidly inspecting her at close quarters. Not just her face but her body, she thought indignantly. To give herself composure she opened the box of pencils and selected one, frowning at the middle distance as if deciding how to draw it. He didn't go away. She could feel the warmth of his body behind her. Gooseflesh suddenly stood out on her neck as a hand touched it, lifting her hair to caress her skin with a roughened hand.

'Pretty,' he said as if to himself, for he was comparing her with Mary Hodgson. This 'un was just a bit of a thing, but he could see the shape of her breasts as she leaned forward. . . .

'Don't touch me!' she said sharply, pulling away and suddenly toppling her stool. She landed on her side and like a flash he was on her, heavy and breathing hard in her ear.

'Keep still, yer little fool!'

Somehow she found the breath to scream – once but loudly. He hit her then and her head fell back, her hat pin painfully digging into her scalp as her hat was pulled off. His hands were everywhere. With a grunt of pleasure he pulled open her bodice and then suddenly thrust under her petticoats and pulled at her drawers. He had watched Mary Hodgson long enough to know that drawers fastened with buttons on either side of the waist. He had pulled hers down in a trice.

She had both hands in his hair, trying vainly to push his red face from hers, screaming in a muffled fashion, convinced that he would kill her. Fear gave her strength and she fought back with her teeth and nails, making it as difficult as possible for him to have his way with her. For now she had realized that he wasn't trying to kill her, but was trying to enter her body. Such a repugnance filled her at this that she knew she would rather die than allow it. And all the time she fought she could hear Mrs Waterman's voice: *They can ruin your life in two minutes*.

Her struggles were almost over. She had no tears left, although her face was wet with them. Feebly she turned her face from side to side, all breath gone.

His hoarse voice in her ear said, 'Shut up. I won't hurtcher. . . . ' and then he gave a cry of pain, as a heavy stick came down on his back.

'Where is Hester?' Joseph asked coming out of the room he fondly thought of as his study; a retreat from the women, a place to smoke and to doze after a meal. But certainly no studying went on there. He had spent the morning writing to Emmy. Getting it off his chest, he told himself. A dignified but fond epistle warning her of the error of her ways. For it had occurred to him in the night (and he had gone quite cold at the thought) that perhaps he had pushed her into the arms of Daniel Wortle. Perhaps by now she had become his mistress and left the little house in Crosby. So this morning he had gone into his study at eleven o'clock and composed this very important letter.

He was afraid she didn't love him enough, he told her gravely in his fine bold writing. That her head was too easily turned by men with wily tongues and more money. Younger too, he added to himself, but didn't put that in the letter. He appealed to her better nature, he reminded her of the good times they had had together and then divulged that he would be over in Liverpool as soon as the Jubilee celebrations were over.

Satisfied that he could not put it better, he opened his notecase and found a stamp. This was one letter he could not put in the hall for John to post in the village.

Glancing out of the window, he saw that it was a fine day. This surprised him for he had been too preoccupied to notice. Well, he would walk down to the village himself and would take Hester with him. That way he would not be too conspicuous; he would be accompanying his niece on her walk. Whistling under his breath he rang for his hat, gloves and stick and then sought out his wife.

'Where is Hester?'

'How should I know?' Ellen retorted impatiently. 'Mooning about on her own somewhere as usual. She's no help to me, that's all I know.'

'Oh, come, Ellen, I heard her ask you at breakfast if she could do something for you. She's a handy little thing – very careful in everything she undertakes and I know she would like to feel she is helping.'

'If you please, sir,' Agnes intervened. 'I saw Miss Hester go into the stableyard a short time ago. Likes to go to visit Mrs Waterman.' She was on her knees in front of a cupboard containing glassware, for she and her mistress had been counting glasses for the reception. Now she scrambled stiffly up, said, 'Thirty-eight, I make it, M'm,' and added: 'Shall I fetch her, sir?'

'No, no, that's all right,' Joseph said quickly. 'I'll find her myself. I want her to come to the village with me,' and he wheeled sharply before Ellen could open her mouth to ask why he suddenly needed to go to the village. Feeling as guilty as a boy, he walked out of the room and across the hall. 'Wiston, have you seen Miss Hester?'

'I saw her just ten minutes ago, sir, going down the rose walk towards the park. Miss Hester likes the lake, she tells me. No doubt she'll be down there now.'

Good God, how they watch us, Joseph thought secretly flabbergasted by this revelation of the Stanhope spying system. Poor little Hester didn't know it, but she had been under surveillance since she left the house! He stepped out into the sun and put on his hat. The rose walk at that time of the day was certainly a delightful place to stroll. He bent over one or two bushes, sniffing them with pleasure and selecting a dark red rose for his buttonhole. Reaching the end of the walk, he stood above the ha-ha and, screening his eyes, looked narrowly over the sun-flooded landscape.

It was then he heard the scream.

A man of quick reactions, he began to walk rapidly down the slope in the direction of the lake. His eyes were far-seeing sailor's eyes and he scanned the landscape alertly, for he was uneasy. A woman's scream – muffled but full of terror – My God, Hester, he thought and began to run. Immediately they came into focus, those two figures on the ground: a blue dress and a man. They were struggling to and fro under the rhododendron bushes.

He reached them just as Hester's strength gave out and her body went limp in Aaron Waterman's arms. He had given a crow of triumph just before he felt the stick coming down on his back. His crow turned to a yelp of anguish and then to stricken cries as Joseph, mad with rage, beat him unmercifully with the cane until it broke in two. 'You dog!' Joseph shouted. 'I'll kill you for this . . . ' His long arms reached down and grasped Aaron by the neck. 'You deserve to die, you cur. . . . '

Hester dazedly watched them, feeling the power of Prickard's fury as, with demonic strength, he hurled the well-built stable boy into the bushes, where he lay blubbering and calling for mercy from the broken stick that cut his bare flesh. Shakily she staggered to her feet, looking round mechanically for her hat, which was hanging from the back of her head.

Joseph straightened, his breath alarmingly short. 'H-Hester, my child, h-has he hurt you?'

She shook her head mutely, too spent to answer, her fear-filled eyes still on Aaron Waterman.

Joseph staggered across to her. 'Wait,' he beseeched her. 'No one must see. Quickly. Your hair . . . hat. . . . ' He pointed to them. Her torn bodice caught his eye and he winced. He suddenly realized that it had been Kelsey he had been attacking, not the half-witted Waterman boy. Kelsey whom he had wanted to kill. But Kelsey was dead and this was his daughter standing with her head down, her hair in disarray, scratches on her face and all the buttons off her bodice. No one must ever know about this – not even Ellen. If ever this got about the chances of a good marriage had gone for good. An unchaperoned girl attacked by the stable-hand. Joseph shuddered. Nothing he could do would save the girl, for the world would regard her as sullied.

Hester tried tiredly to repair the damage. He handed her his own cravat pin and she untidily pinned the front of her dress.

'Put your sketching block in front of you,' he told her. 'That's better, my child. Sure you can walk back with me? Good girl.' He glanced at the blubbering youth under the bushes and, without another word, escorted his niece back to the house. 'We must look as if nothing has happened,' he told her, remembering the eyes that would be watching from the house.

She pointed at his broken stick and with an exclamation he hurled it into the bushes. 'Come along,' he said gently, praying that she wouldn't break down in tears and give everything away. He felt drained; as if he had run a mile and his legs were weak. I'm not as young as I was, he thought with a grimace.

They reached the house and still she hadn't spoken. I shall have to let Agnes into this, he thought. She's not old enough to bear it on her own. Sending her up to her room, he went in search of Agnes.

'Oh, really, Joseph, what a nuisance you are!' Ellen expostulated. 'Agnes and I have a lot to do.'

'Hester has a touch of the sun I think, and has gone to lie down. I feel Agnes should go up to her, my dear.' Casually following Agnes to the foot of the staircase, he rapidly told her what had happened. 'On no account tell anyone.'

She looked at him reproachfully. 'I hope I've more sense, sir.'

'Yes, I know you have. She's very distressed, Agnes.' He turned aside, went into his study and closed the door. Crossing to a cupboard he took down a decanter of whisky and noted with some surprise that his hand was shaking badly as he took out the stopper. He drank quickly and then refilling his glass sat down in his chair by the window. He had wanted to kill that boy. He could have done it easily for it was what he had wanted to do when he heard about Nancy: seventeen and pregnant by that drunken lout, Will Kelsey. But this wasn't Nancy – it was her daughter to whom the same thing had nearly happened. He groaned aloud. Had she encouraged that son of Waterman's – perhaps arranged to meet him there, well away from the house? There were an awful lot of questions to be asked and he would have to go across to the stable cottage and talk to the man. That lad – what was his name? – would have to go. He couldn't give him a character so it would have to be the army or the navy. That and a good thrashing from his father was what young Waterman needed.

'He didn't – hurt you then?' Agnes said quietly. She stroked the dark head of her charge. 'There, dearie, don't take on now. It's all over and that Aaron will get a good hiding from his pa and the sack from the master.' She glanced down anxiously for Hester hadn't answered. She sat on the bed and stared dumbly in front of her, shivering. 'Now let me help you undress and get into bed, Miss Hester.'

Hester moved her head. 'I must have a bath. I feel – dirty.'

Agnes's hand went to her mouth. 'He didn't – ' She sought for words that were delicate enough and yet would express her meaning.

'He put his filthy hands up my petticoat,' Hester said bitterly. She lifted her skirt and Agnes gave a little scream for there was blood all over the dainty Swiss lawn.

'Miss Hester – '

'My uncle beat him about the head. That's *his* blood.' She couldn't bring herself to say Aaron Waterman's name. 'Agnes, I want a bath. Please ask Melia to bring it up.' She dragged herself off the bed and began to take her clothes off, wearily like an old woman, every movement measured.

Agnes hurried to the bell and jerked the handle. Then she helped Hester get out of her corset and wrapped a robe round her shoulders. There was a knock on the door and Melia looked round it. She glanced curiously at the girl who was lying on the bed now.

'Miss Hester has a touch of the sun and is going to bed,' Agnes said in a low voice. 'She wants to take a bath first so get Lizzie to bring up the water.'

'A bath! Why, m'auntie lost all her hair when she was young by taking a bath,' Melia whispered back. 'While she had a temperature see. Worst thing . . . '

'Melia! Do as you're told and look sharp!' Those girls had too easy a time of it, Agnes told herself angrily as she bent and picked up Hester's stockings. But she knew in her heart that her anger was composed chiefly of anxiety, and her troubled eyes went again and again to the still figure on the bed. If only she had cried – Agnes would have known how to deal with hysteria. But this silence – it wasn't natural.

'They do say that vinegar and water's good for the sunstroke,' Melia said as she lugged in the copper hip bath. But a shake of the head from Agnes sent her off with a toss of her curls. When Lizzie had poured in the cans of hot water and the door was shut again, Agnes went across to rouse Hester. She felt her forehead with the air of an expert; the skin was chilled and not hot. 'Come now, dearie,' she said coaxingly. 'The bath's nice and hot and I've put those pretty pink bathsalts in. I'll be back to tuck you up in bed and to draw the curtains. Sure you can manage on your own?'

Hester nodded and went behind the screen. She stood in the bath and scrubbed herself hard, but she felt she could never scrub away the feel of his exploring hands. So that was what men did to you then, she thought with cold distaste. That was how you got a baby. She thought of Sal and the lodger. Uncle Joe and Mrs O'Neill? Perhaps if you loved someone you would not mind, she thought bewilderedly.

Lying on her bed, Aaron Waterman's red perspiring face,

his smell, came back to her vividly and she felt sick. She suddenly longed for Nancy with an acute homesickness. Only her mother could have reassured and encouraged her at this moment. Closing her eyes, she felt a fresh wave of grief wash over her. She was on her own now and there was no use moaning, she told herself fiercely.

When Agnes came back she found Hester sitting up in the chair by the window. 'There, you're better, love!'

'Better? Oh, I'm all right now,' Hester smiled with an effort. 'Shall we choose a fresh dress? I want to go down to lunch.'

Praise the Lord, it had done the child no harm at all, Agnes thought as she busied herself at the wardrobe.

'So I want that son of yours off my land by tomorrow,' Prickard said.

Immovable as a rock, Waterman stood near the study door facing his master. He had never been summoned to the house before, but he was not out of place there. His hands folded in front of him, his lion head erect he looked, Joseph thought with exasperation, as if he were about to take one of his prayer meetings.

'He's no son o' mine,' Waterman said calmly. 'He's Clara's boy. The father never married her.'

'Aha! I rather fancied as much. There you are then; you can wash your hands of him, send him into the army. That'll cool him down a bit — why do you shake your head?'

'It's against our principles,' Waterman said. 'To take up arms,' he explained patiently as Prickard stared. 'The boy's mine now, master. Where we go he go.'

'Don't be a fool, man! You're not going to throw up a good job for the sake of that — that young animal? He's a rough customer, Waterman. There'll be more trouble from him, you mark my words.'

'We shall pray with him . . . burn it out of him with the strap.' The coachman's eyes flickered with religious zeal.

'The Lord will save him from the sin he was born to. Give me what's due to me, sir, and we'll leave tomorrow.' He shifted his feet and drew nearer. 'And the young lady? What shall be done to her, sir? Will you pray with her too? For she too is filled with the sins of the flesh. It was she who led my son to commit this sin against her. . . . '

'Hold your tongue!' Joseph shouted, rising and facing the quiet voiced man. 'How dare you say such things against my niece, an innocent and pure young woman?'

The man's steady eyes burned into his master's. 'She led him on,' he asserted flatly, 'a-flaunting herself in the stableyard every day. The lad was encouraged.'

Joseph's face blackened with anger. 'I don't believe a word of it. If Aaron says this, he is lying. She never . . . ' His voice died away for he suddenly remembered Agnes saying, *I saw Miss Hester go into the stableyard a short time ago.* Without another word he unlocked a drawer in his desk and drew out a cash box heavy with sovereigns. He counted out a week's wages for all the Watermans and added ten more, tipping the lot into the coachman's hand. 'Tell Rickaby you are to have the waggon to remove your furniture. Where will you go?'

Waterman was carefully transferring the coins into a small leather bag. 'To my brother's. He will look after us until I obtain another place.'

Joseph sighed. 'Why are you such an obstinate beggar? The mistress will be very distressed when I tell her you will not stay with us because I can no longer employ Aaron. Won't you reconsider, Waterman? Lady Prickard likes the way you drive the carriage. She feels safe with you. That's a snug cottage you've got too,' Joseph added cunningly.

There was no answering light in the man's eyes. 'I must turn Aaron from his sinful ways. It is the Lord's work I do.' He touched his forelock and went out, quietly shutting the door behind him.

And that is all these last ten years have meant to him, Joseph thought staring at the closed door. He will leave without a backward glance. Then his thoughts went to his niece. So she was a minx if Waterman was to be believed. A minx who had arranged to meet the stableboy secretly and had got more than she bargained for.

Joseph's lips tightened. Then like Aaron she would have to mend her ways. He must find a governess for her immediately, a woman who would keep a tight hand on the girl and teach her ladylike ways. He sighed heavily. Hester was such a taking little thing too; but a baggage like all pretty women. He had never dreamed that Nancy had been carrying on with Kelsey until she ran away with him. And they had the same innocent eyes.

He got up wearily. He would go into Sewerston and see Bracegirdle. The solicitor would know the best way of setting about finding a governess for the girl – but he no longer had a coachman. He swore under his breath as he tugged at the bell.

'Send down to the stables for the gig and young Hawke to drive me. Waterman is leaving,' he added as he saw his butler's puzzled face. He was also going to have to break it to Ellen, he told himself as he took his hat and gloves from the man. She wasn't going to like it one bit, but he hoped she would never hear the real reason for the coachman's departure.

The Watermans must have worked all night for at six next morning the farm cart rumbled down the back drive. Mrs Waterman was sitting up beside Rickaby and the male members of the family, their furniture tied down with rope and the youngest boy, Michael, carrying the family cat. The cottage was swept and clean, the key under the mat. Going in and looking round, Joseph cursed to himself. The best coachman for miles – sober, honest and hardworking. Where was he to find another man like him and with the Jubilee only a week away? For one weak moment he regretted taking his niece in as his ward. Women were the devil at any age and she was going to be a beauty to boot. He shook his head wryly and left the stable yard. There was only one thing for it: she would have to be very closely guarded from now on.

CHAPTER SIX

Seeing Sir Joseph and Lady Prickard composedly receiving their guests on the night of their Jubilee reception, no one would have guessed at the panic and despair that had ruined the hours before. Corked wine; ice cream that wouldn't freeze; the cook in hysterics and Lady Prickard's dress two inches too small round the waist.

'That fool of a woman!' she wailed, meaning the high-class dressmaker she had employed to make the oyster satin dress. Ellen had thought it a magnificent dress and had looked forward to wearing it to confront her neighbours on her first occasion as hostess to more than a hundred people. 'She's made it too small! I shall sue her! The evening is ruined!'

'M'lady, it's not her fault,' Agnes pointed out. 'It fitted a treat when it came home two weeks ago. It's just that you've put on more weight again . . . eh dear, it's as tight as a drum,' Agnes lamented unhelpfully. The dress simply refused to close down the back and Ellen's flesh bulged out of it like over-risen dough out of its pan. She wailed despairingly and Agnes grew red in the face with pulling; all to no avail.

'I can't go to my own party! I won't go in an old dress! I shall have to be ill. . . .'

'Oh, no, mum, you can't do that!'

'Don't you tell me what I can't do!' Ellen had become as stubborn as a disappointed child. 'I shall go to bed until it's all over,' she announced.

'Please let me see what I can do, Aunt Ellen,' Hester begged. She had come to view the new dress only to find her aunt distraught. 'You know I'm handy with a needle and I can move the buttons in no time. Look, you have at least two inches here. We can release these two tucks and no one will be any the wiser.'

'My word, I was glad of your help, Miss Hester,' Agnes told her later. 'M'lady was fit to collapse. You've made a lovely job of that dress and I could see she was pleased. She won't say so, mind, but she's pleased all the same,' Agnes added as she tied the sash of Hester's party dress and stood back with a nod of satisfaction. 'That Mrs O'Neill, whoever she is, knows what's what and no mistake,' she went on, casting a sly glance up at Hester. 'Who did you say she was, Miss Hester?'

'A friend of the family's,' Hester said blandly.

Agnes sniffed to herself, as she watched Hester turning slowly in front of the mirror. White voile with insertions of narrow lace made the bodice of the dress. The skirt was a mass of lacy frills to the hem. A Nattier blue sash, hair ribbon and white stockings with black dancing slippers completed the outfit. Hester regarded herself with the utmost satisfaction. She had put out of her mind last week's unpleasant experience and was preparing to enjoy her very first party. She threw her arms round Agnes's neck, 'Thank you, Agnes darling, for dressing me up. I really look grown-up tonight, don't I?'

'Get away with you. Your hair isn't up yet. You look fifteen, miss, and don't you forget it,' were Agnes's parting words.

In the soft summer night the house stood ready and waiting, its door flung open, banks of flowers filling the reception rooms.

Massed at the head of the stairs were pink Maréchal de Niel roses smelling sweetly. Hester, standing beside her uncle and aunt waiting for Wiston to announce the first guest, could smell them; they were an accompaniment to her excitement and pleasure.

Now John ran lightly up the stairs, to tell his master that the first carriage was coming up the drive.

'Oh, dear, I feel dizzy,' Ellen murmured and fluttered her fan.

'Stop thinking about yourself,' Joseph snapped. 'Hester! Don't lean over the stairs like that! Stand still beside your aunt and remember all we've told you.'

Hester subsided meekly, but she was filled with an excited tingling of the blood. The party had begun.

Among the first arrivals was Lady Ada Woolsey. She had been the only child of the last Lord Girvan and she had married Woolsey, a racehorse breeder and trainer, when she was over thirty and thought by the neighbourhood to be at her last prayers. Her husband had been dead for years, so tonight she was accompanied by her elder son, Gerald, a weedy youth with yellow whiskers and hair that was parted down the middle. He had been sent down from Oxford before completing his last year for having an actress in his rooms all night. Now he lounged opposite his mother in the carriage, looking exquisite in his white waistcoat with a carnation in his buttonhole, and laughing gently as she roundly criticized his way of life.

'That man who has bought my home is only *nouveau riche*,' she said scornfully in her loud voice, 'but who of our own kind has any money nowadays? And you simply must marry money, Gerald. You'll never be able to live in the manner you would like if you don't marry money. Mine has nearly all gone now thanks to your father. There is simply nothing for it, old boy – you must make an effort and get married soon. What else is there? You've no profession.'

'Heaven forbid,' her son murmured with a shudder.

'You've no place of your own and no money unless your aunt Charlotte leaves you hers.'

He was regarding her through narrowed lids which hid

the hard expression in his eyes. He deeply resented their lack of means, which meant they lived in a beastly little house and came out to parties in a hired carriage. 'So you've planned for me to marry the niece, is that it, Mama? Miss Kelsey. What if she's as plain as piecrust?'

'What has that to do with it?' Lady Ada snorted. 'All cats are alike in the dark, Gerald. It's surprising what a sweetener money is too. She'll be rich some day when her uncle dies, for I understand she is like a daughter to him. And he's almost indecently rich – a little sea captain! It's ridiculous – the world's gone mad.'

They got down from the carriage and Gerald offered his mother his arm as they entered the familiar hall of Stanhope. A heavy scent of flowers mixed with the scent of the women guests, as they slowly ascended the stairs to be received. People were looking round with covert interest to see what the new people had made of Girvan's old place.

'Of course most of the good stuff was bought with the house,' Lady Ada informed her friend Mrs Wargrave as they mounted the stairs together. 'These people wouldn't have had the taste, you know. . . .'

'Ssh, my dear,' Mrs Wargrave murmured, blushing, for Lady Ada had the loudest female voice in the North Riding. She exchanged a look of distaste with her husband; it was not in their code to criticize their host while partaking of his bread.

But Lady Ada only shrugged. She was bitterly resentful of the businessman who was now the master of Stanhope. This should by rights be hers, hers and Gerald's. These Prickards were simply interlopers and not one of them.

All the families who had called on Ellen were represented there tonight. There were many young people, for Joseph was anxious for Hester to make friends in the neighbourhood. There were some girls of her age who were not yet out, but for whom this was a family party; that had been emphasized in the engraved invitations. There were few young men and boys as most sons were away at school or university. Master Stephen Fox was among the lucky ones. He had broken his leg in April and wasn't to return to school until halfterm. He was fourteen and still in an Eton collar, and his round face beamed with delight at his unexpected treat. With him were his parents whose property ran next to Stanhope and his two sisters who were fifteen and twelve.

'Such a delightful idea asking the young people,' Mrs Fox told her hostess. 'On such a special occasion too. They will remember it and tomorrow's celebrations all their lives. Marigold, Helena and Stephen – come and be presented to Lady Prickard. And this is your niece? Well, my dear, we're happy to make your acquaintance.' In a stage whisper she added, 'What a very pretty girl, Lady Prickard – such eyes!'

'Just a friendly family affair,' Sir Joseph was telling his guests. 'To toast our beloved queen-empress – but there'll be no speeches I promise you!'

Ellen fanned herself with her fan, her nervous smile coming and going. Unlike Joseph, she was not at ease among these fine folk, as she privately called them. Her voice was falsely genteel even to her own ears, and her heart beat so fast that at times she felt she would faint. If only Joseph wasn't so keen to make a splash in the county she could be enjoying a nice quiet dinner tonight, she thought tearfully. As it was, she wasn't fit to take a bite.

Joseph, who loved meeting people and entertaining them with fine food and wine, was in his element now that the first hurdle was over. His lean florid face wore a relaxed expression of enjoyment that was echoed on Hester's face. Her cheeks were pink with excitement and her eyes were shining. She felt the temperature of the party rising as people met, laughed and talked, and then drifted to form another group.

A beauty, thank God, Gerald Woolsey thought as he watched her narrowly. A child still of course, but only just outside adulthood. What he could teach her! And if she had money too . . . Well, he would have a headstart by making the filly's acquaintance without delay. Walking over to her he said easily, 'Won't you take a turn about the room with me, Miss Kelsey? You've done your duty here quite nobly. I used to live here when I was a child. My grandfather was the old earl.' He smiled charmingly and offered her his arm.

Hester looked cautiously up at the chinless young man with the beautiful silky whiskers. 'Thank you.' She took his arm and they moved away. 'Did – did you use the old school-room when you lived here?'

'Rather. Had an old governess who used to rap me on the knuckles . . . I was a lonely little boy,' he added pathetically.

'There are names carved on the old desk: Jack, Hugh, Gerald and Albert. . . .'

'I am Gerald. Jack was my grandfather. The others are great-uncles.'

She felt a new warmth towards him. 'Why aren't there any girls' names on the desk?'

'Simple. Girls don't own penknives.'

The Hungarian Band, brought all the way from London by her uncle and the cause of much excitement to Hester, was now playing spirited music in the alcove off the drawing room. There was not to be dancing, but several young people were grouped near the band, tapping their feet longingly. 'Shall we go over there?' Hester suggested. She could see that the nice Fox family were already there.

'Oh, no, much too noisy.' He skilfully drew her across the room to the French windows that opened on to a long balcony. It was too early in the evening for anyone to be out there yet. After supper it would be crowded. He felt her turn away and glanced back quickly to persuade her. But she had only stopped to greet a little old lady in black bombazine whom he recognized as old Mrs Weston from Sewerston. Smiling his charming smile he joined them.

'Don't you remember me?' Hester was asking shyly.

Mrs Weston was looking bewildered. 'Haven't we just met, my dear? You are Sir Joseph's niece, are you not? But . . . yes . . . I have seen you before tonight. I couldn't forget your pretty eyes! Let me see . . . I confess I am puzzled.'

'I brought you the bonnet my aunt had made for you,' Hester reminded her guilelessly. 'It was for the Jubilee, but we agreed the colour was horrid. I made you one myself – a pretty greeny-blue and I do hope you're going to wear it tomorrow for the celebrations.'

Mrs Weston was astounded. 'You are the milliner's niece? You?'

Hester nodded. She longed to hear that Mrs Weston loved her bonnet. That bonnet had cost her dear – not that Mrs Weston could know that.

'And you're Sir Joseph's niece too? Kelsey – ah, yes, they will be your father's sisters.' Mrs Weston stared with frank interest. 'You were a half-starved little thing then – I was quite worried about you. No wonder I didn't know you!' She chuckled and said, half to herself, 'Well, well, the world is a queer place to be sure. How are you, Gerald? Your mother here? I must have a word with her.' With a nod she moved on.

Gerald Woolsey had listened to this conversation with increasing fury and amazement. Good God; a milliner's assistant! Is that what he had sunk to? Sir Joseph's poor relation, 'a half-starved little thing'! A Sewerston brat Prickard was trying to pass off as a young lady! Just wait until his mama heard this, he thought with cruel enjoyment. Meanwhile there was a certain amount of fun to be got, for he knew to a nicety what girls like this liked. He firmly led her out on to the balcony which was mercifully still deserted.

'So you're a Sewerston girl, are you?'

'Yes. I was born there. Down on the harbour.' Hester leaned on the balustrade and breathed in the scented evening air.

143

He edged closer, touched her with his arm.

She was jerked into an awareness that his manner had changed. He had suddenly become freer and more familiar . . . she didn't like the way he was pressing against her. . . .

'You're very pretty,' he breathed in her ear. He was a skilled philanderer with women of a certain type, *demimondaines* whom he smuggled into his rooms at Oxford, and to Gerald Woolsey this girl was that type. A cheap harbour brat who was probably experienced beyond her years. With a girl of his own class he would not have attempted familiarity, but then girls like that didn't attract him. He liked common women who were able to give a fellow fun.

'Don't do that!' Hester jerked her head back and looked for an escape route past her escort. Inside the rooms, under the chandeliers ablaze with candles, the noise of many voices rose high and fast like a river in flood.

'Do what, m'dear?' he asked softly, pressing her back into the corner between the balustrade and a wall. He put both hands out and felt for her breasts, his breathing quickening and his head coming down like a beast of prey.

Fear froze her. For a moment the bland fair face of Woolsey became the red perspiring one of Aaron Waterman. This man didn't smell of sweat only of pomade, but his hot eyes were the same. He had trapped her as easily as Aaron had done. She struggled, words bursting from her. 'Leave me alone! don't touch me!' But he took no notice. Then her hand shot out and landed on his cheek with a resounding slap that left a clear pink stain on his skin. As he jerked back she darted round him and into the room where she stood breathing hard, her face white with fear.

Some people near the window had heard the slap; others turned to look curiously at the girl who was so obviously upset and the man who was just emerging from the balcony behind her. There was a telltale mark on his skin and his eyes were furious.

144

Gerald Woolsey saw that his mother was standing a few feet away. He recovered himself quickly and, with an insolent laugh, called out in a ringing voice, 'What do you think, Mama? Miss Kelsey is a milliner by trade. You must get her to make you a bonnet.'

'Good God!' Lady Ada said, staring in the greatest astonishment at Hester. 'A milliner? What on earth are we coming to?'

'And with the manners of one,' Gerald added viciously. He took out a silk handkerchief and wiped his hands with it in a gesture of disdain. But before he had time to put the handkerchief away he found himself swung round in a grip of iron, and a face as angry as his own was thrust into his. Joseph Prickard had advanced on him like a panther from behind. In a voice deep with fury, he said so that everyone could hear, 'Mr Woolsey, I must ask you to leave my house. Lady Ada, you will wish to accompany your son no doubt. I will instruct a servant to call your carriage,' and Gerald Woolsey found himself being propelled ignominiously out of the room by his host. Lady Ada tucked her train under her arm and followed. For once she was at a loss for words, but her face was red with humiliation and anger.

All talk had ceased. For a moment social disaster threatened the Prickards' first party, as people looked from one to the other. Some had heard Gerald Woolsey's remarks and those who hadn't were rapidly told them. The Woolseys were not popular and most people had suffered from them at one time or another. Suddenly Mrs Fox acted. Seeing the young girl who was the centre of attention looking with hunted eyes for a way of escape, she gathered Marigold and Helena to her side and swooped down on her.

'Well, my dear, it's nearly time for supper. Shall we go down? Where is Stephen? Stephen, please escort Miss Kelsey and we will all go down.' Talking easily, throwing remarks to friends, Mrs Fox swept her party out of the room and the tension broke.

'Young Woolsey's a swine.'

'What on earth did he do to make the girl slap his face?'

'My dear, can't you guess? And she's only a child too. He needs horsewhipping,' said one lady vehemently.

'Well, I for one am glad Gerald's been given his congé,' said a young lady feelingly. She had suffered from Gerald Woolsey's attentions in the past.

Joseph Prickard, who had heard Lady Ada's scornful remarks on her arrival, was a satisfied man as he watched her hired carriage trundle off down the drive. Thank God, that troublesome woman was out of their lives for good, he told himself as he started back up the stairs.

Lord Abbotsbury was standing at the top, a look of glee on his rubicund face. 'Very well done, Prickard! Everyone of your guests here tonight will applaud your action. They are such terribly unpleasant people – shouldn't wonder if young Gerald doesn't hang some day. I only hope he didn't frighten your niece – although she's a resourceful little lady by all accounts!'

Laughing together they went back into the drawing room where people were beginning to move towards supper.

It was Ellen who was upset. She had heard enough from her guests to know that Hester had been again at the centre of some imbroglio. Drawing attention to herself! Ellen thought indignantly. The girl was getting above herself; she was the image of her mother and just as spoilt. It was high time she was put into the background and kept there. It would be for her own good, Ellen told herself, using her fan agitatedly. Catching sight of the Bracegirdles, she saw at once what she ought to do.

The Bracegirdles had had hard work in keeping amazement off their faces all the evening. How, they wondered dazedly, did Joe Prickard do it? This was the grandest occasion they had ever attended. It even beat the reception when Edith Bracegirdle's father was made Mayor of Thringley – and that had been a great occasion if you like. Thringley had never seen anything like it. But this – why Abbotsbury couldn't have done better! Alfred Bracegirdle had silently done sums in his head – the man was spending money like water. He must be a millionaire by now, Bracegirdle thought hopelessly. Yet his portfolio in the office gave no such indication – he must have other lawyers and accountants, the solicitor thought and his eyes narrowed. Crafty. Very crafty.

'Oh, Mr Bracegirdle, a moment I beg,' Ellen puffed, catching up with them. 'Forgive me, Edith, but I must seek your husband's advice. We need someone for Hester – a strict governess who will keep her in her place. The girl's getting quite spoilt. It's high time she went back to the schoolroom. I wondered if you knew where I could get such a person. Middle aged at least, and a very strong character.'

Bracegirdle tried not to catch his wife's eye. For here was luck indeed. Their cousin Ethel Rogers was in need of a place. Ethel was all the things Ellen Prickard needed: a former school teacher whose health had broken down. And like stars bursting before his eyes, Bracegirdle saw the advantage of having Ethel part of the Prickard household. Useful, he thought gleefully. Very useful indeed. 'I believe we can help you,' he said, his hand touching his white tie. 'I realize what an anxiety the girl must be to you – with such a background, I mean. Perhaps we could talk over supper? Come, Edith, my dear, let us follow Lady Prickard.' As they went downstairs, he made a meaning face at his wife behind his hostess's back.

It seemed to Hester that she had hardly been asleep at all, before Agnes was waking her for the drive into Sewerston for the Jubilee service at the church. She stretched and moaned, remembering last night and the new friends she had made in the Fox children with pleasure.

'Hurry, Miss Hester. Breakfast is an hour early today,' Agnes chided, superintending the preparation of her bath. 'Now, are you awake? Then I'll go and look after m'lady. Hurry, Miss Hester! You've a ten-mile drive in front of you.'

Her dress had been pressed by Melia who now brought it in. 'Eh, miss, it's lovely,' the girl said wistfully, laying it over the daybed with loving hands. 'And that 'at! Pink's me favourite colour.' Pink muslin with shiny pink spots made the dress, and the hat was pink tulle and roses. Melia had tried the hat on secretly and had longed for John, the footman, with whom she was walking out, to see her in it. 'Come on, miss, the water's getting cold.'

She returned ten minutes later with the breakfast tray.

Hester groaned. 'Melia, I can't eat all that with this tight corset cutting me in half. Butter me a bit of toast and take the rest away.'

'You'll go into a decline, miss,' Melia scolded, but she did as she was told.

'Aren't you coming into Sewerston today?' Hester asked as Melia buttoned the pink dress up the back.

'We're all coming in the wagonette, Miss. Rickaby's getting it ready now.' The girl hopped with excitement. 'We shall be there by the time you come from the church. Oh, miss, isn't it going to be a lovely day? The sun's that hot already.'

It *was* hot. Squeezed between her aunt and uncle in church, Hester felt faint. They were in one of the front pews with the Abbotsburys in the other and with all the prominent citizens at their backs. The pulpit was covered in roses and greenery, and the scent mingled with the women's perfume and the men's pomade until Hester felt stifled. And as the service wore on she could smell people; the strong smell of mothballs and sweat that meant that everyone was in their best. Ellen, who took up two seats, was pressed heavily against her, and when she tried to regain her seat after a hymn it was to find that the small space had vanished altogether.

She was longing to turn round and see if Tommy and his family were in church, but all attempts to do so were thwarted by Ellen.

At last the service of thanksgiving for the reign of fifty

years was over. As the last strains of God Save the Queen died away, Hester turned and looked eagerly about the church. But there was no sign of the familiar red head. Never mind, she thought, I'll see him down in the square. For she was longing to see her friend again, to pour all that had happened in the past two months into his sympathetic ear. She had missed him badly.

As the congregation filed out, smiles of relief were exchanged. The serious business of the day was over, and now they were trooping out eagerly to see what awaited them in the town square. There were many who looked at Hester, remembering her as poor little Hester Kelsey. She looked very different today, they thought. Well, fine feathers made fine birds.

Hester met their curious eyes shyly, for she too was aware that she was very different from the Sewerston girl of only two months ago. She had begged Agnes to let her wear a plainer dress and hat, for she was afraid of frightening Tommy to death when he saw the pink outfit. But Agnes had been shocked. The pink dress and hat had been bought specially for the Jubilee and for the Jubilee they must be worn. 'If you're afraid what people will think, Miss Hester,' she added shrewdly, 'I shouldn't worry. They'll all be done up as right as ninepence themselves. You'll see.'

But nowhere could she see Tommy's red hair and freckled face.

As they walked the few yards to the square, Hester spotted the wagonette from Stanhope disgorging (with squeals and guffaws) the entire staff from Stanhope. Even Wiston was there, and Agnes was beaming and nodding as if to tell her she looked all right in the pink outfit. Rickaby, the carter, had decorated the horses with all their brasses and red, white and blue favours and he had a patriotic cockade on the side of his billycock. Ellen ignored the giggling crowd of retainers, but Joseph and Hester stopped and Joseph chaffed the girls about their smart hats. Melia, Hester noticed, was on the arm of John, the footman, and Lizzie had an escort of stable boys surrounding her. Melia was wearing a blue print dress and a white chip straw hat and looked very pretty, Hester thought. Lizzie sported a parasol. Hester knew all about that parasol – it had been left her by her grandmother and was Lizzie's most treasured possession.

A gasp went up when the new arrivals saw the square. It was transformed, with huge arches of yew and cedar into which were twined thousands of roses and white daisies. Great columns of flowers stood at every corner and in the centre was a magnificent crown made of roses. Long tables were joined together to run the length of the square and back, and women were already serving the food to a long column of people. There were to be several sittings and it looked as if the Jubilee meal would be going on all day. But everyone was good-humoured and the Rising Sun and the Black Bull were doing a roaring trade in porter and beer. Above their heads, the bells of St Margaret's were crashing out a glad carillon. Bunting hung from every window round the square; there was no breeze to lift the flags and the sun was very hot.

Lord Abbotsbury had decreed that the town was to eat together and there was to be no nonsense about a separate table for the leading citizens. Mr Newlands and Mr Beddows had been disappointed, as they had visualized themselves on either side of Lady Abbotsbury. But all was not lost and presently Lady Abbotsbury found herself with the minister on one side and a beaming Mr Beddows on the other, while a discomforted Mr Newlands was taking second best with Lady Prickard. Ellen had seized Hester and pulled her on to the bench beside her when she saw old Hawke, a tankard of beer, his seventh, in one hand making a beeline for the vacant seat on her other side. *That,* she told herself indignantly, she would not stand for.

'We ought to have closed the public houses,' the minister said glumly. He was drinking lemonade, with one eye on old Hawke who had reeled back to the Black Bull for a refill.

'How old *is* that man?' Lady Abbotsbury enquired. 'He

never seems to get any older. I remember him as a child.'

'About ninety-four, I believe. He was born during the last years of the century. He's still as hard as a rock, never washes, smokes that horrible old pipe and drinks like a fish.' The minister sighed, for what use were his lectures (with slides) on the Demon Drink with old men like Hawke still around?

The noise was indescribable. Little boys shouted, babies cried and those waiting to be served kept up a chant of 'We want our dinner! We want our dinner!' to hasten those already eating. Under her parasol Ellen felt she was going to faint. Just look at Joe, she thought indignantly. He was sitting next to a pretty young woman and was saying something to make her blush. 'Hurry up, Hester, we're going home straight after this. . . . '

'Oh, Aunt Ellen, I haven't seen half the people I want to see yet. The aunts . . . ' Hester babbled, remembering them quickly. 'I must say good morning to my aunts. Can I go now? I believe I see them. . . . '

'Very well but be quick,' Ellen grumbled. She was vainly trying to catch Joe's eye to signal her intention of leaving.

'I hopes as you're enjoying the ham, m'lady,' Mr Newlands said proudly. 'Allow me to help you to a morsel more. I've had it for two weeks in brine and I can assure you you won't find finer ham – no, not even in the Court of St James's,' he added triumphantly.

So Ellen, helpless and abandoned by her family, allowed Mr Newlands to help her to a morsel more ham.

Hester looked frantically round, as she shoved her way through the crowd, the pink dress getting crushed in the process. Where was Tommy?

'Well, Hester, so here you are!'

Startled, she turned and there were the aunts all in new Jubilee bonnets.

Hester smiled nervously. She was glad to see Martha and Mary, but what could she say to Aunt Agatha who had a decided sniff on her face?

'I heard you were done up like a fashion plate,' Agatha said, 'and I could scarcely believe it. Lady Prickard must have no sense at all – tricking you out in finery at your age. It's ridiculous.'

'But you look very nice,' Martha said stoutly. 'Very pretty, I must say. Pink's your colour, don't you think, Mary?'

'It suits her quite well,' Mary said, with a nervous glance at Agatha.

'Pink muslin,' Agatha snorted angrily. 'Giving you ideas! What will people think? Your father's only been dead four and a half months. Yon woman's got no more sense than a goose. I saw that at once. I think it's shocking.'

Hester bit back a cheeky retort. She began to back away.

'I hope you're behaving yourself?'

She burst out laughing, all her irritation evaporating. 'Aunt Agatha, what would you do to me if I said I wasn't behaving? Take the cane to me – oh, I forgot! I broke it didn't I? Have you bought a new one yet?'

Agatha's face was suffused with dark red. 'Get out of my way, you good-for-nothing wench,' she said through her teeth and Hester felt the wave of dislike that came from her. 'Come along,' she told her sisters.

Obediently, half-smiling but looking scared, Martha and Mary came on. Hester watched them go without regret.

As they scuttled after their sister, Martha said, 'Well, she's turning into a real beauty, is Hester. She's like her mother.' Mary turned and nodded. 'Very distinguished,' she whispered.

Over her shoulder, Agatha said, 'She'll come to no good, that one, mark my words. She's got it written all over her.'

Hester was still smiling to herself as she walked on. Then suddenly all thought of the aunts faded for there, just ahead of her, were Mrs Hoggarth and Matty. Breaking into a run, she reached their side.

'Why, Hester, is it you? You look very nice, my dear.' Mrs Hoggarth greeted her warmly and then said to Matty,

'Run on and tell your father that Granpa's gone into the Black Bull and must be fetched out at once. Run, Matty.'

'Where is Tommy?' Hester asked breathlessly. 'I've looked for him everywhere.'

'But didn't he write to you? He said he had.'

A cold hand seemed to clutch Hester's heart. 'Write to me? What about? Isn't he here then?'

'Tommy's gone, gone for a soldier. He'll be going out to India at the back end.'

Hester stared wordlessly. She felt her face was set in clay. She tried to speak, but such a sense of loss filled her that she could say nothing. *The back end* – that's what the local people called the autumn. And he was going to India.

'He got restless-like,' Dorrie Hoggarth said, avoiding the girl's stricken eyes. Tommy had said: *I'll never see her again. It won't be the same, Ma, now she's rich.*

'When . . . when will he be coming back?'

'There's no saying. He's signed on for twenty years.' His mother forced herself to say it without tears rising to her eyes. She had to get used to it. Tommy, her darling, had gone away for good. When she saw him again he would be a man. 'Father's promised me I can go and see him before he sails,' she said in a voice of pain and Hester realized that Tommy's mother felt as she did – so empty that it hurt. 'I'm sorry,' was all she could say helplessly, feeling the other woman's pain now as real as her own. 'I thought . . . ' She looked helplessly round at the noisy throng in the square. 'I must go. Goodbye, Mrs Hoggarth,' and she had slipped through the crowd before Dorrie Hoggarth could say any more.

Tommy's mother stared after her. Up till now she could only feel a bitter pity for herself. Now her heart followed the young girl who was walking away from her. She loved our Tommy, she told herself with wonder.

'Hester, come with me,' Ellen commanded. 'I've told your uncle I want to go home so we'll walk back to the carriage.

Heaven knows where that racketty new coachman has got to. I don't think he's going to shape at all.' She looked at her niece. 'What's the matter with you? Have you got a stomachache?'

'Yes – Yes, a stomachache,' Hester agreed with relief. 'Perhaps I've eaten too much.'

'Agnes had better give you a Gregory powder when you get home. I think I shall take one myself. Oh, my head,' Ellen moaned. Her turquoise parasol had not been successful in screening her from the intrusive sun. She would send it back. In addition she was irritated and bored to death and longing for tea in her cool drawing-room. 'Just look at your uncle!' she exclaimed. For there was Joe, enjoying himself hugely in the centre of a crowd of fishermen whom he knew. There was still a common side to Joe, Ellen told herself sorrowfully. He just couldn't forget that he had been a trawlerman. He liked low company, more's the pity. 'Go and get him, Hester. Tell him I have a bad headache and I must go home.' And tapping her toe impatiently she stood and waited, her pout much in evidence.

'Dear Lady Prickard!' cooed a voice and there was Mrs Alfred Bracegirdle in a peagreen taffeta outfit that did nothing for her sallow complexion. 'Such a crowd – and such rough people. I told Alfred that I wasn't going to enjoy it a bit and he promised me I wouldn't have to stay long; but of course it's important that people like us should be seen, isn't it?'

It was a curious thing that an encounter with that snob Edith Bracegirdle always turned Ellen into a Radical. 'I think it's been a splendid day, Edith. I can't think who you've been mixing with, but of course we've been with the Abbotsburys.'

'Oh, don't misunderstand me, I've been with friends too. . . .'

'Who? The Umplebys? I'm sorry I can't stay to see their daughter as the Jubilee Queen but we have to get back.'

Mrs Bracegirdle flushed scarlet. She was a draper's

daughter herself, but now that her father was safely dead she did not consider the local draper her friend. 'The Umplebys? Good heavens, we don't know them. I meant Doctor Dent and his wife and the vicar. I wanted especially to see you about my cousin, Ethel Rogers.'

Ellen looked blank. 'What about her?'

'You said you wanted a governess and Ethel is looking for a temporary post. She's a teacher at a girl's school in the south, but has been home for a term. She's returning to St Catherine's in September and would like to fill this term. She would be most suitable to teach your niece being well educated and *not* a governess by profession. And it goes without saying she's a lady.' Mrs Bracegirdle preened herself. 'So important, especially for your niece. . . . '

'Oh?' Ellen bristled. 'Why particularly?'

'Well, I mean, seeing who her father was. . ; . '

'And who was Miss Ethel Rogers's father? Didn't he help his brother, your father, in that shop you had in Thringley?' The sauce of the woman, Ellen fumed to herself.

Mrs Bracegirdle winced. 'Papa owned a very large emporium in the city. I believe my uncle was on the board. . . . '

'Edith, what rubbish you talk! You're getting sillier every day simply because you've married the only solicitor in this town. I used to make many a purchase at your father's shop in my youth – it had an excellent haberdashery – and your father would serve me himself and I daresay your uncle did too. The way you talk is enough to make a cat laugh. Very well, I'll see your cousin, but I can't do so before July as we're going to see Wilfred next week. Tell her to write to me first. Good day to you,' and Ellen sailed away. Surprisingly, she felt in much better spirits. On the way back to Stanhope she was quite loquacious. It was Hester who was silent, her eyes on the road. The carriage hood was down and a scent of growing plants was wafted in to them. The beauty of the countryside made Hester's heart ache. Or was it something

155

else? It was only when she reached her room that she cried. Despairing tears that only the young know. Oh, Tommy, she thought as she scrubbed at her eyes, won't I ever see you again? Ever?

CHAPTER SEVEN

'There he is! there's Wilfred....'

'Oh, where, Aunt Ellen?'

It amused Prickard to see the two females craning their heads over the side of the hired carriage he had ordered from the Abingdon hotel. They had turned in at the gates and were driving up the tree-lined avenue to the school. It was the summer half-term, and all Ellen's vapours and headaches had disappeared in the excitement of seeing her son again. She had made light of the pokey bedroom at Abingdon, hadn't murmured about the indifferent food and had submitted meekly when Hester offered to do up her hooks and eyes for her.

Now that they had reached the school, Ellen's inanimate face sparkled with excitement. Wilfred was the chief interest in her life.

The Radley boys were men, Hester thought, looking about her with awe. She had expected boys not be-whiskered giants in bowler hats and black suits, or clad like some in white flannels and straw boaters with a pink ribbon round the brim. A fitful sun played on the red-brick buildings, the smooth lawns and the chestnut trees covered in white candles. Despite the grey sky it was warm and everyone was in their colourful best.

The carriage stopped and a boy came forward, taking off his hat. Hester felt a jolt of disappointment – so this was Wilfred. He was the image of his mother with the short broad bones of the Braintrees. His chubby cheeks were pink

157

and his mouth reproduced his mother's pout. His head was covered in tight brown curls and he was quite undistinguished looking.

'Wilfred, love!'

'Hullo, Mama.' Wilfred kissed his excited parent dutifully, wishing she wouldn't be quite so exuberant. He shook hands with his father and then directed a cool stare at his cousin. 'You must be Hester.' He stretched out a hand and took hers; it was plump and clammy, she noticed.

'You're looking thin, love. They don't feed you properly. Goodness knows we pay them enough,' Ellen said indignantly.

'Now, now, Ellen, leave the boy alone.'

Wilfred turned with relief to his father. 'I've asked a friend to join us for luncheon, sir. You suggested it, didn't you?' He led the way to the cricket field which was surrounded by lines of deckchairs. The school, he explained, was playing the old boys' team by tradition. Play had begun at eleven.

A figure rose from the grass at their feet. 'Mama, may I introduce Harry Vivian? My father. My cousin,' Wilfred murmured.

Harry Vivian bowed. He was small-boned with dark hair and a smooth face.

He's too pretty for a boy, Hester thought. Both boys seemed childish compared to the splendid creatures who had been standing about on the drive.

Desultory conversation murmured among them as they professed to watch the game. Hester, who had never seen a game of cricket in her life, had to conceal her boredom. Ellen talked ceaselessly, directing her remarks to Wilfred who sat at her feet facing the game. Watching secretly, Hester saw that he was being dreadfully irritated by these remarks. She felt sorry for him, especially when she saw that the other boy was amused. She also noticed that the two boys had far more to say to each other than to the visitors; a low murmur of conversation ran between them

158

continuously. She wondered what it was they found so absorbing. Uncle Joe was asleep with his eyes open, she suspected.

It was a relief to go to the marquee for lunch at one o'clock. Large family parties crowded in to occupy the many tables, and the unrestricted noise of young voices rose to the canopied roof. Over the cold beef, strawberries and cream and hock, Harry Vivian became very talkative and amusing, making them all laugh – for he had a rapier wit.

How tenderly Wilfred looks at him, Hester thought rather resentfully; for here she was in her best pink muslin and neither boy was noticing her except to pass her something. She stifled a yawn and then sat up and tried to look blasé and adult; for there at the very next table sat the handsomest boy she had ever seen in her life, and he was looking at her. Looking hard. He sat alone with a grey-haired man who ate without talking and looked bored.

She stole another glance and met the blue-eyed gaze again. The boy – he was almost a man – was well-built and very fair, with sleepy eyes that nevertheless saw everything. His manner and voice were languid like the old gentleman's but his eyes, when they met Hester's, danced in the liveliest manner.

'I'll meet you at Tutor's at four,' she heard the father say.

Then – Hester held her breath – the boy was coming across to their table and was greeting Wilfred who seemed astonished. Rather sulkily he introduced the boy as 'Victor Cockayne who's in my Social.'

Young Cockayne accepted Ellen's invitation to sit down with alacrity. It happened that the empty seat was by Hester. It had been so smoothly done that Hester gazed at him with appreciation. He smiled at her as if guessing her thoughts even as he talked politely to Ellen. Then he exchanged remarks about cricket with Joseph. But his eyes never ceased to wander in her direction.

Hester longed to be able to shine in conversation with this

dashing youth whose romantic good looks were so capturing her imagination. He wasn't *pretty* like Harry Vivian, she thought, but handsome. Her heart leapt into her mouth every time he turned towards her and appeared to be about to address her. For what was she to say when he did so at last? What if she had no answer for him? For she knew (Ellen had drummed this in) that she must not on any account talk about her father or Sal or the harbour or the aunts or the millinery shop. After the trouble with Gerald Woolsey, Ellen had given her a lesson in deportment. Young ladies must stick to innocuous subjects like the weather, the flowers and the music that was being played at the party. Anything else was dangerous.

'Do you ride, Miss Kelsey?'

A long breath of relief escaped her. She could answer that one. 'Yes, I love it. I've only just started to learn, but Payton says I'm coming along fast. He says I'm a good 'un to go and that I'll soon have the hang of it. . . . ' She paused uncertainly for he was laughing. Thank goodness, the others were talking and couldn't hear what was being said, for it was obvious she had said the wrong thing again.

'Do go on – oh, I've made you shy again! Don't go back in your shell. I want to hear more of what Payton says . . . he will be your groom, I venture to think? He sounds a man after my own heart.'

'Oh, Payton is nice,' she told him eagerly. 'He's a little man and he knows everything there is to know about horses. He's got a splendid little dog called Sim and he's a champion ratter – Sim, I mean. He lives in a cottage all by himself – Payton I mean – because he doesn't hold with women since his wife ran away. . . . ' She stopped, biting her lip. Why was he laughing again?

He saw she wasn't to be goaded into more talk of Payton, so he leaned towards her and said, 'Now I'll tell you about me. I'm lazy and a thorough disappointment to the Warden, my tutor and my father. They have all told me so. I hate organized games and mathematics and science and I love

160

literature and Greek mythology and Latin verse. I'm going to be a poet, you know.'

A poet! Her face glowed. She had never met a poet before.

'I shall have to go up to Oxford in a couple of years if I matriculate, but I shan't do any work afterwards. Think of it – I shall be free.' His eyes went dreamy as he longed for the future. Then he looked down at her. Such a beautiful little thing, he thought, with such extraordinary eyes. He would write a poem about her – something after the style of Donne. A sonnet to a girl with green eyes.

After lunch the four young people strolled across the park to show Hester the famous Radley oak tree. It was, they informed her, mentioned in the Domesday Book. She, who had never heard of this book, wondered if it was another sort of bible and she pretended an interest she didn't possess.

Ellen and Joseph were left talking to Warden Wilson who was circulating among his guests, overawing most of them with his cap and gown and flowing whiskers.

Victor Cockayne escorted Hester across the marshy ground, while the other two walked ahead, deep in conversation. Seeing her looking curiously after them Victor said, 'It must be nice for Prickard to have you as a sort of sister. He's an only child, isn't he?'

She nodded. 'But I don't know how we shall go on. I never saw him before today. When my father died. . . .' She stopped and a dark flush swept over her white skin.

He looked at her curiously. 'Yes?'

Hester took a deep breath. 'I'd like to tell you,' she said frankly, 'but Aunt Ellen wouldn't like it. Please let's talk about something else.'

He concealed his curiosity manfully and turned the subject. They were approaching the famous oak across rather wet ground. 'Go ahead,' he directed, 'and don't slip off the grass tussocks. They're quite dry . . . ' He broke off, swallowing a curse as he slipped himself and his white buckskin boot sank into oozing mud. Flinging out his hand wildly, he grasped her arm in an instinctive gesture.

Walking ahead, obeying his instructions, she didn't see what had happened. She felt his hand tightening on her arm and instinctively whirled round and hit him with her free hand, completing his discomfiture as he fell in the mud on one knee. 'Yer keep yer hands to yerself!' she hissed.

His astonishment was vast. One knee in the mud, he gaped at her. Why, the little vixen! he thought angrily, getting up and ruefully surveying his ruined flannels. 'I beg your pardon,' he said stiffly. 'I did not mean to touch you. You can see what happened....'

'Ho, I can see all right!' she laughed scornfully, and the eyes he had so recently admired sparkled with anger. 'Why can't you keep your hands to yourself?' she repeated, but in haughty accents now.

Victor's temper rose. 'You are just a silly little schoolgirl,' he informed her coldly, wringing dirty water out of his flannels. 'I wouldn't touch you with a barge pole!'

The other two had turned round and were bellowing from afar with malicious laughter. What fun to see the high-and-mighty Victor Cockayne looking a figure of fun! 'Cockayne, you ought to see yourself!'

'Shut up!' he said savagely. 'I'm going back to change. Perhaps you'll look after your cousin, Prickard.' He raised his hat and turned away.

Wilfred looked at Hester with annoyance, his smiles dying away. He didn't want her along with them. Besides she must have said something to make Cockayne so angry. So he said hurriedly, 'You had better go back to Mama. The ground is too wet for you.'

Her face burning, close to tears, Hester turned back. She was now longing for this day (so much looked forward to) to be over. It was no use, she didn't know how to behave – didn't know what to say to people. She choked, watching the figure of Victor Cockayne hurrying towards his house. She saw him pause to exchange words with friends, gesturing with one hand. Was he telling them some fool of a girl

162

thought I was making advances to her and pushed me in the marsh?

She mopped at her eyes furtively. When his hand shot out to grasp her arm she had thought . . . remembering Aaron Waterman, she shuddered.

'Come along, Hester, we're going for tea,' Ellen said an hour later. She looked sharply at the girl. 'Where have you been all this time? Don't you remember what I've always told you? You mustn't walk about unescorted . . . you're not living on the harbour now, you know. Where are Wilfred and the other boys? Tea is being served and I'm dying for a cup.'

'It appears to me you know nothing. A little ignoramus,' said Miss Ethel Rogers smiling sweetly.

She said the nastiest of things with the nicest of smiles, Hester had discovered this within a day of knowing her. 'Yes, Miss Rogers,' she agreed dutifully.

Outside it was a perfect June day and a bumble bee buzzed against the closed window. Miss Rogers disliked fresh air and the air in the schoolroom was close. Hester tried to keep alert, but her eyes drooped in spite of herself.

Miss Rogers was staring at her, still smiling, but her eyes were icy. Hester felt fear pinching her stomach. This was the second week under Miss Rogers's regime, and each day fear sat coldly in Hester's midriff. Knowing she must not show it, she raised her eyes and met those queer light ones opposite her.

'What are you?'

'A little iggernoramus. . . . '

The ruler came down with a whine on her knuckles. 'Have you no *ear*, girl? No wonder your accent is so atrocious – pure Sewerston and the lower end of it too. Open your book and read. I warn you you will feel this ruler for every mistake you make, so beware.'

Hester curled her hands in her lap, but this was spotted

at once. Both hands must be laid out on the table top. As she stumbled over Doctor Johnson, the ruler came down harder and harder until Hester's hands were red and numb.

Ellen had engaged Miss Rogers after the briefest of interviews in Bracegirdle's office. Miss Rogers appeared to be a very superior sort of person and Ellen was impressed. In her dark grey dress with its crisp white collar, her hair scraped back from her face, she looked businesslike and clever. She expressed herself as a true believer in a strict upbringing for young girls 'to form their character.'

Ellen was relieved to find her quite plain and middle aged. She had no desire to have a pretty young woman about the place for Joseph, she told herself, could not resist a pretty face. Miss Rogers would be impervious to his nonsense. So Miss Rogers had taken up her position at once and Hester was kept out of her aunt's way all day. It was a great relief.

What Mrs Bracegirdle had not told Ellen was that her cousin had been dismissed by her school because she was an alcoholic.

In the school room at Stanhope, Hester saw the dark green bottle that Miss Rogers placed at her elbow each morning. 'Medicine,' she said airily as she took a dose from it every half hour. 'Nerve tonic,' she added as she wiped her lips.

Hester recognized the bottle. This one carried no label but the same smell issued from it that had hung about Will Kelsey. Old Geneva, he had called it. Gin, her mother had said bitterly, throwing it down the drain outside the cottage. Miss Rogers was never drunk or unsteady, but her temper got viler as the liquid in the bottle got less. The slightest mistake brought the ruler down on Hester's fingers. There were times when Miss Rogers came and stood behind her, watching the painful passage of Hester's pen across a clean page. Then Hester would feel gooseflesh stand out on her neck, feel a cold wave of dread as she waited for the inevitable blot and the stinging slap against her face.

Perhaps if Hester had had a closer relationship with her

164

aunt, Miss Rogers would not have lasted a week at Stanhope. But with Joseph away again, Hester saw less of Ellen than usual now she and Miss Rogers ate upstairs in the schoolroom.

Miss Rogers soon realized that Hester rarely saw her aunt and nothing that happened in the schoolroom would be carried downstairs to Ellen's ears. She grew steadily more reckless.

It was only with Agnes that Hester felt free to talk. Agnes brought her arnica for her sore fingers and listened sympathetically, but it seemed natural enough to her that 'the school teacher', as she called Miss Rogers, should beat her pupil in order to get her to learn.

'You'll just have to work harder at your lessons, dearie. You'll be a regular young lady with your French and what not.'

'She drinks, Agnes. All the time. I think it's gin.'

'Miss Hester! Why, that's real bad of you. The poor thing's weakly and has to take medicine. Doesn't she go into Sewerston each week for it? Of course it's not gin – the idea!' And Agnes laughed comfortably as she put the cork back in the bottle of arnica.

Wilfred came home for the holidays in the middle of July. He had only been at Stanhope while they were in the throes of moving. Now that they were settled he appreciated the place to the full and soon found that he enjoyed Hester's company. True, he regarded her as far beneath him in intellect, but out riding it was a different matter. Wilfred, very much a beginner and a nervous rider, was glad of her bracing company when Payton brought the horses round in the afternoons. Hester, who had no fears herself, teased and encouraged him to make greater efforts.

'If you had your right leg twisted round the saddle like me....'

'Hester! Don't you know you mustn't talk about *legs* in

front of gentlemen? Mama will be dreadfully shocked. . . . '

'Then don't tell her,' Hester urged. 'You wouldn't want her worried, would you? How was I to know about legs being forbidden?'

'You don't know anything,' Wilfred said with a sigh. It was obvious that he would have to teach this poor raw little cousin.

Behind them, Payton's nutcracker face wore a grin. In his opinion, Miss Hester made two of the young master who seemed a bit of a milksop. Those white soft hands of his! But he had to change his opinion shortly after this and own 'there was more to t'lad than meets eye.'

It was one of those days when Hester had to be restrained; for a demon of recklessness had gripped her after a bad morning with Miss Rogers. The relief of being out of the woman's shadow and in the soft summer air went to Hester's head like wine. She jumped hedges and raced her horse on the hard roads until Payton lost his temper with her.

'I've told 'ee once and I'll not tell 'ee again!' he roared, catching her bridle. 'If you race Peachy on this hard road I'll have to take 'ee home. You'll lame her, that's what.'

'Yes, for heaven's sake stop it!' Wilfred said shrilly. Her antics were making his own horse fettlesome.

Hester was breathless, her cheeks flushed and her eyes sparkling. Some of the demons had been expelled and she submitted meekly to Payton's scolding. They turned their horses down a lane leading to a village. As usual Hester led the way. Outside the inn, a knot of men were standing with guns under their arms and dogs sitting panting in the shade. It was obvious they had been shooting rabbits and were now slaking their thirst with beer. As Hester passed, one of the men shot out a hand and seized the bridle of her horse. 'Why, if it isn't the little milliner!' he exclaimed.

Hester stared down at the man, recognizing Gerald Woolsey.

'Wonders will never cease. Here's the little milliner looking a regular lady with her horse and groom! I tell you, lads, that's something she is not!'

His companions grinned, pressing forward, scenting fun. They were all three of the same ilk; ne'er-do-well sons of the local landed gentry.

'See a fine lady on a fine horse, eh? You're a dam' good actress, m'dear. Look the part to the manner born!'

'Let me go!' Hester hissed. She jerked the reins and her horse side-stepped, but Woolsey had her by her boot now and was sliding his hand up her leg under the habit. She kicked at him, pushing his hand away. 'Go away!'

Wilfred and Payton had caught up with her now. 'Do you know this man?' Wilfred asked. Woolsey still had his hand up Hester's skirt.

'It's . . . Mr Woolsey . . . ' She was kicking at him with all her strength, but was making no impression. 'I don't want to speak to him . . . Uncle Joe sent him away from our party. . . . '

Wilfred knew now who the man was. 'Let go of my cousin,' he said in his high partly broken voice.

Woolsey brushed him aside like a fly. 'See, lads, the sort of people who are living in my grandpapa's house?' Woolsey rallied his cronies. 'Cits – every man jack of 'em – ow!' for Wilfred had brought his crop down full on the sneering mouth.

'Leave my cousin alone! Take your hands off her!' Raising his crop once more, he brought it down with all his strength on Woolsey's shoulders and head. 'Come on, Hester! Catch hold of her bridle, Payton!' They were away, clattering down the dusty road before Woolsey had found his breath to yell after them. They heard his curses and threats diminishing rapidly in the distance.

'Oh, Wilfred, you were wonderful!' Hester gasped.

'By gor, Master Wilfred, you were quick and all.' Payton added ruefully, 'I oughtn't to ha' let it get out o' hand like. The master put me in charge of you and Miss Hester and I done nothing.'

'Oh, rot, Payton. It was up to me to protect my cousin from the swine,' Wilfred said loftily. He was feeling quite dizzy with achievement. 'The man's a cad of the first water and deserves all he gets. He didn't frighten you, I hope?' he added kindly to Hester.

Hester opened her mouth indignantly and then shut it firmly. It would be a shame to spoil Wilfred's triumph over Woolsey. 'Well, just a bit,' she admitted, 'but I knew you were there – and Payton too.' She threw the disconsolate groom a smile, but he was still shaking his head at his lack of spirit.

When Ellen heard of the encounter, she blamed Hester. Really, how the girl attracted trouble, she thought angrily. Why, Wilfred could have been hurt by that terrible man. All because of Hester. She asked Miss Rogers into her sitting room and expressed the view that Hester needed firmer handling. She was getting above herself. She was spoilt. 'So I leave it to you, Miss Rogers. Please keep a close eye on her. She's a silly little girl and easily gets ideas.'

And Miss Rogers promised she would do her best.

'What's the matter?' Wilfred asked in astonishment. It was Sunday morning and he had just come across his cousin, red-eyed and incoherent in the summerhouse.

For answer she held out her right hand – all the nails had turned blue.

'Good lord!' Wilfred who hated the sight of blood and injury, shut his eyes and shuddered. 'Did she do that? What a beast the woman is! Why, they wouldn't do that to you at Radley even!'

'Will . . . will they come off?'

'Good God, I hope not!' Wilfred said in horror.

'I mean the nails, silly.' Hester blew her nose and looked again at her blemished hand. 'Will they come off and grow again? Or will they always look like this?'

'I once shut my finger in a door and it looked like that.

I was only a youngster. It grew again of course.' He held out his hand, white and soft and plump like a girl's; even the nails were well-kept and shining. What a funny fellow he is, Hester thought, but with affection. He was kind and sympathetic and they were good friends already. 'Why don't we tell Mama?' he added, brightening. *He* told his mother everything after all.

'I did. Just now. She told me it was my own fault and I don't work hard enough at my lessons. She says it's for my own good and I'll understand that presently. But it isn't just that, you know. It's the drink.'

'Miss Rogers? She drinks? You're sure?'

'Like a fish,' Hester assured him firmly. 'Out of a plain bottle that's supposed to hold medicine. But it's spirits. I tasted it one day.'

'Where is she now? This minute? Closeted with Mama? Good. Wait here, Hester, while I nip up to the schoolroom and have a sniff.'

He was gone ten minutes and returned breathless, a smile of intense satisfaction on his round face.

'You look as if you've been at the Old Geneva yourself,' Hester said, still nursing her hand.

'I have. It's gin all right.' He chuckled with sudden glee. 'I've had a brilliant idea. I'm going to concoct a ruse and pay the old girl out. No, I'm not telling you what it is. But just you wait, Hester, just you wait.'

CHAPTER EIGHT

August was very oppressive. A yellow sky pressed down over the moors; the grass turned brown and lifeless and the becks dried up. The sun burned like a brass plate through a thick mist that never lifted. It was a type of sub-tropical weather rarely seen in northern England and people wilted.

The effect on Miss Rogers was alarming. As day after day they woke to another stifling morning and everyone cowered behind drawn blinds, Miss Rogers's temper was stoked to a fine heat. Downstairs, Ellen lay on her sofa waving her fan and drinking lemonade; upstairs, Miss Rogers drank recklessly from her bottle until her brain was inflamed. Hester felt she was shut up in the schoolroom with a dangerous animal who was liable to spring at her at any moment.

Sweat ran down the girl's face and body as she tried to learn her lessons: stumbling over French exercises and arithmetic, hardly finding enough breath to read aloud. Across the table crouched this strange woman, waiting, waiting . . . Near at hand was the ruler – soon Hester would feel its sting on her sore hands.

Now that Wilfred was home, Hester was eating in the dining room again. But Miss Rogers had pleaded ill-health. She was still sadly convalescent, she said, and a tray brought up by that nice obliging Melia would serve her very well. She did hope dear Lady Prickard understood. As Ellen and Wilfred never mentioned her, Hester had given up complaining. Her uncle, the only one who would have understood, she told herself bitterly, was still away in Liverpool. The date of his return had been put back twice by hasty notes posted from the office. So there was nothing for her to do but set her mouth grimly and prepare to endure.

A huge clap of thunder resounded across the park, making the windows rattle. Hester raised her head and looked at her governess, but Miss Rogers was rubbing her forehead, her mind far away. A shiver went down Hester's back – how odd she looked. Through the window she could catch a glimpse of a huge bank of ochre-coloured cloud filling the eastern horizon. Nothing stirred. Suddenly a sheet of lightning lit up the room. Startled, Hester's pen spluttered a fine set of blots across the clean page. Dismayed, she looked up, her hand going to her mouth. Oh, she had done it again! And she had been doing so well up to now. . . .

Miss Rogers staggered to her feet, pushing the chair back and pointing a trembling finger at her pupil. 'You . . . you little fool! Look what you've done . . . all over the page. You're filthy! filthy!' Words choked her mouth as she lifted the ruler and brought it down again and again on Hester's head and face. Outraged, the girl leaped to her feet and glared defiantly at her hated mentor; but it was doubtful if the woman saw her, so blinding and unreasonable was her rage.

Exhausted at last, her thin breast heaving, the woman sank on to the chair. Reaching for the bottle, she didn't even pause to pour a measure into the silver cup she kept at her elbow. Quickly tilting her head back, she tipped the bottle against her lips. The next moment she was incoherently shrieking as blood gushed out of her mouth, down her white collar and grey dress, in a horrifying stream.

Hypnotized with terror, Hester was no match for the governess when she lunged at her crying with her ghastly reddened mouth, 'You little murderess! Just like your father – I'll teach you though!' She was a wiry woman. Plucking Hester up like a doll, she thrust her into the cupboard where the books and maps and pencils were kept. *Click*. The key had turned in the lock and the girl found herself in a suffocating dark place, a smell of chalk and musty paper in her nostrils.

There was no room even to turn and fear ran over her in a cold wave. She tried to control a claustrophobic panic, to save her breath for a plea through the door. 'Miss Rogers, please . . . *please* let me out! I can't breathe. . . . '

There was no sound. Perhaps Miss Rogers was lying dead now? That had been blood pouring from her mouth . . . but was it? Why had Miss Rogers blamed her for it? She suddenly remembered her conversation with Wilfred. *I'm going to concoct a ruse and pay the old girl out.*

Red ink in the gin bottle was a typical schoolboy 'ruse'.

She wriggled, painfully aware that there was very little air in the cupboard. She could hear her heart hammering like a clock . . . suddenly it seemed to stop as the full force of the storm broke over the house. The flash of lightning lit up the interior of the cupboard and she shut her eyes involuntarily. Then came the clap of thunder that rumbled on and on, bringing with it a monsoon-like rain that battered the windows.

The noise of the storm drowned Hester's cries. She guessed that the room was empty and that no one would miss her for hours. The air in the cupboard was, she knew, being used up and she remembered horrible tales of people being walled up alive. Panicstricken tears rolled down her face. 'Help,' she choked and drummed on the door with the back of her heel.

An hour passed. She had stopped crying and was drowsy now. Pins and needles ran painfully up and down her cramped limbs. Then she heard Wilfred's voice.

'Hester? Hester, where are you?'

Feebly, she kicked the cupboard door.

The lock clicked, the door opened, light flooded in and she glimpsed Wilfred's astonished face as she collapsed at his feet.

Ellen had started luncheon when Wilfred charged into the room nearly knocking Wiston down. 'Mama, you must come at once. It's Hester.' He hesitated, remembering Wiston's presence. 'She – has had an accident and Miss Rogers isn't there.'

'What a nuisance. The soup must go back, Wiston. Tell Mrs Crombie I am very sorry but luncheon must be put back ten minutes. Now Wilfred, what is all this nonsense?' she added as she mounted the stairs. 'What has the silly girl done?'

'Mama, you must sack Miss Rogers . . . I know Papa would say so,' Wilfred said as he impatiently followed his mother's slow process along the landing.

'What do you mean?' Ellen had paused to regain her breath. 'Miss Rogers is a splendid woman.'

'Sack her,' Wilfred urged. 'She is an appalling woman. She not only drinks but she's cruel. She locked Hester in a small cupboard and kept her there all the morning. She could have suffocated. She's in a bad state.'

They had now reached the schoolroom. Hester, very pale, was stretched out on the floor breathing unevenly.

Ellen took charge at once. She was in her element with illness of any kind. 'Fetch Agnes and the sal volatile – ask Wiston to unlock your father's brandy. Where *is* Miss Rogers?'

'I'll find out,' Wilfred said grimly. He went across the landing and hammered on her door. There was no reply. Cautiously, he opened it. 'Miss Rogers?'

She was standing in the middle of the room staring dully at him. She was still stained with red ink and Wilfred felt his anger turn to pity. It was obvious the woman had suffered a mental collapse for she made no sign of recognition nor did she move. In her hand she held the empty bottle of gin.

'Sit down,' the boy said gently, leading her to a chair. 'Mama will come and see you presently,' he added and shut the door quickly. Then he collected Agnes, got the brandy from Wiston and ran back upstairs.

Agnes rubbed Hester's hands. 'She's stone cold. Pass me that rug, Master Wilfred. My lamb, what has she done to

173

you? Just look at those fingers, m'lady. That woman wants a right good whipping herself if you ask me.'

Hester suddenly sat up, rejecting the brandy. 'No . . . it's all right. I'm all right. I couldn't breathe.' She put a hand to her head and shivered. Then she looked up at Wilfred. 'Was it you who put the red ink in her bottle?'

'Oh, Hester, I am sorry. I had no idea she would react like this. I only meant it as a warning that we knew. Mama, Miss Rogers must go away today . . . back to her relations at Sewerston. She seems to have lost her reason – it's the gin she's been swigging.'

Ellen looked staggered. '*Gin?* Wilfred, what nonsense is this?'

'I promise you it's not nonsense. Please trust me and go and write a note to Mrs Bracegirdle and I'll get Rickaby to bring the dogcart round and he can take her home. Her trunk can follow,' Wilfred added in a businesslike tone.

'But, Wilfred love, I haven't given her a month's notice. . . .'

'Be damned to that, Mama! I'm sorry but I feel like that. The woman is mad. She must go at once. Put a month's salary in your note . . . yes, I'm sure that's what Papa would do,' Wilfred said with relief. 'She's drinking gin here in the schoolroom . . . can't you smell it? . . . and this morning I put red ink in the bottle. . . .'

'You could have killed her!' Ellen gasped.

'Not her. She's got a cast-iron inside from all that gin.'

Ellen shook her head bewilderedly then looked down at Hester. The girl looked very pale, she thought, remembering with a twinge of conscience that she hadn't listened to Hester's complaints.

'Come and write that note, Mama . . .'

'Yes, Wiston, what is it?'

Wiston was breathing heavily after climbing two flights of stairs. 'The master – the master's just arrived, m'lady. John is getting the luggage in. Sir Joseph has gone upstairs to wash.'

174

A vast relief filled the room. Wilfred took his mother's arm. 'Let's go down, Mama. Papa will know what is best to do.'

Hester was scrambling to her feet, but Agnes restrained her. 'You are not to go down like that, miss. I want you to wash and change your dress – just look at yourself. You wouldn't want your uncle to see you like that, would you now?'

Hester managed a little laugh as she examined her grubby gingham dress. 'Oh, Agnes, we're always so glad to have Uncle Joe home again. Now everything will be all right,' and she drew a long breath of relief.

But it was only when she at last reached the dining room and was enveloped in a hug smelling familiarly of cigars, Russian leather and verbena cologne that she felt the last of her troubles slip away. Uncle Joe had an uncanny way of putting things right, she thought contentedly.

Joseph, sitting at the head of his table again after six weeks' absence, surveyed his responsibilities ruefully. Little did they guess but he had very nearly not returned this time. Emmy had nearly persuaded him at last. 'Not a divorce, Joe,' she had said earnestly. 'Just a separation. You can well afford it. We could have a nice place here . . . a house with a big garden. Don't go back, Joe. Wilfred's old enough to take responsibility now. Stay with me always, Joe.'

How hard it had been this time to tear himself away! It had been one long honeymoon and he had nearly written the fatal letter to Ellen. There was only one life. God knows he had had very little personal happiness until he met Emmy O'Neill. What did a man's achievements amount to in the final reckoning? He had more than enough money for two establishments, for both Stanhope and a home with Emmy.

But he hadn't stayed. All because of Hester. He had taken on a new responsibility, a new young life. Without him, Hester might suffer. He couldn't be sure that Ellen

175

would be kind to the girl and keep her until she was grown up.

It was Hester and not his son who had brought Joseph back. He had stirred in Emmy's arms, known a moment or two of bitterness. But he had come. And now Hester, wreathed in smiles, was sitting next to him and even Ellen was smiling happily. As for Wilfred, well, the boy seemed to have acted sensibly. Perhaps he was growing up at last. Glancing at his son, Joseph felt a faint stirring of pride. There was a lot of good in the lad – if only he could understand him!

For a week Hester had a blissful holiday. Whenever she came across her uncle she couldn't resist running up to him and hugging his arm. 'Uncle Joe, I'm so glad you're home!'

He liked knowing she loved him for she had become a daughter to him, a mixture of Nancy-and-Hester in his mind. Between them there was growing a strong bond.

Wilfred was not averse to her companionship in the small expeditions they made together for he could depend on Hester to make it exciting. He was flattered that she regarded him as an oracle; her own ignorance amused him and he enjoyed enlightening her with the scornful words, 'No, silly, not like that!' Hester took it all meekly, drinking in new knowledge like a sponge. She believed, in those days of her new awakening, that Wilfred knew everything, that she only had to turn to him to get an answer. He enjoyed being her teacher.

They explored the lanes and moors round Stanhope on horseback or in the dogcart. Mrs Crombie would pack hot Cornish pasties, plum cake and cold milk in a can. They would settle by the side of a beck, dump the can in the running water, take the pony out of the shafts and then fall ravenously on the food.

Then they talked. No one but Wilfred had ever heard Hester speak about her life at the harbour cottage. He had lived in the Harbour House with a nurse to take him out. His view of life on the harbour was very different to Hester's. She even told him about the night Will Kelsey had killed Sal and her lover. Somehow, telling it by the stream, with the pony cropping grass nearby and the plump, serious-eyed boy listening intently, the sordid story at last lost its sting. It was as if it had happened to someone else in another life.

She told him about her friend Tommy Hoggarth, but she didn't hint that Tommy had laughed at Wilfred for his golden curls. Tommy, she thought, would like Wilfred as much as she did. For her cousin was kind. There *was* something girlish about him and sometimes she even forgot he was a boy. Like the day she decided to pull off her stockings and paddle in the brown peaty water.

'Hester!' Wilfred said in horror. 'Mama would have a fit . . . no, you really mustn't do that. Don't you know anything?' He turned away delicately as she adjusted her garters and pulled her skirts down again. There was something of the gipsy in this cousin of his.

Hester grumbled but she obeyed him and then lay on her back and looked up into the huge blue bowl of sky. Behind her, larks shot straight up out of the heather, as if pulled on an invisible string, singing shrilly as they hovered. The small brown bees covered the ling and heather, buzzing round her head. She flung her arms wide, laughing aloud. 'Oh, I am so happy, happy, happy. . . . ' she murmured and then fell asleep.

The boy turned on one elbow and watched her. He liked this girl, the cousin he had never heard of until this year. Most girls frightened him. There was something about them . . . a shrillness . . . a cunning that pierced his nerves and caused him to hate them. With boys he was happy – especially one. Dreamily thinking about Harry Vivian he wondered if he could tell Hester. Should he say: there's a boy at school and I think I love him. Would she be surprised, perhaps shocked? There was nothing shocking to him in his love for Harry Vivian. But perhaps Hester would think it –

12   177

odd. Some of the dons at school did, he knew. They were always parting them, putting them in different dormitories, even in to different forms now.

Thinking of Harry, strange feelings filled him. An ecstasy of anticipation. Next week he would be back at Radley and Harry would be there.

It only took a week for Joseph Prickard to find a replacement for Miss Rogers. Ellen, it was obvious, was not going to stir herself. She kept saying vaguely that she would have to do something soon – and did nothing. So Joseph, who now knew everyone in the village, did something instead. He found Miss Crook.

Miss Crook was the curate's sister and for ten years had kept house for him. To everyone's surprise, at the age of fifty, he had suddenly married for the first time a very suitable widow with a little money. Miss Crook was out of a job.

'Two women in that little house will never work,' she told Ellen when she came for her interview. She moistened her lips, a naked look of fear in her eyes; for what was to become of her if she didn't get a post? She was a small woman with a clean pink skin and large trusting brown eyes behind gold-rimmed pince-nez. She was very neat, although her clothes were far from new; and her hair dressed low over her forehead gave her the look of a small intelligent dog.

Joseph sat in the background listening alertly with an air of indifference. Ellen looked helplessly at him once or twice, but didn't succeed in catching his eye. But suddenly he said, 'I want my niece to be taught ladylike ways. I feel sure you can do that, Miss Crook. I don't want a clever girl, just teach her everything you know. Literature, a little French, some drawing. Perhaps it's too late for the piano?'

Ellen looked at him in surprise. It was not usual for Joe to make an impulsive decision, yet here he was assuming Miss Crook was coming. She looked at Miss Crook. What

178

was there about the woman that had made up Joe's mind for him?

Miss Crook had turned and was leaning forward eagerly. 'Oh, I don't think so, Sir Joseph. If Hester is intelligent and interested I can teach her *anything*. I like singing myself and it would give me great pleasure to teach her . . . that is if you decide to engage me,' she added hastily, blushing. 'I daresay you will want to interview other people first. . . . '

'No.' Joseph got up, walked over to the empty fireplace and then faced her. 'How soon can you start, Miss Crook?'

'Today,' Miss Crook said firmly. 'I have not much in the way of luggage.'

'We'll send Rickaby for you at five o'clock,' Joseph said.

It was only afterwards that he realized Miss Crook had not asked what her salary was to be. Was she that eager to come, poor little soul? he wondered, and made a mental note that he would add another five pounds a year to her salary.

The next morning Hester and Miss Crook sat across the schoolroom table and eyed each other rather distrustfully.

'I've seen you in church,' Hester volunteered. 'In the choir.'

'And I've seen you,' Miss Crook retorted with a smile. 'You never join in the hymns. You stand there staring at the stained glass window to the left of the pulpit as if you're seeing something very intriguing.'

Hester's mouth opened with surprise. She went pink. Why, she had never guessed that anyone watched her! 'I make up a story,' she said lamely. 'About the people in the window.' This was not quite the truth. The truth was that one of the angels in the window looked so like Victor Cockayne that she could only gaze and gaze. The angel's face was half-turned towards her; it had a little half-smile on its lips and sleepy eyes . . . Victor Cockayne to the life. She had mentioned it to Wilfred and sent him into a fit of suppressed laughter. And all the time this little woman had been watching her . . . Hester's eyes dropped to her lap.

179

Miss Crook saw her discomfiture and changed the subject quickly. 'I don't know what you have been reading with Miss Rogers, but I thought you might enjoy this,' and she held up a book. It was *The Mill on the Floss*. A smile of pure delight lit up Hester's face. She and Miss Crook would be able to deal together; they had the same taste in literature. Doctor Johnson was gone for good.

PART TWO
Hetty Kelly

CHAPTER ONE

'She's going out again . . . oh, Aunt Ellen, do come and see!'

But Ellen, who was comfortably settled with her embroidery on the other side of the room, refused to move. 'You ought not to peep, Hester, it's impolite.'

'Don't worry. She can't see me. I've found a hole in the lace curtains that's just right,' Hester chuckled.

Ellen shook her head and looked disparagingly round the drawing room of the London house they had taken for the season. A shabby place in her opinion and they were charging enough for it too. She thought of her own cool drawing room at Stanhope and sighed.

It had been Joseph's idea from the first. Now that Hester was twenty she must see something of London life, he said. They had gone abroad as a family every year to Dresden, Vienna, Paris and Rome. But London pleasures were something that Ellen and Hester had only read about. A house had been found in Adelaide Crescent, Knightsbridge, not far from the park and with excellent mews for the horses and carriage. They had arrived in the middle of May and although Joseph had promised to return very shortly from his business trip to Liverpool, he had not put in an appearance and it was now the first week in June. Hester and her aunt were marooned with the servants; for without a male escort they were unable to go about as they would have liked. Wilfred, in his third year at Oxford, was due at any time and Hester was trying hard to curb her impatience. Although they went shopping and for drives in the park, it was becoming obvious to the rest of the household that Hester was very bored.

The young woman living on the other side of the crescent had taken her interest. She was, Hester reported, young and beautiful with the most exquisite clothes. Hester spied on her shamelessly, as she emerged from her house and was helped into a well-sprung landau.

'She's wearing a simply lovely outfit,' went on the reporter from the window. 'It's that new colour . . . eau-de-nil. Watered silk, I think, with frog fastenings . . . and oh, Aunt Ellen! . . . such sleeves! They're *à la mouton* and quite immense. She has ostrich feathers on the most enormous hat. . . .'

It was too much for Ellen. Heaving herself out of her chair, she padded heavily across the Axminster carpet to peer as shamelessly as her niece. 'Well, I don't know!' she gasped. 'Wherever can she be going? She's fit for a garden party in that outfit.'

'She's going for a drive in Hyde Park,' Hester guessed. 'You always wear your best attire for that . . . haven't you noticed? Oh, that must be her husband . . . ' and Hester stared breathlessly at a stoutish man in pale grey who was taking a seat next to the vision.

'He looks half asleep,' Ellen observed. 'Doesn't he have any work to go to, for pity's sake?' A man was not a man in Ellen's opinion unless he had an office to go to.

'I shouldn't think so.' Hester rose from her knees and twinkled at her aunt. 'There, you've been peeping now so you simply can't scold me any more. I wonder who they are? Perhaps Wiston will know. Servants seem to know everything, don't they? Dear Aunt Ellen, can I ring for tea? There's just nothing to do but eat, is there? I do wish Uncle Joe would come back from Liverpool, for I long to go to the theatre properly in the evenings. That matinée was so dull. Confess now, you thought so too. Old ladies and small children and tea trays on our laps . . . oh, it was *dull*!' Hester threw her arms wide. She was longing to experience life; which she privately thought of as Life. Nearly three weeks had passed and Life was at a standstill.

'Yes, ring for tea. I'm afraid you're bored, love. Never mind, there's that nice Mr Bourn and his mother. They've asked us to their At Home on Saturday.' She looked keenly at her niece, but there was no telltale blush. But then, Ellen told herself philosophically, girls didn't blush like they did in her young days. At Hester's age the very mention of a certain man's name would have put Ellen in a flutter. And she wasn't very much older than Hester when she married Joe.

Mr Thomas Bourn was very eligible. Twenty-seven and, since his father's death, the head of a respected tea firm in the city. Joseph knew the Bourns as he knew so many business people, and had written to tell them they would be staying in London for two or three months. Mrs Bourn had called and Ellen and Hester had returned the call last week. Mr Bourn had been there and they had been invited to a musical evening on Saturday at the house in Bayswater. Young Mr Bourn had shown a decided interest in Miss Kelsey.

It would be a splendid thing for the girl, Ellen thought and then sighed. Hester was so headstrong. Young men had fallen in love with her, but she had found something wrong with all of them. Too short, too thin, too fat, too dull. A man was pronounced 'boring' or he was found to have 'lily white hands' – as if a man's hands mattered! Ellen was coming to the conclusion that Hester was going to be difficult to please when it came to the matter of a husband. Her aunt, glancing across at the girl's thoughtful face, wondered once again what she was looking for. With her looks, she had already had many chances of marriage; and Joe still insisted that the girl must be allowed to choose for herself. Ellen realized she would miss her when she did leave Stanhope for, over the years, all her antagonism towards Nancy's daughter had evaporated and nothing was left but good will. Hester was her constant companion and life had become considerably brighter since the girl grew up.

Hester had grown into a tall slim girl with glossy dark brown hair, lively turquoise eyes and a pale skin. She sparkled with life even as she said that she was bored. Ellen had realized very early on that the girl possessed some special magnetism. She had never heard of sex appeal and would have been shocked at the idea. Nevertheless Hester possessed it in a generous quantity. Whatever it was, Ellen tried her best to damp it down. Young men, she told her niece, did not like girls who were too lively and opinionated, but Hester only laughed and went her own way. Poor darling Aunt Ellen was centuries out of date and believed girls should be seen and not heard. Why, they were nearly in the twentieth century!

'After tea,' Hester said as she poured out, 'I'm going for a stroll or I shall *burst*.'

'Hester!'

'Very well, go berserk,' Hester said demurely. 'Don't you think that sounds much worse? And much more dangerous.' She lifted the lid of a dish and saw hot scones. Hot scones in June! Aunt Ellen was amazing. Whatever the weather she was always ready for food. 'Wouldn't you like to go on the river, Aunt Ellen? Will Wilfred take us, do you think?'

Ellen was spreading strawberry jam on her scone. 'I don't know, love. That would be nice, wouldn't it?' she added hopefully; for Hester with her cup in her hand, was wandering about the room like a prisoner in a cell. 'Go for that stroll . . . not far and not too long or I shall be worried.'

'Twenty minutes, I promise.' She ran blithely upstairs for her hat and encountered Agnes.

'Now, Miss Hester, where d'you think you're going? Has m'lady said you could go out on your own? That hat's too smart just for a walk. You'd best wear the panama.'

'Agnes, you're behaving like a gaoler. Please stop badgering me or I warn you I'll have hysterics.'

'Get on with you! You don't know what the hystericks

186

is! Those gloves aren't clean. Give them here. Take these and for mercy's sake don't forget your parasol. It's like a baker's oven out there. I've never seen such a place – not a breath of air and only early June. What's it going to be like next month? Has m'lady thought of that? I'm not saying nothing but I reckon we should never have left Stanhope . . . not for so long . . . not for two and a half months. . . .'

Hester heard her voice fading as she ran downstairs. Wiston was in the hall. 'Do you want a cab, Miss Hester?'

'No, Wiston, I do not,' Hester said firmly. 'I'm going for a stroll and please don't say I shouldn't, for if I don't go out for ten minutes I shall . . . ' She paused, eyeing his raised brows. 'I shall run amok. Very nasty.'

It was hot in the street. Hester strolled slowly on the shady side of the crescent, wondering who lived behind all those stiff lace curtains. Beyond the crescent was a redbrick square of much more imposing houses built early that century. She came out into Knightsbridge and found a throng of people pushing her off the pavement into the gutter. There was a smell of horses, a din of traffic and clouds of dust. She turned down a quiet sideroad and wended her way home. The beggars on every corner made her feel sick – crippled children, white-faced and hollow-cheeked, old blind men, toothless women with babies wrapped in shawls. She had emptied her purse before she had gone many yards.

Reaching the square again, she drew a breath of relief as she strolled under the trees, grateful for their shade and the quiet of the little open garden where one could sit on a bench for a while. Drawing little patterns in the dust with the point of her parasol, she sighed. It was a dreadful thing to admit, but she was already disillusioned with London. The over-furnished house with its closed windows was suffocating. The days passed, punctuated by heavy meals, a drive to the park, a rest in the drawing room with a novel to yawn over. Oh, why couldn't they go back to Stanhope?

I ought to feel grateful, she scolded herself. Uncle Joe

wants me to enjoy London. I'm getting spoilt – but I'm so *bored*.

She caught herself sighing again, jumped up and began to walk very fast across the square and into the crescent. At the corner she stopped and her face lit up. A cab had stopped outside their house, Number 18, and . . . yes . . . it was Wilfred! She picked up her skirt and half-ran towards him.

Wilfred saw her and burst out laughing. 'Hester, if you could see yourself! You're scarlet. Who's chasing you?'

'No one, you idiot. I'm just so pleased to see – ' She faltered to a stop, for another man had got out of the cab and was snatching off his hat. She recognized him even after five years for he had not changed much.

'You remember Victor Cockayne, don't you? My cousin, Hester Kelsey.'

Hester bowed, a distant expression on her face. Even though she recognized him, she hoped he did not remember her.

He was smiling, looking quite friendly. 'How many years since we met, Miss Kelsey? Those flannels of mine never recovered, you know!'

Hester's colour brightened and she gave him a frosty glance. But Wilfred remarked, 'Jove, you were a little idiot in those days, I don't know how we endured you.'

'Well, you did and I'm still here,' Hester snapped. 'How nice to see you again, Mr Cockayne. I suppose you and Wilfred are sharing a cab because you're both out of funds and have only just managed to get home?'

'You are absolutely right, Miss Kelsey,' Victor Cockayne said gravely, the corner of his mouth twitching. 'We only managed to leave Oxford this morning before the bailiffs caught us.'

Wilfred was grinning as he directed John with the luggage. 'She's got a pretty sharp tongue, my cousin. Pinch Hester and out come her sharp little claws. I tell you what she did once . . .'

'Goodbye, Mr Cockayne, I think my aunt is waiting for me.' She bowed and sailed up the steps and past Wiston into the house.

Victor Cockayne was staring after her. The delicate looking boy of Radley days had turned into a fair young giant with a pale skin and lazy eyes. There were lines at the corner of his mouth which could look hard when he was not smiling; it was the face of an experienced man now. Beside him, plump Wilfred with the querulous voice looked a youth, yet there was only a year between them. Victor turned towards his friend and said explosively, 'Why, you idiot, she's a beautiful girl now! Why didn't you tell me? We haven't invited her to my sister's dance next week . . . look, you'll have to bring her. I'll square my mother about it.'

Wilfred shrugged. 'I just think of her as my cousin and an awful little pest at times. I suppose she's more like a sister than anything. As for being beautiful . . . she's not bad but . . .'

'Good God, Prickard, she's a stunner, a divine woman. . . . ' He caught the footman looking interested (for John had never learned not to take an interest in Mr Wilfred's friends), suppressed the rest of his speech and got back into the cab. 'I'll post the invitation as soon as I get home,' he promised as the cabby whipped up the horses and they rolled out of the crescent.

A young woman in acid yellow satin was singing a soulful song. 'Farewell – fare thee well – fare*well*!' she trilled.

Sitting on the hard horsehair sofa Hester was using her fan; for the air in Mrs Bourn's drawing room was suffocating. Her aunt, she noticed out of the side of her eye, was smothering a yawn. Wilfred had escaped from the room and was laughing and talking with another man in the hall as they drank weak claret cup.

Their hostess kept time with her fan, her eyes closed,

her lips curved in a satisfied smile. She believed her musical evenings were renowned in Bayswater and had already informed Lady Prickard of this fact. The song finished, she opened her eyes and beckoned her son to the piano. 'Thomas is going to sing a sea shanty,' she announced. 'Miss Dutton will accompany him.'

Mr Bourn was a pale young man, rather narrow of shoulder with large feet and hands. As he opened his mouth and a deep bass voice issued from it, Hester saw her aunt's amazed face and irresistible laughter welled up inside her stays. Agnes had tight-laced her firmly and she had not been able to eat much supper, which was the object of the exercise. Young ladies, Agnes said, should have appetites like little birds. Feeling laughter bubbling frantically inside her, Hester looked wildly round for escape. The sofa shook and Ellen was nudging her indignantly. With a tremendous effort Hester brought her over-developed sense of humour under control. It was really too bad of Mr Bourn. He ought to have warned them that he possessed a bass voice that rightly belonged to a red-faced sailor weighing twenty stone. It was too unexpected of him.

Having presently got herself under control, she rose to meet her hostess who was approaching her. 'Now, Miss Kelsey, I feel sure you perform. What shall it be? A pianoforte solo or a song?'

'How kind of you, Mrs Bourn, but I brought no music.'

'But cannot you sing or play without music, my dear? Come, I will not condone any excuse.' She tapped her young guest playfully with her fan. 'And where is Mr Prickard? Will he not sing a duet with you? I feel sure he has a fine voice.'

'Indeed, Mrs Bourn, my cousin is quite unmusical and neither sings nor plays,' Hester said, smiling but firm. Wilfred, she knew, would be furious if she let him in for a performance in front of the polite Bayswater guests who spoke to each other only in undertones and smiled so uneasily. Wilfred's tastes ran to ribald songs suitable for

190

smoking evenings. She glanced round the room and realized everyone's eyes were on her. They all knew who she was – the niece and ward of one of the richest men in England. How suitable for young Mr Bourn and how clever of old Mrs Bourn to capture the young lady!

Hester was wearing dark red, the bodice embroidered with beads, the full skirt showing off her tiny waist. In her hair shimmered a pair of ruby butterflies set on silver springs. She looked elegant and sophisticated, a different creature from the silent young girls sitting tongue-tied in their mothers' shadows.

Mrs Bourn laughed affectedly. 'Now that's altogether too bad of you! I'm sure Mr Prickard has a charming voice – he has such a soulful face. Come, Lady Prickard, help me to persuade your young people.'

Catching Hester's baleful eye, Ellen stuttered nervously.

Then some devilment entered Hester's head. This gathering was the most boring affair, the food indifferent, the wine weak. Mrs Bourn was an insufferably pushing woman, Thomas Bourn unendurably self-satisfied. He was at her elbow now, bowing and smiling, urging her to grace the proceedings (as he put it) with a song. They wanted a song – were indeed pestering her for a song: well, they should have one.

'There's only one song I can remember without music,' she said sweetly and Ellen looked up apprehensively. Taking a lace handkerchief out of her little beaded bag she stepped hesitantly into the centre of the room. The guests rustled expectantly. Playing with the wisp of lace she began to sing in a shy little voice:

> A smart and stylish girl you see,
> The Belle of High Society,
> Fond of fun as fond can be –
> When it's on the strict Q.T.
> Not too young and not too old,
> Not too timid and not too bold,

191

But just the very thing I'm told,
That in your arms you'd like to hold. . . .

Suddenly, Hester's shy manner fell away from her. Her voice changed and became raucous and she waved the handkerchief as she danced (showing a great deal of ankle).

Ta-ra-ra-*boom*-de-ay,
Ta-ra-ra-boom-de-*ay*,
Ta-*ra*-ra-boom-de-ay,
Ta-ra-ra-boom-de-ay!

It was only two nights ago that she and Wilfred had gone to see Lottie Collins sing this song, which she was making so famous at the Tivoli theatre. It was a lifesize imitation.

'I don't suppose we shall get asked there again,' Ellen said glumly as they drove home. The fixed eyes and grim mouth of her hostess had not escaped her. 'You looked a thoroughly bad lot when you sang the chorus, Hester. I didn't know where to look.'

'I don't believe Lottie Collins does it better,' Hester averred shamelessly.

Wilfred was still choking with laughter.

'Wilfred, how can you? Hester has done for us with the Bourns.'

'Thank God,' Wilfred emerged from his handkerchief to say. 'Mama, I nearly died there. That woman in yellow had a moustache.'

'Wilfred!'

'I swear it.' He shuddered. 'As for Bourn himself, a more humourless fellow I've yet to meet. As for the food . . . ' He gripped his large waist anxiously. 'I hope the fish hasn't given me ptomaine poisoning and as for the claret — it came from the grocer's and had been watered. No brandy had been near that cup. Hester has done us a favour. Really, what was Papa up to, getting us acquainted with those middle-class tradespeople?'

Ellen gaped at her son. Never before had there yawned such a gap between them. She had been impressed by the Bourns' house . . . they were evidently both rich and safe. They had, in Sewerston parlance, done well for themselves. And here was Wilfred pouring scorn on the tea merchant's family, calling them *middle-class* as if they were murderers, poor things. Well, she didn't know what things were coming to. For it was dawning on her very gradually that Wilfred had been brought up to be landed gentry. He thought of himself as the scion of a well-known family. He would be a baronet one day. Their poor beginnings would have melted away in the mists of time. A feeling of hot pride seized her and she threw the Bourns to the wolves. He was quite right; they were dreadful people.

'Where is Papa, may I ask? Does he never take a holiday?'

'Now, love, you know he does. He's very busy just now . . . I'm not sure what it is, but it's something quite vital,' Ellen said hastily. The name *Mrs O'Neill* came and went in her mind. It was, she knew with bitterness, that woman and not business that kept Joe from his family.

'Don't forget that Hester and I will want the carriage tomorrow night, Mama. We're going to the Bridlingtons' dance.'

Warm pride filtered back into Ellen's veins. There! that's what she meant! She hadn't guessed that that nice Victor Cockayne was an earl's son – Wilfred took it all so easily. Up in Yorkshire the Bridlingtons were a big name. To Wilfred it seemed perfectly natural that he should know them. To Ellen it was something of a miracle, for her aunt Lucy Baines had once been a kitchen maid at Filey Park. She remembered being taken in through the back door of the kitchen when she was in long petticoats. Mrs Tawse, the housekeeper was called . . .

'What are you thinking about?' Hester murmured in her ear.

'Nothing, dear, nothing at all . . . just of my bed for I'm more sleepy than I can say.' Ellen shut her eyes firmly, willing herself to forget the past and making herself remember that she was the wife of the rich and powerful baronet, Sir Joseph Prickard. But it meant a strange division of soul.

Lady Amy Cockayne was kneeling on the floor of her mother's sitting room, arranging the seating for the dinner table next day, when her youngest brother came in.

'I hear that Caro Elliot has fallen out,' Victor said, sitting on the edge of a small table and swinging his leg.

'Her little brother has diptheria and so all the Elliots are unclean. It's ruined their season and they're all going down to the country tomorrow. I was thinking of telephoning Miriam Hexham. . . . '

'I'd like you to ask Miss Kelsey. Hester Kelsey.' Victor savoured the name with pleasure. He had thought of the girl for a week and now here was this superb chance. He leaned over the table chart. 'Mama doesn't object . . . I've sounded her out already.'

Amy raised her fair brows, a small smile on her lips. She had, like her brother, sleepy eyes that could look alarmingly alert at a moment's notice. 'Really, Victor, you're incorrigible. You know how you boys can twist Mama round your little fingers. Who is Miss Hester Kelsey and why don't I know her?'

'She's perfectly respectable and eminently eligible,' Victor said airily. 'Also very beautiful. I was at school with her cousin. She's lived with the family all her life as she's an orphan. Sir Joseph Prickard is said to be one of the richest men in England. Lord, Amy, how I long to be rich,' Victor said, sliding off the table and strolling about the room with his hands in his pockets. 'I'm so sick of being short of money at Oxford. I've run into debt again and haven't dared tell the governor yet.'

'Are you looking for a rich wife, Victor? You know what Papa thinks about that! He values breeding above everything.'

'Breeding!' Victor's tone was savage. 'Are we to go on interbreeding until we die out?' He recollected himself quickly, for this was not a subject he ought to be talking about to his young sister.

She had flushed but said warmly, 'Well, I agree with Papa. It would be insufferable to bring into the family some impossible – however much money they bring with them. Who is Miss Kelsey?' she repeated stubbornly.

'I told you. She is the ward of one of the richest men in England, Sir Joseph Prickard. He's come up from nothing in Sewerston. . . . '

'Sewerston?' Amy repeated in amazement. 'Where we went the year we all had the measles?'

Victor laughed. 'The same, my dove. Great men have a habit of springing from places called Nowhere. Take Disraeli. . . . '

'Is Sir Joseph Prickard a politician then?'

'No, he is a very successful business man. He owns Prickard's Lines – you know, the big ships that carry people across the Atlantic. His son was at Radley with me and is with me up at Oxford . . . different college though. He and his cousin are coming to your ball and I've asked Mama if we can invite Miss Kelsey to dinner in Caro's place. She said yes, as I've already told you, so don't look down your nose at me.'

Amy toyed with her pencil as she inspected the table plan. 'What a nuisance you are, Victor! Caro was next to Hornsea and he won't want an unknown girl next to him. He won't utter a word and the poor girl will have a thin time.'

'That's easily remedied. Put Mabel Porter next to Hornsea. They can be dumb together.' They both laughed. Their brother John, Viscount Hornsea, was famed for being a sticky conversationalist.

'Very well,' Amy said and Victor kissed her.

'You're a darling, Amy. I'll do the same for you some day. Wait until you see Miss Kelsey. She's a stunner.'

'She had better be after all the trouble she's given me,' Amy retorted rubbing out names.

Hester had dressed with special care, causing Agnes to peer suspiciously at her. She was usually without vanity, but tonight she fussed over her hair and took particular care in the exact placement of a pair of sapphire and diamond butterflies, which had to quiver delicately in her massed dark hair. The dress she had chosen was turquoise satin overlaid with tulle. Skilfully cut to show off her small breasts and white throat, it was low on the shoulders and tight in the waist. There was nothing of the awkward debutante about Hester. While most girls had been shut up in the schoolroom with a governess, Hester had been travelling in Europe. She had picked up three languages, been climbing in Switzerland, to the opera in Dresden, spent two months in Florence looking at pictures and had had most of her clothes made for her in Paris. She was twenty and had the self-assurance of a young married woman. But she was about to fall in love – she owed it to herself frankly. Victor Cockayne had been at the back of her mind for years and meeting him again had rekindled her feelings. There was an iridescence about the girl tonight that Agnes noticed. She looked her loveliest with her soft eyes and hair and skin. And the uncertainty of her feelings gave her a very appealing look.

Not that Wilfred noticed. He was totally concerned with his own appearance and with borrowing his father's gold studs for the front of his shirt.

'But we gave you a set for your eighteenth birthday,' Ellen protested, even as she unlocked the safe for Joseph's studs. He had fortunately taken his diamond ones to Liverpool. Ellen privately thought them vulgar, but no doubt *that woman* would approve of them.

'I know, Mama, but I've lost two lately . . . thanks awfully,' he added, hurrying away to finish dressing.

Heavens, he must be in deep at university, Hester thought. He never loses a thing – he's like a fussy old woman with

196

his possessions. Depend upon it, he's sold them to raise money for gambling debts or horses. She smiled indulgently, sitting carefully on a sofa waiting for Wilfred and the carriage which was to drop her off first at Lady Bridlington's, as Wilfred was going to another dinner party. There were to be twenty-four to dinner, the gossip columns had told their readers, and eight hundred to the ball afterwards. A marquee had been built out over the garden and 'the Countess of Bridlington, once the most beautiful debutante of the season herself and daughter of the Duke of Sherborne, was bringing out her only daughter, the Lady Amy Cockayne.' The heir, Lord Hornsea, would be present as well as the Hon. Martin and the Hon. Victor Cockayne. As an afterthought, the columnist had mentioned that of course the Earl of Bridlington would be at his wife's side.

Ellen had read it avidly, gloating to herself. Their Hester was dining with the family beforehand! She must remember to tell Edith Bracegirdle when she wrote next.

'Wilfred's going to make me horribly late,' Hester complained. 'The one thing I can't abide in my dear coz is his vanity. He looks at himself for simply hours.'

'He was like that when he was a little chap,' Ellen admitted, smiling to herself over her embroidery. 'He couldn't bear to get himself dirty and he would make Nurse change his little suits if they got at all rumpled.'

Hester groaned. 'I suspect that that is exactly what he's doing now – changing his little suit. Oh, Wiston, please send John to tell my cousin we are already late,' Hester called down the well of the stairs.

'A woman's voice should always be gentle and soft,' Wilfred said coming up behind her. 'Yours, Hester, is the nearest thing to a gong that I know. Yes, Mama, don't remind me again. Sandwiches in the study when we return.'

'You are the limit,' Hester complained. 'I shall be late at Lady Bridlington's and I don't know them. She will think it so rude. Goodbye, Aunt Ellen, I shall see you tomorrow, but not at breakfast I think.'

Although she was late at the Bridlingtons, she was not disastrously so. Relinquishing her white velvet cloak and adjusting her long gloves, she was announced by the butler to a tall fair woman not unlike Victor except for her rather vacant eyes.

The room was full of chattering people. For a moment or two, conversation was suspended as everyone looked at the self-possessed young woman standing in the doorway. 'Gad, what a girl,' a man murmured. 'Who is she?'

Lady Bridlington had clasped her hand, vaguely murmuring, 'You know my husband? Miss Kepple, Marcus.'

'My name is Kelsey – Hester Kelsey,' Hester smiled.

Victor was quickly making his way towards her. 'You look divine,' he murmured. 'I like the insects in your hair. I am to take you in – oh, they are already going down.' He held out his arm and she tucked her hand in it. They had never been so close – except when I pushed him in the mud, she thought with an inward tremor of laughter.

The dining room was lit by candles in silver gilt candelabra down the centre of the table. Between them were tall epergnes tumbling roses and maidenhair and stephenotis in sweet-smelling confusion. The long windows at both ends of the room were open to the soft light.

'Tell me which is your sister?' Hester asked.

'If you can see through the roses, she is the fair girl in pale blue and white. Awful dress isn't it? She thinks so too – it simply kills her colour. We're an awfully pale family, aren't we? Mama of course chose it and as Amy refused to wear white, it had to be pale blue which is worse. Now your dress is perfect.' His eyes admired her frankly. She is the most beautiful girl I've ever seen, he thought. So different too. Nothing of the timid debutante about her.

Hester's more worldly air had not escaped Lord Bridlington's attention. His pop eyes inspected her broodingly, as she sparkled up at his youngest son. Who the devil was the girl? And how had she got here? Too pretty for her own good, no doubt about that. Victor seemed to be on very good terms with her. Even, Hornsea, that notoriously slow starter, was staring at her.

Hester, unaware of the misgivings of her host, was having a delightful time. On her other side was a tall cadaverous-looking young man with very sleek black hair and a moustache. She took a hasty peep at his place card and saw that he was a Captain Crown. He was, he told her, in the 8th Hussars and just back from three years in India.

India. She thought of Tommy Hoggarth at once. It was strange how when she least expected it, Tommy came into her mind. 'I had a friend serving in India.'

'Oh? What regiment?'

'The Green Howards.'

'Oh, a county regiment,' Crown said, losing interest.

Their small-talk languished and Victor turned eagerly to her again, taking up their conversation where it had lapsed. They seemed to have so much to say to each other, she thought joyously.

From the head of the table Lord Bridlington's eyes brooded.

They rose at ten-thirty and Amy took the girls upstairs to her bedroom. They crowded on to the bed and chattered like starlings. They all seemed to know each other very well from childhood. Amy, conscious of Hester as the outsider, tried to draw her into the circle, but without much success. The others only smiled vaguely at her and continued their conversation. Rather proudly, Amy showed them to the new bathroom on this floor, and this prompted one of the girls, a sharp featured girl they called Connie, to drawl, 'Do you realize, my children, that there are only chamber pots at the Palace? Who goes on Thursday to the Drawing Room?'

'Me.'

'Me too.'

'Oh, Connie, is it true?'

'Mama told me so it must be.' There were giggles at this. 'I am not to drink anything at all from breakfast onwards.'

A plump girl said in a complaining voice that, from sheer

nerves, she always needed to go more often. 'But of course it would be awkward without Nannie or someone to hold one's train out of the way.'

Hester listened in surprise. Ellen, who used euphemisms for every function of the body, would have been horrified to hear such plain talking from girls about to be presented to Her Majesty. It struck her (and not for the first time) that the lines of behaviour laid down by her aunt were usually not those of the upper classes.

The girl called Connie turned to her suddenly and said, 'And you, Miss Kelsey, when are you to be presented?'

Hester smiled round on them (for something in Connie's tone of voice had fixed their attention) and said easily, 'Oh, I shall not be presented. You see, I am middle-class and not eligible.' She was intrigued to see Connie's mouth curl with satisfaction. 'My uncle, whose ward I am, is a shipowner, so I don't think I could possibly be allowed in the Palace, do you?'

They giggled nervously, not sure if she was joking.

Amy said quickly, 'We must go down. It's eleven o'clock and people will be arriving. Come on,' she added good-naturedly to Hester and held out a hand.

They trooped downstairs to the first floor where Amy was just in time to stand with her parents, for guests were arriving. Victor, his fair hair gleaming under the chandeliers, was talking to another man. When he looked up eagerly, Lady Constance Courage (whose mother had sounded her about an alliance with the Bridlingtons) called out 'Victor!' rather proprietorially.

But he wasn't looking at her. He was smiling up at that middle-class girl in the too-smart dress with real jewels in her hair ('Only after you are married, dearest,' her mother had explained to Connie. 'Till then, only pearls and fresh flowers.') and stretching out a hand to claim her for the first dance.

Connie Courage's small mouth turned down. Her eyes became pinpoints. *Middle-class interloper*, she thought with fury. Too well dressed, too sophisticated altogether. *Vulgar.* The pity of it was Victor didn't seem to realize it at all – but men never did. She conjured up a sweet smile of submission as Captain Crown came to claim her.

'Do you know you are the most beautiful girl in the room?' Victor said as they circled in a waltz, Hester holding the hem of her dress clear of the floor. 'Where have you been all these years? Why did I lose sight of you?'

She raised her brows mockingly. 'Did you really want to know me again after I pushed you in the mud? Those beautiful flannels ruined? We didn't come to Radley for the next Gaudy. I was in Dresden with my governess, going to the opera and living with a nice family to learn German.'

'You speak it?' He was surprised. Most girls were such ninnies and came out at eighteen without having been outside the schoolroom.

'Of course. Then it was Chantilly for six months at Madame Bressier's school, with weekly trips to Paris to see museums. Oh, I haven't been idle, I assure you!' she finished demurely. 'Three voyages to America were somehow fitted in between. My uncle went frequently, you see, sometimes taking Wilfred, sometimes me.'

'How I envy you!' he exclaimed. 'I would love to see America.'

'Why don't you go this vacation? On my uncle's boat The *Golden Jubilee*? It's tremendously comfortable.'

He smiled thinly. She was obviously too rich to know, that even families like the Bridlingtons had not the cash to spare for younger sons to go gallivanting about the world.

She danced next with Captain Crown and then with three of his brother officers whom he introduced to her. But Victor claimed her again before the first supper and they went down to it together. He had never met a girl who so attracted him. They had such a lot to say to one another. They danced again, and this time he danced her into the conservatory that was built out over the dining room. He skilfully placed two chairs in a corner, well-screened by a climbing jasmine,

'I am so glad we have met again,' he said in a low voice.

Her heart leaped despite herself and her breathing quickened. She looked at him mutely; he took her hand and carried it to his lips impulsively.

'Don't . . . please do not do that. You must not.'

'Hester . . . can I call you Hester? We have known each other since we were young, after all. And you pushed me in the mud when we first met!' He laughed, his eyes shining at her through the dim light. He came nearer and her heart broke into a gallop, nearly choking her in its flight.

She drew back and took her hand out of his. 'Do you still write poetry?'

He lounged back in his chair. 'After a fashion. Nothing's ever good enough though. I struggle to express what I feel and when it's down on paper it's merely banal. Have you ever taken drugs?' he asked after a pause. 'The effect is amazing. Words pour out of me – I can't get them down fast enough. It is so fascinating. Words and images haunt me for hours afterwards.'

'I don't suppose it can be very good poetry if it is written under the influence of drugs,' Hester demurred. 'What sort of drugs?'

'Hashish mostly. And I can't agree with you. Some of the best poetry written this century has been written by drug takers.'

'Does Wilfred take drugs?' she asked abruptly.

'I'm sure he has done. Most men have at Oxford. It's fashionable at the moment. I assure you it's an experience.'

She shook her head adamantly. 'No, I would never try hashish or any other drug. It would not be me. I wouldn't care for that.'

He looked at her thoughtfully. Perhaps that was why she fascinated him, he told himself. She was so decided, so certain, so strong.

'Would you be very kind and fetch me an ice?' She fanned herself, watching him over it. She needed time to think. Was she going to let herself fall in love in earnest? This man was having a strange effect on her. He was impulsive and was trying to sweep her along with him. Did she want to be swept?

'Of course. I won't be two minutes.'

She watched him go. He was passing on the other side of the glass when she saw his father stop him. There was a small square of glass missing behind the potted plants, and Hester could quite clearly hear what was said.

'Here, Victor, a moment. Who is that new gel in the blue dress with the thingummies in her hair? Your mother doesn't seem to know. You have been dancing several times with her this evening and it won't do, you know, won't do at all.'

Victor glanced over his shoulder and saw through the glass that Hester's head was turned the other way. In a low voice, he said, 'She is Hester Kelsey, a cousin of a chap I was at Radley with.'

'Radley? Pshah!' Lord Bridlington made a sound of disgust. 'A new school full of tradesmen's sons. I was a fool to let you go there . . . a whim of your mother's. Too dam' High Church too. Kelsey eh? Who are her people?'

'She hasn't any. She is a ward of Sir Joseph Prickard.'
'Who?'

'The Prickard Line. Oh, come, Father, you must have heard of him. He is one of the richest men in England. You would like me to marry a rich girl, wouldn't you?'

'It depends who she was. Remember, m'boy, it's blood that counts. I don't want any jumped-up tradesman's daughter in my family. My God, no. The Prince may be setting the fashion for Jews and businessmen to enter Society, but it won't do, m'boy, it won't do. Pretty gel and all that, but hardly one of us, eh?'

'I think you're a shade old-fashioned, sir. Blood without money could see the end of the Bridlingtons. . . . '

'Poppycock! We shall survive. We always do.'

Hester heard it all and burned with indignation. So Victor thought she was rich, did he? A suitable match because of her money? But she hadn't any money, only her quarterly

203

allowance! But of course it was Uncle Joe whom Victor was thinking of, Sir Joseph Prickard of the Prickard Line. One of the richest men in England, he had told his father. 'You would like me to marry a rich girl, wouldn't you?' She jumped up, aware of dismay and chagrin taking the place of the warm feelings she had felt for Victor. So great was her feeling of fury that she said, 'Oh, the wretch!' out loud, and was immediately pounced on by Captain Crown.

'There you are, Miss Kelsey? Isn't this our dance?'

It wasn't, but she smiled at him and accompanied him back to the ballroom. When next she saw Victor, he was dancing with Connie Courage, smiling into her face, his coat tails flying. She went down to supper with another young Hussar and laughed and talked with animation. When Victor approached her again she told him her card was full and so it was. She didn't have to sit out one dance.

But when at three o'clock, just before the second supper, Wilfred asked her if she was ready to go home, she nodded briefly and went to fetch her cloak and to thank her hostess.

She was silent as they drove home, her face turned to the dim light of the dawn that was etching the outlines of the roofs.

'Balls are over-rated entertainments,' Wilfred said with a yawn.

They opened the front door of Number 18 and at once noticed the silk hat on the hall table.

'Uncle Joe's come back!' A great wave of thankfulness filled Hester. London would become bearable now that her uncle had come. She could feel secure again, knowing that she had him to turn to when she was in difficulty. Would he help her to understand the attitude of Victor and his father? She would have to tell him – or would she? Her first thought had been to tear upstairs and see if he was awake; but with second thoughts, a new feeling of vulnerability made her hang back.

A figure appeared at the head of the stairs.

'Hullo, Papa,' Wilfred called softly.

Joseph came down to them smiling. He was wearing a long green brocade dressing gown over his stiff shirt and trousers. 'Well, my children, so here you are!' He kissed Hester and clapped a hand on his son's shoulder. 'Don't wake your mother, Wilfred, she doesn't know I am home. I only arrived an hour ago. I went to a City dinner on the way.'

'Uncle Joe, I'm so glad you've come at last. You will stay a few weeks, won't you?'

He laughed gently, his eyes evasive. 'We shall have to see, my child. I'm a busy man and there are no holidays for me. Did you have a good term, Wilfred? I wish you would write more frequently. Your mother expects it. What is the damage this time? I see you are wearing a new dress suit — very nice cloth too. When can I expect the bill?'

'Well, I am a trifle overdrawn, Papa,' Wilfred admitted. 'But not nearly so much as some of my friends.'

'So we must be thankful for small mercies, eh?' Joseph said drily. Wilfred's predilection for fine clothes and the speed with which he followed the latest fashion never ceased to amuse his father. 'Now go to bed both of you. I shall see you at lunch.' He watched them go up the stairs, Hester turning to throw him a kiss, then he went into the study behind the dining room and poured himself a whisky and water. A deep sigh shook him. It would be hard on them when he left; but they were adults now and he would leave them secure. Wasn't that enough?

He sat down on a chair near the window, dragging the curtain back so that the pink light of dawn fell on him as he sipped his drink. He couldn't go on living this secret life with Emmy indefinitely. Living in snatches. He needed her all the time now, for he had discovered that he loved her. He knew everything about her: her temper, her hysterical fits, her sensuous delight in their physical life, her transparent nature, her silly little lies. And he loved her. He shrank from telling Ellen, but she would have to be told soon. She would refuse to divorce him and make a terrible

205

fuss. There would of course be a scandal, but Emmy didn't mind that so long as she could be Lady Prickard some day. People would soon forget, she had told him blithely. He knew this to be untrue. It would be the end of his social climb, but he no longer minded that. He had made money – a terrible lot of money – and he was tired. Only he knew how tired he felt now. Sick of it all. He only wanted Emmy and a new life in the Lancashire countryside; for he fully intended buying a place where she could be Lady Prickard in style.

He buried his face in his hands. Oh, God, what a lot would have to be gone through before he was free!

CHAPTER TWO

There was seldom anyone in to lunch at Fitzherbert Square, although Lady Bridlington sometimes had a lunch party for her women friends and their daughters. The men of the family never stayed at home, and if they had no engagements they lunched at their clubs.

The morning after the ball, Victor came downstairs carrying his curly-brimmed bowler in one hand and his stick and pale grey gloves in the other. The hall was a hive of activity as the staff cleared up after the night's festivities. As he walked to the door he was waylaid by his father, who bounded out of the library like a cuckoo out of a clock.

'There you are, m'boy! Don't see half enough of you when you're home. Care to lunch with me at the club?'

'That's very kind of you, sir, but I have an engagement.'

'Not that gel? The one with the thingummies in her hair?'

'No, Father,' Victor said patiently.

'Oh? Well, come in here a moment, Victor. Want to speak to you.'

Victor followed his father into the library and stood waiting.

'Well, shut that door, boy. Can't hear myself speak in the racket that's going on. Thank God, that affair is over. Your mother's thought of nothing else for weeks.' Lord Bridlington sat down and twiddled with a letter opener on a writing table. Victor continued to stand silently, a mulish expression on his face for he had guessed what was coming. He was going to be talked to seriously.

'Sit down, Victor.'

He complied, putting his hat and gloves on a nearby chair. He was conscious of a flame of anger beginning to burn inside him.

'I was glad to see you heeded my advice and didn't dance with that Miss Kepple again.'

'Kelsey, Father. Hester Kelsey.'

'That's what I said. Looked a bit of an adventuress to me.'

With a supreme effort Victor controlled his anger. 'I thought an adventuress lived by her wits? I can assure you Hester Kelsey has no need to do that. She is rich. They are much richer than we are for all our acres. She is a very nice girl, who has travelled all over Europe and is not tongue-tied like her contemporaries. As for heeding your advice, I never gave it a second thought. Miss Kelsey had overheard our conversation and simply dropped me flat. Unfortunately for us, there is a hole in the glass which Venables had hidden with those infernal plants of his. She heard every word. I felt thoroughly ashamed.'

'Ashamed? Nonsense. Just as well she overheard. It saves a lot of trouble. We shall not pursue the acquaintance.'

'You may not, sir, but I certainly shall if she will allow me to.'

They stared at each other, puzzled anger in the older face, defiance in the younger one. Sons were the devil, Lord Bridlington told himself glumly.

'I simply say the gel is not from a family we wish to know. It was a mistake to ask her to your sister's ball. . . .'

'Personally I consider she adorned it.'

'Don't interrupt!'

Victor pressed his lips tightly together. Then he retrieved his hat and gloves and rose.

'I haven't finished yet! Hang it all, what's the hurry? Can't you spare me ten minutes?'

'This is not proving a very fruitful conversation, sir. We are unable to agree on any point. I think Miss Kelsey a

208

delightful person. She has travelled on the Continent and to America. . . . '

'America!' his father said with loathing. 'What in God's name did she want to go there for?'

'Isn't it a trifle old-fashioned to try and keep the new people out of Society? Times are changing, sir.'

'Rubbish! This is simply the Prince's influence. Your generation have become tainted with his radical opinions. God help us when he becomes the sovereign. Look at his friends: Americans, financiers, Jews and tradesmen. English society is being ruined by their differing values. Damn it, they are even getting into the clubs – they'll stop at nothing. I won't have them in my family and I give you fair warning. Don't bring those people here again – you understand?'

'Perfectly, sir. You do realize that your ban includes a great many of my Oxford friends? I shall be meeting some of them this afternoon at the Rhymers' Club. . . . '

'Poets! Affected nonsense. Really, Victor, I sometimes think you are a greater fool than poor Hornsea.'

'Without doubt, sir. John is really your better bet, so perhaps it is just as well I'm not your heir.'

'Look here, m'boy, don't let's quarrel. Can't you interest yourself in that nice gel Connie Courage? Westchester would settle a large sum on her, I know, and I could give you a house in Yorkshire. She would make you an excellent wife and would be one of us.'

'Connie is a nice girl, Father, too nice for me to marry without caring for her.'

'I can see you have become a Bohemian in thought and outlook,' Lord Bridlington said gloomily. 'Just look at that hat! Whoever made you a hat like that wants shooting.'

'Mr Lock made it. I believe he makes yours? I must go now, Father, or I shall be late. Are you dining in tonight? Perhaps we can have a game of pool afterwards. Good-bye.'

The boy treats me like a half-wit, his father thought

staring moodily at the closed door. What a pretty pass things had come to when one's son stood there trying to make one look small. Victor was a rum 'un, no doubt about that. Not interested in games or sport or the Yorkshire estate. Poetry! Hang it all, his ideas would be the death-knell of England's ruling classes if they spread.

Shuddering within himself, he heaved himself out of the chair and prepared to sally forth to lunch.

Victor had meant to walk briskly to the Cheshire Cheese; for after the ball he felt in need of air and exercise. But it was now so late he had to hail a hansom. As they trotted through the traffic, the bell jingling, he sat deep in thought, going over his conversation with his father. It was all such nonsense, he thought wearily, but it had gone on for so many hundreds of years that his father's generation could not accept that things were changing fast. The power and the glory were slipping away from the aristocracy. Men and machines were going to count in the future. To say that Hester was not a suitable young woman to bring to the house, to become friendly with, even to fall in love with was such arrogance – and all because her uncle was a rich man who had worked once with his hands. Hester, Victor told himself, as they were held up by a huge tide of horse buses and hansoms in Trafalgar Square, was as well-mannered as his own sister.

The sun was beating on the roof of the hansom, making it a stuffy box. He took off the hat that had so offended his father and fanned himself with it. He could feel his collar wilting – not that the members of the Rhymers' Club would notice it, for their own clothes were invariably shabby. London in summer was insupportable, he thought irritably; yet every summer they and others like them came up from Yorkshire and stayed the required two months in the hope of marrying off their daughters.

Victor closed his eyes against the glare and thought of

210

Oxford: the river with the willows reflected in the pellucid water, bowls of shade under the elms in the college garden and the spires shimmering in the golden haze of evening ... the utter peace of the place. ...

'Cheshire Cheese, gov'nor!' the cabby bawled through the skylight – the cove had gone to sleep by the looks of him.

Victor opened his eyes, clapped on his bowler and threw a coin upwards. 'Keep the change!' Now he was here his mood had changed to pleasure and excitement. The Rhymers' Club met in a room on the first floor and he clambered up the bare wooden stairs and opened a door. Smoke from several pipes curled towards the ceiling. They were all here and he was the last to arrive. Tankards of beer stood on the scrubbed tables and, with chairs tilted backwards, the Rhymers were in session.

Ernest Dowson paused in the middle of reading one of his poems and gave Victor a friendly smile. Victor smiled apologetically back, crept to a chair and sat back to listen raptly.

The poet, who had left Oxford four years earlier without taking a degree, was the leading light of the Rhymers. He was a slight pale young man of about twenty-four with a weak mouth and chin. It was a vulnerable and feminine face dominated by a pair of tortured blue eyes. Someone had likened him to Keats, and there was a look of the earlier poet about the face. He was wearing a shabby brown jacket, very rubbed at the elbows, and his grey and white trousers were loose about his thin shanks. His hands holding the paper were large and well-kept and looked as if they ought to be on another body.

Near him sat his friend Arthur Symons who had looked reprovingly at the late arrival. 'Go on, Ernest,' he prodded gently.

Dowson gave him a smile full of pathetic charm and began to read again in a rather thin voice.

'Ah, Lalage! while life is ours,
Hoard not thy beauty rose and white,
But pluck the pretty, fleeting flowers
That deck our little path of light:
For all too soon we twain shall tread
The bitter pastures of the dead:
Estranged, sad spectres of the night.'

A sigh went round the group as Ernest Dowson folded his scrap of paper. The poem was very much in the sombre mood of the day. It was exactly what Victor was always struggling to produce, and he looked somewhat enviously at the small shabby figure sitting so quietly under a shower of praise.

'I thought of calling it *Amor Profanus*,' Dowson added when the voices had died down.

Amor Profanus: yes, exactly right, they nodded round the table.

There was a knock on the door and the pot-boy arrived with more beer, a large crusty loaf with a Stilton cheese beside it and a hunk of cold beef with a jar of pickles. Everyone gathered round and ate and talked until the noise rose to the smoke-stained ceiling. Victor felt contentment creeping back into his mind. Here he was on familiar ground and completely happy.

It was three thirty when he sent his name up to Lady Prickard and followed the butler upstairs to the drawing room.

The portly figure of his hostess came towards him holding out her hand. She remembered him very well, she assured him. 'Your ball was a delightful occasion last night, Mr Cockayne. Your mother must feel gratified that it was such a success.'

He smiled. 'I hope so. It has been talked of for months in the family! Amy is the only girl, you know.' He looked

212

round the room as he sat down and put his hat and gloves on the floor; there did not seem to be an inch of room elsewhere for them.

Ellen saw his glance and said hastily, 'This is a hired house, you know. Very shabby is it not? But it was all we could get at such short notice. I was telling Sir Joseph only this morning that I was quite ashamed of receiving my guests here. I wish you could see Stanhope, Mr Cockayne! It is a beautiful place.' Poor Ellen knew she was talking too much and saying the wrong things. Why didn't Wilfred or Hester come and rescue her, she wondered indignantly.

Victor smiled his charming smile, sensing the poor woman was flustered and nervous. She was certainly very much the rich merchant's wife. How his father would have crowed if he had been here, he thought ruefully. Presently, Wilfred came in and then tea arrived and Ellen pressed her guest to eat; he looked much too thin, she said.

Victor wondered where Hester was. Unable to resist saying her name he said, 'I wondered if you and Miss Kelsey would come with me to a play tomorrow night, Prickard? There is rather a good one at the St James's – by that fellow Wilde, you know. Would you ask your cousin – if she is in? I could call round for the tickets on my way home.'

'Wiston, where is Miss Hester?'

'I don't recall seeing her today, m'lady. I will ask Miss Bentley.' He went out of the room with his heavy tread and found Agnes on the upper landing. She was sponging and pressing the dress Hester had worn the night before.

'Eh, this London,' she panted as Wiston's face loomed on the stairs. 'I don't know about you, Mr Wiston, but I'm starved for a taste of moor air. I can hardly get my breath.'

'A little rain might help,' Wiston agreed. 'Where is Miss Hester? She's wanted in the drawing room. A Mr Cockayne has called. He looks a nice young fellow,' he added in a less official voice. 'Wants to take Miss Hester to a play.'

'I'll see she comes down,' Agnes promised. 'She's out of sorts today – black imp's on her back I say.'

Hester was sprawled in a chair in her room reading a book. She refused point blank to go down when she heard who had called. Agnes cajoled and threatened, but she remained stubborn. 'I don't want tea and I don't want to see Mr Cockayne. I wish people would leave me alone.' She raised the novel as a barrier across her face and Agnes had to admit defeat. 'Late nights, that's what it is,' she observed irritatingly to the book. Hester pretended not to hear. But presently she went to the door and opened it; she could hear Victor's deep voice on the stairs. He had a nice voice, she thought wistfully – the wretch, she added quickly. She was done with him. All he was interested in was Uncle Joe's money.

She had written her thank-you note to Lady Bridlington and, when she heard the front door bang, she went down to her uncle's small sanctum behind the dining room. He was writing at the little desk, but looked up with a smile when she requested a stamp for her letter.

'You look tired, my child. Who was that who called?'

'Oh – just a friend of Wilfred's. Uncle Joe, you promised to take me to the theatre. Can't we go to the Gaiety to-morrow night? Oh, Uncle Joe, you are nice!' She kissed the top of his head and flew upstairs to tell Ellen.

'But Victor Cockayne has just called. He wants to take you and Wilfred tomorrow night to see a play of Mr Wilde's,' Ellen protested. She inspected the inside of a sandwich: smoked salmon. She ate two quickly and poured herself another cup of tea. She had hardly had a bite to eat, she told herself self-pityingly, with that young man to entertain. Now she relaxed and made up for lost time. 'He came to see you,' she added reproach-fully, 'even I could see that. Your uncle will have to take us another night.'

'Oh, Aunt Ellen, he can't – he's already sent John to get the tickets for the Gaiety!'

'The Gaiety? Mrs Bourn said that it wasn't at all a suitable place for ladies....'

'Mrs Bourn!' Hester exclaimed with scorn. 'I hope we haven't to listen to Mrs Bourn's opinion of the theatre – she and her son never go. They told me so. Wilfred says that their opinions are quite *démodé*.'

Ellen sighed and gave in. Wilfred poured scorn on so much in their lives at the moment that she was quite losing heart.

'Besides I don't want to be taken to the theatre by Mr Cockayne.'

'But he's such a charming young man....'

'I've come to the conclusion,' Hester said angrily, 'that charm is the most over-rated of qualities.' Those words of Victor Cockayne's continued to haunt her: *her uncle is one of the richest men in England.* Charm indeed! He was a fortune hunter, pure and simple.

So Victor's invitation was hastily refused and they went to the Gaiety the next night. Wilfred tried to opt out of the expedition; he was annoyed with Hester who was not making the most of her opportunities. The Bridlingtons, Wilfred considered, were their only entree into Society and it was too bad of Hester to behave as if she didn't care.

Joseph took him aside: a party of three would be an embarrassment just now with those secret plans of his for the future. 'Look here, old chap, I think your mother would like you to come.'

Wilfred looked stubborn. It was Hester who should be made to give way – how his father did spoil her! But he gave way in the end with a rather ill grace. The burlesque at the Gaiety was not to his taste, he reminded his father with dignity.

'But you will come? Good. Capital.' His father's heartiness seemed a trifle overdone to Wilfred.

So he sat beside his mother divided from his father by Hester. She was simmering with excitement to be seated in the famous theatre at last. The balcony was crammed with heads, the boxes filled with beautifully dressed women, their jewels glinting and gleaming in the light of the chandeliers. Above the boxes came the upper balcony and at the very top (nearly out of sight) was a gallery that seated hundreds for sixpence a seat. Imagine being on that stage and playing to a full house such as it was tonight! The cardinal red curtains with their gold tassles would be parting soon and there she would be, in the centre of the stage. . . . She subsided with a secret smile. Her childhood dream – how close it seemed tonight.

The audience seemed to be purring with anticipation. The show tonight was *Cinder Ellen up-too-late*. Once the famous Nellie Farren had been its star, but she had been forced to retire a few months ago, crippled with rheumatism. Her part had been taken over by an unknown actress and the show had nearly failed. But now Lottie Collins of *Ta-ra-ra-boom-de-ay* fame had come in to it for the summer and was ensuring its success. With her was Fred Leslie, inimitable, charming and handsome. Only those behind the scenes knew that he was already suffering from the disease that was to kill him before Christmas. The audience loved him and, when he came to take his curtain calls after every act, only those nearest the stage saw the beads of sweat and the ghastly pallor under the make-up.

'Isn't he glorious?' Hester exclaimed, clapping until her hands were sore. 'I've quite fallen in love with him.'

'Some of the jokes are not suitable,' Ellen pronounced. Mrs Bourn had been right all along, and she had allowed herself to be persuaded by Hester against her better judgement.

Joseph smiled indulgently at his niece. His heart felt heavy, although he gave no sign of depression and teased her lightly. Next week he would be going back to Liverpool – on business. But this time he would not be returning to his home. He would go up to Stanhope to collect his things and then he would be gone for good. He turned his head away from Hester's eager eyes, determined she should not see the pain in his face. His heart was heavy. Coming out

216

on a family party like this made what he proposed doing seem so infamous.

'Uncle Joe, it's starting again!' Her long slim hand was tucked in his arm. He squeezed it convulsively. She took this as a sign of his own enjoyment of the burlesque, and sent him a swift understanding grin. Then her eyes were riveted on the stage, on the beautiful girls moving like swans across it to the sound of the haunting music composed by the fat little German conductor. And she wished with all her heart that she was one of them.

In the second interval Joseph took Wilfred to the bar. They returned in ten minutes accompanied by a beautiful well-dressed woman and a stiff-looking man. Hester looked up and her heart skipped with excitement, for here was their beautiful neighbour from the other side of the crescent.

'My dear.' Joseph bent over Ellen. 'Here are some friends of mine who tell me they are living close at hand in Adelaide Crescent. Lady Bland, this is my wife. Sir John and Lady Bland, Ellen. And my niece Miss Kelsey.'

Ellen's eye caught Hester's. *Well, I never!* Ellen's eye said. Hester's eyes gleamed with delight. What a perfect evening this was turning out to be.

Lady Bland was prettier and much younger close at hand. Hardly more than a girl. Her husband, that silent man bowing without warmth, was a much older man. She wore ice blue satin with flowers in the corsage. Her eyes were brown and twinkling and her hair was the colour of a new penny.

'We met Sir Joseph last year on board the *Golden Jubilee*,' she explained after a bit. 'We were all at the captain's table, you know. We were such a merry crowd! I do wish you had been there, Lady Prickard.'

'I am a very poor sailor and not at all strong,' Ellen said quickly. 'My niece has been several times – my son too.'

Lady Bland smiled at Hester. 'May I call tomorrow?' she asked Ellen hastily as the bell rang at the end of the interval.

'Pray do. We shall look forward to it.'

217

'Oh, Wilfred, isn't she attractive?' Hester whispered, watching their new acquaintances going back to their seats.

Wilfred shrugged. 'If you like that type,' he returned indifferently. Hester looked at him indignantly. Wilfred was always so critical; what type of woman did he like?

Hester dressed with care next afternoon, putting on a pale grey foulard with white lace round the collar. She sat in the drawing room turning over the pages of a novel with one eye on the house across the crescent. She was so glad they had met the Blands at last. Sir John wasn't such a stick as Aunt Ellen had thought; for he had spoken to her in quite a lively manner when they met in the foyer while they awaited their carriages.

'You like burlesque, Miss Kelsey?'

'I do indeed. Of course this is the first one I have seen. Perhaps they are not all as good as this?'

'George Edwardes usually puts on a very good show. My wife – ' his eyes strayed to his wife as she chatted animatedly to the Prickards ' – was in the chorus here before we married.' He had bowed and left her side before she could follow this up. A Gaiety girl – Hester could talk of nothing else as they drove home until Wilfred protested about her 'school-girl enthusiasm', as he termed it rather scornfully. 'Going into transports over a vulgar woman like that. . . . '

'Vulgar? Oh, I can't allow that.' She appealed to her uncle. 'Didn't you think Lady Bland very beautiful and fascinating, Uncle Joe?'

'Of course. She wouldn't have been in the Gaiety chorus if she wasn't. George Edwardes knows how to pick the girls – he's famous for it. I haven't yet met a Gaiety Girl who was in any way ordinary. I have met several on my voyages because they go to America on tour, you know.' His eyes flicked briefly in his son's direction. There was something very cold about the boy. Most young men would have been eating out of Cissie Bland's hand in five minutes. Yet there

218

he had stood looking bored . . . Joseph had a brief moment of misgiving. There were men who were not completely male. A pity if Wilfred was one of those. He would like to see his son married and with a son of his own to inherit the title and Stanhope. He had worked hard to found this family. It would be unkind of Fate to blot out his efforts in one generation.

Hester glanced up at the clock in the glass case. Aunt Ellen wasn't yet down from her rest, so if Lady Bland came now they could have a long talk before tea. There was so much Hester longed to know about the Gaiety.

The door opened. 'Mr Cockayne,' Wiston announced.

Hester felt her heart leap in her breast as she confronted Victor Cockayne. He, on the other hand, seemed completely in charge of the situation.

'Good afternoon, Miss Kelsey. I'm so glad to find you in this time.'

'Good afternoon.' Hester sidled to the door. 'I'll just tell Aunt Ellen you are here. . . . '

'No, please don't. Won't you talk to me a moment?'

They stood facing each other; his eyes were pleading but hers were deliberately blank.

'I have offended you in some way and I have come to apologize. Please tell me what I've done – I've been a blundering fool, I fear.'

Oh dear, how good-looking he was – how charming . . . She bit her lip and took a deep breath. 'You haven't offended me, Mr Cockayne. I couldn't accept your invitation to a play because we had a prior engagement. I hoped Wilfred would have explained.'

'He did – but I still think I have done something that has pained you in some way.' His eyes searched her face, pleading with her to remind him of the conversation with his father she had overheard. He longed to explain that his father's outlook was not his; that he did not condone one of the sentiments expressed.

219

'Will you come to the play on Friday? I could get Amy and someone else to make up a party.'

She remained silent. He saw a refusal tremble on her lips. Glancing swiftly at the door, he seized her hands, shaking them a little. 'Hester – that's how I think of you – you are hurt, I know. You overheard my conversation with Father. But you cannot blame me for his out-moded opinions! You will think him a snob and I'm afraid that, although I love him, I have to think so too. He is a very proud man – proud of his ancient family, anxious that his sons should carry on all the old traditions – like marrying the daughters of his friends! What he doesn't understand is that the world – even our own little part of it – is changing all the time and never more swiftly than now. We are going to marry whom we please and the social classes are going to be mixed as never before. I choose my own friends and in his heart he knows it.' He stopped, wondering if he had said too much. It was so difficult to explain the old order's outlook that the Prince of Wales was helping to destroy as much as anyone. He could find no answering warmth in her face. Hopelessly he dropped her hands. 'Try and understand. My father, who is the fifteenth earl, is terrified of newcomers like your uncle because gradually the power is passing into their hands. So he tries to hang on to the fringe of a passing world.'

She looked at him squarely. 'Does it mean that every time I go to your home – if I am ever invited again – I must feel an outsider?'

He laughed. 'You gave no sign of feeling like that! I heard many people ask who the beautiful girl was. Besides did Amy make you feel at all miserable?'

'No, of course she didn't. I liked her very much.' She thought a moment. 'It isn't as if we are thinking of marriage and that is all your father is worried about. We only want to be friends.'

He smothered a smile at her candour. 'Do not be too sure of that!'

She looked into his face and a slight flush stained her skin, but she said composedly, 'No, friends only, please. We hardly know one another.'

'And you will come to the theatre? Oh, I am so glad.' He heaved an exaggerated sigh of relief and they were both laughing when Ellen came in followed by the footman and tea.

Ten minutes later Captain Crown was announced. He seemed rather taken aback to find Victor there. 'I thought you said you were going to the Rhymers' Club this afternoon?'

'My dear chap, I do lead a normal life between poems, you know,' Victor retorted. His eyes narrowing, he watched Denis Crown being charming to Miss Hester Kelsey and Miss Kelsey responding in a very friendly fashion. Good Lord, she couldn't really like that affected ninny, could she?

'I have called to invite Miss Kelsey to a river party on Sunday,' Captain Crown told Ellen.

'It sounds delightful,' Ellen commented, handing John the cups to take round. 'And who is to chaperone you?'

'My mother. She is spending a week in London at the moment. She will call for Miss Kelsey at three on Sunday and we shall go up to Hampton Court and picnic. It will be delicious on the river,' he assured Hester. He waved away the milk and sugar being offered him and bent his full attention on Hester. He had liquid eyes that had a trick of holding your attention. When she had danced with him at the ball, she had noticed approvingly that he danced beautifully. What she was not to know was that he was in need of a rich wife. His debts had become almost insurmountable.

'Lady Bland,' announced Wiston.

Hester sprang up and went to meet her new friend. 'I am so glad you have come.'

'I said I would come today and here I am.' She took Ellen's hand. 'I have been so eager to make your acquaintance. Was it not the greatest luck we should meet last night? And to find that we already knew Sir Joseph – oh, the greatest piece of luck. He made sure that we had such a delightful time on his beautiful steam ship – why, Captain Crown, how are you?'

Captain Crown bowed over her hand. He looked somewhat disconcerted.

'Do you know Mr Cockayne, Lady Bland?'

Victor had come, out of the shadows to bow. Cissie Bland looked at him narrowly. 'We have not met, I think, but I have heard of you, Mr Cockayne from a mutual friend. Rosie Lock.'

He raised his brows. 'Rosie Lock of the Gaiety. Why yes, I remember her very well. When I was in my first year at Oxford we used to come up regularly to the good old Gaiety. How is Rosie? It must be two or three years since I saw her.'

'She died.'

The room was startled. Hester saw Captain Crown look alertly at Victor Cockayne. Ellen clicked her tongue. 'How sad. She must have been quite young?'

Lady Bland sat down and took off her gloves. 'Very young and very sweet. We were in the chorus together.'

Crown leaned forward. 'I suppose there is a new generation of mashers outside the old stage door nowadays? How quickly time goes! One's palmy days are soon over. I have been out in India for the past three years and don't seem to have caught up with the news even yet.'

Cissie Bland nodded at him over her cup. 'I remember very well that supper party you gave at Romano's – oh, all of four years ago. I married a year later. I go backstage at the Gaiety to see the girls from time to time – I miss the life, you know.'

This was Hester's cue and she found it hard to restrain her eager questions. The two men left soon after this, Victor reminding her once more of their engagement on Friday.

'You know Mr Cockayne quite well?' Cissie Bland asked. 'Because I feel I must warn you, Miss Hester, he has not got a good reputation.'

Ellen was startled. 'We have known him for years. He was at school with my son.'

'Then I'm even more sorry to have to tell you this. He is a heartless philanderer, the cause of Rosie Lock's suicide.'

'Suicide? Oh, surely not,' Ellen protested.

Lady Bland nodded her head vigorously. 'She was an innocent creature, poor Rosie, and she took his blandishments seriously. He wanted to marry her, he said, and she believed him. They used to go away together for weekends. She adored him. Then, quite suddenly, he dropped her and she didn't see him again. She wrote several times and he didn't answer the letters. She became very depressed and took an overdose of sleeping powder.'

There was silence in the room for a moment or two.

'How horrible,' Hester said quietly. 'Poor girl. But Mr Cockayne must have been very young then. He is a year older than Wilfred, my cousin, so that makes him twenty-two now. Three years ago he was nineteen, surely not in a position to offer marriage to anyone. Do you think she took him too seriously?'

'I am sure she did. But that does not excuse his conduct. He treated her badly by ignoring her after being such a close friend – even her lover.'

'Oh dear,' Ellen said. 'I am sorry to hear that. It sounds very wild.' What a blessing her Wilfred was not like that, she thought comfortably as she took another piece of cake.

'I don't know him well enough to defend him,' Hester said, 'but surely most young men sew wild oats at some time? It was a thousand pities that the poor girl was so affected by his conduct though.'

'He mixes with a Bohemian crowd,' Cissie Bland said significantly. 'Still if he is Mr Prickard's friend I will say no more.' She smiled her brilliant smile and tapped Hester on the arm. 'Will you drive in the park some afternoons? I should so like that. I am a great deal on my own. Sir John has his club – not that he isn't a very attentive husband,' she added quickly. 'But for years I have been used to the

223

companionship of the other girls at the theatre and I miss it. Now I must go.'

'A thoroughly nice young woman,' Ellen declared when the door had closed behind her guest.

Hester smiled rather absently. The whole afternoon had given her food for thought.

CHAPTER THREE

After only a week Hester felt she had known Cissie Bland for years. They drove in the park most afternoons, both in fashionable toilettes, their little parasols keeping the sun off their faces. The trees made great green caves and somewhere inside the cool shadows a military band played popular tunes. One could take tea at small round tables and then stroll near the Achilles statue at the fashionable hour of five o'clock.

Hester was glad to have Cissie as her guide, for Lady Bland certainly seemed to know a great number of people, especially gentlemen of leisure who greeted her with marked delight.

'He used to be one of the stagedoor "johnnies",' she would say confidingly of someone. 'Then he married a rich woman and, lord, what a change! I shouldn't have known him – poor soul. So dull now.'

During these drives and strolls Hester learned a great deal about the Gaiety and Cissie's life before she married. Her father had a small business in a Midlands town. 'He made a bit of a fuss when I joined the Gaiety chorus – Papa's a deacon in our chapel at home – but my mother soon got him round. She pointed out how the Guv'nor takes care of all his girls. . . . '

'Who is the Guv'nor?'

Cissie stared and then laughed. 'Why, I thought everyone knew the Guv'nor! George Edwardes, my dear. He's a stickler about etiquette. No one got past old Tierney the doorkeeper who hadn't an invitation and a proper introduction, and no gentleman was ever allowed anywhere near the dressing rooms. Even the actors are on the other side – no hanky-panky there! And when I married John, Papa was ever so pleased of course. He gave me a good send-off and a thousand pounds – there, what do you think of that?'

The Gaiety was still Cissie's ruling passion. She still went there often to see her friends and knew everyone in the chorus and every change that was made. Hester guessed that she hankered after the old life and was bored to death with her middle aged husband almost at once.

'The bouquets I would receive. . . . ' She sighed and shook her head. 'Once I was sent a little vine hung with grapes. It took two men to carry it in . . . I could have married Lord Dover,' she went on after a reminiscent pause. 'And Captain Hugo Pember – he's got a terribly rich father. Then there was the Duke of Toro – a Spanish duke and handsome as a dream. He sent me a bicycle of all things.' She gave a little screech of laughter. 'Lord, I did have fun.'

Most people would have been bored by Cissie's talk because she only had one subject. Not Hester. Hester was the ideal audience, for she hung on every word.

'I remember the Duke of Clarence took a box one night and sent us all huge bouquets. Poor lad. Fancy dying like that and poor Princess May widowed before they were married – oh, look, Hester! There's Mr Gladstone.'

Hester craned her neck over the side of the landau and found herself looking almost directly into a stern old face with the familiar Dundreary whiskers. He was waiting to cross the busy carriageway and a younger man was rather anxiously at his elbow.

'Eighty-two, my dear, and going blind; but John says he's going to be Prime Minister if they get in next time.' Then she rallied her friend.

'Come now, Hester, I'm doing all the talking as usual. What about your cousin's friend, Mr Cockayne? I hope you have seen no more of him?'

Hester smiled. 'But I have! I like him very much and his sister too. We went to the play last week. It was *Lady Windermere's Fan*. No doubt you've seen it? It was very affecting,' Hester said dreamily. Some lines early on in the play had haunted her ever since: *I wish I had known it was your birthday, Lady Windermere. I would have covered the whole street in front of your house with flowers for you to walk on.* Ah, if only Victor would say that some day! He was capable of it, being a poet. They had talked about it in the carriage going home and Victor had agreed it was a beautiful idea. Amy had spoilt it by saying the new municipal workers would have swept up the flowers as rubbish in no time. She was a very practical person and not at all like Victor. So Hester had caught Victor's eyes and they had smiled in sympathy.

Hester thought about Victor Cockayne a great deal now. They had met twice since the theatre: at a supper party at the Savoy to which he had taken her and again at tea in Adelaide Crescent. Then next week she was going down to Henley to stay with Captain Crown's mother for three days for the Royal Regatta. Little prickles of anticipation ran along her veins when she thought of it. Victor Cockayne was to be in the party.

Finding Cissie Bland's eye on her (speculative behind the smile) Hester quickly said, 'I do wish you would take me behind at the Gaiety. I would be overjoyed – ah, say you will,' she added coaxingly, for her friend was wavering.

'Well, we could go now – mind, I mustn't be late for we are dining out tonight.' She poked the coachman's back. 'The Gaiety, Anderson.' Then she looked at Hester and nodded her head. 'You will love it,' she predicted solemnly.

The Gaiety, unlit and closed, looked dirty and run down. Hester who had only seen it at night was secretly amazed; what a dreadfully shabby place. They stopped in the street at the side and Cissie led the way through the door – the famous stage door where the mashers and johnnies swarmed each night after the show. There was a little office inside with a window. Cissie poked her head in.

'Good afternoon, Tierney. Can I run up to see the girls?'

A white-whiskered face appeared at the window and looked Hester up and down. 'Afternoon, m'lady. You'll have to sign the book.' He shoved a greasy-looking book on to the sill and they both signed.

Beckoning, Cissie led the way. She was wearing a pale biscuit tailored suit and her enormous sleeves were brushing the dirty walls of the narrow corridor, but she didn't even notice. Her face was alive with pleased anticipation. The smell of the old theatre acted on her like a tonic.

Hester sniffed the air wryly as she followed. The stone-floored corridor smelt vilely. She bumped against huge wicker travelling baskets, barely visible in the dim light and murmured, 'What's that funny smell, Cissie?'

'Lamp oil, mice and meths!' Cissie threw back blithely. 'And a bit of grease paint for good measure – here we are.' She opened a door very quietly, assumed a deep voice and said, 'A-HA!'

There were squeals. 'Cissie, you dam' fool! You've made me burn Flo's hair!'

'Oh, my God, she has! Girls, she's fried me!'

Peeping over Cissie's shoulder, Hester saw a tiny room filled with three young women in various states of undress. One had been using the curling tongs on another's head and there was a strong smell of methylated spirits and burning hair.

'Belle, you fool!'

'T'was Cissie who was the fool . . . bursting in like that. . . .'

'Shut up all of you. I've brought a friend to visit you. This is Miss Hester Kelsey. Flo Hughes, Belle Collins and Lily May.'

The girls grinned at her. 'Come in and shut the door. There's a howling draught,' Lily May complained. She was lying on a horsehair sofa clad only in a peignoir, and was languidly eating sandwiches and drinking champagne. One bottle was empty and she began to open another, directing Belle Collins to fetch two more glasses. 'Lord Hewlett sent me a case. Go on, dear, have a glass. Champagne's good for you. Gives you a lovely lift.'

The bubbles ran up Hester's nose and she laughed as she drank, for the champagne was delicious and had been cooled on the stone floor, as Lily May explained.

'Well, what's the news, girls? How's the Guv'nor?'

'Just the same, bless him. I love that man,' Flo declared. She was busy covering her over-frizzled hair in front with a well-placed flower. 'He sent me to his own dentist last week – that expensive chap, Fraser – and he did a beautiful job on my front tooth. Look.' She bared her teeth proudly. 'Nothing but the best for us girls as the Guv'nor always says. You joining the company?' she added.

'Me?' Hester shook her head. 'Oh, no. I can't dance or sing – well, I do sing a bit but I'm not good.'

'Pity. We're short of girls since Phyllis James got married.' Lily May selected another sandwich and allowed her dark eyes to cover Hester's figure thoroughly. 'I'd say you are just the type the Guv'nor's looking for. What d'you think, girls?'

Hester had to endure four pairs of eyes inspecting her.

'I've thought so from the first,' Cissie said quickly. 'Tall and stately just like he wants them.'

'And very well-dressed,' Belle murmured. 'Got to be able to wear your clothes well, m'dear – that's what he always says.'

'This show is coming off in July and there's to be a new production of it in October. We've heard Lettie Lind is to have the lead as Lottie's contract is up and she's going into panto. So we're all having a holiday.' Lily May sat up, emptied her glass and added calmly, 'I'm thinking of marrying Hewlett.'

The others stared at her. 'He's been married before,' a voice murmured.

'I know. He's asked me up to Scotland for his shooting

229

party in August.' She smiled. 'Of course I had my tweeds made months ago.'

'You are a dark horse, Lily!'

'Well, dears, we can't go on for ever, can we?' Her eyes flicked over Cissie. 'Even if marriage is a bore, it's safe.'

'Well, don't forget to ask us to the wedding,' Flo said brightly. 'I don't know about you others but I'm starving.' Opening the door, she shrieked: 'Jord-y!'

A thin woman in a jet bonnet and a dusty black dress appeared. 'Now what d'you want? I'm in the middle of pressing. . . .'

'And we're in the middle of dressing,' Flo retorted. 'Be a love and run across to the Four Feathers and fetch me a pie and some porter. I've got to eat or I'll collapse on stage.'

'Where's the money?'

'Anyone got a bob?'

The others shrugged. Flo scrabbled like a squirrel among the mess on the dressing shelves. 'Someone's taken a tanner . . . I kept it under this jar. . . .'

Hester had opened her purse. 'I've got some silver – you can pay me back another time,' she said hastily to Flo's effusive thanks.

'You're a trouper – knew it the minute I clapped eyes on you.'

As they walked downstairs, Cissie whispered, 'You had a success with them. Lovely girls, aren't they?' She looked at her fob watch and gave a little scream. 'Oh, my God! It's half-past six! It takes me at least an hour and a half to dress. Anderson will have to go like hell or Johnnie will have my guts for garters.'

Lord Bridlington and Victor had been playing billiards after dinner with Amy as marker.

'Ten o'clock. Time you went up to bed, Amy,' her father said.

Amy, who had yawned secretly once or twice, kissed him

230

and left with alacrity. Lord Bridlington strolled over to a tray and poured a drink. 'Whisky, Victor?'

'Thank you, sir.'

They drank together. Victor felt there was something in his father's air of resolution. Oh, lord, not another lecture surely?

Now his father was pulling a letter out of his trousers pocket. It had been folded into a small square and he took time to smooth it out again. The gas sconces on the wall were lit because it was a wet dark evening. He went to stand under one, motioning to his son to join him. 'I want you to hear this. Since you pigheadedly insist on seeing that gel Miss – er – Kelsey, I have set some enquiries going.' He tapped the letter. 'This should interest you.'

'Enquiries? From whom, Father?'

'Our man of business up in Yorkshire made them on my behalf. He knows a lawyer fellow in the gel's home town. Chap called Bracegirdle – it's a good northern name. He has written very fully. . . .'

'I think it's infamous!' Victor expostulated. 'No, Father, I don't want to hear.'

'Don't be a damned young fool!' There was a look of satisfaction on Lord Bridlington's face that Victor couldn't miss. Poor Hester! What had she been up to? He listened as his father knew he would.

Bracegirdle had omitted nothing: the girl's birth and parentage, the double murder and suicide. Her short career as a milliner's assistant. It was all there. And there was more.

The young woman would seem to have inherited her father's dangerous nature (wrote Alfred Bracegirdle), for when only fifteen she had made a serious attempt to murder her governess by poisoning her drink. Fortunately it was discovered in time and the whole affair hushed-up. The governess suffered nervous prostration in consequence and was unable to obtain another post.

231

Folding the letter, Lord Bridlington looked triumphantly at his son. 'Told you she was a wrong'un, didn't I? I can smell 'em a mile off. Those thingammies in her hair,' he added disparagingly.

Victor was staring at him in disbelief. 'Father, you don't believe this rubbish? Poisoning her governess forsooth!'

'Are you suggesting that lawyers lie? Of course it's true. The uncle's a brigand, too. Cut anyone's throat to get to the top. I tell you this, Victor, if you continue to see this girl, I shall take away your allowance and you'll have to come down from the varsity. I mean what I say.'

Victor spread his hands. 'Father,' he began helplessly and then stopped, an old familiar lassitude creeping over him. What was the use of arguing? His father held the aces. Besides, it couldn't all be lies. Those murders – the lodger and the second wife. Good God, it was the seamy side of life all right. A clear picture of Hester came into his mind: cool and beautiful with perfect taste and good manners. It was unbelievable that she had come from a slum only a short time ago. He had been in danger of falling seriously in love. Now (as his father had guessed) a fearful doubt had crept into his head. Was she as false as her smile? An adventuress after all? 'But I shall be meeting her at Mrs Crown's for a Friday to Monday, Father.'

'There is your chance to make yourself perfectly clear. You must shake yourself free. Don't worry too much about the gel. That sort never come to any harm. Too dam' thick-skinned.'

For the weekend at Henley, the little party met at Paddington and travelled down on the one-thirty train together. Denis Crown, Victor Cockayne and Wilfred escorted Amy Cockayne, Connie Courage and Hester.

From the moment of setting eyes on her alighting from the Prickard carriage, Lady Connie had eyed Hester with suspicion and alarm; it was evident that she had not expected her to be one of the party. Very unwarily, not realizing that Hester had very sharp hearing, she muttered to Denis, 'Why on earth has your mother asked that girl? She isn't one of us.'

Denis reddened with annoyance and pointedly walked up to Hester to greet her with a message from his mother.

Connie tossed her head angrily, her baleful eyes taking in the pale grey tailormade and the neat grey hat with white feathers that the object of her disparagement wore. Connie herself wore a brown skirt with buttons to the hem, and a yellow and white striped blouse that was not the same yellow as her hat. Everything had been chosen by the Duchess of Westchester herself who believed she had perfect dress sense. Hester thought poor Connie looked like a wasp. Getting into the first class compartment, Connie beat Amy to a corner seat facing the engine and opened the Tatler. Denis Crown talked to Amy and Hester, and Wilfred joined in occasionally. But Victor was withdrawn and remote. Hester had noticed his depression immediately. He had avoided looking at her after their first greeting and sat as far away from her as possible. Presently, folding his arms and shutting his eyes, he whiled away the journey with his own thoughts. As a travelling companion, Hester thought with amusement, he left much to be desired.

If only his father had left well alone, Victor was thinking and groaned to himself. It was too unbelievably awful for words. Trust the governor to leave no stone unturned. It was the sort of background he couldn't have invented. Poor Hester. He squinted at her through his lashes as she chatted and laughed with his sister. What a strong character she must have to have got through all that unscathed – if she was unscathed. What was she really like under her laughing face? Was she the dangerous schemer his father thought her? He felt again – as he often did when a problem presented itself – the lassitude that stopped him fighting for something he wanted. Lord Bridlington had ordered his son 'to chuck Henley', but Victor had refused. When he learned that Connie Courage was to be in the party, his father had relaxed and nodded. Very well; he should go. The boy wasn't a fool.

So everyone in the railway compartment was in splendid spirits except Connie and Victor. At Henley station a barouche and a victoria were waiting to take her guests to Mrs Crown's house set in the woods off the Fair Mile. Denis Crown put four of them in the barouche and then turned charmingly to Hester, 'You and I, Miss Kelsey, will beat them to it in the victoria. A sovereign we get there before you, Prickard!'

'What about my maid?' demanded Connie, indicating a crushed-looking female who was standing by the luggage.

'Begging your pardon, Miss,' the coachman said turning round in his seat, 'but Mrs Crown has arranged for the young woman to come up in the station wagonette. Just you wait there, m'girl, and the porter will see to you,' he added to the maid.

'Oh, what an idiot you were to bring Yvonne,' Amy said impatiently. 'Good heavens, Connie, can't you manage for three nights without her? You're giving Mrs Crown an awful lot of trouble. It's only a small house, you know. . . . '

'Oh, you are a beast to me, Amy!' Connie said tearfully.

'Amy,' said Victor's weary voice. 'Leave Connie alone there's a good girl.'

'If we're to win the wager I suggest we start,' Wilfred suggested.

The little town was gay with bunting for the regatta. Flowers hung in baskets from the lamp standards and wreathed the bridge; while all the shops had made special decorations of their own. They glimpsed the river where marquees and stands were full of people; for the racing had started two days previously. They would see only one day of it, but that being the final day, great crowds were expected.

Mrs Crown was herself at the regatta, the maid informed them on arrival. Tea was waiting for them on the ivy-covered verandah overlooking the charming garden and the wooded slopes beyond. It was cool and shaded and the girls decided to sit down in their travelling costumes and Amy poured out. There was no sign of Denis Crown and Hester until they were half way through the tea, when they came out of the house laughing. Denis gave Wilfred a sovereign.

'Lost but worth it! Don't you agree, Miss Kelsey?'

'I do indeed. We have had the most delightful drive through a wooded road to the sweetest little village – several villages in fact. I had no idea Oxfordshire was such a lovely county.' She took her cup from Amy and began to describe where she and her host had been. Victor watched her. What a capacity for enjoyment she had. Connie would have come back complaining of the heat and the flies and the noisy roads. Suddenly Hester looked up and met his eyes. Deliberately, like a slap in the face, he moved his away. She bent her head to sip from her cup, a faint colour running under her pale skin. She had begun to suspect that Victor was avoiding her. Now she knew he was. He had turned to Connie Courage and was carrying on an animated conversation with her. The intimacy that had grown between them during the past month seemed to have disappeared, Hester thought bewilderedly. Was this how it had been with Rosie Lock and probably many others with whom he had flirted heartlessly? It serves me right, Hester told herself sturdily. Cissie did warn me. Anyway, why should I care? But her heart didn't seem to understand; it ached like a wound in her breast. Pride alone stiffened her body and made her smile and talk normally to the others. She didn't look again in Victor's direction.

Mrs Crown and her other guest, Major Webber, arrived back just before the dressing bell and found her guests still in the garden. She was a widow, a delicately pretty woman with a misleadingly helpless air. In reality she was an excellent manager of her small income, and managed to do marvels on nothing. But she had been brought up to look idle and everyone thought she was. Denis, her only child, was her chief concern – for him she would do a great deal.

These little house parties cost a lot but she managed; she always would. Dick Webber, a bachelor and once a brother officer of her husband's, was always glad to come down to Henley as her escort, but he irritated Denis who always sulked when he was about.

'Why on earth ask him, Mother?' he asked in an undertone as they went upstairs to dress.

'My dear, the numbers would be all wrong at dinner – you know that. Besides, I need an escort in the Stewards' Enclosure. Now Denis darling, be good. Poor Dick does mean to help, you know.' She beckoned him to shut the door of her bedroom. Sinking on to her dressing stool she said frankly, 'I like Miss Kelsey. She would be quite suitable and is within your reach. Amy and Connie are not. She has money you said?'

'Her uncle with whom she lives has made a fortune. The Prickard Line of Liverpool among other things.'

Her eyes were eloquent. She nodded and he smiled, pleased that he was pleasing her.

'She is beautiful, isn't she? If I've got to marry a rich girl, what luck if it is Hester!'

'Money is essential,' his mother nodded. 'Otherwise, my dear, you cannot remain in that expensive regiment much longer. It will mean the City for you.'

'You could sell this house if the worst came to the worst.'

She looked up at him, concealing her anger, aware that he lacked heart and was selfishly concerned only for himself.

I've spoilt him, I suppose, she thought as he left the room. For one thing he has no idea what sacrifices are involved in giving a weekend like this. The pinching and scraping beforehand. The training of poor quality staff so that they played their parts well. The excellent food and wine . . . A sigh shook her as she unclasped her pearls. He will always want the best in life, she told herself wryly, because that's what I've brought him up to expect. She hoped devoutly that the Kelsey girl liked her son. The marriage would come just in the nick of time. He had a mountain of debts, poor

236

darling. She had worked hard for something like this — nothing must go wrong now.

Hester was leaning out of her bedroom window breathing in the scented evening air. It was at moments like this that she realized how much she missed Stanhope. Only two more weeks and she would be back there again. She sighed quickly. Leaving London meant that she would not see Victor any more. Victor. He had begun to mean a great deal to her. But did she mean anything to him? Apparently not. Why otherwise was he avoiding her eyes?

Next door she could hear Connie Courage being querulous with her French maid. Hester made a hideous face at the dividing wall and, catching sight of herself in a mirror, broke into helpless laughter. Had she not all the symptoms of jealousy that she so decried in others? Pull yourself together, girl, she admonished herself and began to feel better immediately.

Joseph Prickard finished packing documents in his Gladstone bag, locked it and put the key on his watchchain. Then he stood deep in thought. He realized that he was behaving in rather a cowardly fashion by slipping away from his family without a farewell; but he also realized that he could not stand any raw emotion at the present time. To all intents and purposes he was simply leaving London two weeks ahead of the others. They knew he was going to Stanhope. They expected he would be there when they themselves returned in July.

But he would have left Stanhope by then. For good. When he walked out of Stanhope a few days hence it would be for the last time. He would not see any of them again. Ellen. Wilfred — and Hester. At the thought of Hester he winced. What a hostage to fortune he had made when he took in Nancy's daughter and began to love her as his own child. He dreaded leaving her.

Yet he had known for some time that there was only one

way of doing this thing that must be done. He must leave in the manner that would make them despise him. It was the kindest way of doing it.

Ellen would no doubt weep for the sake of appearance and say (he could hear her saying it) that her mother had always known it would happen; he had never loved her – never! Wilfred would be astounded, for he knew nothing about his father's private life. Astounded and probably disgusted, for he seemed to have little sexual feeling for women himself. To give up a life of power and influence for a woman – for love – would be beyond his comprehension.

Joseph looked round the room, a sad half-smile on his lips. He loved Emmy – perhaps a great deal more than she suspected or than she loved him. He longed above all else for quiet contentment with her for the rest of his life. He knew he could no longer go on without her. He needed her naked body close to him every night. God! how he missed her when he was away from her, counting the days to his return. He was getting older. There would be no other women in his life now. He was fifty-five – that wasn't too late to have some life, some real human life, before he became too old.

One last glance round the room told him that he had left nothing behind. Putting out the gas, he went slowly upstairs. It was late, the house was silent. But as he turned the corner of the landing he saw that there was still a light shining in Ellen's room. He looked at it frowning, then turned and went into the drawing room. Putting the document case down, he went across to a tray of drinks and helped himself to a whisky and water. He drank it quickly and followed it with a second stronger one. Then he walked resolutely across the landing to his wife's bedroom. There was only one more thing he must do.

'I shall be away early tomorrow so I'll say goodbye now,' he said and kissed her on the forehead beneath her be-frilled boudoir cap.

She was searching among the papers on her overcrowded

bed table. 'Will you give orders to have the kitchens re-painted before we return? A nice bright yellow. And here's a list for Melia to order from Sewerston. Mrs Crombie has made it out, you see. And these are Wiston's instructions for the maids . . . and another list from Mrs Crombie . . . oh, and she says the stove is not so good as the one we have here. Perhaps we could have one like it. That's its name, she says, so will you order Larkins to see to it?'

Bemused, he put the papers in his pocket without looking at them.

'It's very quiet without the young people, isn't it?' she went on. 'They have enjoyed their stay and seem to have made some nice friends. But I'll be glad to be back in Stanhope, won't you?'

'I am afraid I shall not be there long, Ellen, I'm a busy man.' He turned away, hesitated, then turned back to face her again. 'There is just one thing. If anything should happen to me, you and the boy are perfectly safe for life. I've seen to that. There is no need to worry.'

She looked directly at him for the first time, startled, unable to grasp his meaning. Her round smooth face was frozen with surprise. 'Joe, you're not ill?'

'No, nothing like that, but there are such things as railway accidents, my dear. I just wanted you to know that *whatever happens* you are safe for life and can remain at Stanhope. I know you are fond of the place,' he added hastily as he saw her about to speak. 'So there is nothing to worry about.'

'How you startled me! As if I ever doubted we should be all right. I know what a good business man you are. You have done ever so well, Joe. Wilfred is a lucky boy with his future assured.'

He flushed. It was years since she had praised him in such terms. Hurriedly, he moved to the door to prevent her saying more. 'Goodnight then, Ellen.'

Blue sky with a few well-placed clouds heralded a fine morning for the last day of the regatta. The girls came downstairs at eleven in their best outfits; for Saturday in the Stewards' Enclosure was a very fashionable day.

Hester wore a white muslin dress that Mrs Crown's maid had pressed carefully. The huge puff sleeves stood out proudly like a butterfly's wings. A large black hat with two white ostrich feathers, long black gloves and a white lace parasol completed the outfit. Under the brim of her hat, her white skin and brilliant eyes were shown to the best advantage.

Denis Crown greeted her at the foot of the stairs. He seemed to have been waiting for her which rather surprised Hester. She thought she had made it quite clear that she had no wish for a flirtation. 'By Jove, Miss Hester, you're looking very well!'

She smiled at him. 'Thank you. Am I the last? Have you been waiting for me?'

'No, my mother is not yet ready herself. The others are getting in the carriages now. Come, I will see you in.'

But the other carriage was already moving off. She could see Amy and Connie facing Victor and Wilfred as the horses turned left at the gates. She felt quick disappointment. She had hoped so much that by this morning Victor's low spirits would have disappeared and that he would have been waiting for her . . . Instead, Denis Crown was smiling at her, helping her into the second carriage. They were soon joined by Mrs Crown and Major Webber. It did not occur to her to wonder why things had been so arranged that she was driving with the family, and they hadn't asked Lady Connie or Lady Amy. However it was pleasant to be with people who seemed pleased by her, who were ready to laugh and chat in as friendly a fashion as she could wish. Denis went further – he admired her with his eyes.

There was no sign of the others as they strolled in the enclosure.

'Never mind, we shall meet for lunch,' Mrs Crown said, stopping yet again to greet friends and introduce her party.

Major Webber appeared to be quite a personage and most people knew him and addressed him as 'Jumbo'.

'He's an Old Blue and a member of Leander,' Denis told Hester. She wondered what on earth he meant.

Races were taking place at half-hourly intervals. Denis and the Major would rush to the water's edge and shout, 'Well-rowed, you fellows! Very well done.' Or they would suck in their lips and shake their heads sombrely. Fortunately, Mrs Crown did not pay the slightest attention to the racing, which relieved Hester of the pretence of doing so.

They went to the Leander Club for lunch and there, waiting outside in the hot sun, were the other half of the party. Connie was very cross that they had not been allowed in because they weren't members, and her face wore a peevish look as she grumbled under her breath.

Major Webber was the member and he led the way with a flourish. Victor, Hester was forced to notice, made no move to stroll by her side and again she felt a little chilled at his deliberate neglect. Instead he bent his head to something Connie was saying.

His sudden devotion to Connie had not escaped his sister's attention, and she voiced her annoyance in an undertone to Hester, as they went upstairs to the ladies' room. 'Victor seems to have made up his mind about Connie. I'm not at all fond of her nor is Martin, my second brother. Hornsea wouldn't mind marrying her though, but she won't look at him so I suppose it will be Victor. I shall marry whom I please,' she added as Connie emerged from the lavatory and looked at her in quick curiosity, having heard the last remark.

Mrs Crown laughed. 'My dear Amy, all young things start out thinking that! I'm afraid parents are wily old birds. We generally get our own way, you know.'

'Oh, Mrs Crown, that's awfully cynical!'

Hester locked herself in the lavatory. To her horror, she could feel tears pressing against her eyelids. *I will not cry. I don't care a button. Cissie said he was a heartless flirt. I should have listened.*

There were other men in the world, she reminded herself, mopping her eyes. Only one filled her horizon at the moment though.

They all exclaimed over the salmon-pink carnations grouped in the hall, reproducing the exact colours of the Leander Club. There were epergnes full of them on the luncheon tables. The dining room smelled pleasantly of flowers and the good smells of cold salmon and cucumber. Hester sat between Denis Crown and Wilfred, and avoided looking at Victor who sat directly opposite. That line from Wilde's play kept recurring to her: *'I would have covered the whole street . . . with flowers for you to walk on.'* She felt sick with misery, yet managed to laugh and be gay. So brilliant was the smile she directed at Denis Crown that his spirits rose with a bound.

By Jove, he told himself, it looked as if he had a great chance with the darling girl. It would be wonderful to have enough money at last to stay in the regiment and play polo again, he thought, as he talked to her about her home in Yorkshire.

'Stanhope? I thought that was the Girvans' place?'

'My uncle bought it five years ago when the last Lord Girvan died.'

'Does he shoot?' He had visions of a grouse moor in August.

'Oh, no. He's very much a business man.'

'Isn't that rather a waste? A lovely old place and all those acres and he doesn't shoot or fish. . . .'

'But Wilfred does. Wilfred is much more of a countryman than his father. We ride too. I shall be glad to be going home on the fifteenth. London is all very well but the air seems so stale after Yorkshire.' She drank some hock, her eyes far away. At Stanhope she would forget Victor, she promised herself. The ache would stop and she would throw herself into the satisfying old life again.

'I'd love to see it,' he hinted.

'Then you had better make friends with my cousin,' she laughed.

He was disconcerted, for he had hoped that she would ask him up in the autumn . . . get her aunt to write to him. He would have leaped at the invitation. He ate in silence while she leaned forward to answer a question from Major Webber. Then he returned to the siege again. 'If I came to stay with friends in the neighbourhood, would you ask me over to see Stanhope? I know old Girvan's grandson, Gerald Woolsey. We were at school together.'

Her face was suddenly cold. What a tight little circle these upper class people revolved in, she thought. 'I – have met him. He is never invited to Stanhope, I'm afraid, so if you stayed with them I'm afraid we should not meet.'

He was staggered. Upstart business people rejecting people like the Woolseys! He smiled wryly and temporarily abandoned his pursuit. But he meant to return to the attack later.

In the afternoon, the heat became so exhausting to the women that Mrs Crown suggested they returned to her house for tea. Hester happened to glance at Victor and was horrified to see how white he looked. Unobtrusively, he mopped his brow, smilingly attentive to his hostess as they got into the carriage. But she noticed how he leaned against the cushions as they drove away. She was thoughtful as she followed Amy into the second carriage. Perhaps he was ill? Could that explain his behaviour? But she knew that it couldn't, that he had made it plain yesterday that he preferred Connie Courage's company to hers. His pale face with the eyes closed, leaning back in the carriage kept coming back to her uneasily – like a figure on a tomb, she thought with a shiver.

They had tea on the cool verandah and after the girls had gone upstairs to rest before changing for dinner, the men talked and smoked.

'Sorry there's no billiard room,' Denis said, adding with

a deprecating shrug, 'A house this size doesn't run to one. But we could play bridge after dinner.'

'Don't fuss, old chap,' Victor murmured. 'We're perfectly lazy and happy. Are you going to Scotland soon? We leave on the twentieth and I can't say I'm sorry. London doesn't suit me – drains my energy.'

They glanced at him, wondering at his pallor. Hope he's not back on the hashish, Wilfred thought and said aloud, 'You are coming back to Oxford for your fourth year, aren't you?'

'I suppose so. The thought wrings my withers rather, but I'm expected to take some sort of degree. What does one do then? No, Major Webber, please don't suggest the army. Two subalterns in the family are enough. I am not cut out for it.'

'Marry a rich wife then,' Major Webber said slyly. 'It solves everything.'

They laughed and Victor murmured, 'There's something in it of course. You're all right, Prickard. You have Prickards Lines waiting for you.'

Wilfred reddened. He was not sure there hadn't been a sarcastic note in Victor Cockayne's voice. 'Oh, I don't suppose I shall work there,' he said hurriedly. 'It just keeps us comfortably that's all.'

Victor laughed and sat up. 'How wise to leave all the hard work to your pater, old boy, and reap all the pleasant benefits. A rich father or a rich wife? There's nothing to choose between them.'

'Well, the Duke of Westchester owns half London,' Denis said with a smile.

There was a general laugh as they went upstairs to dress.

Denis knocked on the door of his mother's room. She was already dressed and looked cool and elegant, in black and green. He sat on the bed and stared at her, thinking that she was marvellously preserved for forty-five. Why the deuce didn't she marry again? 'Mama, why don't you and the major make a thing of it? Heavens, he's been dancing attention on you for years and was a friend of Father's in the regiment. I find him a bit irritating as you know but he's a kind old fellow, I daresay, and you're still fairly young.'

She had turned and was staring at him. 'My dear boy, I thought you knew.'

'Knew what? Good God, he's not married already is he?'

'Denis, don't swear. Of course he isn't. He is – odd. Your father told me years ago. He only likes other men.'

He stared at her, horror stretching his face. Then he leaped to his feet. 'The filthy swine! How can you have him here? Mama, you must send him packing. I won't have it!'

'Sit down, Denis, and be quiet. Of course I shall continue to invite him here if I like. This is my house not yours. He is useful to me. He has a carriage which he lends me, and the entrée to the Leander Club. He also pays me well for staying here. . . . '

'He pays you? Mama, I can't stand it. It's too horrible.'

'Don't be a fool,' she said curtly. 'How else could I afford these weekends? Afford to entertain like this?' Calmly, she pressed a diamond ornament into her hair. 'Don't pretend to be ignorant of my circumstances, Denis darling. I think you know only too well that I am not at all rich and that's why your allowance is smaller than your friends'. As for poor old Jumbo's weakness . . . '

'Don't! Women shouldn't talk of such things . . . shouldn't know of them.'

She looked at him mockingly. 'Then we won't. What progress have you made with Miss Kelsey? She's got charm, I think. I like her.'

'She's not out of the top drawer. I found that out this afternoon. Her uncle is a business man.' If he had said a murderer and a thief, his tone would not have been more contemptuous.

She nodded calmly. 'I realized that before we invited her. If she were well-born and had all that money you would not have a chance, my dear. You mustn't expect everything. Someone has done a very good job on her. Her manners are easy, she's intelligent and would make you an excellent wife. I don't care what Miss Kelsey's origins are,' she added in a harder voice. 'I'm sick and tired of seeing you poor. If you married her, I could have the full use of my income again.'

He stared at her speechlessly. So this weekend had been arranged with one object in mind; the capture of Prickard's niece and the dowry she would bring. His pride ruffled, he got up and walked stiffly to the door. 'I don't want to be late for dinner,' he said sourly and walked out.

She stood looking at the closed door with a bitter half-smile. What a child he still was! He knew nothing of life and its struggles – nothing at all. She had sheltered him, taking all the hard knocks and hiding from him anything that might upset him. Now he couldn't respect her. If he married Miss Kelsey, he would soon be a stranger to her, his mother. He would soon forget how much he owed her, how much she had sacrificed for him. He wouldn't even like her very much. Adjusting her face, she went down to her guests.

On the upper landing, Major Webber was knocking at Wilfred's door. 'Oh, my dear fellow, sorry to trouble you but I wonder if you have a spare dress stud? I've mislaid one of mine – can't go down like this, y'know.'

He sat down on a chair and they smiled at each other.

'Where can we meet in London?' Major Webber asked.

After dinner, a bridge four consisting of Amy, Denis, Major Webber and Wilfred sat down on the verandah and became engrossed in their game. Mrs Crown sat near at hand embroidering a fire screen. Victor sat on a deckchair between Connie and Hester. Connie's conversation was so bright it set Hester's teeth on edge. Presently, Connie discovered that the midges were biting and she went back on to the verandah to sit beside Mrs Crown and began to tell her all about the Duchess of Westchester's charity fair to be held next week in aid of the match girls.

Hester saw her go with relief, for during dinner she had

decided to tackle Victor if she got the chance. Here then was her chance. She rose. 'Do let us go for a stroll under the trees, Mr Cockayne. What a delightful garden this is. And the most perfect evening too.'

He could not refuse to accompany her however unwillingly. They had not gone twenty yards before she said quietly, 'I have to ask you: have I done something to spoil our friendship?'

He glanced at her miserably in the half-light, wishing this opportunity hadn't arisen. 'Nothing at all. I hope we shall always be friends.'

'But we are not friends now – only acquaintances.'

A shadow crossed his face. 'I'm sorry you feel that.'

She threw him an angry glance, stumbling a little on the uneven grass. Dew was rising through her satin slippers and staining them, but she no longer cared. If she had to follow him through the river to get an answer to her question she was prepared to. 'Of course I feel that!' She turned her face away, unable to find the right words. Why didn't he help her instead of remaining stiff and unfamiliar?

He could sense her distress. 'It has nothing to do with you . . . with you personally. My father arranged many years ago that I should marry Connie Courage. I really am not free. . . .'

She whirled round to face him. 'You're going to marry that fool of a Connie because your father tells you to? I don't believe it.'

'You mustn't call her that. Connie is . . . is a nice girl and I've known her all my life.'

'You don't love her. You never will. You're not made for each other – we are! Victor, tell me you feel it, too?'

'Don't say it, Hester. You will hate yourself if you do.'

'I'll regret it more if I don't say it. I haven't been brought up like you and Connie or Denis. I don't believe in hiding my feelings until it's too late. I love you. There, it's out. You care for me too. I've known that for a whole month.

247

Victor, we've only got one life – don't waste it – ah, I beg of you don't waste it!'

Her face was very near his. All her earlier resolutions to be calm and dignified and to hide her heart had gone, swept away in the passion that had taken hold of her. He could see the pale glimmer of her skin, her rippling dark hair and those eyes that fascinated him – all so near him that he could smell the scent rising from her dress. He stared at her for a moment and then he gave a sigh that was almost a groan and pulled her to him. Their breath was loud in their ears, their voices low and strained.

'Oh, Victor, I knew it! I knew it!'

'Hester, I love you . . . I'll always love you.'

He could feel the warm curves of her body pressed close to him in a passionate response to his words. He covered her face with his lips, dwelling on the curve of her jaw which he loved and the small brown mole at the corner of her mouth; never dreaming that her passionate response was astonishing her as much as it was him. She had been half-afraid of the physical side of love until she met him again. Men who pawed her like Gerald Woolsey, men who tried forcibly to have their way with her like Aaron Waterman, had deadened something in her. Until now. Close to Victor, in his arms, she would have lain on the grass and given herself to him if that had been his wish.

Connie had tired of sitting on the verandah and had begun to wonder uneasily where Victor and Hester had got to. She sauntered down the garden expecting to find them strolling up to the house again.

At the bottom of the slope the garden ended in a low hedge. Beyond were fields deep in hay and beyond them were the woods. Here, oblivious to the world, stood two figures locked in each other's arms, the girl's pale dress and the man's fair hair glimmering in the dusk. Connie stopped, her mouth falling open. She said their names but no sound came. Then she turned and stumbled back to the house.

Victor suddenly pushed Hester from him. 'No,' he said,

248

'no, Hester. We mustn't. This changes nothing. I won't have an affair with you and I can't offer you marriage.'

Her eyes were huge. 'But why?' she cried. 'You've said you love me!'

He took her hand, kissing it. 'It can never be, my dear. Don't ask me why – I wouldn't hurt you for the world.'

Then suddenly she knew. Somehow he had discovered her background. So now she was not a fit match for him. Her lip curled back. 'You don't know the real meaning of love!' she cried bitterly. Catching up her skirt she walked back towards the house, her head bowed.

He watched her go, the line of his jaw tight. She was a child in the ways of the world, he thought with pity. She had everything and yet nothing.

He sank on to the grass, suddenly feeling as if his life blood had drained out of him. There was a rushing sound in his ears and he felt panic sweep over him. This had happened before – at Oxford last term. I must be ill, he thought. I shall have to visit the quack when I get back to London.

He lay quite still, feeling the dew soaking into him, and willed life into his veins. Overhead spun a myriad of stars and he felt as if he were spinning with them.

'Victor! Where are you?' Denis Crown's voice seemed to come from afar. 'Good God, what's up? Too much wine at dinner?'

Victor shook his head. 'Don't make a fuss,' he managed to say. 'Get me some brandy and then help me back to the house.'

'It's all right, everyone's gone to bed,' Denis assured him. 'Hang on, old fellow, I won't be a second.'

CHAPTER FOUR

Tea and Ellen were waiting in the drawing room on their return.

'I don't want any tea,' Hester said hurriedly. She put her hand to her head. 'I have a frightful headache. Do you mind if I go and lie down?'

Ellen was astonished. She had never heard the girl complain of a headache in her life. 'Very well, dear. You certainly look washed-out. Tut! late nights are the ruination of a girl's beauty,' Ellen lamented. 'There's a note on the table over there. It's for you from Lady Bland.'

Hester tore it open. 'She has asked me to lunch on Wednesday. Is that all right?'

I've asked George Edwardes from the Gaiety and his wife Julia (Cissie had written in her large undisciplined sprawl). And a baby guardsman to make up the table. But take no notice of him. It's the Guv'nor I want you to meet. Do come.

'Hester looks fagged out,' Ellen said when the girl had left the room. She handed her son a cup of tea, rather enjoying having him to herself. 'Was it a nice weekend?'

Wilfred shrugged. 'So-so. Yesterday was a bit of an anticlimax. Victor Cockayne had to return to London and Hester was obviously not well. Then Connie Courage took to her room after church and that left a very depleted party.'

'Good heavens, I hope it isn't a germ of some sort,' Ellen

said uneasily. 'I do hope you will gargle, Wilfred. I don't think London is at all a healthy place.'

'Oh, I don't suppose it's much.' Wilfred helped himself to more cake, for like his mother he loved sweet things. 'Mama, I'm out to dinner tonight. Some people I met at Henley. You had nothing special planned, had you?'

'No, dear, nothing.' But Ellen concealed a sigh. No one seemed to care that she was so much alone, she told herself, with some self-pity. Everyone was becoming increasingly engrossed in their own lives. She didn't know half Wilfred's friends. London had had a very unsettling effect on him and he never seemed to be at home for a meal.

After he had left her to go and take a bath and change, she solaced herself with more tea and cake, staring ahead, her mind empty. 'Yes, take the things away, Wiston. Will you tell Mrs Crombie that I shall be dining alone again. Miss Hester would probably like a tray of something light sent up to her room. She has a headache.'

'Very well, m'lady. Here is the evening post.' Wiston held out the salver.

There were a couple of invitations and a letter from Joe. She moved across to the window and looked for the paper-knife she kept on the table. It was, she saw now, raining gently and that was why it was suddenly so dark. She could hear the hansoms jingling past the opening to the crescent and a man plaintively calling his wares under the window. London was a sad place on an afternoon like this, Ellen thought, and sighed her deep heavy sigh that spoke of her boredom.

She opened the invitations first. Mrs Bourn again – well, fancy that, Ellen thought with the first smile of the afternoon. There was also an invitation to a river party, but of course they would be back at Stanhope by the end of next week so neither invitation could be accepted. Then she opened her husband's letter.

His fine sloping hand was easy to read even without her spectacles.

Dear Ellen,

The time has come to tell you that I am deeply in love with another woman. You have never met her but I have known her seven years and she has come to mean a great deal to me. Her name is Emily O'Neill and she is the widow of one of the officers employed by the Line.

I shall leave Stanhope on Tuesday for the last time. It is now solely for your use and Wilfred's. I earnestly hope you will keep Hester with you until her marriage. I know you are now fond of the girl. I have made arrangements so that she will not be a drain on your income.

Our marriage ended years ago so you will not miss me. I hope you will agree to make our separation legal. Bracegirdle will see to it.

Joe.

Ellen's mouth had dropped open as she read. The man had gone mad! Was he really proposing to ruin himself for a trashy woman called Emily O'Neill? Oh, she knew very well who she was – that woman he had been keeping in Liverpool. Well, let him have her and the misery that would surely be his because of her, Ellen thought viciously. She stumbled across to the bell to summon Wiston. Wilfred must come down at once and be told. . . . She stopped, crushing the letter convulsively.

Don't do anything. Don't tell anyone. Destroy the letter. Pretend you never received it. Let *him* do the explaining to Wilfred – and to Hester too.

A feeling of relief came over her. Without re-reading the letter she tore it into small pieces and pushed them into her leather writing case. Then she went back to her chair and picked up her embroidery.

But inside her body, under all her clothes and flesh, something was trembling and weeping: a younger Ellen who had once loved a tall spare man, plain Joe Prickard who was rising in the world. Twenty-three years they had been married – October 1869. She had worn a cream dress trimmed with braid and buttons. There were feathers in her cream bonnet. Joe had said she was pretty enough to eat – and he was hungry. The great fool. They had been so much in love.

Tears were running down her plump cheeks, tasting like salt in her mouth. It was too cruel. Everyone would know that their marriage had been a miserable masquerade for years. How they would gossip in Sewerston!

Anguish twisted in her, turned to rage and began to dry up her tears. Well, in the eyes of the world and his family, Joe had done for himself, she told herself with some satisfaction. It was to be hoped Emily O'Neill was worth it, she added angrily.

But she knew in her heart that it was the exact opposite that she hoped for. Meanwhile she would behave as if she had never received his letter.

Cissie's baby guardsman turned out to be a chinless boy who goggled at Hester throughout lunch and stuttered when he spoke.

She found George Edwardes's eyes on her several times too; sleepy blue eyes that were nevertheless examining her with interest. He was a well-built man with a petulant voice that held a hint of Irish brogue. His dark hair and moustache were flecked with grey and he wore his good clothes carelessly. His wife Julia, a former actress, was a friendly woman who was putting on weight now, but once must have been beautiful. She talked incessantly of her two small children to anyone who would listen. She and Cissie seemed to know each other well.

Hester was glad she had dressed with care in a blue ribbed silk dress and jacket with Flanders lace at the throat and wrists. Her small hat was covered with pink roses and tilted forward over her eyes. But her face lacked its usual happy vivacity, and when she smiled it was mechanical. She had just spent three of the unhappiest days of her life. She cried herself to sleep at night and woke heavy-eyed and listless next morning. And all the time she had had to conceal her feelings from Agnes. Ellen had seemed to notice nothing and was rather depressed herself. It was time they all went back to Yorkshire, she kept saying, and Hester had pretended to agree. But she dreaded leaving London for then she knew she wouldn't see Victor again. While they remained there, she nourished a tiny hope that he would get in touch with her.

She was not ashamed of having declared her love for him, she told herself defiantly over and over again. And he did love her – he did! She had told him proudly that she hadn't been brought up to conceal her feelings. And he had kissed her with passion and whispered that he loved her . . . he would always love her. But he couldn't marry her. Then she realized (for he didn't have to spell it out) that he knew about her father; the double murderer. He knew that she had been born in the slums. That she was simply pretending to be a lady. Somehow he had got hold of the whole story. The worst of it. The part that kept cropping up again and again, that was held against her so unfairly – for it had been none of her doing. Didn't they realize that?

If Victor knew the real meaning of love, she told herself stubbornly, none of it would matter.

'So you liked *Cinder-Ellen*, did you?' George Edwardes said. He glanced at her, wondering what had caused that faraway look in her wonderful turquoise eyes. Then he directed his attention to the smoked salmon on his plate, for he saw that the girl was having difficulty in concealing her tears. 'Rich food is very bad for you, you know,' he said conversationally. 'I never touch it myself. I hope you don't eat much of it? Green apples every day – simple things like that. They are the answer to most ills.' The butler was offering more sauce and he poured it liberally on his plate.

'I should get very hungry,' she demurred, smiling at him, making an effort to be normal. 'I'm afraid I like food.'

His eyes ran over her appreciatively. 'Ever thought of

going on the stage? The Gaiety chorus like our hostess?'

She laughed. 'No, never – at least only in dreams! I think my uncle would have a fit if I suggested such a thing. He loves the stage and actors but not for his own family I think!'

'He is your guardian I take it?'

'Yes. Sir Joseph Prickard of the Prickard Line. Have you met him?'

He was looking at her, nodding. 'I have indeed. I was up in Liverpool last year to welcome my company home from New York. They had had a great success on Broadway in *Ruy Blas*. Your uncle was on board that trip and gave a splendid party for them. We had Nellie Farren with us then – poor little Nellie.'

'What happened? Did she die?'

'As good as, poor little soul. She became so crippled with rheumatism that she'll never walk a stage again.' His face had become sombre. Then he looked at her, forcing a smile. 'Do you believe in luck? There's been a hoo-doo on me and my company. I hope we are coming to the end of it now.' His attractive smile was back on his face. 'Turquoise blue – that's the colour of your eyes and it's my lucky colour. My luck's going to change – I can feel it in my bones.'

'*I* bring you luck?' she asked ruefully and shook her head. 'I can't bring luck even to myself!'

He saw the dejected look had returned to her face and he watched her thoughtfully as she turned to answer her host. A beautiful girl who was having an unhappy love affair, he told himself.

They didn't speak again until he and his wife were on the point of leaving.

'Miss Kelsey, I'm going to give you my card,' he said in a low voice, scribbling on it. 'If ever you change your mind and want a job, show this to the doorkeeper and he'll see you get an interview with me. If I'm not there, my assistant Mr Malone will see you.' His eyes looked deeply at her. 'I'd like you in one of my shows. Think about it.'

She thanked him, rather bewildered. What an extraordinary man, she thought. Does he usually set about getting girls for the Gaiety this way?

'Well, Cissie, my dear, I'm sorry to break up the party but I'm a busy man. Julia can stay if she likes. . . . '

'And how am I to get home if you take Turner and the brougham?' Julia Edwardes asked with asperity.

'But isn't the Guv'nor *walking* everywhere these days?' Cissie asked with an innocent air. 'I'm sure he told me he was doing it for the good of his health – I know he advised me to take it up myself!'

'He did it one morning – one morning only,' Julia said. 'Then he got back in the brougham – but he tells me it will be the making of me.'

'Now, now, Julia, no tales out of school.'

'Wait,' Cissie murmured in Hester's ear. She shook the young subaltern's hand. 'So glad you could come, Mr Vaughan. Remember me to your mother, won't you?'

As the door closed after the last guest, she turned to Hester and said; 'Well?'

'He gave me his card and suggested I try for a job at his theatre.'

'What did I tell you?' Cissie was triumphant. 'I'm delighted for you. What a career you could have,' she added wistfully, knowing that her own chance was gone for ever.

'Cissie, can I talk to you?'

'Just let me get rid of Johnnie,' Cissie hissed. 'I'll send him for a nap to the smoking room. Wait here.'

Presently she returned to find that Hester had wandered into the window embrasure to stare down at the almost empty crescent. There was a dejected set to her shoulders that made Cissie click her tongue. 'What's the matter, dearie?' she asked in the voice she used to her intimates.

Hester gave her a weary smile, her eyes dark. 'I went away last weekend and made a discovery: my past is always going to colour my life.'

'Your past? My dear, you're not old enough to have one!'

'I mean my background. I want to tell you about it.'

Cissie sat quietly and without a great show of astonishment. She had heard much worse, although she didn't tell Hester so.

'It's made me realize that despite Uncle Joe's money and all he's done for me I am barred from marrying into the class of society I have become used to mixing in.' She swallowed painfully as the misery of Saturday night returned to her. The smell of the mock orange in Mrs Crown's garden and Victor's gentle voice piercing her like a knife. . . .

'That's rubbish! Why, I know girls who've come from nowhere, who hardly know who their own fathers were, who have married into the aristocracy and no harm done. You're speaking of Victor Cockayne, aren't you? Well, I did warn you.'

'Yes, I remember, Rosie Lock,' Hester said in a low voice. 'He told me on Saturday – I made him tell me – that although he loves me he can never marry me. He knows everything about me – my father murdering two people – and everything. He can never go against his father's wishes, he says. And I love him,' she ended sadly.

'It's the Bridlington pride,' Cissie said scornfully. 'The old man's stuffed with it. I'm sorry for young Cockayne – he's going to have a hell of a life if he doesn't throw off his father once and for all. So he's to marry Lady Constance, is he? I wish him joy of the union. They'll beget a dozen dull children . . . ' She stopped for tears were rolling down Hester's cheeks. 'Oh, damn the man!' she said crossly. 'I wish you could see him as I see him: charming but weak, with a strong streak of Bridlington pride. He's not worth crying over . . . listen to me! I've seen more of life than you have. In a few months you'll look back and be thankful you never married him.'

Hester was staring at her. 'Do you really believe that? I wish I did. I don't suppose I shall ever forget him, however hard I try.' She tried to smile and choked. 'Perhaps I had better take up Mr Edwardes's invitation and become a Gaiety Girl – something in my own right.'

Cissie was beaming at her. 'Hester, I know the Guv'nor. When he looks at a girl the way he looked at you, I know what he's thinking. *Would I sleep with her?* – and his answer was *yes!*'

'Oh, Cissie!'

'My dear girl, it's well-known,' said Lady Bland calmly. 'It's the first thing he asks the fellows when they beg him to see a little girl they've spotted in panto. "Would you want to sleep with her?" and if they shake their heads then he won't even give the girl an audition. The moment I set eyes on you, Hester, I knew you were the Gaiety type. There's something about you – call it style perhaps – yes, loads of style and something that makes the men look at you twice.'

Hester laughed as she prepared to depart. 'Thank you, Cissie, you've made me feel better.' She kissed her and went down the steps with a slightly lighter heart. Cissie was right. She must try and forget Victor. Walking home quickly, she was followed by a beggar, a boy so thin and ragged it hurt to look at him. He was offering her matches and she emptied her purse into his palm. His wizened face froze with shock and she fled from his thanks. There, but for Uncle Joe, she thought incoherently, she might have been selling matches herself. She hammered on the front door and almost fell into Wiston's arms.

'Has that lad been bothering you, Miss Hester?' Shoo! Away with you before I fetch a copper!'

'Oh, no, no! Please don't frighten him, Wiston. Just look at him. That might be you or me out there.'

Wiston pursed his mouth. By no stretch of the imagination could he see himself in the beggar's shoes. He shook his fist at the boy and closed the door firmly.

'But Hester, your uncle will never allow it!' Ellen wiped the nervous perspiration off her upper lip with a wisp of cologne-scented lawn. She hated argument at the best of times. 'How can you want to be a chorus girl after all he's done for you? Turned you into a young lady we're all proud of? No, he wouldn't hear of it, I'm sure.' Guiltily, she thought of the torn-up letter in her letter case. Would Joe care if his niece went on the stage? she wondered wretchedly. But she must try and forget the letter – forget it existed. 'A Gaiety Girl, indeed,' she added, trying to rally her forces once more.

'But it isn't quite what you think, Aunt Ellen. Gaiety Girls are special. They don't have to sing or dance or kick their legs in the air . . . at least not always, indeed not often. They are a new sort of chorus girl. They move about the stage in beautiful clothes, and if there's any singing it's done by real singers behind the stage . . . '

'Then what does he pay them for?' Ellen asked suspiciously. 'I don't like the sound of it at all. I'll see what Wilfred says.'

Wilfred of course expressed himself with proper horror. The older he became the more pompous he grew – or so Hester accused him. Joseph had noticed it with wry amusement; Ellen with a great deal of pride. Wilfred, she confidently told herself, knew what was expected of them now that they had risen in the world.

'You're a silly girl, Hester, even to think of such a thing. People like us don't go on the stage.'

'People like us?' Hester repeated mockingly. 'Oh, Wilfred, what an idiot you are! Money doesn't make us different, you know; we only hope it does. I don't suppose my background is nearly so good as some of the Gaiety Girls. I shall always be my father's daughter despite what has been done for me by Uncle Joe.'

Wilfred looked uneasily at his cousin. 'I hope you don't intend going about talking like that? Because you'll simply be dropped.'

'You're not my guardian and I don't have to listen to you,' Hester pointed out.

'I shall tell Papa what I think,' Wilfred retorted loftily.

259

He took out his gold watch and squinted at it. It had been given him for his twenty-first birthday last December and he used it to terminate conversations, Hester had noticed. Rather sulkily, she went upstairs to help Agnes pack. They were standing in a sea of tissue paper and arguing the best method of packing three enormous hats when John came upstairs with a bunch of pink roses that had just arrived for Hester.

She buried her nose in them. Their scent was quite heavenly, she thought, and took up the card attached to them by blue ribbon.

Hope you have enjoyed your stay in London. Victor.

She looked at the card for a long time, her breath ragged. She must not cry, she told herself fiercely, only too aware of Agnes's eyes on her. With a gesture of finality she tore the card into small pieces.

But the roses she couldn't destroy. They stood by her bed all that week and when at last they died and were removed, she felt relief. Now she could begin to forget him.

As the carriage turned in through the gates of Stanhope, Hester pulled the window down despite the rain that was falling.

'Only for a moment, Aunt Ellen. Smell it. Isn't it beautiful? If I were blind I should know I was back at Stanhope. Nowhere else smells anything like it.' She was glad to be back; now life would return to normal.

The house came into sight, it was not shining and white today, but a dull blue-grey, its shallow roof bright green under the rain. Under the leaden sky the cypress trees near the house looked almost black.

How beautiful it was! Hester thought once more and her spirits rose. She glanced back at her companions. They seemed indifferent to Stanhope's charms. Wilfred was gathering up the books on jurisprudence he had been yawning over (the first time he had opened a book this vacation) and Ellen was looking up into the luggage net and wondering if she had left one of her parasols on the train. Returning to Stanhope after nearly three months and smelling its verdant scent obviously meant nothing to them.

They were all in bed early that night after their long journey. But Ellen couldn't sleep. She got up at last and padded into Joseph's room across the landing, carrying a lamp which she held high, to inspect the few possessions he had left behind. Every cupboard and drawer was bare. So it was true then. He was gone for good.

A feeling of disaster overcame her and she sobbed silently. How was she to manage without a husband to look after her? He had had many faults, but he had always seen to her comfort and shielded her from tiresome chores. And if he had really gone – and it looked like it – then how was she to break it to the children? What am I to do? she thought wildly, looking round the empty room. Oh, the disgrace! How could he do it to her?

'We're at sixes and sevens downstairs this morning,' Agnes announced gloomily, coming to wake Hester. 'So you'd best have breakfast up here, Miss Hester, and keep out of t'way. Mrs Crombie's temper is sharp as a knife this morning. Those girls have let things get very slack in the kitchen. As for the rest of the house, I don't know I'm sure. They've been drawing their wages for nowt, I'd say.'

When Melia arrived with the tray, Hester saw that her eyes were red. 'Oh dear, has Mrs Crombie been scolding you?' Hester asked.

More tears rolled down Melia's cheeks. 'It's not that, miss. I can take any amount of tongue from Mrs Crombie. It's John. You know, miss, John the footman. He's not coming back. Gave in his notice in London 'cos he means to stay. And we was engaged!' Melia wailed. 'Going to be married next year we was . . . ' She wept loudly into her apron. 'An' not a word to me if you please. One postcard that's all I had with a picture of London – looked horrible, I thought.'

'Well, I do think it's too bad of him, Melia. Never mind,

261

there are lots of other nice young men about. Rickaby's sweet on you, I know. . . . '

'*Rickaby!*' Melia said scornfully. 'He's only a carter and smells of straw and horses. John was a lovely boy – so clean in his ways.'

Eating her solitary breakfast, Hester found herself sighing. It was no use pretending – London had been a disaster to some of them. She could give Melia good advice; could she take it herself? Victor was seldom out of her mind. That time in Mrs Crown's garden – it had been the first time she had encountered passion and she had been astonished at her own reaction. She possessed feelings that up till then she hadn't known existed inside her. Since that terrible evening, these feelings had ached and ached like a sore place that would never heal. She shrank a little from the memory of her body that night; a vessel borne along on a tide of feeling that had nearly proved disastrous to them both. She had wanted to tear off her clothes, to feel his body close to hers . . . At the memory she put her hands to her hot face. Was that what being in love did to one? 'Oh, Victor, Victor,' she murmured brokenly as a fresh wave of misery swept over her.

The rain had cleared overnight leaving a pale sky and a fresh wind. She put on her garden cape with the hood. She would go and see Miss Crook. A visit to her former governess always did her good, for Miss Crook was a tranquil person. She now lived in the little village house where she had once kept house for her brother. Joseph had bought the place and given it to her for life.

Hester found her already at work in her small garden. Her hair was grey now, but her eyes were as young and trustful as ever behind the pince-nez. She put down her trowel and greeted Hester with a kiss. 'My dear child, how good to see you again! Well, did you enjoy London? You look suitably wraithelike after your sojourn there.'

'The thing about London,' Hester complained as she sat down on the iron garden seat beside Miss Crook, 'is the air.

It chokes the lungs. I can't imagine what it's like when they have winter fogs. Miss Crook, how can people live there? No wonder the people look so pale. We used to gasp like fishes some days. It suited Wilfred in a funny sort of way. He now looks thoroughly prosperous and about thirty-five. Such whiskers! And here is a little London offering.' She laid a small parcel in Miss Crook's lap.

Miss Crook flushed with pleasure. 'Oh, Hester, these are lovely. Such soft white gloves – my dear, you shouldn't have done this.'

'Think how nice they will look on Sunday at church,' Hester smiled. 'And you have such pretty hands. They pay for showing up.'

Miss Crook spread her hands. 'Well, I confess they are my only beauty and I'm wickedly proud of them and cover them with gloves when I work out here or in the house. Come, let us go inside.'

They went indoors to the neat parlour with its sprigged curtains and wide-boarded floor that was polished like glass and covered here and there with Indian rugs. It was a sparsely-furnished room and looked as if it belonged to the last century and not the 1890s, for Miss Crook had inherited her few pieces of furniture from her grandmother. Everything shone, wearing a cared-for air and there were flowers and plants in profusion. Hester loved coming here. There was something in the air of the little house that calmed and soothed her. If ever she were to become an ageing spinster, she often told herself, she would live just like Miss Crook. In many ways she envied her already. Nothing seemed to ruffle the tranquility the woman had built up.

When lemonade and sponge fingers were brought, Hester took off her cape and told Miss Crook what was in her mind – she wanted to become a Gaiety Girl.

'You see, it's no use pretending any more. I'm just a fraud.'

'A fraud? My dear child, in what way?'

'You've helped to give me the outer trappings of young

263

ladyhood – oh, yes, some of the inner ones too! – but it's who you were when you were born that matters when it comes to – to marriage.'

Miss Crook looked at her searchingly. 'Surely that depends on a lot of things,' she demurred.

'I wasn't born a lady, I'm from the slums. If I had stayed with the aunts I should have become a milliner. I might have married one of the local boys – Tommy Hoggarth,' she said, a stab of remembrance hardening her expression. 'Instead Uncle Joe and his money plucked me up and turned me into quite a good imitation of a lady. Because of him I've mixed with people who are socially far above me. And I can never marry them. Until the other day I thought I could – I honestly thought so. I fell in love – I can't tell you who it is – but everything fell to pieces when he told me he couldn't marry me – because of who I am.'

'How very disagreeable,' Miss Crook said quietly. 'It surprises me a great deal. Even the great families are receiving quite ordinary girls into their circle nowadays. And you are a very beautiful girl, Hester. Also I have educated you and I have no false pride about my abilities: you are well-read, you speak French and German and you have travelled widely. Besides this, you are the ward of a very rich man. Whoever he is, the young man must be a fool and I advise you to forget him as quickly as possible. Ah, you think me hard, I can see. But don't let one unhappy love affair spoil your outlook on life. Wait, Hester. Don't act hastily and go on the stage and perhaps be very unhappy.'

But Hester's face remained sombre. The bitterness of Victor's rejection was with her again, turning like a knife in her heart. 'In London we were only on the fringe of everything. Aunt Ellen's Yorkshire accent was more pronounced than ever, and people like that notice you know. You think it bad of me to speak of it, don't you? We were outsiders and I realized it. It made me uncomfortable. The only real friend I made was a former Gaiety Girl – I also met Mr George Edwardes from the Gaiety. With people like that I could be myself. They wouldn't have minded what my background was whereas Lord Bridlington. . . . ' She stopped.

'The Bridlingtons are notoriously proud,' Miss Crook nodded. 'And increasingly poverty-stricken; so perhaps it was nice of them not to try and snatch a rich bride for their son.' Miss Crook realized that whatever she had experienced had hurt Hester badly. The young man had a great deal to answer for, she thought with concern, if his actions damaged the girl's security. It was a frail enough security that had been built up after the unhappy start to her life. She had fallen in love with the wrong man and been hurt.

'I could go back to London tomorrow and be taken on at the Gaiety. . . . '

'No, Hester, don't do it. You owe it to your uncle and aunt to do what they want and I'm sure they wouldn't be in favour of this scheme. Wait until Sir Joseph comes back and then talk to him about it. I've always found him a very reasonable person, haven't you?'

Hester nodded. 'I love him too much to hurt him,' she agreed.

Miss Crook ached over the new bitterness in the young face opposite her. Hester had always looked so happy – it was sad to see it vanish overnight so to speak. She was very young still and the bruise would show.

'But I know I'm in a cage and I want to get out of it,' Hester said, getting up and putting on her cloak. 'Don't you see? If I should fall in love again and the same thing should happen . . . ' She shivered suddenly. 'Never again do I want a man to tell me – oh, so regretfully! – that although he loves me he cannot marry me because I'm a fraud. I'm not a young lady in spite of my fine clothes, but only Hester Kelsey from Sewerston whose father was a murderer – oh, don't look shocked, please. We must call a spade a spade. In future I shall make certain I announce who I am before I get intimate with anyone.'

'Oh, my dear,' was all that Miss Crook could say help-

265

lessly as she followed the girl to the door. It was obvious to her that Hester had lost confidence not only in herself but in the future.

Settling down at Stanhope took them almost a week. Late July was oppressive and grey. It rained a little each day. Hester wandered about, amazed to find herself bored now that she was at home. She quarrelled with Wilfred and accused him of being pompous and boring. Now, instead of riding with him, she sent notes to the Fox family to meet her on the boundary of the two estates. Stephen was a large young man of nineteen learning to run the estate; Marigold was engaged and seldom turned up for their ride and Helena, poor plain Helena, had grown into a bore who could only talk about things that happened in the village. But they were useful when the twin devils of boredom and depression had Hester in their grip. Wilfred just sat in his room most of the day. He said he was working for Oxford, but in reality he smoked and dreamed the mornings away and grew heavy with too little exercise.

If they had not been so engrossed in their own feelings, Wilfred and Hester would have noticed that Ellen had become very quiet. Bottling up her secret trouble, Ellen actually lost weight for the first time since Wilfred's birth. But no one noticed except Agnes, who decided that London had been bad for her mistress's constitution and brought her trays containing calf's foot jelly and Bovril.

One day, Hester went into Sewerston with Ellen who had the larder at Stanhope to refill. Leaving her aunt talking to Mr Newlands of the Farm Products Centre, she strolled across the square. If she was to be a Sewerston girl then she must examine her roots, she told herself grimly. She called first on her aunts, but the shop was closed and there was no answer to her ring at the doorbell. She looked at the three hats displayed in the window. One was marked *Bargain 10/-* and was made in dusty velvet. There was an old-fashioned bonnet on the other side and, in the centre, a terrible creation in straw, feathers and fruit with the proud claim: *London Style!*

She suddenly realized how infinitely pathetic the old women were; none of them had ever left Sewerston in their lives, so had they copied their 'London style' from a magazine? And what dreadful hats they were! Who would wear them? She had the uneasy feeling that probably no one did any more.

She turned to walk down Chaundler Street to the harbour and the row of cottages where she had been brought up, but before she reached the bottom of the street she knew she couldn't face it. There were too many ghosts haunting the harbour area; some day she would go but not today.

Back in the square, she saw that her aunt was now having an absorbing conversation with Mr and Mrs Beddows, and Mr Beddows was holding up a splendid salmon for Ellen's examination. Hester walked across to Willy Hoggarth's shop, and stepped boldly inside. There was no sign of any of the family, she saw at once, only a bored girl dusting the display cases. Mr Hoggarth had branched out: there were shelves of children's annuals, shelves of novels, a cupboard full of toys. China filled other shelves round the shop, all a far cry from the days when Tommy ran round the town delivering the *Yorkshire Posts.*

'Yes?'

'I was wondering if Mrs Hoggarth was about?'

'Through there. Just knock and she'll hear you.'

Mrs Hoggarth knew her at once. 'Well, Hester, what a sight for sore eyes! It must be four or five years since I saw you last.' Mrs Hoggarth's hair was now quite white and she had put on weight. What a shock she'll be to Tommy when he next sees her, Hester thought as she sat down and began to recount all that had happened in the intervening years.

'I called on my aunts but they weren't in. Have you seen them lately?'

Mrs Hoggarth shook her head. 'Not lately. They keep

themselves to themselves. I don't think they do much business and I daresay are living on their savings now.' She sighed. 'It's hard on women without men, Hester. There's nothing at the end but the workhouse.' She rose suddenly and searched the mantelpiece. 'I heard from our Tom last week. He's still out in that India and no signs of coming home yet although he's had the chance. He's doing well, you see, and is soon to be married.'

'Married?' Hester repeated and her heart fell like a stone.

'To the sergeant-major's daughter. He's done very well for himself,' Mrs Hoggarth said proudly, 'she seems a lovely girl by all accounts. Violet Porter – that's her name. Let me see, what does he say . . . *She's nineteen, Ma, and only a bit of a thing. I can put my hand round her waist . . .* (that's Tommy all over!) . . . *Her dad is going to set us up when we come back home but I'm in no hurry. I like the life out here and so does Vi . . .* (This bit concerns you) . . . *Do you ever see Hester Kelsey, these days? Wish her the best if you do.* So isn't it funny you called? But that's how things happen, don't they?'

Hester nodded brightly, her face stiff. 'I'm delighted to get news of him. Please tell him how pleased I am to hear he's getting married. He – he was my best friend when I lived here, you know.'

She was still smiling brightly when she parted from Mrs Hoggarth, promising to call again soon and hear the latest about the wedding. But as she walked slowly across to the carriage she felt sick with shock. What was the matter with her? She was in love with Victor Cockayne. Tommy was just a dear friend. They hadn't seen each other for years, not since the day she had set out, a ragged girl of fifteen, to go and live at Stanhope and become a fine young lady. Much good it's done me, she thought bitterly and then felt ashamed. She owed her uncle everything. Just because Tom Hoggarth was to marry some creature called Violet Porter was no reason to turn on her benefactor and wish she had never been transported to another class. But she felt as if the bottom had dropped out of her world. She owned to herself that she had hoped one day to find Tommy waiting to give her the same warm friendship he had given her in the past. What a fool she was being!

CHAPTER FIVE

The telegram came at breakfast at the end of their third week at home.

Wilfred was already consuming a quantity of bacon and eggs when Hester came down to the dining room. He had propped *The Times* up before him and was reading about the pending election. To everyone's astonishment Mr Gladstone was proposing to come back for a fourth time at the age of eighty-two.

'G'morning,' he mumbled, his mouth full.

Hester helped herself to kedgeree at the sideboard. As she glanced out of the window to see what sort of day it was turning into, she saw the telegraph boy alighting from his scarlet bicycle and undoing the leather pouch at his waist. Hester considered his little pillbox hat – should she have one made in velvet? The Princess of Wales looked charming in hers – 'Wilfred, there's a telegram arriving. Perhaps Uncle Joe is coming home at last.'

'I hope you're right,' Wilfred grunted, spreading butter thickly on his toast. 'I've simply got to get next year's allowance straightened out. Five hundred really isn't enough and it's no wonder I've so many unpaid bills. Why, some fellows run their own victorias, you know.'

Wiston came in, bearing a salver. 'I don't know whether this is for you or m'lady, Mr Wilfred. Shall the boy wait for a reply?'

'I don't suppose there will be one,' Wilfred slit open the orange envelope. He read rapidly, blinked, then read it again.

Hester glancing up because of the prolonged silence, saw that he was suddenly very white. She put her fork down.

'What is it?'

'It – it's about Papa. He's *dead*.' Wilfred looked at them, incredulity on his round face. His father – dead? That extraordinary alive man? There must be some mistake.

Hester's voice was saying the same thing – but very shakily. She snatched up the telegram and read it. 'Oh, Uncle Joe! Uncle Joe!' she cried. She buried her face in her hands, rocking to and fro in grief and pain and shock. 'It can't be true. Wilfred, say it isn't true?' She raised her head in half-hope. He moved across to her and patted her on the shoulder.

'I'm afraid it is, Hester. Will you tell them in the servants' hall, Wiston? Sir Joseph died suddenly during the night while in Liverpool.' He picked up the telegraph form. 'This is signed O'Neill. It must be from his landlord; he had rooms out at Crosby.'

'O'Neill?' Hester looked up into her cousin's face, but it was obvious that the name meant nothing to him. So Uncle Joe had died in Mrs O'Neill's house. Well, if they didn't know who Mrs O'Neill was they shouldn't learn from her.

'You will be going straight up to tell her ladyship, Mr Wilfred? – I mean, Sir Wilfred?' Wiston asked. 'Miss Hester had better tell Miss Bentley.'

A new sensation possessed Wilfred, overcoming the first shock. My God, but Wiston was right! He *was* Sir Wilfred now. And all this was his. It was a powerful sensation and he tried hard to conceal his feelings in the face of Hester's distress. Not that he hadn't been fond of his father . . . but how wonderful to be free, to be the master here, to have all the money he needed. He nodded at the butler, new dignity in his bearing. 'I will go and tell my mother now – oh, Hester, do stop,' he added irritably as Wiston left the room. 'You'll make yourself ill.' For Hester was sobbing in what her cousin considered a very violent fashion.

She made an attempt to quell her sobs, but she was trembling so violently that she was shaking the table. She got up

271

and gave him a watery smile. 'I will try. Go and tell Aunt Ellen.' When he had gone, she went across to the window and looked out with tear-blurred eyes. All this beauty he had given them, but how little he had seen of it himself! For every summer he had taken his family somewhere – to Europe or America. His restless spirit had driven him relentlessly on, never allowing him to relax and enjoy what he had earned in life. Worst of all, he had never been happy with his wife. She realized at last (now she understood the relationship between a man and a woman) that a precious ingredient had been missing from his life. Was it this perhaps that had engendered the extraordinary drive that had sent him to worldly success – a success that at the last could have meant little to him? If he had been contented, he probably would not have gone on to conquer so much. Now he was dead in the early fifties, twenty years younger than the old queen . . . 'Oh, Uncle Joe,' she said softly, 'I hope *she* loved you well – that Mrs O'Neill in Liverpool.' She swallowed a sob. I shall miss him dreadfully, she thought. He spoiled me. I had only to ask him and he gave way to me – how good he was to me.

And realizing that all her thoughts were in the past tense now, she broke down and cried loudly in the silent empty room. Instinct told her that something good in her life had come to an abrupt end.

Wilfred found his mother eating her usual hearty breakfast in bed. The room smelled stuffily of cooked food and last night's medicine. The windows were tightly shut and the heavy brocade curtains not fully drawn back. He waited for her to swallow a piece of toast and then said quickly, 'Mama, I have bad news for you.' He looked at the bed table and saw that the usual small wicker-covered flask of brandy was standing there. It might well be needed, he thought uneasily. He took the telegram out of his pocket and held it out to her. 'It's about Papa.'

She put a hand to her mouth. 'I haven't my spectacles. What is it?' she said in a muffled voice.

'It's from someone called O'Neill....'

Her reaction startled him. Snatching the form out of his hand, she shouted, 'Don't read it! Don't believe a *word* that wicked woman says. . . . ' She screwed the form into a ball and threw it across the room.

Pulling himself together (because for a moment he had been too staggered to utter a word), he shouted back, 'But you don't understand! Papa is *dead*! He is *dead*!'

She leaned back on her pillow as if suddenly weak. 'Dead? Are you sure?'

'It says so in the telegram.' He bent and retrieved it, then proceeded to read it out to her. She had closed her eyes and he did not see a long breath of relief escape through her lips. She had been rescued at the last minute by death. No one now need ever know that Joe had left her, she thought. Not even Wilfred. Opening her eyes and finding his fixed anxiously on her, she said feebly, 'I've had a dreadful shock – oh, what a shock it has been.'

He was puzzled, remembering her words: *Don't believe a word that wicked woman says* – yes, he was sure that that was what she had shouted. 'Do you know the person – a woman you said – who sent this?'

'It's – a friend of your father's, the widow of one of his captains I believe.' She gave no other explanation of her outburst as she began to sob. 'I . . . I'm just dreadfully upset. Don't leave me, Willy.'

He took her hand. 'Of course I won't, Mama.'

Behind her tears was a vast relief. Joe was dead. Joe could no longer disgrace her, make her a laughing stock in the eyes of the world. She was now his widow and people would sympathize with her. There would be letters of condolences, a big funeral – and that woman would have no part of it at all.

Wilfred was holding her hand. 'Don't worry, Mama, you've got me to take care of you. Do you realize I am now the second baronet?' They smiled at each other in deep understanding.

'You'll make a splendid one, Willy.'

Yes, he really believed he would. Already his head was full of schemes and changes. It was quite taking the sting out of his sorrow. Of course he would miss his father badly – that went without saying surely? – but he would be much more of a country gentleman than poor Papa had been. There would be country house parties here – *his* friends at last. He thought of Major Webber and nearly smiled outright. Then he took out his watch and consulted it frowningly. There was already an air of power and decision about him. 'I shall have to go across to Liverpool today. I must get hold of Bracegirdle – there are a hundred things to be seen to. There is a midday train from Sewerston Junction. I will telegraph to Bracegirdle to meet me there. Mama, you will be all right? Hester will stay with you. Today is Thursday – we can't possibly hold the funeral before next Wednesday at the earliest. So many people will want to come.'

She was sitting bolt-upright in bed suddenly. 'Willy, do you have to go to Liverpool? Can't Mr Bracegirdle go and see to everything?' There was panic in her eyes and he stared curiously at her.

'Of course I must go,' he said shortly. 'There are a hundred things to see to. And I must collect Papa's body.'

She shuddered. 'That woman,' she mumbled. 'Have nothing to do with her – don't listen to her lies whatever you do. Promise me, Willy love, not to listen to her?'

'Now, Mama, don't distress yourself. I will send Agnes to you.' He kissed her and left. How oddly she was behaving – it must be due to shock and grief.

In response to the new baronet's telegram Alfred Bracegirdle, breathless and with a shaving cut on his chin, met him at Sewerston junction. In one hand he held a small overnight case and in the other a large Gladstone bag filled with documents. He had left his office in disarray, his engagements for the rest of the week cancelled, his filing cabinet in total disorder. But he had managed to reach the junction in time.

In the train they talked business in a quiet compartment. The new baronet seemed to be a sensible enough young chap, Bracegirdle thought. He looked enviously at the chubby face under the tweed cap. My God, what the lad was inheriting, he thought with awe. Probably more than a million. And he wouldn't be affected by this death duty bill those damned Liberals were trying to get through Parliament. Poor Joe had died in the nick of time it would seem. Before opening the Gladstone bag he leaned across, until his cadaverous face was within an inch or so of Wilfred's, and said in a low voice, 'You do understand about Mrs O'Neill, I trust?'

Wilfred stared at him. 'Understand what?'

'She was your father's mistress.'

The young man's face froze. 'His *mistress*?'

Good God, was the lad that innocent? Bracegirdle spelled it out. 'He had lived with her for years. And it had come to worse than that. He wanted to marry her. You knew he had left home for good this time?'

Numbly, Wilfred shook his head. He felt sick; sick and frightened and filled with hatred. *His father. Mrs O'Neill.* He closed his eyes and felt nausea rising.

Bracegirdle watched him with unconcealed interest. 'Oh, yes, he was quite determined to marry Mrs O'Neill! He wanted your mother to divorce him. He was quite determined,' he repeated.

Wilfred turned on him. 'Determined or not,' he said in a choking voice, 'my mother would never have agreed. It was disgusting of him to suggest it to her. He must have been mad.'

'He wrote to me only last week,' Bracegirdle went on relentlessly, taking no notice of the interruption. 'Apparently he had not received a reply from Lady Prickard and he asked me to go and see her. I didn't relish the task I can tell you so I had put it off. But if your father hadn't died

275

there would have been nothing for it; I would have had to go.' He looked at the floor. 'Divorce is a terrible step, Sir Wilfred. I'm thankful we have been spared that.'

Wilfred glared at him. What did he mean *we*? It would have been his mother and himself who would have suffered from this ghastly middle-aged madness of his father's. And people had thought that Sir Joseph Prickard was the most astute man in the north! How he had fooled them all. Imagine ruining the whole structure of his life for a *woman*! Demented was too kind a word. 'I would never have forgiven him,' Wilfred said scornfully. 'Nor would my mother.'

'So you don't know what he intended doing about it?'

'No.'

Bracegirdle sighed and averted his eyes. There was a queer look in the lad's eyes, he thought. He wouldn't make a good enemy. Well, poor Joe was dead so it was to his advantage to make up to the son. Business was business after all.

They travelled in silence for some time then Wilfred burst out, 'I tell you this, I am never going to let my mother know that I have heard anything. Do you understand? It is never to be mentioned. If I hear it has been talked about in Sewerston, then I shall change my solicitor.'

Bracegirdle blinked in astonishment. Well! There was a vicious temper under that boyish exterior, was there? He filed the knowledge in his brain, leaned forward and said earnestly. 'You need have no fear that I will betray a client's confidence, Sir Wilfred.' Heaven help Edith if she had dropped hints over the teacups anywhere! He would have to warn her. He had an uneasy recollection of betraying a confidence or two while in the marriage bed. He went on smoothly. 'I need hardly remind you that we shall have to meet the lady in question today. It must be in her house that your father's body is lying – that is if he died in the early hours of this morning.'

'You have no need to remind me,' Wilfred snapped. 'We shall meet the undertakers there – I telegraphed Munro, the manager of the Line, to see to that – and then we shall leave at once.' He pointed to the Gladstone bag. 'Is my father's will in there?'

Bracegirdle brought out a twenty-page document – the will that Joseph had made the year after Hester had become his ward. The date was April 1888. Wilfred was named as the sole heir and two trust funds had been set up: one for Ellen's lifetime, the other until Hester was either twenty or had married.

'And what then?' Wilfred demanded. 'She was twenty last spring.'

'Then she inherits one thousand pounds for her immediate use. . . .'

'Only a thousand pounds?' Wilfred said blankly. 'That won't go far. Am I supposed to provide for her? I think that's very unfair.'

'No, Sir Wilfred. The income from the second trust fund will be hers, a very generous gesture to a young woman who was not, after all, your father's daughter,' Bracegirdle hinted softly.

Wilfred agreed wholeheartedly: it was too much in his opinion.

It was late when they arrived at the Adelphi Hotel. They found Munro, the general manager of the Prickard Line, awaiting them. He was a swarthy man with very black hair and whiskers and clad from head to foot in black, with a crêpe band round his top hat. He looked askance at the new owner of the Lines in his tweed suit and cap. Wilfred was conscious of being considered careless, which made him brusque with the manager.

Mr Munro was a man of few words himself however. He sat in almost total silence, watching them eat an indifferent dinner of brown Windsor soup, roast beef and steamed jam roll. Outside it was a hot August night and Wilfred had to wipe the perspiration off his face. Munro had declined to join them. He had eaten his tea at six o'clock he told them austerely.

Wilfred felt sick from the heat and greasy food. The

277

excitement and grief of the day had fatigued him to the point of exhaustion. But he had made up his mind that his father's body should not remain another night in 'that woman's' house. Although it was after eleven, they took a growler on the long drive out to Crosby. The manager told them that the undertakers would be meeting them at the house.

They stopped and, by the street lamp, Wilfred saw a tiny house with a monkey puzzle tree in the garden. The curtains were drawn close, but a faint light showed through an upper window. So this was the place; so this was his father's love-nest, Wilfred told himself, his lip curling scornfully. Distaste and jam roll lay heavily on his stomach as he led the way up the brick path and rattled on the door. Bracegirdle accompanied him and Munro stayed behind in the growler. Wilfred had seen him light up a cigar which annoyed him. The fellow would be sitting there puffing at his ease, while they had the disagreeable task of interviewing the woman.

A little maid, her eyes like saucers, opened the door to them and led them upstairs to a small stuffy sitting room.

Two black-garbed men nursing their crêpe-banded hats, rose as one and bowed. Wilfred nodded to them. 'I'll be with you presently. You stay here, Bracegirdle.' He turned to the girl. 'Where is Sir Joseph's body?'

The girl's red hand pointed in the direction of a door across the landing. 'In't there wi' her.'

Wilfred braced his shoulders and turned the door handle quietly. The room's only light came from a small lamp on a chest. The room was a bedroom. On the large double bed lay a figure: very flat, nose pointed upwards. Wrapped in a sheet it looked like a figure carved on a mediaeval tomb. Wilfred stared down into the face, unable to recognize the father he had known in this majestic figure of death.

There was a movement on the other side of the bed and he started back. 'Mrs O'Neill?'

The figure didn't reply. One of her hands lay protectively across the dead man. Wilfred bent towards her. 'Will you

278

come outside?' he said in a low voice as if his father were only resting. 'I want to talk to you.'

By the light of the lamp he could just see the movement of her eyes. She neither moved nor spoke. Wilfred opened the door and went out.

The undertakers rose again at his entrance. 'About the arrangements, sir,' one of them murmured.

He looked at them with irritation. Why did they have to whisper? He dealt briskly with them in a normal voice: the body must be made ready for the journey across country by an early train next morning.

Alone again with Bracegirdle he said uneasily, 'The woman – she's sitting in there with my father's body. She hasn't moved.'

Bracegirdle sucked in his cheeks. 'Tricky, that. What if she makes a scene when they try to remove the body? That's how it takes some people. Best summon the maid to persuade her to come and talk to us.'

But Polly refused pointblank to go into the room with the dead. 'No, sir, I daresn't – I daresn't – ' she wept, holding her apron to her eyes.

'I will go myself,' Bracegirdle said. He was in the room five minutes; but when he emerged it was with Emmy O'Neill. Wilfred stared at her, wondering what his father could have seen in this ageing woman. Her fuzzy reddish hair trailed on her shoulders and she was still wearing the peignoir she must have put on in the early hours. Patches of broken vein stood out on her white cheeks and her eyes were hollow and empty.

'Come and sit down over here, Mrs O'Neill,' Bracegirdle said, leading her gently to a chair. 'This is Sir Wilfred Prickard, Sir Joseph's son.'

She fixed Wilfred with a stare. 'You'll be like *her*. There's nothing of him in you.' Losing interest in him, she swung round to the solicitor and said in a hoarse voice that shook from emotion, 'What's to become of me now? That's what I want to know. I was to have been his wife. . . .'

279

'Never!' Wilfred said sharply.

She wagged her head. 'Oh, yes, I was. He promised me.'

Bracegirdle made a slight warning movement of his head in Wilfred's direction and said 'Now, you've nothing to worry about, Mrs O'Neill. Just tell us what happened.'

She began to sob, burying her face in her hands. Her voice was blurred. 'We'd been to the music hall . . . had a bite to eat and a bottle of wine afterwards. We were lying there talking . . . his arm was round me like always . . .' Her voice broke. 'We had gone to bed early . . . he said he was tired . . . and then in the middle of talking . . . he just stopped. Just like that. Then . . . then I couldn't hear his heart . . . such a strong heart he always had . . . and I cried out, Joe, are you all right? He didn't say anything. I had to find the matches . . . oh, God, it was awful. Just silence and me fumbling about in a panic trying to light that damned lamp. When I did, I could see he was dead. He looked just like poor Sam – that's my late husband. His eyes were open and he just lay there.' She raised her head suddenly and turned wildly on Wilfred. 'He's *dead* I tell you! What's to happen to me now?'

Wilfred exclaimed under his breath and blundered out of the room. They heard the front door slam and she started to her feet. 'The little bastard! Making that racket and his pa lying in there!'

Bracegirdle pulled her back into the chair. 'Sit down, Mrs O'Neill, I want to know a great deal more. You summoned the doctor, I take it?'

'I sent Polly. She didn't want to go out in the dark, but I kicked her out and locked the door after her. When they returned, he told me there was nothing to be done.' Sobs racked her again. 'Oh, Joe, oh, Joe, what am I to do now?'

Bracegirdle sighed. He feared that Mrs O'Neill was now playing to the gallery and the sooner the interview came to an end the better. When he rejoined the others waiting in the growler, he saw that Wilfred was sitting with his arms folded, his chin sunk on his chest. Munro threw away his cigar and gave Bracegirdle a significant look.

As they jolted off, Wilfred said (with a shudder in his voice): 'That woman. . . .'

'Quite. You won't have to see her again, Sir Wilfred. I've sorted one thing out. He had been seeing this doctor who lived quite near. High blood pressure apparently. The man said this sudden death was not unexpected as he was in a pretty bad way. But you know how your father was about health – he always tried to laugh it off. He had obviously had a warning but refused to take any notice. There will be no difficulty about a death certificate. He signed it straight away and the undertakers have it. So it's plain sailing,' he added quietly in Wilfred's ear.

The young man nodded. Thank God, no one need know about Mrs O'Neill. There would be no inquest or enquiry of any sort.

Munro leaned forward. 'Perhaps you'll give me my instructions about the office staff, Sir Wilfred. Several will want to come to the funeral. Should we close down for the day as a mark of respect?'

Wilfred turned to him with relief and they discussed the future of the Prickard Line for the rest of the journey. But when Munro had left them at the hotel, Bracegirdle touched Wilfred's arm. 'About Mrs O'Neill. There's no provision made for her in the will. . . .'

'I should dam' well hope not!' Wilfred said indignantly.

'Exactly so. Nevertheless, I feel certain your father intended doing something for her. The woman is entirely at your mercy. She has no means at all. The house is in her name and Joe – your father sent her a generous sum every month. Now that will stop. She tells me she has very little money in the house and she hadn't received a cheque for this month yet. . . .'

'She won't get a penny from me.' The words were rapped out.

Bracegirdle bit his lip. 'It's not for me to say.'

'Exactly so,' Wilfred mocked him coldly. 'This is **my**

281

business. She will never get a penny from me. She can go to the Poor House for all I care.'

Stanhope's drawing room was a sea of black. The funeral was over.

Like Ellen, Hester had worn a veil draped over her hat and face. She had shed bitter tears behind it as Joseph's coffin was lowered into the earth. She wondered if Ellen was crying too behind her veil and had taken her aunt's arm. But the arm had been rigid and when they turned away, Ellen had reached for her son's support to lead her back to the carriage.

As she tried to talk to obscure relations who had stayed for tea, Hester felt misery lying like lead on her spirits. It was, someone remarked with satisfaction, the biggest funeral in the district for twenty years. It made old Lord Girvan's look a shoddy affair. The self-made Joseph, sturdy and unpredictable, had been well-liked for he had been generous with time, money and sympathy where needed.

Wilfred looked at the relations with impatient scorn. They were from the backwoods, he thought gloomily, skilfully avoiding his great-uncle who had been gleefully telling everyone he was thirty years senior to the dead man and look at him, still going strong! Why on earth didn't they go? Wilfred wondered.

Ellen had provided a traditional funeral tea for all those who had come from afar. They ate heartily, looking round with interest on their kinsman's possessions. They wandered over the house and garden – it might have been a fête and not a funeral.

'I don't believe they're ever going to go!' Ellen wailed under her breath to Miss Crook.

'May I suggest something, Lady Prickard? Go up to your room and lie down and leave everything to me.' And firmly Miss Crook saw to everything: the hired carriages were suddenly at the door and the black stream of people began to pour down the steps. They had had a day that would be talked of for a long time in remote farm houses and small villas – the day our cousin Sir Joseph was buried.

The day after the funeral Alfred Bracegirdle waited impatiently in a small room off the hall at Stanhope. As he had left after the funeral, Wilfred had said in a low voice: 'Can you come at eleven o'clock tomorrow? Apparently there's another will. . . .'

This piece of information had taken Bracegirdle horribly by surprise. Another will? But *he* was the family solicitor! It was he who held the secrets of Joseph's financial affairs. Tossing sleepless by his wife's side that night, he had begun to have terrible doubts. Joe had been a wily old fox. He had never believed in keeping all his eggs in one basket. Bracegirdle had suspected years ago that transactions were taking place in which he had no part.

His heart had sunk to his boots as Wiston showed him into this small room and not into the study. 'Sir Wilfred has a gentleman with him, sir. Would you care for the newspaper? I will give Arthur instructions to bring you coffee at once.'

'No – no coffee. Nothing. Who is in there with him, Wiston?'

'A Mr Owen-Davies, sir. And a clerk.'

Owen-Davies, eh? Bracegirdle swallowed something sour. He knew the name only too well. It belonged to a large law firm in Liverpool – Owen-Davies, Chantry and Swindon. Big people. Restlessly, he paced the room, bitterness growing with every minute. Another will meant that his firm would not have the lucrative job of proving it. The twenty-page document signed four years ago (and which he had brought with him) was now just so much rubbish. It could be cut up for the staff lavatory for all the worth it held. He growled under his breath, knowing now that Joseph had realized long ago that some of his secrets had been leaked. Well, in a small town like Sewerston it was impossible not to have one or two confidants, Bracegirdle argued. There had been the little matter of the harbour land he had thought Joseph needed for expansion . . . He sighed heavily, shaking his head at the perfidy of his old friend.

It was a quarter to twelve before Wiston appeared again.

'Will you come this way, sir, please?'

Bracegirdle allowed his long face to show bitter displeasure as he was shown at last into the study. Wilfred sat in his father's chair. His face looked paler than usual and he toyed nervously with a silver letter cutter. Opposite him sat a red-faced man with grey whiskers. A clerk sat at a small table holding papers.

Wilfred introduced the two men briefly. 'Mr Owen-Davies made a later will for my father,' he explained. 'It was made two years ago.'

Bracegirdle slumped into his chair. 'I knew nothing of this.'

The fat man had a high thin voice: 'Sir Joseph had used my firm increasingly in the last five years. His business had expanded considerably and become more complicated.' He smiled deprecatingly and turned to Wilfred. 'We are – er – experts in company law. Shall I go over the points again, Sir Wilfred? For the benefit of your own lawyer.'

Wilfred nodded wordlessly.

Something's rattled him all right, Bracegirdle thought with sour satisfaction. The young cock's not so sure of himself as usual.

'In a nutshell then, the shipping company called the Prickard Line is to be inherited in equal shares between Sir Wilfred and his cousin, Miss Hester Kelsey. If Sir Wilfred has no issue, then the two halves of the company come together again and descend to any children there might be of Miss Kelsey's.'

There was a brief silence while Bracegirdle struggled with chagrin and fury. Joseph had never breathed a word of his intentions to him. He had made him look a fool.

'But I have already said my cousin knows nothing of business. She is only a girl,' Wilfred began in a complaining voice. He glanced at Bracegirdle. 'My father must have been mad!'

'I hope you are not making a serious allegation, Sir Wilfred?' The high voice had lost none of its smoothness. 'I can assure you that your father was in full possession of his powers up to the day he died. I had seen him myself the day before when he had made a codicil to the will. . . .'

'A codicil?' Both men leaned forward.

Owen-Davies snapped his fingers at the clerk who came forward at once with more papers. 'It concerned a trust fund he wanted set up for Mrs Emily O'Neill.'

Wilfred's breath almost stopped. Was there to be no end to the shocks he was receiving from this smooth-tongued lawyer?

'It was on exactly the same lines as the trust fund for your mother.'

'The same?' Wilfred echoed feebly. His blood pounded suddenly in his head. 'Then it is infamous! That woman was no better than a whore! And she's to be treated in exactly the same way as my mother!'

'I think that was what he intended, yes. Mrs O'Neill had been his mistress for many years. He felt he owed her a great deal. If they had been married she might have done even better, may I remind you. She is to receive the house and the income from a trust. It will give her a very handsome income.'

'Oh, no doubt she'll be able to keep a carriage and pair now!'

'I'm sure of it. She is safe for life. But then so is Lady Prickard, for your father has stipulated she is to remain at Stanhope if that is her wish.'

'I consider it an insult to my mother!' Wilfred said shrilly. 'I shall fight it.'

'I don't advise it, Sir Wilfred. Dirty linen and all that. It's a small sum when one takes into account the total of your father's possessions.'

'How much?' Bracegirdle leaned forward eagerly.

Owen-Davies looked at him coolly. 'It will take us some time to assess. He had lately acquired a cargo-carrying fleet of ships belonging to Berry Brothers. Used mostly on the Australian route. Then there are his shares and Stanhope and some farms in the north of the country, occupied at present by some relations. And you can thank God, Sir Wilfred, that that infamous death duty bill has not been through Parliament. If it ever becomes law, it will impose an eight per cent duty on the first million. Of course with Gladstone back in power it will be on the statute book in a year or two.' Mr Owen-Davies shook his head sorrowfully. 'It's a terrible thing to say, but your father died just in time. You and your cousin will be in a very favourable position financially.'

'There appears to be no need for me to stay,' Bracegirdle announced, rising and gathering up papers.

Wilfred nodded dully. He felt sick, as if he had received a blow to the heart. Only a few hours ago he had felt confident: he was the new head of the Prickard Line – his father's heir. And now he had to share it with silly little Hester, a girl, only a half-cousin.

When both solicitors and the clerk had left, he climbed the stairs to his mother's sitting room. She was sitting by the window doing her embroidery and her eyes were anxious as they met his.

'Well, love? They stayed a long time.'

He nodded, going to sit on the windowseat. 'Mama, I have something to tell you – it's about Hester.'

She listened in petrified silence, her mouth slowly falling open with horror. 'Joe must have been mad – it was wicked of him! But I should have guessed it – he always intended giving Nancy's girl the same as his son,' and she laughed bitterly. She felt that she hated Joseph now he had slighted their only child.

'Stanhope is mine though,' Wilfred pointed out.

'And with half the income to run it on! Hester can set up

as a fine lady tomorrow and snap her fingers at us.' All her affection for Hester (carefully built up over the years) was crumbling in the face of this blow. 'Does she know yet?'

'Not yet. Owen-Davies said I could tell her though. He will be writing to all the beneficiaries in about a month. There's a lot to be seen to first.'

Ellen got up and joined him at the window. 'Don't tell her yet. Leave it to him to do. There's no hurry.' For now suddenly she was clinging to the notion that something would transpire to prevent Hester coming into her fortune. Joint owner of the Prickard Line – it was monstrous. In five minutes this piece of information had blotted out Ellen's five-year relationship with the girl. She felt that Hester was to blame in some way. 'I couldn't bear her to know yet. Goodness knows she's full enough of her own importance as it is. It's time she realized she's not the daughter of this house, only a relation we took in out of the kindness of our hearts. It was madness – I always thought so and I blame myself for allowing it. The little snake in the grass!' She wept suddenly into her wisp of a handkerchief. 'Oh, what a lot I've had to put up with . . . if only my mother had known the half of it! Even you don't know the half of it, Wilfred love.'

'But I do.'

She was startled and stared at him blankly.

'He has left the woman the same amount as he left you.'

She screamed with anger. 'That whore! My God, what a wicked man he was! I'm glad he's dead! I'm glad!'

'Mama, for God's sake calm yourself!' Alarmed, he had sprung to her side and attempted to lead her back to her chair. 'You mustn't worry yourself, Mama dearest, you're going to be very well off and you're to stay here with me for the rest of your life. And I shall be a rich man – as rich as my father was in a few years, Owen-Davies says. Business is doing so well I shall make up the income. . . .'

'Yes, and Hester's income will be just as big! As for *that woman* words fail me. I've got to say this, love: your father was a bad man. I was the best of wives and look how he treated me in the end!' She wiped her eyes. 'I'd like to go away for a bit. For a little holiday. Just you and me. We could go to Baden Baden and take a cure. Ah, say yes, love! Just you and me,' she added coaxingly. 'We can leave Hester at home here and Miss Crook can come and keep her company.'

'Very well. It will do us both good to be out of the way for a while. Hester will have learned about my father's wishes by the time we return, and being away will solve a great deal. Now, Mama, the gong went some time ago. Let's go down to lunch.'

'I shan't be able to swallow a morsel,' his mother predicted tearfully. 'Not a morsel.'

Before she left for her holiday, Ellen had disposed of most of Joseph's possessions which had arrived home from Liverpool in three trunks, four hat boxes and a packing case. She locked herself in his bedroom and went through everything carefully, turning out every pocket and scrutinizing every paper. There was nothing incriminating to be found, she realized at last; that woman had been there before her and had brushed the clothes and packed everything between layers of tissue paper. She did not appear to have kept anything, Ellen saw with disappointment. She had longed for an excuse to have a wrangle with this unknown Emmy O'Neill. Dispirited, she replaced the clothes and then directed Wiston to dispose of them in any way he wished. Yes, the few possessions in the packing case too.

'Oh, Aunt Ellen, before everything goes could I have something of Uncle Joe's? Something to remember him by?' Hester pleaded as the trunks were carried downstairs.

Ellen shrugged. 'I've given everything to Wiston. You'll have to ask him.' She had kept nothing herself and Wilfred had only taken the diamond dress studs. Neither of them wanted any reminder of Joseph Prickard, they told each other indignantly for, fed by his mother's resentment, Wilfred was beginning to think he had been badly done by, slighted in the eyes of the world.

So Hester hurried downstairs to the kitchen wing and found Wiston and Mrs Crombie in the middle of an uninhibited discussion.

'She couldn't have cared at all for the poor master. Take it out of my sight, she says. . . .'

'Fancy!' Mrs Crombie caught sight of Hester and signalled to Wiston.

'Oh, Wiston, before everything goes, could I have something of my uncle's ?' Hester asked breathlessly.

Wiston's eyes softened. 'Of course you may, miss. What would you like?' They opened the trunks and, on hands and knees, inspected Joseph's handsome possessions. Mrs Crombie, arms akimbo, watched them; shaking her head lugubriously and clicking her teeth at the sight of every familiar object. 'Eh, the dear master! To think he'll never use any of these lovely things again!'

Seeing his silver hair brushes, Hester took them in her hands. She felt tears rising in her eyes, for they held a faint scent of his favourite hair oil. Then she put them down. 'I don't want anything valuable,' she said hurriedly.

Wiston took the brushes with the entwined J. P. on them. The bristles were set in ebony and the whole backed on heavy silver. He had had his eye on them for himself but he held them out to Hester. 'They should be yours, Miss Hester. Sir Wilfred doesn't want them. Some day you might have a son of your own to give them to. I think Sir Joseph would like them to go to him.'

Awed, Hester thought of a son of her own one day using Uncle Joe's brushes. 'Do you really think so, Wiston? But would it be greedy to ask for his cigar case as well?' She held out the worn Russian leather case Joseph had always kept in his pocket. There were still two cigars inside. 'Doesn't the smell of them bring him back,' she choked.

'There, there, dearie.' Mrs Crombie wiped Hester's tears

familiarly with the corner of her white apron. 'You loved your uncle – we could all see that.'

Hester nodded, scrambling to her feet. 'Oh, Wiston, don't you think we ought to send something of his for Mrs O'Neill to keep? I'm sure she would like something to remember him by.'

Startled, they could only stare at her. How on earth did Miss Hester know of the woman?

She was bending over the trunks, searching for something and presently found what she wanted – Joseph's green brocade dressing gown. 'There! That she would like I'm sure. And his card case. I'll write her a note and we can pack them up down here and Arthur can take them to the post.' She looked up, encountering their eyes. 'Did you think I didn't know? But you must remember I'm no longer a child.' She nodded her thanks and went out through the baize door.

Mrs Crombie heaved a sigh. 'Well! To think she knew all along and there's Miss Bentley telling us not to let on. Well, it's not up to us to make her any wiser, poor Agnes. She'd have a stroke if she found out Miss Hester knew.'

Wiston nodded. 'I wonder what will happen to Miss Hester now that master's gone?'

Mrs Crombie shivered. 'The Lord knows. Poor child, I wouldn't be in her shoes, dependent on them upstairs. Thank God, I've m'own two hands to work with,' she added as she bustled back to the kitchen.

Although Hester was relieved not to be asked to accompany them to Baden Baden, nevertheless she was sad. Here was another outcome of her uncle's death: they were, it seemed, no longer a family. Or at least she was not a member of it. Ellen and Wilfred were now the family. She was just a relation. Almost a stranger. It hurt her, but it made her think hard about her future. That she couldn't continue as the daughter of the house was daily becoming obvious. If she continued to live at Stanhope, an embarrassing situation would soon arise. She was almost at the end of her quarterly dress allowance and the necessity of asking Ellen for money filled her with abhorrence.

It was when she was at her lowest, sitting in her bedroom, that she suddenly remembered George Edwardes's card. If you ever want a job, he had said. Her heart lifted, became light and hopeful again. She went into her sitting room and wrote at once to Cissie Bland. Could she come up for a week and stay with her?

Cissie's reply came by return. Sir John was shooting in Northumberland and she was on her own getting her autumn clothes made. She would send Anderson to meet the five o'clock train on the following Thursday.

Hester went rather timidly to see Ellen.

'London again? Lady Bland?' Ellen shrugged. 'Oh, very well. I don't suppose we shall be back for three weeks at least. Do you propose staying so long?'

'I don't think so. But Miss Crook will come and keep me company when I return, I feel sure. You know she is always willing to. I hope you have a lovely holiday in Germany. Don't worry about me at all. There's just one thing. I haven't enough money for the train fare. I've very little of my quarterly allowance left.' She stammered a little. How difficult it was being, asking her aunt for money! She had never felt timid with Uncle Joe – but had she ever needed to ask him? She could not remember one occasion. 'You'll be needing money, my girl,' was how he had put it, digging into his sovereign purse and pouring them into her palm while she feebly protested. There was no doubt Uncle Joe had spoilt her, she told herself wistfully.

Ellen was unpicking yellow ribbon off a black hat; Agnes was to drape it in black crêpe for the journey. Now she held it out to Hester. 'This is what I have to do now I've lost my husband – retrim my old hats. Yes, you may well stare,

291

Hester. There's not the money there was and *you* ought to know the reason why.'

Hester winced. Did her aunt mean that she had cost her uncle too much money to bring up? He had certainly given her the best of everything for over five years. 'I'm very sorry, Aunt Ellen. If we're going to be poor I had better get a job. Wilfred too. I don't suppose he'll be going back to Oxford now?'

'Don't be foolish – of course he is going back. He must get his degree next year. And how you take me up! I didn't mean we were going to be poor – *I* am going to be poorer of course but there, my life is almost over. I hardly matter now. As for getting a job,' she added, seeing Hester was about to speak, 'I should wait and see. There's no sense in rushing things.' She regretted now that she had spoken in the way she had. The girl was such an impulsive creature – just like her silly mother. 'Now you're not to do anything until we return and have talked things over.'

Hester said nothing.

'You had better ask Wilfred to give you some money. If you don't travel first class, you can travel quite cheaply I believe.' Why should we advance the girl more money? she asked herself with a return of bitterness. She's going to be one of the richest women in England – money that's rightly mine and Wilfred's.

Wilfred too gave her mysterious advice as he carefully counted five sovereigns into her palm. 'Now, Hester, don't do anything silly in London, will you? I don't know why you are going back so soon. I shall expect you back on the twentieth. There's a great deal to be talked over: the future and so on. Do nothing until you have seen me again. Do you understand? And whatever you do, travel first class. You are less likely to get molested. Really, Miss Crook ought to be accompanying you, I think.'

'It's nice of you to worry, Wilfred,' Hester said. She smiled affectionately at him. There was no vice in Wilfred; he was just such an old woman that she couldn't help smiling sometimes. 'If I don't turn up again you had better enquire for me in South America – now don't look shocked. Miss Crook has told me all about the White Slavers, you know.' She kissed him lightly and went to pack.

CHAPTER SIX

Cissie was delighted to see her again. Hester's visit was just the distraction she had been looking for. It was very hot in London and the rooms were airless as they sat long over dinner and then talked until midnight in the drawing room. Cissie had been on her own for a fortnight and had had no one to talk to. Talk gushed out of her like water out of a geyser.

'I can't tell you what I felt when I heard about Sir Joseph's death. If John were here he would tell you that I cried – positively *cried*. Your uncle had such charm, you know. He looked at women as if he really liked us. . . .'

'He did,' Hester agreed, smiling. 'He liked women to be pretty and appealing and clinging – he was a trifle old-fashioned, you know.'

'Old-fashioned?' Cissie paused uneasily. 'But I'm all those things! Does that mean I'm old-fashioned too?'

'Yes, Cissie dear, it does, and that's why you are so popular with gentlemen. They admire you for just those qualities. The New Woman stands on her own feet and doesn't wear corsets and smokes. I think it very likely that I shall turn into a new woman. . . .'

'Hes-ter!' Cissie shrieked. 'Don't you dare! It would ruin you. George Edwardes would never have you in his chorus so where will you be then? He is like Sir Joseph was – he likes womanly women,' Cissie ended, tossing her head and eyeing herself in the mirror.

'That reminds me, is he back from abroad yet? Did you find out?'

'No, but we can call round at the Gaiety tomorrow and ask Tierney. The Guv'nor goes on the Continent every summer for about seven or eight weeks, looking for new plays he can turn into a Gaiety burlesque. He finds some stodgy play in Berlin, brings it home and Meyer Lutz composes a score. Then the Guv'nor begins to change the thing scene by scene till its author wouldn't recognize it and that, my dear, is a Gaiety burlesque.' Then she added thoughtfully, 'But you could see Pat Malone – no? Well, I agree. If you have a card from the Guv'nor himself it's better that you see him.'

They called at the Gaiety next day to make sure. There was a new doorman there, a large neatly-dressed man with grey hair, a bulbous nose and a walrus moustache. He and Cissie eyed each other suspiciously. 'Where's Tierney? The poor old darling hasn't died, has he?'

'No, madam. Only retired. I'm James Jupp, late sergeant-major 8th Hussars. Can I be of service in any way?'

'I'm Lady Bland. My friend, Miss Kelsey, has a card to see the Guv'nor – I was in the chorus myself, you know,' Cissie confided.

The late sergeant-major looked appreciatively at the two pretty young women. 'I'm sorry but Mr Edwardes isn't expected until next week. Mr Malone is in. . . . '

'No, we'll call back next week,' Cissie said firmly. It was clear to Hester that she intended managing the whole affair.

Jupp watched them leave. The little milady was very pretty with her bedroom eyes, he thought. The sort to kick up her legs in a good dance. But she wasn't a lady born – that was obvious. Now the other was altogether different. Well-bred and elegant. Looked as if she could open bazaars. Came from a good family, no doubt, and wanted to get in the chorus. Well, they took all sorts at the Gaiety. For his part he preferred the little rogue – and Jupp gave a fruity chuckle before returning to his work.

So there was a week to be got through. The two girls

amused themselves discreetly for Hester was in mourning.

'Black suits you,' Cissie said enviously.

Hester shook her head mutely. Cissie, for all her charm, was insensitive. Didn't she realize that Hester had only to look down at herself to remember her uncle's death? That a great wave of misery overcame her at times because Uncle Joe was dead? The future was uncertain and bound to be different now.

George Edwardes's office was in a side street opposite the Lyceum Theatre where Sir Henry Irving was playing Macbeth. Hester, feeling as if she were going for an operation, showed his card to his secretary. She read the message scrawled on it and then took it across to a man who was sitting at a table littered with manuscripts. He was a handsome man with a handlebar moustache and very blue eyes. When he spoke it was with a pronounced Irish brogue. This was Pat Malone, the Guv'nor's chief assistant.

He came forward and shook her hand, his eyes noticing at once that this beautiful creature was very nervous, in fact was trembling.

'Mr Edwardes is engaged on the telephone at the moment. Please come and sit down.' With practised charm he began to talk to her, drawing her out until she had quite forgotten her nervousness and was laughing with him. By the time the Guv'nor himself came through the door she was completely relaxed and was soon reminding him of their meeting at Lady Bland's. He nodded. 'Miss Hetty Kelly, isn't it?'

Later she was to learn of his inability to remember names. Now she laughed. 'No, Hester Kelsey.' But Hetty Kelly would be a good stage name, she thought mischievously. She realized almost at once that today she was meeting a very different man from the urbane luncheon guest; his eyes were alert under the deceptively drooping lids and there was a hard and decisive note in his voice.

'Come through, please.'

Yes, it was being just like a visit to the doctor's, she thought as she seated herself across the desk. Malone and the secretary, Emilie Reed, had followed and were sitting unobtrusively in the background.

'I usually hold auditions every morning at ten-thirty,' the Guv'nor said. 'But since I asked you to come and see me, I won't ask you to come back tomorrow. Now, let's have a look at you, m'dear.'

She rose to her feet and walked to the spot he indicated. Her heart was beating loudly in her ears as she felt the three pairs of eyes running over her very thoroughly. A faint blush began to stain her skin. Edwardes noticed it and that the skin was warm and moist as a child's. Those eyes – ah, he remembered those eyes in his lucky colour. There was a strength in the mouth and chin that he liked to see. A strong will helped a girl to success, he told himself. She had a beautifully balanced body, that swayed naturally and gracefully as she walked up and down at his behest. Yes, she had the quality that made a man want to sleep with her, he thought, and looked towards Malone to see his thoughts reflected there. 'Why are you wearing black?' he asked her suddenly. It suited the girl, the high collar with its delicate white frill outlining the oval face to advantage. 'Are you in mourning, m'dear?'

'Yes, for my uncle who was my guardian. He died last month.'

And suddenly he remembered everything. Prickard's niece. So the poor little devil had been cast out on the world, had she? And that was why she now wanted a job.

'I should have remembered. I read about it in the papers. He was a good man,' he added soothingly, for the girl's eyes were being hastily lowered. He saw her swallow painfully. 'Would you mind taking your hat off?'

Her hair had no need for the usual 'rats' and frizzling, he noticed with pleasure, being luxuriant and a dark and shining brown. He began to feel mounting interest, even excitement. Here was a girl who, under his guidance, might become a professional beauty and the talk of London. Had she any talent? No matter. She would have to be taught how to make herself instantly noticeable.

George Edwardes knew all about girls – he was a supreme picker of beautiful women; but every time he found a new one, he was filled with fresh excitement.

'Can I see your legs?'

She paused in her walk and regarded him with disbelief.

'Your legs, m'dear.'

She raised her skirt a few inches and pushed out a narrow, elegant foot shod in black glacé kid. A white frill of petticoat coyly concealed her ankle.

'More.'

Four inches of leg emerged. Hester shut her eyes thinking of Ellen's outrage and disgust if she ever discovered that she had shown her leg to a strange gentleman. . . .

'Very nice. But I meant your legs, Miss Kelly. You do possess legs, I suppose?' A little smile softened his words.

She tried to smile back. 'Oh. Oh, yes – my legs.' She raised her skirt a few more inches. Wasn't that enough for the man?

'Up to your knees, Miss Kelly.'

Drawing a deep breath she showed him her legs. I shall just pretend he's the doctor, she told herself firmly.

'Yes, very nice. Excellent. Eh, Pat? Sit down, m'dear.' He sat on the corner of his desk and looked at her kindly. 'I've come to one conclusion: you won't do for my show at the Gaiety.'

Disappointment – sharp as a knife – pierced her. 'I won't?'

'I'm putting on a new production of Cinder-Ellen-up-too-late and I've found a new dance at the Moulin Rouge in Paris that I intend putting in the show.' A quick smile crossed his face. 'It will mean showing a lot of leg! Petticoats and garters will be on display – not your style, Miss Kelly, I'm afraid. But I think my new show at the Prince of Wales will suit you very well. It's what I call a musical-comedy and it will be filled with elegant girls. I think it will be just your cup of tea, Miss Kelly, so if you'll present yourself at the theatre for rehearsal. . . . '

298

'No,' Hester said firmly. 'I'm sorry but I only want to go to the Gaiety. And you're quite wrong about me: I shan't mind showing my legs at all when . . . when I've got used to it. You'll see, I promise you. Please, Mr Edwardes, put me in the Gaiety chorus.'

The Guv'nor's eyes twinkled suddenly. 'Dancing the can-can?'

'Yes,' said Hester firmly. 'I shall be Hetty Kelly and quite a different person then. Anything else will be an anti-climax.'

He began to laugh. 'An anti-climax, she calls it! My beautiful new show at the Prince of Wales!'

'Oh, I didn't mean to be rude but you must understand how I feel,' Hester began.

He waved his hand. 'Yes, yes, I take your point. Eleven o'clock sharp at the Gaiety tomorrow then. Miss Reed will have your contract all ready for signing. Thirty shillings a week I pay my girls, three pounds if they become one of the Big Eight – and that will be up to you, m'dear. Miss Reed, give her the list of lodging houses, will you? I don't suppose Miss Kelly has anything permanently fixed. And before you go, Miss Kelly, let's hear you sing a little song for me. Pat, knock up a number the little girl might know.'

Malone seated himself at a battered piano and she looked through some music and pointed out a song for him to accompany her. If they had asked her to sing ten minutes earlier, she told herself, she would only have been able to croak. Now she began to sing *Ta-ra-ra-boom-de-ay* with verve; for wasn't she almost a Gaiety Girl herself?

Edwardes listened with unconcealed amusement. 'Not bad at all. I can see you know how to sing. Someone teach you?'

'My governess. She's very musical, you know.'

To her amazement, both men burst out laughing. She could see that even the silent Miss Reed was smiling. She shrugged her shoulders – this was a strange new world she was entering and no mistake.

299

She felt very much the new girl when she presented herself at the Gaiety next morning. Jupp was kind and sent a boy to guide her backstage. Everyone was assembled there. She crept on, aware of being stared at by the other young women who all seemed to know each other.

It seemed very strange to be standing on the famous stage and looking down on to the auditorium.

'Ladies!' Malone came on, clapping his hands for silence. 'Mr Edwardes has a new dance routine he wants you to learn. Mr Bertrand is here from the Empire *corps de ballet* and he's brought with him a young lady who will demonstrate the *can-can*.'

The girls gathered round as Mr Bertrand signalled to the pianist and the dancer came on. She wore very full short skirts, black stockings, a very tight bodice cut low and long black gloves. On her head was a plumed hat. To the Girls she looked very odd and Miss Lily May, a tall dark beauty who usually spoke for them all, was heard to say 'Good heavens above!' in a very disdainful voice.

The dance began and Hester caught her breath. Such a display of high kicks and bare thighs she had never seen before. It was danced by the young woman with a bravura that added to the shock. Hester glanced at the others and saw her own stupefaction reflected on their faces. Now the girl was working up to the climax of the dance, stamping and spinning like a top, then whirling round holding out one leg by the ankle. Suddenly she turned, tipped her petticoats over her head and displayed her bottom to the audience before finishing with the splits, her hands high over her head.

'Bravo, my dear!' called the Guv'nor, clapping his hands enthusiastically. 'Now, girls, I want this dance learned in a week so you will have to work hard.' He was chuckling to himself. This girl from the Empire was almost as good as La Goulue at the Moulin Rouge. Seeing La Goulue's performance (sensual and bawdy and drawing huge audiences) had given him the idea of introducing the *chahut* (as it was known in Montmartre) to his own Gaiety Theatre. If only he had a tall male dancer like Valentin-le-Desosse to go with the most talented of his dancers! But he couldn't expect it, and it was enough that he was going to be the first man to introduce the *can-can* to English audiences.

'Mr Edwardes, may I speak to you?' Lily May, wearing Lord Hewlett's diamond engagement ring, had stepped forward. She was elegantly dressed in biscuit silk with black braiding, and the hat on her head would have passed muster at Ascot. She pointed a quivering finger at Daisy Riley from the Empire who was gasping and grinning on the edge of the stage. 'If you expect us to make a display of ourselves *like that* then you are sadly mistaken. Am I not right, girls?'

A murmur of assent answered her.

'Nothing on God's earth will make us do it.'

'No, nothing,' chanted the chorus.

Miss May's eyes sparkled angrily. 'Nothing like this has been seen at the Gaiety before and to expect us to perform this – this *lewd* dance is quite disgraceful. I am speechless.'

'I wish to God you were,' the Guv'nor murmured under his moustache. Zidler of the Moulin Rouge wouldn't put up with Miss May for a minute, he told himself glumly and sighed – he hated scenes. 'Don't you like it, m'dear?'

'It's disgusting. Isn't it, girls?'

'Yes, it's disgusting!'

Mr Bertrand spread his hands and shrugged. Englishwomen; such Puritans. He signalled to Daisy Riley to go and change, and then he walked across to the pianist and prepared to go on with the ordinary work routine. The Guv-'nor watched him, frowning. Bertrand threw his hand in too easily. He would not give way without a fight. . . .

'We quite refuse to do it,' Mis May assured him confidently.

'What if I sack the lot of you? What then?'

Miss May smiled slowly and behind her the others snickered. Where would the Guv'nor get thirty more such beauties before the opening night in four weeks? Get them and train them? *Beauty with class,* one theatre critic had written of them, and they did not want to forget it. They were not the *corps de ballet* at the Empire; hard working professional dancers who sweated it out every night. They were the Gaiety Girls, the darlings of the rich young men who swarmed to see them; they were the young ladies whose dignified bearing turned them in no time into duchesses and marchionesses. That common *can-can* from Montmartre was not for them. The Guv'nor must have been mad to think so.

The Guv'nor sighed sadly. 'Well, Bertrand, what are we to do? I want that dance in my show and they don't want to do it.'

Bertrand nodded wisely. 'Perhaps a more genteel version will be agreeable to the ladies?' He glanced at Lily May who inclined her head.

'A much more genteel version,' she said in an unyielding tone of voice. 'The petticoats not to be lifted higher than the knee. No flesh displayed. And those splits are out – too vulgar.'

The men looked at each other. What was left was a mere drawing room dance. 'Very well, m'dear,' the Guv'nor conceded.

Mr Bertrand clapped his hands. 'Five minutes only for you to change out of your street clothes! I promise you that you are going to work at this dance until it is almost as good as the original – but without legs,' he added hastily, meeting Miss May's steely eye.

Dearest Aunt Ellen,
I hope this won't be too much of a shock but I shall not be returning to Stanhope as I have got a job. I am now in the chorus of the Gaiety Theatre – I still can hardly believe it, I am at present with Cissie and looking for lodgings. . . .

Ellen gave a gasp and cast the letter from her. Leaning over, she pulled hard on the bell and when Agnes appeared she said hastily, 'Ask Sir Wilfred to come and see me at once. Tell him it's urgent.'

Wilfred groaned when he got the message. He was in the middle of his usual large breakfast, but threw down his napkin and stalked in a martyred fashion to his mother's bedroom. He was beginning to find her rather a trial to live with. The German holiday had not been an unqualified success. She had been didactic and difficult and had made him feel like a small child again. There had been a charming young Austrian count at the hotel with whom he had struck up a quick friendship; but his mother had taken a dislike to Count Blomberg and had ruined everything. In short, she had been a nuisance. So he stood in her bedroom and scowled sulkily.

'There! Read that.'

Wilfred's expression changed as he read Hester's letter. 'In the *chorus?*' he said in a high voice of indignation. 'She must be mad! Tell her to come home at once, Mama. I can't have my cousin in the chorus!' He looked at his mother accusingly. 'There you are – we should have told her about her inheritance before she left. There's a letter from Owen-Davies for her downstairs – no one has thought of sending it on. I shall go up to London tomorrow and see her. She will have to come home of course.'

'Oh, Wilfred, you can't leave me on my own! Send her a telegram. Both of you deserting me at a time like this – ' Ellen wept, holding a handkerchief to her eyes. There was more in the same vein, but Wilfred was learning to withstand his mother now. He sent Hester a telegram, but only to tell her he would call on her in two days time. He would stay at his club (of which he was now a very new member) and have some fun, he told himself, before going back to Oxford. Heaven knows he deserved some after that dreadful month in Germany.

Cissie Bland had no time to be bored now. Sir John wrote to tell her he would be back at the end of the week, and she telegraphed him not to hurry home on her account. In fact, she told Hester, his arrival would be rather a nuisance now

303

when she was suddenly so busy hunting for lodgings for her friend. Every morning, she and Hester set off with a list of lodgings to be inspected. Just before eleven, Hester was dropped at the Gaiety and Cissie continued the search on her own, enjoying every minute of it and remembering wistfully the years when she had been a Gaiety Girl and Lord Dover had been so ardent.

After three days, Hester felt quite an old hand as she signed Jupp's book and ran up the stone stairs. She tried not to notice that her muscles were aching alarmingly. Mr Bertrand came in each morning to teach the chorus and he was very exacting. Sometimes the girls had to grit their teeth, the muscular pain was so bad; but Bertrand only told them scornfully that they were all too fat and lazy. 'But it is coming – ah, yes, we have a good dance,' he beamed at the end of the morning.

Hester shared a dressing-room with two other girls. Katy Cochran was a jolly little brunette with a sunny nature that nothing seemed to spoil. But Belle Collins was a cold Nordic blonde who had taken an instant dislike to the new member of the chorus and spent her time goading her. At first Hester had been glad to find a girl she knew and reminded Belle that they had met before. She shrugged and said nothing, but her eyes were full of spite. Keeping out of Belle's way soon became Hester's most compelling task.

The producer in the early stages of rehearsal was Pat Malone. George Edwardes came in now and again and sat in the front stalls, changing everything that had been done so far. 'Now, you're all good boys and girls,' he told the cast warmly, 'but we're going to have to quicken the pace. Let's cut a few lines and see how we go, eh?' Sometimes rehearsals went on in to the evening when the Guv'nor took over. When that happened, they all got extra pay. He also saw that everyone ate well. Buns and tea didn't produce beautiful women, he told his girls, and arranged for them to eat for half-price at Romano's.

Hester liked the evenings when they ended up at Romano's. Every one stared openly at the Gaiety Girls and many young men tried to scrape up an acquaintance; but they got short shrift from the older members of the cast who were in charge. There was always a very mixed crowd in for supper: racing men, journalists, soldiers and young peers; the staff of the Pink'un even had their own table. The girls wore their most beautiful dresses and no one would ever guess that they had been working hard all day and that they ached with fatigue.

The new *Cinder-Ellen* (the show that had got off to such a bad start eighteen months ago) promised to be a great success. There were new clothes, new songs and a new star! Letty Lind was one of a talented band of five sisters who were all on the stage. She was small and pretty, with a tiny little voice and a huge personality that reached out over the footlights and quickly brought her fame. Opposite her, Fred Leslie was to play his old role. Dark, thin and handsome, he had great charm and the Gaiety Girls adored him. He tried (not very successfully) to hide the fact that he suffered chronic indigestion and stomach pains. It was known that George Edwardes was uneasy about him; but Fred laughed it off and sang and danced with all his old verve.

On the morning of the fourth day of Hester's new life, Wilfred arrived. Hester, summoned from her room, went down to meet him wearing a stubborn expression. If he had come to take her home he was in for a shock, she told herself belligerently.

But Wilfred greeted her mildly and sat for ten minutes boring them with his account of four weeks at Baden Baden. It was only when Cissie left the room that he produced a letter and put it in his cousin's hand. 'This came for you. I know all about it, but it will probably come as a big surprise to you.'

The envelope was large and had the name of a firm embossed on its flap. She opened it wonderingly and drew out a letter with a cheque pinned to it. The cheque was for £2,000. She gasped and read the letter quickly. Then again. Then she looked up. 'But I don't understand.'

Wilfred smiled indulgently. 'Oh, come, Hester, it's simple

enough. You and I are the new joint owners of the Prickard Line. You're rich. That cheque is only the beginning. There'll be lots more before long.'

Her mouth was dry. 'It can't be true! Why? I don't know anything about business. . . .'

'Of course not, silly.' Wilfred was feeling warmly superior. 'You don't have to. Munro will look after it for us. Of course when I come down from Oxford I shall work in the firm. I think I might open a new branch office here. I know Father was thinking of it. But you don't have to do anything; you're just a sleeping partner,' Wilfred added loftily.

She was silent for a moment or two, staring at him with large eyes, the letter clutched to her. The cheque, he noticed impatiently, she had torn off and it had floated down on the carpet. Retrieving it, he placed it reproachfully in her unresisting hand.

She was thinking that she knew why her uncle had done this strange thing and made her an equal partner with Wilfred. It was to ensure that she remained a member of the family, that with his death she didn't drift away and become lost to them. Tears flooded her eyes. He had treated her exactly as if she had been his own daughter, she thought gratefully.

'For heavens sake, don't blub, Hester! What a one you are for the waterworks!' Wilfred shook his head at her. 'Most girls would be dancing for joy instead of leaking like you.'

'Do you mind about this, Wilfred?'

'Mind? Not in the least,' Wilfred said and to his surprise found it was true. Away from his mother, he felt no animosity toward Hester. In fact, he was beginning to think it was a jolly good idea of the pater's. Hester wasn't a bad sort. They had always got on and, after all, there was a great deal of money to be divided between them.

'Does it mean I can buy a house?'

'Half a dozen,' Wilfred assured her, waving his hand.

She jumped up and kissed him. He stiffened and drew back as he always did if one touched him, Hester noticed.

306

What a funny fellow he was, she thought affectionately.
'Then will you come and find one for me? Cissie and I had no
luck looking for lodgings, so I'm sure we shan't do much
better finding a little house for me. I mean to ask Miss Crook
to come and live with me – I'm sure she would.'

'You're not going on with that Gaiety nonsense, are you?'

She nodded her head vigorously, her mouth smiling. He
got up, shaking his head, and retrieved his hat and gloves.
'You'll soon tire of it,' he predicted confidently.

The little period house in Markham Square was desperately
shabby. It had been empty for nearly a year and the mice and
spiders had taken over. It had a dark green front door with a
lion's head knocker, dark green peeling railings and two
steps worn in the middle. 'This won't do,' Cissie said deci-
sively.

But Hester was already unlocking the door and entering
into her kingdom. Without seeing it, she knew she had come
home. After a week's fruitless search, Wilfred had given up
and gone back to Yorkshire. But the two girls had gone on
doggedly each morning and Hester had shaken her head at
every house. Until this one. She turned round and beckoned
Cissie, her face full of mysterious excitement. The little
house smelled of mice, but it was dry and it welcomed her.
The rooms were small with carved ceilings, and there was a
most unusual drawing room on the upper floor that stretched
from front to back, and had a pair of glass doors that opened
on to a roof garden. Hester knew at once that she must have
it.

'How much did that man at the agency say the people were
asking for this place?' Cissie asked. '£800? What a scandal –
daylight robbery I call it. If you really feel you must have it –
I don't think much of it myself – then you could offer him
£600. I'm sure John would think that too much,' she added
virtuously.

Hester smiled for she had noticed how Cissie (who never

mentioned her husband most days) was now continually dragging his name into the conversation to reinforce her points; especially to discourage. All Hester knew was that she must have the house at any price. She loved it already.

That evening, the house secured, she sat up late writing to Miss Crook. Sir John had given her a stamp and it went off first thing the next morning. Three days later, Miss Crook arrived in London accompanied by seven trunks – two of her own and five of Hester's. An army of women were scrubbing out the house and William Whiteley, the Universal Provider, had sent round two men to lay carpets. A long column of Whiteley's carts and boys on bicycles delivered everything that was needed for a home. When the curtains were up, Miss Crook sent round to the local domestic agency to secure a cook and a couple of girls. While she was interviewing them, Hester went round her domain in a happy dream. This doll's house was hers – her very own. The little dining room had dark red paper on its walls and chintz curtains covered with roses and green leaves. Upstairs, the drawing room was full of sunshine, encouraged by dark gold walls and yellow and white curtains. The windows on to the roof garden were open and Hester filled her small watering can and tenderly watered the plants. Next spring she would have jasmine and roses here, she promised herself. Then she sat down on the little iron seat and dreamed again. To be free, to have her own home and to have darling Miss Crook to share it – yes, she was happy, she assured herself.

But then a wistful look crept over her face. What if she was sharing this with Victor? That would be true happiness – that would be a dream fulfilled. Victor. He would be back at Oxford next week and Wilfred would be seeing him. Would he ask after her? Would he even remember her? she wondered with sudden bitterness.

Two days later, eating a hasty breakfast before taking a cab to the Gaiety, she opened the *Morning Post* and saw the announcement of his engagement to Connie Courage.

'Hester, you really must eat something,' Miss Crook scolded. 'What has happened to your appetite? The show opens tomorrow and you won't have the strength to dance.'

To pacify her, Hester buttered a piece of toast. There was to be a full dress rehearsal that afternoon so for once she was home for lunch. Feeling Miss Crook's eye still on her, she took a spoonful of soup. But for days she had hardly been able to swallow. The hope that had kept her going, the hope of meeting Victor again had melted away for good. He was to marry Connie Courage. Lying sleepless in bed at night she kept on repeating, 'But he loves me – I know he does – he loves *me*.' Her bitter unhappiness haunted her eyes; there were dark shadows under them and she was very quiet.

'I think all this has been too much for you,' went on Miss Crook. 'If your health is going to suffer, then you should leave the Gaiety. That man sounds a slave-driver – Hester! you haven't touched it,' she added, as the parlourmaid (a stout Cockney girl called Sarah) removed the plates. Then she stopped, for she saw that Hester was trying valiantly not to break down in front of the servant. 'Don't bring the next course until I ring, Sarah, please.' As the door closed, Miss Crook got up and took a chair nearer Hester. 'I don't want to nag you, my dear, but you're not eating enough to keep a fly alive. Won't you tell me what is wrong?'

It was a relief to do so, Hester found. Miss Crook listened in silence. Then she said musingly 'One wonders why it has to be; but everyone has at least one unhappy love affair in their lives. Even I! I was very much in love with a gentleman who was a friend of my brother's. He married someone else and I thought that life was finished. But it wasn't. There was still so much happiness to be found that presently I hardly thought at all about my trouble, and after a few months I was ashamed to find that I had forgotten him. I worked hard and gave myself no time to think, and pride forced me not to ruin my health or spoil my looks just because one man did not love me enough.'

Hester wiped her eyes. 'As I am doing,' she agreed with a sniff. 'But I'm not hungry – truly.'

'Nonsense,' said Miss Crook briskly and rang the bell. 'Roast lamb is your favourite. Eat a little, my dear, and tell me if you don't feel better afterwards. It's wonderful how much easier it is to bear our troubles on a full stomach.'

The dress rehearsal that afternoon taxed everyone's endurance. Seated in the middle of the stalls, George Edwardes proceeded to make changes. Lines of dialogue were altered, entrances were delayed and for one scene he calmly proceeded to include a dance and a song. It was no wonder that Malone's eyes smouldered like coal in his pale face and Meyer Lutz, the composer and conductor, threw a temperament and threatened to walk out.

'You've all been such good boys and girls,' the Guv'nor announced before he sent them home, 'that I'm going to give you all an extra week's salary. Make a note, Miss Reed. Now, goodbye everyone. Early to bed tonight, eh?'

There were butterflies in Hester's stomach when she arrived at the theatre next evening. Long queues for the gallery had already formed and there was an air of excitement in the dressing rooms. The girls had seen huge bouquets arriving and being piled up near the stage door; but they knew that Jupp wouldn't let them have them until the show was over.

Hester wished she had persuaded Wilfred to come up from Oxford and to bring friends. But the Blands had taken a box, and had invited several friends and Miss Crook to share it with them. Afterwards they were all going to dine at the Savoy.

It was one thing to dance to an empty theatre, she found, and quite another with the rows of expectant faces turned towards the stage. Hester forced herself to look out on the sea of faces as she turned and swayed and strutted to the music. Dressed as shepherdesses, as friends of Cinder-Ellen's and finally in the decorous *can-can* at the end, they went through their paces. Letty Lind and Fred Leslie were a perfect team and the house rose to them. But as Hester passed Leslie in the wings at the end of their dance, she saw his terrible pallor and the sweat pouring down his face. He smiled courteously and charmingly at the girls and assured them they had been 'absolutely bewitching, my darlings'.

'He's a nice bloke,' Katy said warmly as they took off their make-up and costumes at the end, 'but I know the Guv'nor's worried stiff about him. He might caper about all right on the stage, but afterwards he looks fit to pass out. Let's hope nothing nasty happens to ruin a nice long run for the show. . . .'

'You're a comfort,' Belle grunted, struggling into her day dress.

'Hey, aren't you going to celebrate, Belle?'

'No, got to get home. So long, girls.'

'It's because of her little girl,' Katy said. 'She's been left to bring her up. Her husband went off to Australia with the company three years ago and never came back. Touring in *Little Jack Shepherd* they were – men! We're daft to marry, I always say. You watch it, young Hester. Let 'em take you out to the Savoy Grill or the Café Royal and give you a nice apartment and a string of pearls but *don't marry them*. Once they've given you a child, they lose interest in you and are off after another pair of bright eyes.'

Hester wondered if Katy spoke from experience herself. She was older than either herself or Belle and lived in dread of losing her job in the chorus. It was strange that, despite their closeness in the last few weeks, none of them really knew anything about the other.

'My, but you look like a young duchess,' Katy added generously when Hester had changed. 'I like those glass things in your hair.'

Glass things! Patting the ruby and diamond butterflies into place Hester said 'You look lovely too, Katy. Who is taking you to supper?'

'Heavens, I don't know,' said Katy. 'I shall have to see who's waiting in the hall. Don't forget to ask if there are any flowers for you, will you?'

Left alone in the dressing room, Hester looked round on the unshaded lights, the tins of greasepaint, the cold cups of tea and all the muddle left for the dressers to clear up. 'I'm a pro,' she said aloud and felt the first surge of happiness for days.

Going home in a cab from the Savoy at dawn, she was startled to see early editions of the papers were on the streets, and to read on the flapping posters that Tennyson was dying.

'He is old, of course,' Miss Crook said sadly. 'But what a shock to the nation!'

CHAPTER SEVEN

By the end of the first week of *Cinder-Ellen* the whole company felt rather jaded. The show was a success and reaction had set in. Now everyone had something they wished to bring to the notice of the Guv'nor. Even George Edwardes's easy-going temperament must have been tried at times by the small squabbles that broke out.

Unlike Katy, Belle was unfriendly and seemed to resent the presence of the new girl in their dressing room. She seemed unable to leave her alone. She teased her and pushed her into the smallest space on the dressing shelf; so that Hester had to make up with only three inches of mirror. Blatantly, without asking, Belle made use of Hester's possessions: her brush would disappear, her powder puff, the small housewife she kept for running repairs – anything and everything that Belle needed she took and didn't return. And it was never taken from Katy; only from Hester.

Hester, never good at pouring oil on troubled waters, stood up boldly to the dressing room bully, seeing in the tall Nordic-looking girl the face of Aunt Agatha who had also enjoyed bullying. It was a pity that the beautiful Belle with the ethereal face should be so detestable, she thought one evening as she stepped out of her skirt and into the frilly petticoats of her can-can costume, the last item of the programme every night. Hurriedly, she did up the hooks and eyes, then the small buttons. There was a loose blouse next and over this a red and striped corselet top. It was not an easy costume to put on in ten minutes, with the dressers running from room to room and with never enough of them or of time.

Belle was always ready first. Now she stepped over to Hester's chair and picked up her underwear. 'I never saw such drawers in all my life,' Belle said scornfully.

Still busy changing, Katy and Hester turned and stared at the pair of drawers Belle held in her hands. Katy thought they were particularly nice drawers in finest Swiss cotton with pale blue threaded ribbon and three rows of frills around each leg. Hester was so used to them that she could not for the life of her see what Belle found to criticize. Ellen and Agnes had spent five years impressing on her that a lady was known by her drawers and petticoat, that a lady must be as well-dressed underneath as on top, that fine lace and embroidery and tiny pearl buttons were absolute essentials.

'Don't tell me you came by them honestly!'

Hester's head jerked up. 'What do you mean?'

'Oh, I've offended our Miss Goody-Goody have I?' She scornfully pointed to the lace on the drawers. 'Don't tell me you bought these on your salary, ducks. A nice gentleman, was he? Old perhaps, but with plenty of golden boys to spend on little Hetty? He would be just your type, Miss Hetty-head-in-air!' With a jerk of the hand she ripped all the lace off one leg.

Hester sprang at the mocking face and pulled at the carefully piled-up hair. Hairpins were showered in all directions as the heavy golden mass collapsed round Belle's shoulders.

'Girls! Girls!' Katy interposed urgently. 'We've only got a couple of minutes to curtain call. . . .'

But they were locked in battle and deaf to her entreaties. Belle was giving little screams of rage and Hester was breathing hard, as all the frustration of the past weeks came to a head in the most primitive of fashions. Then, bunching her small fist, Belle brought it down with a resounding crack on the side of Hester's face.

Hester sat down hard on the floor, her hand to her face. Her head rang and she could see stars before her eyes. 'Oh, you vixen! You've broken my nose!'

'Just look what you've done, Belle!' Katy was on her knees inspecting the damage. Blood was pouring from Hester's nose and spilling on to the white blouse, so Katy snatched up a towel and attempted to stem the flow. Between them, they plucked Hester off the floor and propped her against the wall where she visibly sagged. 'Get me the cottonwool – Mr Malone's going to wring both your necks for this – just see if he doesn't. Now, Hetty, stop wailing – you're not really hurt and anyway you shouldn't have pulled Belle's hair down. Belle, push that cottonwool up her nose and help to fasten her bodice.'

'Oh, my God,' Belle faltered, 'she's got blood on the bodice – what shall we do?'

Both girls seemed dazed by what had happened and it was left to Katy to direct operations. With urgent hands, she and Belle finished dressing Hester just as the call boy came along the corridor banging on all the doors and calling out.

'You don't look too bad,' Katy said breathlessly, pushing Hester before her down the spiral staircase to the wings. 'Keep the cottonwool in your nose whatever you do, Hetty.'

They reached the wings. There was the brilliantly-lit stage awaiting them for the finale. Crash! went the music as, arms entwined, they pranced on to the stage and began to kick their legs in the air. In half a minute the plug of cottonwool had fallen out of Hester's nostril and blood began to pour down in earnest. She was choking with it – pulling herself free she fled into the wings and into Malone's iron grasp.

'What's this? What have you done?' he demanded unsympathetically. 'Good God, what a mess! Where's Jordy? Tell her to get an ice pack for Hetty – the girl's bleeding like a pig.'

Lying on the horsehair sofa in the dressing room, Hester allowed herself a few self-pitying tears as Jordy, clucking like a metronome, put an ice pack on her face. 'My, you're going to have a black face tomorrow,' she predicted ghoulishly, 'Mr Malone, I reckon this girl's been fighting,' she said to the producer as he looked round the door again. 'I know a bloody nose when I see one.'

315

'Well, have you?' His hard cool eyes raked her.

She nodded miserably.

'Who with? Don't pretend you walked into a door for I shall soon find out the truth. All three of you who share this room will come to my office before the performance tomorrow night. Now you had better go straight home before the others come off-stage.'

Hester was only too glad to make her escape. Barely dressed she threw her evening cloak on and tied a shawl round her face. Nursing her sore face she got into a fly. 'Got the tooth-ache, have yer?' the sympathetic cabby asked her. 'Best to have it out, that's wot I say.'

Miss Crook was sewing in front of the drawing room fire. She sprang up in alarm when Hester came into the room. 'My dear girl, what has happened? Lie down on this comfortable sofa and I'll get Sarah to fetch you some tea before she goes up to bed. You're home early tonight, no, don't try and talk,' she added as the blood began to flow again as Hester struggled upright.

After tea and toast and a great deal of sympathy, Hester began to feel better.

'That young woman should be ashamed of herself,' Miss Crook said indignantly, when she had heard the story.

'But I did pull her hair.'

'Yes, and showed a sad lack of control, Hester. But that caused no blood to flow. I'm afraid you're among a rough lot of young women. . . .'

'Truly, they're not! Most of them are awfully nice. It's only Belle Collins. She detests me. I think she's an unhappy girl — she never smiles and makes jokes like Katy. Well, I shall probably get the sack tomorrow,' she finished gloomily and began to shed more tears. What an ignominious way to end a short career at the Gaiety — sacked for fighting. She could hardly sleep all night for thinking about it.

But apart from being dressed down with a few crisp words from Malone, nothing much happened. He fined her and

Belle (because he had of course found out the whole story) a week's wages and sent them away.

'Thank God it's no worse,' Katy commented as they finished changing into their shepherdess costumes.

'We've been lucky,' Hester agreed.

Belle said nothing. But at the end of the evening's performance they found her in tears, huddled on the sofa and not bothering to clean the greasepaint off her face.

'Now what's all this?' Katy demanded, giving her a little shake. 'It's not like you to make a fuss over nothing, Belle. Malone will have forgotten it all by tomorrow. There's nothing to worry about.'

Belle uncovered her ravaged face. 'That's all very well, Katy Cochrane, but who's going to buy my child food? Who's going to pay my rent? I owe for last week as it is. I had to buy boots for Posy – oh, a dozen things. Lamp for the heater. That room we've got is like a morgue this weather.' Tears began to rain down her cheeks again.

Hester bit her lip, her eyes meeting Katy's warning ones. Don't sympathize, Katy's eyes telegraphed. So she finished dressing and said goodnight. But she didn't go down into the hall. Instead she waited for Katy to join her and they walked down the cold corridor together. 'Where does Belle live? I'd like to go and see her tomorrow morning.'

'What? Put your head in the lion's mouth?' Katy stopped dead and laughed. 'Well, I'll say this Hetty, you're a devil for punishment. If you offer to lend Belle money, she'll kill you!'

'I wouldn't be such a fool. I know what Belle's like. But I've an idea I can help her another way. I feel responsible, you see.'

Katy shrugged. 'Don't say I didn't warn you. Well, ta-ta, dear, I can see my escort waiting for me.' She ran lightly down the stairs and warmly greeted a chinless young man in an evening cloak. Most of the girls had escorts that evening for supper at Romano's or the Savoy Grill. There were many other young men standing under the gas jets watching

317

the girls leave but they knew better than to accost any. It was only by a proper introduction that they could meet the Guv-nor's Girls, and Jupp had an eagle eye for any who tried to take a short cut. So although they looked eagerly at Hester as she hurried past them to her waiting cab, no one dared approach her and she sank thankfully into its dark interior, hiding her bruised face under a silk shawl. It had been easy enough to disguise it under greasepaint but, uncovered, there was a dark green bruise from nose to eye.

Miss Crook was already in the dining room when she got home at eleven-thirty and the meal, a light supper with white wine and fruit, was on the table. As they ate and talked together, Hester found her idea growing in her mind. Presently she revealed it to Miss Crook and to her relief found her enthusiastic. 'I'll go and see Belle tomorrow morning then,' she said.

The house where Belle lived turned out to be a shabby slice of a house squeezed between two larger ones. It had peeling railings and a front door standing permanently open to the street. Urchins played on its six dirty steps. The railed-off area was full of rubbish and a sign in the window proclaimed *Rooms to Let*.

Hester picked up her skirt and, passing the staring children, boldly entered the hall. It smelled vilely of dry rot, rats and dirt.

A bedraggled old woman lumbered out of a door and stared suspiciously. 'Wot you want?' Wisps of greasy hair fell from a man's cap worn back to front and a coarse apron was pinned to her bulky bosom. Her bare hands were wet and scarlet to the elbows and she smelled like the house.

'I'm looking for Mrs Belle Collins – does she live here?'

'Oh, 'er. You another of them actresses, are you? Them and their fancy clothes and not a penny to rub together. . . .'

Hester looked the woman up and down, assuming a haughty air. 'I am the Marchioness of Sewerston,' she said disdainfully. Extracting half a crown she offered it with the tips of her fingers. 'Show me her room and quickly.'

The woman cringed as Hester had guessed she would. Bobbing a curtsey, she went to the foot of the stairs and pointed. 'Second floor on left.' Then she made off with her half-crown, whining, 'Mrs Collins owes me for the rent. I'm a poor old woman and I don't like being cheated. . . . ' Her grumbling voice faded as she returned to her lair; but Hester noticed she left the door ajar – no one would leave without the landlady's knowledge.

The landing was uncarpeted and very dirty like the stairs. A small grimy window was the only point of light. What a place, Hester thought, as she found the right door. How much worse London slums were than Sewerston's! Rapping on the door, she waited.

The door was thrown open defiantly. 'I've told you already – oh, it's you,' Belle broke off and stared. A little girl clung to her skirts, one thumb firmly fixed in her mouth. Belle looked as if she had been crying – she certainly did not look her usual elegant self. Her hastily pinned-up hair straggled across her face and she wore a large apron over a shabby brown dress. 'What do you want?' she demanded aggressively.

'Behold, the Marchioness of Sewerston,' Hester announced and minced past her reluctant hostess. 'Or so I told the old hag downstairs! I had her eating out of my hand at the sight of half a crown and an air of disdain. Oh, can I come in, by the way?'

Belle shrugged, banging the door behind her. 'If you can find anywhere to sit in this dump . . . I'm packing.'

'I'm glad to hear that,' Hester said briskly. 'This is a hell-hole.' She took off her gloves and held out a hand to the child. 'What's your name? Shall I guess? Jemima? Hilda? Mary?'

The child's scared face broke into a smile. She removed the thumb from her mouth. 'Posy.' She had a pale and delicate little face and looked about three years old.

'Her name's Primrose.' Belle thrust a hairpin back into her hair with a gesture of utter weariness as she sank down on the bed. It was a sparsely furnished room but very clean; in sharp contrast to what Hester had seen of the house. She remembered from the past how difficult it was to keep a place clean when there was no water except one cold tap downstairs. Yet the room smelled fresh and aired, and never had she seen Belle anything but dainty and fresh. She wondered how on earth she had managed it, living here.

The child had come to lean against Hester's knee, to finger the dark green silk braiding of her costume. 'Pretty,' she murmured.

Belle smiled tenderly at her child. 'She loves pretty things,' she said. 'Not that she sees many.'

'She's too pale, Belle.'

The old angry look returned to Belle's face. 'Well, what do you expect, you fool? She hardly ever goes out unless I take her before I go to the theatre. I have to leave her with that old bitch downstairs who takes my money and keeps her prisoner in this terrible house. I believe she doesn't even give her the food I provide but eats it herself.'

'You don't leave her with that dreadful woman, do you?'

'What else am I to do? But that's all come to an end now. I owe two weeks rent and she says I've got to go. God knows where. I was going to ask the Guv'nor to help me but – well – having just blotted my copybook I felt I shouldn't ask him for a loan. It would have cancelled out the week's salary Malone had just docked.' Rather ashamedly, she inspected her visitor's face. 'God, that was a black eye I gave you! You must bruise easily. . . .'

'Bruise easily! You hit me with your bare fist and now say I bruise easily! That's why I'm wearing this veil – still I didn't come here to reproach you. . . .'

'I should hope not! You started it. . . .'

'*Belle!* Shut up there's a good girl or we'll start all over again. When are you leaving? Today? Good, because I've come to ask you to join us.'

'Join you?' Belle asked suspiciously.

'Yes. My friend Miss Crook has a charming small house in Chelsea and she has a room to spare which she's willing to give to you and Posy.'

'What is she? The madam of a bordello?' Belle sneered.

Hester's hand itched to slap that sneer off. What an impossible and prickly person Belle Collins was! 'If you knew Miss Crook you wouldn't suggest such a thing. She's just – philanthropic. She is also rich enough to indulge her whim of having people like us to stay with her. It won't cost you a penny.'

For once Belle was speechless.

'Of course you can leave as soon as you find another apartment,' Hester went on. 'It will just be a breathing space while you look round. I like it there so I don't see why you shouldn't. It's near the park and there's a safe garden in the centre of the square where she can play. Think of Posy, Belle,' she added, picking up the child and hugging the thin little body close. 'Think how much better it will be for her.'

Belle's mouth began to quiver and suddenly she was sobbing into her hands. 'Oh, God, it's been an impossible dream to me! A decent place for Posy – someone kind to care for her when I'm not there. I've dreaded having to go on tour. . . . ' Her voice became incoherent.

Hester walked to the window and lifted the child in her arms to look out on the drab roofs, pointing to a pair of pigeons strutting and cooing along a gutter. 'Cushats,' Posy said pointing. 'Mrs Flanagan calls them cushats.' Her clear precise speech amused Hester.

'How old are you, Posy?'

'I'm four – aren't I, Mama? Four last birthday.'

'Yes, love.' Belle had blown her nose and was composed again. She joined them in the window. 'My mother used to look after Posy,' she said. 'Then she died this spring and I was left on my own – *he* went years ago,' and she nodded towards a photograph she had been about to pack.

Hester could see the likeness to the child in the large eyes of the man who was her father. But he had a weak mouth under his silky moustache. But for the moustache it would have been a girlish face.

'That's my papa,' Posy said pointing. She struggled out of Hester's arms to go across to the picture.

'He left me before she was born,' Belle said in a low voice. 'We were out in Australia touring in *Little Jack Shepherd* with Nellie Farren and Fred Leslie. He married me when he knew I was pregnant, then he ran off and left the show.' She shrugged. 'Australia's a good country to lose yourself in. I'll not see him again.' As she went to close the lid of the portmanteau on the bed she suddenly confronted Hester, her face suspicious and wary again. 'You're not paying for me at this Miss Crook's, are you? For I won't have that.'

'Now how on earth could I on thirty shillings a week? Don't be idiotic. I've got a cab outside. Put on your hat, Belle. Where's Posy's jacket? And look,' she opened her purse, 'Miss Crook sent this to pay the back rent if any – go on, Belle, it's only a couple of sovereigns.'

'I can see you ending in the Poor House. You don't know the meaning of money,' Belle scolded. 'A cab waiting, if you please.' She looked round hastily. 'I'm not leaving that old skinflint anything she can take to the pawnbroker,' she explained and Hester burst out laughing. Belle frowned at her, then reluctantly began to chuckle with her. Laughing together (even Posy laughed and clapped her hands) they shut the door on the unsavoury little room.

The cab ride was a delightful treat to Posy. She craned her head to watch every passing horse and carriage; to point at the dogs being exercised by their owners. When they turned into the square, a barrel organ happened to be playing. Her cheeks became quite scarlet with excitement for there was a little monkey in a yellow fez!

When Belle saw the house in Markham Square, a small sigh of relief escaped her; it wasn't imposing at all, just a snug little house with a fat and smiling parlourmaid in starched cap and apron opening the door to them. Upstairs in the drawing room a small white-haired woman rose to greet them. She had kind eyes behind pince-nez and in next to no time Posy was showing her a prized doll that was called Gertrude and had real hair. Tea was waiting with boiled eggs and muffins and strawberry jam, for the new arrivals would be hungry after their journey, Miss Crook said tactfully.

Posy ate her food with pathetic eagerness and drank two cups of milk laced with tea. Then she curled up on the sofa with Gertrude and fell asleep while the three women talked together in the firelight. Soon it was time for the girls to leave for the theatre; but first Belle carried Posy to the new drop-sided cot beside her bed and undressed her without waking her. Miss Crook said the door would be left ajar and a night-light burning in a saucer. 'Don't worry, my dear, I shall look after her but I don't think she will wake.'

Belle tried to express gratitude but Miss Crook seemed embarrassed; so she contented herself with saying earnestly that Miss Crook was a human sort of angel.

'Belle's moved into my lodgings,' Hester told Katy as they made up in the dressing room. 'With her child.'

Katy's mouth fell open. She gazed at Hester. It was evident that she found the news astounding to say the least.

On Saturdays, the Gaiety played to capacity houses and although the show ended at eleven o'clock, most of the girls did not get home until one or two in the morning. They were usually taken out to a light supper of foie gras, chicken and champagne at Romano's or the Café Royal. Then a private carriage would take them home and, although they might allow their hands to be kissed on parting, no young men were allowed inside their houses.

There was extra verve in the *can-can* on Saturday nights. A whole day and a half of delicious leisure lay ahead. So they kicked and tossed their heads while sweat glistened on their breasts. And when the audience roared 'Encore!' they went into the routine all over again.

One Saturday night early in November, they ran off the stage to find real drama in the wings. Fred Leslie, the male star of the show, was lying on the floor among the stage props at the feet of a dozen helpless onlookers. He was trying to bite off groans and his eyes were closed in his ashen face. Ten minutes earlier, he had been out there raising laughs and sighs; now looking old under the greasepaint, he was in obvious agony.

Letty Lind was on her knees beside him, still in her gorgeous ball dress as Cinder-Ellen. 'Oh, Fred! Oh, Fred!' she cried. 'Oh, Guv'nor, thank God, you've come! What shall we do?'

'Keep calm, m'dear. I've sent for my doctor and he'll be here any minute now.' George Edwardes raised Letty Lind and supported her. 'Now, you run along, little girl, and we'll see to Fred.'

Pat Malone chivvied the gaping chorus. 'Get to your dressing rooms, you girls. There's nothing you can do here.'

They went, their tongues silent for once. 'What will happen to the show if Fred's ill?' Belle whispered inside the dressing room.

'There's Willie Drew, his understudy. . . .'

'Him? People aren't going to pay to see him – it's Fred they love. The Guv'nor will have to get another big name or we'll fold.'

'Perhaps he'll be better by Monday?' Hester suggested.

The others withered her with their looks. 'If there's one thing I can't stand it's a bright and cheerful face at the sight of disaster,' Katy said caustically. 'It's obvious you're new to the business, Hetty, or you'd be smelling ruin like Belle and me.' She thrust a flower into her hair and regarded herself in the mirror. 'Well, I must go. I've got my Russian count waiting downstairs. He *says* he's cousin to the Tsar. Think it's true? I like this thing he gave me,' she added and held out the flashing pendant that was suspended round her neck. Belle inspected it as well while they debated whether or not the bauble was real. Behind them, Hester smothered a laugh. They pretended they knew everything, these Gaiety Girls with their Russian counts and peers waiting humbly to take them to supper; but they didn't know a real, enormous diamond when they saw one on the end of a gold chain.

'Depend upon it, it's paste,' Belle assured Katy. 'Still, it looks good and who's to know?'

As usual, Miss Crook was waiting up for them with a hot meal and Hester went in to the dining room with her. She was telling her about Fred Leslie when Belle, who had gone to look at Posy, came in and said, 'Hetty, have you left your window open upstairs? There's a draught wailing like a banshee under your bedroom door.'

'I haven't been up,' Hester said, helping herself to rabbit pie.

'It's very unlike Sarah to leave the window open,' Miss Crook said. 'She makes up the fire before going to bed – Hester, you had better go up and see.'

Belle had spoken truly. There was such a strong draught of air that Hester had to push the door of her room open and it flew out of her hand and banged behind her as the curtains billowed. The room was full of smoke from the fire and she ran to close the wide open window, the cause of all the trouble. Then she stopped dead, a shiver of horror convulsing her. As the curtains swayed, she could plainly see a pair of dirty boots sticking out below the chintz. The top drawer of her dressing table lay open; someone had removed her red leather jewel case. There was no sign of it.

She backed to the door, opened it with a wrench that nearly tore off the handle and bundled downstairs crying, 'Oh, come at once! There's a thief in my room!'

'Posy!' Belle shrieked. 'If he's touched my Posy I'll kill him!'

She dashed out of the room and Hester subsided on a chair. Miss Crook poured her a glass of wine and took up the poker. 'Come, we must investigate.'

Hester armed herself with the tongs; holding their hems clear of the floor they went rapidly upstairs. Belle was standing on the landing holding her sleepy child in her arms. 'You're never going in?'

'Certainly we are,' Miss Crook said firmly, her voice trembling a little. 'Are you ready, Hester? *Now.*'

But the room was empty. They wrenched back the curtains and found the window yawning to the night. The red jewel box lay behind the curtain, empty. They roused the servants and searched the house from attic to cellar. Then they bolted every door and window. Annie, the cook, had collapsed with terror and had to be revived with brandy.

'He must have known we was a passel of women!' she wailed. 'Oh, m'am, we'll have to get a man somehow!'

Hester was looking to see what had been taken. Her favourite pieces were her watch and chain and the perfectly matched pearls her uncle had given her, both of which she was wearing. 'But I do regret my beautiful butterflies I wore in my hair.' For Victor had loved them, those jewelled insects that trembled on thin gold springs when set in the hair. And then with a glad jump of her heart she remembered that they were in the leather dress box she carried with her to the theatre. The burglar could have all the other things, she thought blithely, as long as her butterflies were safe.

'I didn't know you had all that jewellery,' Belle said curiously. This Hetty was something of a mystery, she was thinking.

'I had an indulgent uncle,' Hester said. She was too tired to fence with Belle. Let her think what she liked.

Miss Crook sent everyone to bed. 'I don't propose sending anyone for the police on a night like this,' she said firmly. 'It's far too late for women to be out on their own. Sarah shall go as soon as she gets up tomorrow.'

The girls slept late next morning. When a tall melancholy policeman presented himself at nine o'clock he couldn't understand why he was not to be allowed to visit the scene of the crime, Miss Kelsey's bedroom.

'Not at present, Sergeant. Miss Kelsey is in the show at the Gaiety and needs her sleep. Can't you be looking outside the house? I'm sure you'll find all sorts of footprints there.'

'I have already done so, mam. You've been asking for trouble in my opinion. There's a dustbin and a pile of boxes in the back yard that any thief worth his salt would use.' The policeman wet his stump of pencil and wrote something in his notebook with an air of triumph.

To Miss Crook's relief, a fly presently drew up outside and a man whom Sarah announced as Inspector Trumper walked into the room. The policeman immediately stood up and collected his helmet, meekly accepting the inspector's suggestion that he return to the station and sort his information.

Inspector Trumper was a thickset man with grizzled hair and moustache. He shook her firmly by the hand, holding his bowler at his side, his bright blue eyes looking round the room and missing nothing. He listened patiently while Miss Crook told him she was reluctant to rouse Miss Kelsey just yet. Could he wait a few minutes? The parlourmaid had just taken her breakfast in. 'She is in the show at the Gaiety and Sunday is her only rest day. Would you care for a cup of tea while we wait?'

Inspector Trumper thanked her. Sitting down by the fire, he listened to the story of the burglary with an impassive face, nodding and holding his hands out to the blaze. When the tea came he put in three lumps of sugar and stirred vigorously, looking appreciatively round the room as he did so. 'This is a nice room – got the woman's touch,' he observed. 'I miss that since my wife died. You do, you know. The place at home now – well, it's too neat. You can see it isn't lived in. You don't realize what a woman does to a house until she's no longer there.'

Miss Crook murmured sympathetically. Through the window floated the sound of church bells – well, she would have to miss matins this morning, she thought regretfully.

'Has your wife only recently died?' she asked, refilling the inspector's cup.

'Been gone six months now. I live on my own. I'm usually very busy,' he added. 'Our station's one of the busiest although I say it myself. What with bit fakers, bludgers, breadsmen and prigs, there's never a dull moment. That'll be like a foreign language to you, m'am, and you can thank your lucky stars for it. I tell you, this London's a dark place, a devil's kitchen, and the one half doesn't know how the other half lives.' He drank his tea gloomily. 'Full of lost souls – the devil's own.'

Miss Crook sighed, for the inspector's glumness was affecting her. 'Indeed, you are right. I feel the responsibility in a house full of women. The house belongs to Miss Kelsey and I look after them all.'

'And very well you do it, madam, by the look of things,' Inspector Trumper told her. 'And a good cup of tea that young woman makes. No, I won't take any more, thank you. When Miss Kelsey is finished with her bedroom,' he hinted delicately.

'I will go and see if she's ready for you.'

Hester was putting the finishing touches to her toilet.

'My dear, there's a charming police inspector out there – quite a fatherly man. He's waiting to see the window and to talk to you. Are you ready?'

Summoned, Inspector Trumper shook hands with Miss Kelsey and heard her version of the burglary. Then, watched anxiously by both women, he inspected the window bay, muttering under his breath. 'Could be the work of a snakesman while the kidsman waited below,' he was heard to murmur and they looked at each other. 'Could be an inside informer.' He straightened and looked at them. 'Can you trust your servants?'

'Most certainly,' Miss Crook said warmly. 'There are only two now, as I had to sack the kitchenmaid the first week she was here. She was dirty and unreliable.'

'That sounds more like it,' the inspector said briskly. 'I'd like to go down to the kitchen now, m'am.'

Miss Crook nodded. A button on his coat was hanging by a thread, she noticed, and her hands itched to sew it on.

'Well, thank you, ladies. I'll let you know developments.' He started to follow Sarah downstairs then turned. 'And thank you very much for the tea, Miss Crook.'

'He is a nice man,' Hester said. 'If anyone can catch our thief Inspector Trumper will. But did you notice that button?'

'The poor man's a widower,' Miss Crook told her.

The next day at three-thirty, he returned. Of course Miss Crook offered him tea and they sat by the fire, the inspector giving Posy a ride on his knee, and had another enjoyable talk. Hester and Belle were out shopping and by the time they returned, the inspector had departed again. Miss Crook said regretfully that he hadn't found the burglar, but he felt sure their former kitchenmaid had had a hand in it. She had noticed that the button had fallen off; which was a pity as coat buttons were difficult to match.

It was Thursday before he turned up again. Sarah now greeted him like an old friend and tea arrived promptly. Accepting a slice of plum cake, he ate it with enjoyment. 'Now that's something I've not tasted for months – a good old-fashioned plum cake. Eileen, my wife, was a first-rate cook. You'd have liked her, Miss Crook, everyone did.'

She nodded, feeling pity for the big man who seemed so lonely. 'Have you no children? A daughter, perhaps, to look after you.'

He swallowed the last of the plum cake and nodded. 'Two girls, both married, one in Australia and the other in Canada. Fat lot of use to me they've been. I tell you, Miss Crook, children are mighty ungrateful. You bring up a couple of girls to be a blessing to you in your old age, and they're off almost before they've put their hair up.'

'It's natural, I'm afraid. Young people marry and then have lives of their own.'

He looked at her. 'You didn't.'

'No, I had a brother to look after. He was a clergyman and life was very busy. Then when he married rather late in life, I took the position of governess to Miss Kelsey.' Why am I telling him all this, she wondered, amazed at the way her tongue was running away with her. Good heavens, the man's got a genius for finding out about one – and quite painlessly too. 'More tea, Inspector?'

He stayed until five o'clock. When he left, he wrung her hand and said he couldn't remember when he had enjoyed himself so much.

He called a week later, a satisfied smile on his face. Before Hester's eyes, he emptied his pockets and there were her jewels. She gave a squeak of excitement. Belle jumped up to look at the pretty baubles lying on the chenille cover of the table.

'Good heavens, Hetty, are they real? They must be worth a fortune!'

'Your former kitchenmaid, one Ellie Smith, had this little lot buried under the floorboards of the room she shared with a notorious character called Dan Nelson.'

Their cries of 'Oh, Inspector, you're wonderful!' seemed to please him. His smile got broader and he was prevailed upon to take a cup of coffee. When the girls took Posy out to the park, he was still there.

'He's sweet on her,' Sarah told Annie down in the kitchen. 'What did I tell you? And she's putting a button on that coat of his.'

'A very good sign,' Annie said, sighing sentimentally.

CHAPTER EIGHT

Fred Leslie died of malignant typhoid on December 7. The Gaiety company was stunned by the news and the theatre closed down for a week's mourning. When the funeral procession wound up the Strand on its way to Charlton cemetery, all the traffic came to a halt. As the six plumed horses pulled the glass hearse past the waiting crowds, a low murmur followed it like a groan. He was only thirty-seven and his handsome face, his wit and his élan were known to a wide public.

Belle and Katy, Hester and Flo Hughes rode together in a hackney carriage and Flo wept all the way there. She was like that, she kept telling them, as if they were not expected to have her sensitivity. Snow lay on the ground, a dirty London snow that was the colour of mud, and a keen wind with hard particles of ice in it bit into their faces as they wound in a long black line into the cemetery and past the open grave.

It was a relief when it was all over and Hester and Belle were dropped off in Markham Square, leaving Katy to face the rest of the journey alone with the sobbing Flo. 'I'll have strangled her before we get home,' Katy said, grim-faced.

Hester went shiveringly into her house and felt the caress of warm air with relief. 'Let's go up to the drawing room and thaw out,' she said, leading the way. Outside the drawing room door, they paused and exchanged a glance. They could hear a male voice.

'It's *him* again,' Belle hissed. 'I told you he was courting her and you wouldn't believe me. Mister Inspector Trumper knows a good thing when he sees it. He's just after her money.'

Hester laughed, shaking her head. 'Why shouldn't he care for her when she's such a darling?' she asked as she opened the door. Then she stopped, a little shock running over her as Victor Cockayne rose and came to take her hand. Wilfred was also there, busy eating hot scones; he suffered a kiss from Hester and half-rose to bow at Belle. Miss Crook boiled more water in the little silver kettle and made fresh tea for the newcomers. 'My dears, you look frozen. What a terrible day for a funeral. Do move up, Wilfred, and let the girls get to the fire.'

Posy, wearing a red velvet dress, was having tea on a little stool, her dolls beside her.

'Well, Posy, haven't you a kiss for Mama?' Belle demanded. The child got up and hugged her, shyly glancing over her shoulder at the men who were a novelty in her life. 'No, sit here near me,' Belle directed possessively.

Miss Crook and Hester tried not to exchange a glance. Belle's possessive attitude to her child irritated them both, although they did their best to hide it. It was as if she suspected them of trying to usurp the child's affection.

'We're staying for a few days in town,' Wilfred explained. 'At the club. Term ended yesterday and, as we've kept the required number of nights, Victor and I thought we'd come up to town. I'm going up to Liverpool to see Munro on business next week. You'll be at Stanhope for Christmas, won't you, Hester? Mama expects it.'

'My dear cousin, Christmas is the busiest season in the theatre! We shan't even get the day off.'

'But that's absurd! I'm not going to spend Christmas on my own at Stanhope,' Wilfred said querulously.

Hester only gave him half her attention. Over the rim of her cup she was covertly watching Victor talking to Miss Crook. His face was averted. It seemed to her that its outline was much thinner than the last time she had seen him. He looked not only thinner but older, and his lips were set in a straight line. Remembering the last time they had met, a little nerve quivered in her body. Did *he* remember? she wondered with a spurt of bitterness.

Just then he turned and met the bitter look in her eyes. She saw then that he did remember. Coming across to her, he drew up a chair at right angles to hers and said in a low voice, 'How are you, Hester? I hear you're working at the Gaiety.'

'Yes, haven't things changed?' she said with forced brightness. 'You must come and see the show and bring Lady Connie. I hear I must congratulate you, Victor, for you are to be married shortly.'

'Thank you but we have made no plans, set no definite date.' He hesitated, seeking for words. 'It has been ordained for a long time – ever since we were in swaddling clothes, I think!'

She didn't reply, but looked searchingly at his face, wondering why it had lost the golden look of youth in so short a time. Have I changed so much? she wondered. 'Have you been ill?'

He flushed, glancing quickly at her. 'Not really. I had some disorder of the blood last autumn but I'm much better now. Do I look ill?'

She nodded. 'As if you are just recovering from an illness. That is why I asked.'

His eyes looked down at his clasped hands. 'I've been unhappy,' he said under his breath. 'Good God, you must realize that!'

But she would not meet him in the shared intimacy of remembering that night in Mrs Crown's garden. A veil came down over her eyes and she did not reply. Instead she turned to Wilfred and engaged in banter with him. He was putting on weight, she told him, and was beginning to look quite middle-aged.

'Females are all the same,' Wilfred grumbled. 'You're either too fat or too thin. Yes, I'll have that piece of cake, Miss Crook. What a delightful house you've found in

London,' he added slyly and Hester breathed a sigh of relief that he was remembering to keep up the pretence that the house was Miss Crook's. She hoped very much that he hadn't taken Victor into his confidence, that Victor didn't know the true state of affairs. Somehow that was important.

They were rising, taking their leave. 'Thank you for my tea, Miss Crook,' Wilfred said. They kissed and he added, 'It is good of you to give young Hester a home and I know she's grateful. I hope you don't let her have a latchkey? You do?'

Really, he was over-doing it, Hester thought with exasperation. There was a strange expression on Victor's face — puzzled, surprised. They clasped hands briefly, exchanged a look. Then he was gone and misery filled her. She had been too busy to brood for some weeks. If only he hadn't appeared in her life again! What a strange thing love was. One could go on loving in the face of every obstacle. Her feeling for Victor Cockayne was beginning to hurt again like a disturbed wound.

'Wilfred has no idea or he wouldn't have brought him,' Miss Crook said, breaking in on her thoughts. She put out her hand to touch Hester's cheek. 'Mr Cockayne still loves you. When you were talking to the others, his eyes followed you with such an expression of longing. . . .'

'But he has only to remember who my father was to make everything all right again,' Hester said bitterly. 'I'm sure he feels quite justified in ruining both our lives. Oh, I wish I could hate him,' she cried and tears began to roll down her cheeks. But she knew that whatever Victor did, however badly he treated her, she would go on loving him and the pain of it was something she must get used to in the years ahead.

A letter in the morning post requested Miss Hetty Kelly's presence in Mr Edwardes's office next day. Hester, reading the summons over breakfast in bed, cast the bedclothes from her with a shriek of 'Sarah! Sarah! Bring my bath at once, please!' For it was after nine and the appointment was for ten-thirty. What could he want with her? Whatever happened she mustn't be late. She had slept badly, Victor's thin unhappy face had haunted her. Would it make a difference if he knew she had enough money for them both? But she would hate him to marry her because she was rich! Besides, she did not believe money was the main reason he was marrying Connie Courage. True, it was an arranged affair but Victor had struck her yesterday as a man who could not make a stand. Perhaps once he had not been like that – languid and indifferent, making few plans for his life. The uneasy feeling that there was something wrong with him returned to her. If only she had the right to help him!

She flung open her wardrobe door and inspected her clothes. It would have to be the grey tailormade with the chinchilla cap and muff. It wasn't new, but the soft grey suited her.

Hurrying out of the square in the teeth of a bitter wind, she saw the old flower woman with her basket sheltering under the bare trees. 'Devon violets, lidy. Suit you a treat this morning.' She laughed and bought a bunch to pin to her muff; their faint mossy smell rose to her nostrils as she sat in the fly that was taking her to Wellington Street and she felt in better spirits. Even the thought that perhaps the Guv'nor was about to give her the sack could not deflate her.

When she was sitting across the desk from him, George Edwardes thought she looked like a spring goddess with the violets in her lap. He smiled, remembering that those lovely eyes were his lucky colour, and God knew he needed luck at this very minute with Fred in his grave and no one to replace him.

'I want you in my Big Eight,' he said without preamble. 'Mabel Sylvester fell on the ice yesterday and broke her ankle. You'll take her place. You'll get three pounds a week from now on and you'll have to move your dressing room. I shall want you in every morning to rehearse all this week.

335

There are three dances and several songs to be learned. Think you can do it?'

'Of course,' she said composedly. Excitement was beating colour into her cheeks. The Big Eight. They were the most glamorous girls at the Gaiety and she had been chosen to join them! 'Thank you.'

He smiled, satisfied. 'Right. Miss Reed will see that you are fitted for your clothes. The theatre will be closed until Monday but we shan't be idle. We've a lot to do.'

Going back to Markham Square, Hester remembered Belle. Belle had been at the Gaiety much longer. How would she take this?

But Belle made a great effort to be pleased. It was true that her face fell and she bit her underlip and when she smiled it was with difficulty. But she said, 'I'm glad for you, Hetty. You did me a good turn getting me in here, so I won't be a jealous swine and wish you dead.'

Hester let her breath run out. 'Oh, I am glad to hear you say that, Belle!'

'As for the money,' Belle went on, 'I've saved such a lot since I've been here that I'm beginning to feel quite rich! What's the gossip from George Edwardes's office? Have they found someone to take Fred's place?'

'Miss Reed says they are hoping to engage a comedian called Payne. Edward Payne.'

Belle clapped her hands. 'Teddy Payne is just the man! He's a Cockney with a lisp. The show will go on now and perhaps in the spring we will go on tour with it.' She glanced over her shoulder and whispered, 'Miss C. is going out tonight. With him. I tell you he's got his eye on her and we'll be out of this place by the spring.'

Miss Crook, her cheeks pink, told Hester herself. 'Inspector Trumper has asked me to go to the play. Isn't it kind of him? I feel sure he would have preferred a music hall – perhaps the Empire. What shall I wear, Hester? My black?'

'Oh no, your lovely dark green velvet of course.'

'No, no, it's much too good.'

'Darling Alice, what are you keeping it for? This is an occasion!'

Miss Crook looked at her with pleasure. 'You've called me Alice! Oh, Hester, how nice it sounds from your lips! We're no longer governess and pupil – but friends.' She leaned over and kissed her ex-pupil. 'I shall wear the green,' she announced.

Victor turned into the club in Pall Mall of which his father had recently made him a member. Giving his hat and over-coat to a steward and avoiding contact with other members, he walked slowly up the stairs to the reading room. From the portraits lining the stairs, rows of past Prime Ministers looked down on him, as he dragged himself up with one hand on the bannister. He could feel his heart going *tick-tack, tick-tack* like a very fast clock. He got breathless and tired so easily yet, only half an hour ago, an eminent heart specialist had pronounced his heart to be quite sound. 'The trouble lies elsewhere,' he had said, looking over his glasses at his patient. 'The blood needs a thorough investigation. I suggest you visit Dr Arnold Parry, our foremost authority on diseases of the blood.'

So tomorrow he would see Dr Parry, in the hope that he could solve this mysterious malady that had haunted him for a year.

There were only two old men in the reading room and both were asleep. Victor took up *The Times* as a cover and retired to a window seat. It was dusk, half-past three on a December afternoon. The hansoms and private carriages carried lighted lanterns that danced like fire-flies in the fading light. He looked out, but saw only Hester's face as it had looked two days ago: startled and glad and then bitter. He knew that his love for her was unchanged, as strong as ever. Not even agreeing to marry Connie had managed to erase it. Perhaps from this unhappiness of his, something good would trans-pire; he might at least achieve good poetry. Poems – whole

337

notebooks of them – littered his Oxford rooms, but nothing memorable had yet come from his pen. He was a merciless self-critic and he knew his poetry was not in the same class as his friends, men like Arthur Symons and Ernest Dowson. It was mere verse, coming from the head and not the heart. It was Arthur who had said of him at the Rhymers' Club, 'Victor has two sides: the English country gentleman and the poet. Which will prove the stronger?'

He put *The Times* down for suddenly his hands were shaking; a trembling weakness was coming over him again. This accursed illness that was flowering in his body now seemed to be taking root in his mind, and he was finding it increasingly difficult to concentrate.

Reaching into a waistcoat pocket, he found the box containing the pills the quack had advised him to take at times like this. They made him stronger for a time and he measured them out through the day like a miser counting his money.

He had asked Symons to dine with him and afterwards they would go to the Gaiety. He had told Symons he knew a girl in the chorus and Symons (a poet who wrote of the ballet girls and the music hall) had jumped at the chance. After his last encounter with Hester, Victor had been in a ferment of impatience to see her again. He had thought he could forget her, but now he knew his love for her burned as steadily as ever. He could feel it beating like a second heart – and a good deal stronger than his real heart, he thought wryly.

Waiting for the pill to work, he sat quietly watching the blossoms of light springing up along the whole length of Pall Mall, as the lamplighter wended his way with the lighted rod.

'By God, she is beautiful!' Symons said leaning forward in his seat as the Big Eight, clad in ball gowns of different hues, danced with their mirrored images in a kaleidoscope of colour under the arc lights. 'She is the most beautiful of them.'

'Yes, I do believe she is,' Victor agreed with pride. His

eyes followed Hester's figure as she dipped and swayed, her dress spinning out round her twinkling feet.

He was obviously not the only man who thought her beautiful, for in a box to the right of the stage stood a large man with a bushy brown beard who was pelting her with flowers as she danced. That the flowers were meant for her alone was obvious; for he took careful aim and reached his target every time, bellowing 'Bravo! Bravo!' as he did so.

Hester kept a fixed smile as his flowers hit her in the face and breast. She knew who he was – Katy's Russian count who had transferred his allegiance to her.

'And you can have him, dear,' Katy had assured her. 'He smells vilely of garlic and pomade.'

But Hester had no intention of 'having' him. When his cards arrived imploring her to have supper with him, she refused his invitation. Unfortunately this only seemed to fan Count Livinsky's ardour to fever pitch. Baskets of flowers and fruit arrived each day, with jewel boxes concealed inside. She kept the fruit and flowers and returned the jewels, wondering who would get them next.

'Let's go round to the stage door and ask her to supper,' Symons suggested at eleven o'clock. 'She can bring a little friend.'

Victor hesitated. 'I doubt very much if she will come.' But he sent his card up and they waited among the throng in the hall; watching the girls as they came down, gracious as queens in their splendid gowns, furs and jewels, and gave their hand to the chosen one of the evening. Yes, they were beautiful, Victor thought, but in his eyes Hester outshone them all. If she came tonight – he felt anticipation leap up like a flame. To sit near her, to talk to her – but he was engaged to Connie and Hester would not come. He said so to Symons who remained airily *insouciant*. 'Rubbish, my dear fellow, these girls will go anywhere for their supper. We'll take them to the Café Royal and give them champagne – plenty of champagne,' he said gleefully.

Jupp leaned out of his box and bawled, 'Mr Cockayne?'

'Yes?' Victor strolled across and leaned on the ledge.

'Miss Kelly regrets,' Jupp said dryly and handed back his card. On the back she had written: *How kind of you but impossible. Hester.*

It had cost her something to refuse. Hope had stirred in her for one wild moment. Then commonsense took over; if he were free again this would not be the method he would choose to tell her. She was just a Gaiety Girl, and he thought he could take her out to supper and no harm done. As she wiped off her make-up, she could not see her image for tears.

It was not long after this that a bouquet of pink and white carnations was delivered to her dressing room. Unlike the chorus, the Big Eight had their flowers delivered, for they were second only to the stars. *Will you have supper with me? Denis Crown.* She turned the card over and scribbled recklessly, 'Yes.'

It came as a pleasant surprise that Denis Crown had recognized Hester Kelsey in Hetty Kelly of the Big Eight. He must, she thought, have been in the audience tonight.

But that was not how he had found her; he had in fact tracked her down quite deliberately.

He had forgotten how beautiful she was. Strange that he should think of her money first, and only remember that she was beautiful as an added bonus. He came forward and kissed her hand. 'My dear Hester, how lovely you look!'

She glanced at him, wondering at his freedom of manner. Had he been used to using her name? She thought not. But he was part of that enchanted summer last year when she had been young and in love. She now thought of herself as older and more cynical; she knew how to handle men and not to expect too much. So she smiled and asked coolly after his mother and talked lightly of life at the Gaiety as they sat over supper at Romano's.

'I've been at the Curragh for three months,' he told her, motioning the waiter to refill her glass with champagne, although she had hardly touched her first glass. 'Now that I have got a spot of leave I'm back in London. Got a small apartment and a man to look after me.' In reality, he had two rooms off Oxford Street and the man was his landlord. He was in deep waters in regard to money and his mother was proving unexpectedly obstinate. 'What made you do this, Hester?'

'Do what, Captain Crown?'

He looked at her quizzically. 'Oh, come, it's Denis surely?'

'Very well, Denis. And you may call me Hester,' she added pointedly; for he was now squeezing her elbow and sitting too close for comfort. She shifted her position as he repeated, 'Why become a Gaiety Girl? There was surely no need?'

'Need?' She looked up quickly. 'No need to earn my living you mean?'

'I've been given to understand that you are now co-owner of the Prickard Line with your cousin.'

She stared at him. 'Where did you learn this? Who told you?'

'It's true then? Major Webber told me. You remember him? He's very thick with your cousin Wilfred, you know. No secrets from each other and all that!' He gave a little laugh.

She began to eat cold salmon with indifference, letting her gaze wander round the room. She hadn't answered his question, he noticed. Not directly. He leaned towards her. 'You can trust me, Hester. I shan't tell a soul.'

'Who else knows? Does – does Victor Cockayne know?'

He nearly said, Good God, I hope not! but stopped himself in time. Shrugging he said, 'I've no idea. Have you seen anything of him lately? He's engaged to Connie Courage, you know. Poor devil!'

'Oh, Connie will make him a good wife I'm sure. . . . '

'I wasn't thinking of that. He's got something wrong with him. The doctors can't fathom it. I'm told he looks rotten.'

She felt fear squeeze her heart. 'He is ill?' Thin and pale, his face rose before her as she had seen him last. 'Not TB?'

'Something like that I believe. He crocked up that weekend at Henley and I had to put him to bed.'

'I didn't know,' she said slowly.

'I want to see a great deal of you this leave, Hester. May I?'

She looked at him without seeing him. 'Of course,' she said mechanically.

He was pleasant to be with, a gay and witty talker who made her forget her anxiety about Victor. She dined with him several times, alone or with another officer and a friend of Hester's, Milly Silver, who shared her dressing room. He had only got a month, he reminded her and he meant to see a great deal of her.

'I'm in love with you, Hester,' he said earnestly in the cab one night. They had halted outside the front door of her house.

She looked at him in the dim light and laughed. 'No, Denis, you're not. We're simply friends. You just think you ought to tell me this. Goodnight.'

He got out and helped her down, accompanying her to the door. 'Do you like making me miserable?' he asked pathetically.

'Denis, please.'

'Hester, I want to marry you.'

She sighed. She knew he was not in love with her but with her money; she had guessed his interest in her last summer. She knew this, but how could she be cross with such a charmer? 'I wish you wouldn't say things like that, Denis. I shall have to stop seeing you.'

'Oh, don't say that! Oh, Hester, that would finish me!'

The cabby cleared his throat loudly.

Lowering his voice, Denis said urgently. 'I know you like my mother. She is up for a few days staying with me. Will you come to tea tomorrow? She would like to see you again.'

'Why didn't you tell me before? I would like to see your

342

mother again. She gave me such a good time at Henley last summer. Now, Denis, I shall come only on condition that you don't keep asking me to marry you. Promise? Then four o'clock tomorrow. Will you call for me here? I shall have to go straight to the theatre after tea.'

He promised, kissed her hand and drove away. As she shut the door and went softly upstairs, she thought how happy she would have been at this moment if it had been Denis she loved – and not Victor.

He called for her punctually next day and she noticed at once that he was in tremendous spirits. Looking out of the window when the cab stopped she said in surprise, 'Is this where you live?' For the house was a shabby one in a shabby street. Children played on the pavement and there was a noisy public house across the street, from which came the sound of voices raised in song as well as a stale smell of beer. It was already dark, but still light enough for her to connect Huntriss Street with Sewerston harbour.

'Oh, it's nice enough inside and not being in funds I had to find somewhere cheap,' he said easily.

The room he led her to was certainly better than she had expected from the outside. A fire blazed, there were flowers and a table set for tea.

'Let me take your wrap,' he said, his hands lingering on her shoulders.

'Where is your mother, Denis?' she asked quietly; for a suspicion was being born that this was to be a tête-à-tête, the last thing she wanted.

'She has obviously not returned from shopping,' he said and smiled at her as he put the kettle on the hob. They sat talking in the lamplight, waiting for the kettle to boil, and still Mrs Crown did not put in an appearance. He made the tea and suggested they start. 'It's no use waiting for Mama when she's Christmas shopping,' he explained.

The tea was good and so were the crumpets dripping with butter. He made no attempt to be amorous, but sat on the opposite side of the fireplace in a deep chair and talked amusingly of his time in Ireland. She realized that his mother was not even in London, that he had made it the excuse to have her round in his lodgings – an apartment was too grand a name for the room. No great harm had been done, she thought, but he ought not to have lied to her. Looking at her watch, she suddenly exclaimed at the time. 'I must go. It's gone six o'clock and I shall be late at the theatre.' She rose, looking round for her wrap, but he sat immobile not attempting to help her. 'My wrap, Denis, please.'

'Sit down, Hester; you're not going anywhere.'

She stared at him and saw that his face had changed. The good humour and laughter had left it; he looked grimly determined.

'That door is locked. The landlord has instructions not to pay attention to anything that goes on here – I have paid him well for that. I intend keeping you here all night, so that by tomorrow you will be glad enough to marry me.'

Her astonishment dissolved in laughter. 'Oh, Denis, you fool! What a stupid idea! You must know me well enough to know that I shall simply break your window and scream for help! You can't be serious?'

'People round here are used to women screaming out of windows,' he assured her, and now he was smiling quietly. 'I shan't harm you. I only want to marry you. I *must* marry you because I'm in deep waters. I have mountains of debts, but worse than that I have gambling I.O.U.s that I cannot meet and I shall have to resign my commission. So you see, Hester, I am quite desperate. I shall make you a good husband, never fear. I'm sure we shall get on very well.'

She sat down hard and stared at him. He had thought it out quite carefully it seemed. She had been going out to dinner with him, to supper at the Savoy and Romano's, and all the time it had been leading up to this. She suddenly felt furious with herself for falling so easily into the trap he had laid. 'You have forgotten one thing,' she said in an even voice. 'Even if you keep me here for a week I shall never consent to marry you.'

'You talk like a fool,' he countered. 'Your reputation will be gone and you know it.'

'The reputation that was Hester Kelsey's perhaps,' she said and began to smile. 'But Hetty Kelly, the Gaiety Girl, has nothing to lose. You've made a very grave mistake, my friend. Shall I tell you who I am? The daughter of a double murderer? A penniless girl from the slums? Ah, I see you didn't know that! I see now I should have told you. Other people know – Victor Cockayne for instance. He wouldn't marry me, you know. Am I really the sort of woman you want for a wife? What will the other wives in the regiment think when I tell them who I am?'

'I don't believe you,' he said angrily.

'Then ask our mutual acquaintance, Gerald Woolsey, if you don't believe me.'

A coal fell in the grate and light ran across the wall. By this and the soft light of the one lamp she could see his face quite clearly, see the uncertainty and chagrin in it. She stepped across to him and held out her hand. 'Give me the key of this room at once.'

For answer he hid his face in his hands and groaned. 'Oh, God, what am I to do? Why don't you marry me, Hester? I don't care about your background – I swear I don't.'

'No, you care only about my money,' she agreed. 'It's a very great deal of money, you know, and you would certainly have a very good time with it. But you won't have the chance, my friend. After tonight, I never want to see you again.' She wondered if he was going to refuse her, but after a minute he slowly put his hand in his pocket and gave her the key of the door. The last she saw of him he was sunk in his chair staring into the fire.

Hurrying into the street, she looked for a cab rank, knowing she was going to be late for the theatre, a crime that would bring Malone's wrath and probably another fine down on her head. At last she found one and directed him to the Gaiety,

345

with the promise of double fare if he got her there quickly. As they bowled along she found herself pitying good-looking Denis Crown who had been spoilt all his life.

CHAPTER NINE

At Christmas Hester gave Posy a kitten. It was black with bright green eyes and came with a basket, a blanket and a brush. When the child ignored her other presents in favour of the kitten, Hester realized she had made a mistake. Posy barely looked at the new doll her mother had given her and although Belle said nothing, her blue eyes became distant and cold for she was a jealous mother.

'I'm afraid she will not be a good one,' Miss Crook said, shaking her head. She had observed Belle's tug-of-war with her child over the kitten. Belle declared it was dirty and must live in the kitchen. It was only when she was at the Gaiety that the kitten came back upstairs. 'She wants the child to need no one but her, to turn to her for everything. Have you noticed how curt she is with Sarah because she can see Posy is fond of her? It's hurtful to Sarah who is being so helpful. You ought to speak to her, Hester.'

But Hester had become rather a coward where Belle was concerned. Let sleeping dogs lie was her philosophy, she told Miss Crook with feeling. Secretly she knew that there was more in Belle's attitude than met the eye. There was Inspector Trumper. Belle made no bones about disliking the man she called 'Miss Crook's policeman with the big feet'. She took childish pleasure in decrying him in front of Alice Crook who, having learned self-control in a hard school, pretended not to hear.

January was a bitter month of snow and ice. Ellen, who had been invited to spend New Year in Markham Square

347

(for Wilfred was going to Paris) wrote that although she would be 'alone', she had decided not to travel in such weather. 'I know I must get used to my lonely life,' she wrote reproachfully, 'nevertheless I do think you should return to Stanhope to look after me. Remember all your uncle did for you. It is your duty to live here.'

'*Duty!*' Hester said glumly, showing the letter to Miss Crook. 'Daughters have had their lives ruined by so-called duty and I am, I suppose, a sort of daughter to Aunt Ellen.'

'She is lonely. It's understandable.'

'I realize that. I suppose you wouldn't like to go to Yorkshire for a short holiday in my place? No, I thought not.' Hester smiled mischievously. 'What would Inspector Trumper do while you were away?'

Miss Crook laughed and shook her head reproachfully. A faint colour crept into her cheeks and she sought for the right words. 'Would you think it strange – do you think I am too old to contemplate marriage?'

Hester flung herself at her former governess and whirled her round the room. 'Darling Alice, how glad I am! Oh, how lovely to have a policeman in the family – for you are my family, you know. And he's a dear. I like him immensely. We shall all get on famously together.'

'My dear, you've knocked off my spectacles! Yes, he is a dear man and I've grown very fond of him. He is lonely without his wife and with both daughters in the colonies. But, Hester dear, we shan't live here, you know. I couldn't ask him to do that. He is a proud man and wants to provide me with my own home – ah, don't look like that! We shall see each other often.'

Hester sat down on a stool, her face sober again. 'So you'll go away and I shall be left with Belle.' She twisted her face as if tasting something bitter. 'We shall fight – I know we shall. You are forever pouring oil on troubled waters and keeping the atmosphere sweet. Belle isn't a cosy person and I fly off the handle too easily. But I mustn't burden you with that. Let's make plans. You'll be married from here, won't you?'

'I should like that. Leonard wants us to get married at the end of March or beginning of April. He's having the house at Streatham done up. . . .'

'Oho! you have been making plans, haven't you? He's quite right,' she agreed, although her heart sank at the prospect of the house without Alice Crook. 'There is no point in delay. Ask him to supper on Sunday and we'll make plans together, for I insist on giving the wedding breakfast and buying you the nicest trousseau obtainable.'

'My dear child, that's much too much. . . .'

Hester slid off the stool and knelt at Miss Crook's chair. Her face was serious. 'Alice, don't try and stop me, please. For six years you've been my friend and mentor, the person most like a mother to me. Aunt Ellen has never been that. I can tell you this now. It's to you and my uncle that I owe everything. You have turned a raw little girl into the semblance of a lady. More than that, you've helped me to absorb the right values, I think. I know now that money means very little if you cannot be happy within your self. It can't buy one contentment. It can't buy one the person one loves – for I could never love a fortune hunter, you know.' She let her face break into a rueful smile. 'And now I must go and break the news to Belle. I suspect she won't be pleased! Then Sarah shall bring up some champagne and we shall have a toast.'

Hester's method of telling Belle was a bare announcement followed by the grim warning: 'And if you run down the inspector and make Alice unhappy I'll box your ears, Belle Collins.'

But Belle was too disturbed by the news to let her waspish tongue run away with her. What was going to happen to them when Miss Crook left the house? she wanted to know. 'It's her house after all. I knew it would come to this and I should have to turn out again. I wish I'd never come.'

Hester took a deep breath and told her the truth.

The truth was not palatable to Belle. 'Do you mean to tell

349

me I've been living in your house and on your charity?' she demanded shrilly. 'I would never have stayed a minute had I known! You've not been straight with me, Hetty.'

'For heaven's sake, don't talk such rubbish. Charity is the wrong word. I wanted to fill the house with friends. . . . '

'*Friends* indeed! You can hardly call us that!' Belle sneered, her temper getting the better of her. The revelation that Hetty Kelly was a rich young woman filled her with jealous hatred. It seemed to her that Hester had too much already – now all this was hers as well. She had been packing her bag for the theatre. Now she abandoned the task and confronted Hester, her hands on her hips. 'It's humiliating, that's what it is. You're younger than me and not married and here I've been living free on your charity and I don't even like you! Well, I'm not having it. I shall find new lodgings.'

'You're talking nonsense. Think of Posy . . ; think how well she's done since she came here. . . . '

This was fatal. Belle drew herself up and hissed. 'So you think I wasn't looking after my own child properly? You think it's all your work, yours and Miss Crook's and that impudent Sarah's? Oh, it's nothing to do with me – me who's been working myself to the bone for her child since that rat, Bert Collins, abandoned us! That settles it. I'm taking my daughter away next week.'

Hester went into her bedroom, banged the door and wept. They were all deserting her: Alice, Belle and Posy. She was to be left alone with the servants. She threw herself on the bed and cried bitterly, suddenly terrified of being left on her own for the first time since she was fourteen and Sal and her father had died.

Inspector Trumper came to supper and Hester found she liked him more and more. His simplicity and obvious devotion to Alice Crook comforted her; it was easier to be glad about the impending marriage after this. The inspector's eyes shone proudly on Alice, and he wore the satisfied air of a man who had accomplished a great feat.

'I never thought she would have me,' he confided to Hester. 'But I made up my mind the first time I met her.'

Hester told herself gloomily that she was beginning to feel more and more like Jane Austen's Emma, who tried so hard to be pleased when Poor Miss Taylor got married, but in reality could only think of herself. Miss Crook however only laughed when she told her this.

'You won't miss me at all after a week . . . oh, no, you won't, so don't look disbelieving! Annie and Sarah are good girls who now know their jobs thoroughly and I think you can rely on them. Besides, you will marry yourself before long – perhaps sooner than you think.'

The smile on Hester's face faded. She stopped making wedding lists and sucked her pencil rather pensively. 'I don't think so. I love a man who can't marry me.'

Miss Crook again felt the tinge of dismay that always accompanied her remembrance of Hester's love for Victor Cockayne. If only the girl could be swept off her feet by another man! It might make her forget the humiliation of loving a man without hope. Hester had so much to give she thought, looking with tenderness at the girl who had been her charge and for whom she still felt a certain responsibility. If only Victor Cockayne would keep out of her life and give her time to recover, Alice Crook thought with exasperation.

She was therefore justifiably indignant when in late March, Wilfred wrote to ask them both to spend a Sunday at Oxford. 'I have asked Victor to lunch with us along with a couple of other friends,' he wrote.

It was only a week before the wedding, Miss Crook pointed out, hoping to deter Hester. But Hester's shining, hopeful eyes were her answer.

'Oh, Alice, please come with me. I would so love to see Oxford and I can't go alone. As for the wedding, well, we've done everything but order the flowers. Please, please come, dear Alice.'

Miss Crook took the girl's hands firmly in hers. 'I wish you would try and forget him, Hester. Try and remember that Mr Cockayne is to marry Lady Constance in the summer.'

'I want to go,' Hester said in a low voice. 'I must see him again. I promise this will be the last time. I promise.' Pleadingly, she fixed her eyes on Miss Crook's face, and when she saw an expression of acquiescence begin to dawn she smiled with relief. 'I promise,' she said for the third time.

There were only two Sunday trains and they had to rise early to catch the nine o'clock from Paddington. Hester's luminous skin seemed to burn with an inward fever. It made her laugh and talk like an excited child as the slow train wound its way through a wet spring landscape. It took two hours to reach Oxford where Wilfred, wearing a natty check suit recently delivered by his tailor, met them in the best of spirits. He had a cab waiting to take them round some of the sights of Oxford. They saw Christ Church and stood in the Great Quadrangle better known as Tom Quad; they saw New College because Miss Crook's father had been up there in the 1840s, the Sheldonian and the Radcliffe Library and then went as far as Magdalen to see the tower. By this time it was nearly one o'clock and Wilfred began to be anxious about his luncheon guests who had been asked for one-fifteen. So the cab was paid off and they entered his own college with its ivy-covered walls and quiet quads – giving it a deceptively monastic air.

'I've arranged lunch in my rooms,' Wilfred said, rubbing his hands at the prospect of roast beef and Yorkshire pudding. 'Sharp, my scout, will have seen to it. He's a capital fellow. Wish I had him at home instead of old Wiston – well, Wiston's such a misery, Miss Crook. He's forever stopping me with "Sir Joseph never had it so" or "Sir Joseph wouldn't like that, Sir Wilfred." The bally man forgets I'm no longer a child. I've ordered claret; will that suit you?' He was leading the way up a narrow oak staircase and throwing warnings back at them over his shoulder. 'Be careful of this corner. There's a rough bit of wood here . . . don't slip on it. . . .'

'Almost exactly as if we are octogenarians,' Hester whispered.

Miss Crook frowned at her and, as they entered his set of rooms, said, 'Well, this is nice, Wilfred!'

The room was warm and bright with flowers and a large fire leaping up the chimney. A table was laid for six people and sparkled with silver and glass in the sunlight. There had been an obvious attempt to tidy away books and papers; pipes and tobacco had been banished to the top shelf of a bookcase. As the women exclaimed and praised, Wilfred expanded with delight. 'Capital set-up, isn't it? I shall be quite sorry when I go down for good in June. Oxford gets into the bones, you know.' He showed them his bedroom where they could wash and leave their outdoor clothes. When they emerged, it was to find two of the guests had arrived and were advising on the claret which Wilfred had forgotten to decant.

'Curse Sharp,' he grumbled. 'The fellow has a memory like a sieve.' He then recollected himself in order to introduce Dr Scoreby, his tutor, and Stephen Wood, a tall shy youth with a girlish complexion who peeped at the women, and then took a seat as far from them as possible.

Hester talked with one hopeful eye on the door – perhaps he wouldn't come . . . perhaps he had refused the invitation and Wilfred had forgotten to mention it . . . perhaps he didn't want to come. . . . She chatted to Dr Scoreby who stared at her wordlessly, his head sinking slightly all the time. She hardly knew what she said for one half only of her mind was engaged. She paused mid-sentence as the door opened – but it was only Sharp, come to ask if he should serve the meal as it had passed one-thirty.

'Victor Cockayne's not come,' Wilfred explained to his guests. 'I think we must start without him – yes, serve it, Sharp, we're all of us peckish.' He inspected the table and uttered a cry. 'The horseradish, Sharp! Absolutely essential.

Send the boy down to the kitchens at once.'

So they sat down and Hester's heart seemed to sag in her body, all its spring gone. They had just begun to eat when the door opened quietly. 'I'm sorry I'm late,' Victor's voice said.

'My dear fellow, we had quite given you up. Cut Mr Cockayne some beef, Sharp.'

Apologizing to her, Victor slipped into the vacant seat beside Miss Crook. He threw a smile at Hester then bent his full attention on the elder lady. She had nursed a prejudice against him for some time, but Hester could see her mood melting towards Victor as the meal progressed. She herself ate in silence, happiness threatening to take her appetite away. He had come; he was here. She was as aware of him across the table as if he sat beside her, touching her. I am ill, no, I am sick with love, she thought tremulously, quite amazed at herself. I wish he had stayed away for he is going to marry Connie Courage.

She tried to listen to Dr Scoreby who, having thrown silence from him like a discarded garment, now poured out words as if nothing would stop him. He was telling her of his recent visit to the Vatican and what he and the Pope had said to each other. ' . . . so I said to his Holiness . . . yes, just a touch more of that excellent beef, Prickard, thank you . . . I said I had made a study of that very pope and I offered to send him my poor little effusion – Horseradish? Well, just a touch more. . . . '

Hester raised her eyes and met Victor's across the table. A message without words passed between them.

I love you still.

And I you.

'How interesting,' she said to Dr Scoreby, and smiled so dazzlingly that he lost the thread of his story.

After the meal, when Sharp and the boy had cleared everything away, Wilfred proceeded to make coffee on a spirit lamp. Hester found Victor beside her. Across the room, Miss Crook was listening to Dr Scoreby's tale about the Pope, while Stephen Wood hung round Wilfred like an acolyte.

'Hester, I've been longing to see you again.'

'Victor.'

It was enough. Each knew the other's feelings now. Presently, finishing their coffee, Victor said in a loud social voice, 'You must allow me to show you the college, Miss Kelsey. The sun is out so it won't be too cold for a stroll.'

He had taken the room by surprise and Miss Crook's eyes, warning and anxious, briefly met Hester's. Outside a thin March sunlight warmed their faces as they strolled round the quad. The grass in the centre was a vivid green and the window boxes outside the Master's Lodge held a few frail flowers. There was a scent of growth in the air that said winter was past.

'How beautiful it is,' Hester said as they walked.

He agreed, then said in a low urgent voice, 'But don't let us waste time in banal talk I have so much to say to you, I prayed you would come today although I don't deserve it!' He stopped and they faced each other. 'I have no right to speak yet – not until I'm free. All I can say at the moment is that I have asked Connie to release me.'

She was taken utterly by surprise and could only stare speechlessly.

'When I hear from her there will be so much I shall need to say to you,' he said gravely. 'I've been a fool – indolent and immature – and now suddenly I am an adult and free. That is the only explanation and apology I can make you. There is still my father to see. I realize it won't be pleasant, but I am not going to shirk telling him and my mother that I must make my own decisions in life. In the Easter vacation I shall come to you in London. Will you receive me kindly?'

'With – with the greatest gladness,' she said in a low voice, not daring to look up now. For suddenly it was too much joy to bear and she wanted to cry freely, alone from his eyes even. They stood apart although he longed to take her in his arms. He looked round impatiently; perhaps if it had been night it would have been possible, he thought. Now he could not even stretch out a hand and touch her.

After a moment or two they moved on. Both were now happy and silent, warmed by a tide of feelings that they had last experienced in the garden at Henley. But there was contentment now, a sense that the future was there waiting for them.

'When I get my degree this summer I shall be free. I shall be able to earn a living without my father's help. How should you care to be a schoolmaster's wife, Hester? We shall be poor, but I know we can manage. You see, I've thought it all out,' he said eagerly, his thin face flooding with colour.

She knew then that this was not the moment to tell him that money need never worry him again. 'I should like it above everything,' she assured him warmly. Then she added because she must: 'Are you better in health, Victor? Forgive me asking, but Denis Crown told me you had been ill.' His face was very thin, she thought. His neck too. He had lost much weight.

He shrugged impatiently. 'I believe so. Half the quacks in London have been trying to solve the puzzle of my sudden decline! I think myself that unhappiness has been eating me away – it's not so fanciful when one remembers that people have died before now for love! But when I'm free – when we can tell the world we love each other and the awful worry of it is behind me, then you'll see I shall be well again.' He smiled so hopefully that she pretended to be reassured. But his gaunt appearance continued to haunt her even when they parted. As they retraced their steps she said hardily, 'You haven't forgotten my background, have you? That is still the same.' She was determined that this must be resolved once and for all. 'My father was an unhappy suicide and murderer and I was brought up in the slums of Sewerston.'

'I haven't forgotten, but I know that it no longer matters. I know *you.*'

She stopped and stared at him. It was a moment of supreme triumph. She had won him because of herself, not

356

lost him because of her father. They stood in the spring sunshine smiling at each other, unable to express their joy with a comforting embrace. The sun came out and touched them gently and for the first time they noticed how loudly the birds were singing.

Miss Crook married her policeman at the beginning of April and Wilfred gave her away. Ellen came up to London for the wedding, but declined to stay in Markham Square. She had brought Agnes with her and they stayed in the hotel in Dover Street that she liked to use. But she called at the house daily to criticize the arrangements Miss Crook and Hester had made for the wedding, and to suggest new ones that were far too elaborate. Miss Crook wanted a quiet wedding with a wedding breakfast for twelve and the food cooked and prepared by Annie and Sarah; who in the event excelled themselves with calf's-head soup, lobster salads and boiled fowls, not to mention a Wiltshire ham and raisin sauce, wine jellies and iced puddings. There was a three-tier wedding cake and a great deal of champagne selected and donated by Wilfred, who did not trust his cousin's judgement with regard to wine.

The Reverend George Crook married them in a spirit of melancholy disapproval. Mrs Crook told Ellen in confidence that George feared his sister was marrying beneath her and would live to regret it.

Inspector Trumper had a fellow police officer to stand up with him and both his daughters sent cables from Australia and Canada. He looked a happy man when at last he drove away with his wife for a week's honeymoon in Cornwall. Alice, in dove grey and a hat with roses, looked quite young and pretty as she waved from the cab that bore her out of Hester's life. But Hester, determined to send her away untroubled, managed to smile and laugh until the end. It was only as she turned back into the house that she wished the wedding guests in Jericho.

But far from departing they were enjoying another glass of champagne all round.

'You're going to miss her, Hester,' Ellen said unnecessarily as she turned again to the table and began to select a plateful of titbits. 'Lady Bland, another lobster patty? Wilfred, you hardly ate a thing, my dear, so busy you were. Come and have something, I beg.' Ellen (considering the breakfast had made a very poor show) was now firmly taking charge and sending Sarah scurrying to fetch more iced pudding.

The Reverend George Crook collected his wife and took his departure, as stiff and unbending as when he arrived. 'Three glasses of champagne he had,' Cissie giggled, 'and as sober as a judge to the end. I've always maintained the clergy have heads like rocks.' Ignoring her husband's signals for departure, she was settling down cosily with Belle Collins for a gossip about the Gaiety.

'Sarah, take a bottle of champagne to the kitchen,' Hester directed 'And look, Mrs Trumper left you these – one for you and one for Annie.' There were pretty gold brooches in the white tissue packets that she was putting in Sarah's palm. 'And you needn't clear anything up until this evening. I want you to enjoy the wedding day.'

'Those girls of yours are spoilt, Hester,' Ellen observed before Sarah had time to leave the room. 'You don't know how to treat staff. They'll never respect you if you give them champagne and treats.'

'Yes, Aunt Ellen,' Hester murmured dutifully. She would go on saying, 'Yes, Aunt Ellen,' until tomorrow when Ellen departed, but she marvelled at her self-control. Had Ellen always been so interfering and irritating? or had she, Hester, grown up and away from her at last?

Two weeks later Belle had gone.

'I wish you wouldn't nag me,' she told Hester crossly, 'as if

358

I didn't know what I was doing. I can look after my own child, thank you very much.'

'Oh, Belle, I wish you wouldn't go! Without Alice I feel quite lost. Don't you miss her too? Without you and Posy the house will be empty.'

'Without Miss – I mean Mrs Trumper – ' Belle corrected herself hastily (for they were still unused to thinking of her as the inspector's wife), 'Posy would be left with the servants and I couldn't allow that.'

'How can you say such a thing? Annie and Sarah are splendid with her and so kind. She loves them both. . . . ' Too late, Hester stopped – that was the worst thing she could have said. Belle would not tolerate Posy caring for anyone but herself. So the cab rolled up and Sarah carried out the luggage and hugged the little girl for the last time. 'There, lovey, you'll remember to come and see us soon, won't you?'

But Posy in her red velvet bonnet and coat had no eyes for anyone until she had found her kitten. She squirmed in Sarah's arms calling out 'Blackie! Blackie! Where is Blackie? Oh, Mama, we haven't got Blackie. . . . '

Blackie had been shut in the kitchen at Belle's direction. The new landlady had stipulated no animals. Hester found tears rolling down her cheeks as the cab rolled away, with Posy still shrieking for Blackie and beating on the window with her fists.

'There, don't take on so, Miss Kelsey,' Sarah said, sniffing loudly herself. 'We're all going to miss the child – Annie's quite cut up and couldn't see her off. It's to be hoped she likes the new place, poor little soul.'

No one mentioned Belle. Although the servants had done so much for her child, she left them no present and indeed barely said goodbye. Hester suspected that never having had servants made Belle uneasy with them. 'We ought not to have got so fond of her,' she sighed, returning to the dining room. The little cat, released from the kitchen, bounded up the stairs and on to her lap, mewing and rubbing her face anxiously against Hester's arm. She hugged it convulsively, remembering how Posy had cried for her kitten. How could Belle do it? she wondered. Uprooting the child once again and planting her amongst strangers – it was cruel.

Hester wept again, tears dropping on to the black fur on her lap. She felt utterly dispirited. Apart from anything else, she had heard nothing from Victor. In the Easter vacation, he had promised, he would get in touch with her. Daily, she had risen with the hope that there would be a letter in the post. He had neither written or called and she knew that the Oxford term had started last week. She wondered uneasily if Connie had refused to release him. What did a man do then? Or had Lord Bridlington proved too strong for his son once again? She veered from despair to anger as the days passed and Victor made no sign.

On her way to the theatre that night, she directed her cab to Fitzherbert Square and stopped it outside the Bridlingtons' house. But it was obviously still unoccupied, its windows shuttered inside. The family would not come up to London until next month; they had arrived earlier last year because of Amy's coming-out ball.

'Drive on,' she told the cabby, sinking back in her seat. It was only a year since Uncle Joe took the house in Adelaide Crescent, she was remembering; only a year and yet her life had changed out of all recognition. She shivered suddenly, aware of an uneasiness she couldn't explain.

Three nights later Jupp, hanging out of his little office, called out, 'There's a letter for you, Miss Kelly. Came by hand.'

She approached slowly; she saw at once it was from Victor. That neat and tiny script with the classical 'E's' could only belong to him. She thanked the doorkeeper absently and hurried upstairs with the envelope held tightly in her hand. It had come at last. She banged the dressing-room door and leaned against it. Milly, thank God, had not yet arrived. Slitting open the envelope she scanned the letter – it was little more than a note – anxiously. She blinked, trying to take it in. What did he mean? *It is no use. You must forget me and that I ever spoke as I did. I have left Oxford for good and have gone to live in Normandy. Victor.*

Normandy? Was he mad? And how could she forget that he had spoken, told her he loved her? Anger chased dismay away as she hurried downstairs again to Jupp. 'Can you remember who left that note for me? Please. It's important.'

'Oh, I can remember all right, Miss Kelly. Know the gentleman well. He writes poetry about such places as these.' Jupp jerked his head at his surroundings. 'Often round this stage door to see one of you ladies is Mr Symons.'

'Mr Symons?'

'That's right. A nice young gentleman. Lives in Fountain Court, the Temple – seen it on his card many a time. Not that he's in law or anything. Just lives there and writes he tells me.'

'Thank you. That's very helpful. You can't remember the number in Fountain Court, I suppose?'

No, Jupp couldn't. But he assured her the gentleman's flat would be easy to find if she was thinking of sending a message. There were not many of them, and no doubt there would be a card with his name on pinned to the door. She thanked him again and hurried back to change into her costume for the opening scene of *Cinder-Ellen*. But all the time she changed and Milly chattered, she felt a sense of urgency and anxiety. Something was wrong. Why else would he go down from Oxford within a month or so of taking the degree he needed so badly? It was folly. What was causing him to behave in this fashion? One thing she determined on: she was not going to tolerate being kept in the dark any more. Tomorrow she would go to see this Mr Symons and find out why Victor had left England.

In the Temple the trees were full out (for it was sheltered here) and pools of blue shade lay under them. She walked carefully over the uneven cobblestones looking for Fountain Court and when at last she found it, she stopped to look at it appreciatively: a charming stone court with a fountain playing in the centre and a bench to sit on under a group of trees.

Her heart beat nervously as she climbed the stairs and examined cards pinned to doors. It took her ten minutes to locate the card that said *Arthur Symons* and she knocked timidly on the black door. No one answered. Outside she could hear the iron ring of heels on the cobbles. Someone called out a greeting. A door slammed and feet ran down the stairs below her. She knocked again, very firmly this time, until her gloved knuckles ached. Presently footsteps shuffled inside and a cross and sleepy voice called out, 'Who the devil's there?'

'Hester Kelsey, a friend of Victor Cockayne's.'

The unseen occupant seemed to be digesting this, then his voice said resignedly, 'It's terribly early, you know.'

'It's gone eleven.'

'Well, you'll have to wait. I'm not dressed or shaved yet – I'm hardly awake. Can you go and sit in the courtyard for ten minutes?'

She remembered the bench under the trees and she made her way there, laughing a little at the absurdity of the situation. She was to sit here meekly while the unknown irate voice dressed and shaved! Yes, it was ridiculous, but if she learned something about Victor's movements in the end then it would be worthwhile. Where he is concerned I shall always be willing to wait, she thought with painful clarity.

She looked up at the sky just visible through the leaves, and at the water sparkling in the stone basin round the fountain, and gradually a new peaceful feeling took the place of the angry frustration she had felt since yesterday. There was a timelessness about this place that calmed her. A pair of barristers passed, their bags over their shoulders and so absorbed in their conversation that they did not even glance her way.

Fifteen minutes later she climbed the stairs to the black

door again. It was now ajar and a voice called out, 'Come in! come in!'

She found herself in a narrow passage with doors on either side. The chink of china from the room on the left directed her there. A tall slight young man, with dusty-brown hair and moustache, was setting a tray on an already overcrowded desk.

'My apologies for not being able to receive you when you first called, but I never go to bed before three,' he explained. 'This is my *déjeuner* – the coffee's good. I learned to make it in France.' He looked at her appraisingly. 'Of course I recognized you as soon as I saw you walk out to sit on the bench. That's Hetty Kelly from the Gaiety, I told myself. The name Hester Kelsey had meant nothing of course. That must be your real name? Hester: that's the name of Victor's girl but Hester *what* I never knew.' And he looked at her quizzically.

'Please make no mistake, Mr Symons. I am not *Victor's girl*. I am simply a friend of his, but I am concerned to hear he has gone down without taking his degree. Gone to live in Normandy he says in his note to me.'

'Well, as a *friend* of his, Miss Kelsey, I am afraid I can tell you little.' He was pouring coffee for them both and, as he handed it to her, he looked at her coolly. 'I am in Victor's confidence, but I am not free to divulge his reasons to anyone who asks for them.'

She took the coffee and sipped it. 'You are making it hard for me. I have no *right* to ask you to tell me all you know about Victor. He is after all engaged to be married to Lady Constance Courage.'

Symons began to butter a roll. 'No longer. The engagement was terminated two weeks ago. By mutual consent of course. You say you are not Victor's girl, Miss Kelsey, but that is not my information. Victor wanted to marry you – the first time he has ever been serious about a woman. This singular betrothal to Lady Constance was doomed from the first and I told him so.'

She put down her cup and spread her hands in a gesture of bewilderment. 'Then why does he now write and tell me that I must forget him? That it is no use and he has left Oxford and gone to France?'

He got up and, with his hands in his pocket, looked out of the window. He was silent for nearly a minute and she watched his back, her throat quite dry with fear. For suddenly she knew – instinct told her – that he was about to give her unpleasant news. Because he had to deliver a blow he couldn't look at her.

'He wanted to go away and fade from everyone's memory,' he said slowly. 'To spend the last few months of his life free of commitments of any sort. . . . '

'The last few months of his life?' she repeated in a whisper. She stood up and leaned on the desk. 'What do you mean?'

'He saw a specialist a few months ago and again in the vacation. He confirmed that Victor is suffering from an incurable form of anaemia – he cannot live a year.'

From a long way away she heard him say, 'There! I knew it was too sudden. Now don't faint on me, my dear.' She felt him guide her back to her chair. As she lay back in it, he thought she looked as if she herself were dying, dying from a mortal wound. Her face and throat were ivory; her unfocussed eyes were without expression. Symons, cursing to himself, hurried out to the kitchen for water and he held her head as she drank from the glass.

'And you wanted me to believe he meant nothing to you,' he chided her gently.

She pushed the glass away and covered her face with her hands. In a muffled voice she said, 'It's been my dread all along – there was so obviously something wrong. Oh, God, how am I to bear it?' she asked in a despairing voice. 'I love him so much. I can't go on without him.' She looked pleadingly in his face. 'He has always been young and vigorous – he can't be dying. They've made a mistake.'

'He has accepted it as a fact,' he said gently. 'He stayed here last week because he didn't want to be alone and he got

364

over it here. We made plans, and he went away cheerfully to Dieppe to join some mutual friends of ours with whom he can live quite cheaply. He didn't want you or his parents and family to know why he had gone – the poor fellow is so tired of recriminations. His father has washed his hands of him – those were his words – simply because he wouldn't marry Connie Courage. He cut off his allowance and made it impossible for him to return to Oxford. Victor had nowhere to go so he came to me. . . .'

'He could have come to me!'

Symons shook his head. 'No man likes to go to a woman from a position of weakness. Especially if he loves her. After the family row he didn't want them to know about his . . . illness. He didn't want their pity. It had been a bitter quarrel, it seems. He was exhausted when he came here, and I'm thankful he went off last week in a better frame of mind. He gave me the note for you, to be delivered after he had gone. I have heard from him and he has settled in very well and is enjoying a new sort of freedom. Don't disturb that.'

'You expect me to accept this situation quietly?' she asked scornfully. 'I won't do it! If he has a year, then we'll spend it together.' She got up and collected her bag and gloves. 'If you won't give me his address in Dieppe I shall simply go and search for him myself. He'll be in the old quarter no doubt – oh, yes, I know Dieppe and the cafés where the poets and painters congregate.'

They looked at each other. Then with a shrug of resignation, Symons opened a drawer and took out a letter. 'Well, if you're prepared to throw away your reputation and go off alone to Dieppe . . .'

'My reputation?' She threw back her head and laughed, but there was little mirth in it. 'I long ago lost that if I ever had one. I'm just an ordinary girl from a slum. No one is ever going to have to worry about my reputation. Besides I'm from the Gaiety and people expect a Gaiety Girl to have no morals! It's very comforting when you're a dancer because you know you've lost before you've begun. So what are the odds?'

He smiled at her. 'Then there's no point in keeping this from you.'

She took out her little ivory note tablet and rapidly copied out the address from the back of the envelope. She thanked him mechanically. He had the feeling that she was barely aware of him now and was impatient to be gone.

'What about your contract at the Gaiety? If you break it your career there is finished. I know George Edwardes won't tolerate that. What will you do for money?'

'Money doesn't matter. I have enough.'

Poor girl, he thought. She has probably got a small nestegg that will keep her for a few months. He went to the window and watched her as she walked out of Fountain Court, over the cobblestones and past the fountain. The leaves made a pattern on her plain green dress and she looked like any beautiful young woman out for a walk. Only he knew the terrible burden she carried with her; for the angle of her head and the steadiness of her footsteps gave nothing away.

CHAPTER TEN

Twenty-four hours later she had completed her arrangements. Annie and Sarah would stay behind and look after the house, for she was determined to travel alone to France. Dressed quietly, people would take her for a governess going to a new post.

She had broken her contract at the Gaiety. 'It's a matter of life and death,' she told the Guv'nor.

'Or of a man, m'dear,' he said caustically. His own love affair with an actress was not going well and he was in a cynical mood. 'If you walk out in the middle of the show I shall never employ you again. You're finished. Understand?'

She understood, but she folded her lips and stood her ground and he looked at her and groaned to himself. When a woman looked like that he knew it was all up. Well, he would just go ahead and promote someone from the chorus.

'Would you consider Belle Collins, Mr Edwardes?'

'Belle?' He shook his head. 'The story of Belle's life is in her face. It's lost its bloom. You take care the same thing doesn't happen to you, m'dear. Troubled love affairs play havoc with a girl's looks.'

Now it was the next morning and she had a passage booked on the midday packet from Newhaven. She was taking only the clothes she would need: practical clothes like jumper coats and linen skirts. A wrap, a plaid rug and her own pillow, some linen sheets, a spirit stove and several books made up her luggage. In a basket she had collected invalid comforts for Victor: a hot water bag not easily come by in France, a thermometer, a feeding cup, aspirins, beef tea and calf's foot jelly from Jackson's.

'Goodbye, miss,' Sarah said tearfully, seeing her into the cab. 'You take care now in that abroad. Some nasty things 'appen. And if Sir Wilfred asks after you I'm to tell him you're on 'oliday with friends.'

'Quite right, Sarah. On no account is Sir Wilfred to have my address.' For she had visions of Wilfred fussing across to Dieppe in order to make a scene. Come what may, she intended to stay with Victor until – until the end. Not that she could believe he was so seriously ill. Not until she saw him with her own eyes would she believe that.

The cab took her to West Croydon station where she was in plenty of time for the Newhaven boat train. Sinking back into a corner seat, she breathed a sigh of relief. By this evening she would be in Dieppe. The new one-funnelled steamer *Sussex* had cut the long crossing to three hours.

There was misty sunshine in France, and a fresh little breeze to lift her spirits. As her cab carried her to a quiet little *pension* off the Rue St Jacques she could smell the familiar blend of drains, freshly-ground coffee and the fish market. The *pension* was the sort of place a timid young governess would stay at en route to a new job. It had a black and white tiled floor with pot plants in the bow windows which, in turn, were shrouded in yellowing lace curtains. The proprietor sat in a glass cage and watched the comings and goings of her lodgers with a shrewd eye.

'I trust you had a good crossing, mademoiselle?' she said, her small black eyes taking in every detail of Hester's travelling costume. Perhaps she thought them of too good a quality for the newcomer from England, for her face took on a decided sniff. Plainly dressed, certainly, she was thinking, but what young person seeking a post could afford such exquisite cloth and cut?

Innocently unaware that she was arousing suspicion in Madame's heart, Hester replied that the crossing had been excellent in the new swift little ship. Madame nodded and handed her the key; following her with her eyes as Hester carried her own bag up the narrow staircase.

Up in her room, Hester rang for hot water. When no one answered the bell she gave a wry smile – of course there would be no chambermaid in a place where one only paid a few francs a night. So she washed in cold water and brushed and re-coiled her hair. Changing her blouse for a crisp linen one, she donned the all-enveloping cloak she had worn for the crossing. Pinning on a golf cap, she surveyed herself critically in the spotty mirror. No one would give her a second glance, she thought with satisfaction. She looked like a French working girl hurrying home to supper.

She set out to walk, carrying her basket of invalid foods, but on enquiry at a nearby cafe, she found to her dismay that Victor's lodgings were in the Pollet, the old part of Dieppe near the fish quay and harbour. So she hailed a cab and presently it deposited her in a greasy street reeking of stale fish. She looked round in dismay. Why on earth had he come *here* of all places to die? Behind an iron gate was a flagged-stoned yard filled with a few sickly plants in pots. A pair of cats crouched on the step leading to the door. A woman wearing a dirty apron over her black dress came out to empty a zinc pail of dark grey water, which she threw into the yard, causing the cats to bolt. Hester shook the gate which was locked. '*Madame! Madame, s'il vous plait. . . .*'

The woman stared at her.

'I am looking for Monsieur Victor Cockayne. Is he at home?' Hester asked in French.

'Monsieur Cockayne does not live here,' the woman grunted and turned away indifferently.

A young girl thrust her head out of a window and inspected the stranger. Leaning out cautiously she whispered 'The English milord has left us.'

'Do you know his present address?'

The girl hesitated and the mother, turning round suddenly, shrieked angrily, 'Yvonne, go back to the kitchen at once. Do you want to burn my tarts?'

'Please, mademoiselle!' Hester implored.

'I do not know the address but each day he is at the Café des Tribuneaux with his friends....'

'Yvonne!'

The girl vanished and Hester turned away. She was sick with disappointment. To have come all this way to lose him again. She tightened her lips. She wasn't going to give up. She would stay in Dieppe until she did find him, however long it took. She had dismissed her cab and none were to be found in this unsalubrious area so, shifting the heavy basket, she began to trudge back across the bridge to the main part of the town. It was here she at last found a cab to take her to the Place du Puits Salé, where the cabby assured her she would find the café she sought.

'*Voilà*! Les Café des Tribuneaux!' said the cabby triumphantly.

She leaned out to inspect the tables where people lolled in the evening sunshine. Her head ached in the bright salt-filled air and she screwed up her eyes hoping to see Victor's familiar face. But he was not there.

'What other cafés are there?'

'What, in Dieppe? Why, there are many cafés, mamselle. You wish that I take you to them all?'

'No, only those popular with English poets and artists.'

'Ah, poets!' The cabby shrugged eloquently. 'Well, there is the Café Suisse and the Hotel des Arcades....'

'Take me to them, please.' Her voice was crisp, belying her spirits which had sunk completely. Something was beginning to tell her that she was on a fool's errand. She was never going to find him.

Both cafés were in the shadow of the railway which ran like a tram from the harbour through the town.

'Café Suisse, mamselle.'

Again there were tables on the pavement under a bright awning. Here sat a bohemian collection of men in dusty velvet jackets and crushed felt hats. She got down and looked eagerly about her. The cabby, she noticed, was watching her slyly, no doubt suspecting her of a hundred vices . . . She bit her lip and decided to pay him off and continue the search on foot. She returned to give one more look at the café. Men at nearby tables watched her with unconcealed interest. A beautiful young girl, plainly dressed and carrying a heavy basket, an anxious expression on her face, could not fail to arouse their interest.

'*Un café*, mademoiselle?' one young girl urged, grasping her cloak. 'Come and sit here.'

'No, thank you,' she said in English, and a man turned round and said 'Good God, Hester!'

She ran to him, her face flaring with excitement and relief. 'Oh, Victor – oh, Victor at last!'

'My dear girl, what on earth are you doing here?' Like this?' and he indicated the cloak and the basket, his face a mask of astonishment.

She hardly heard him. Her eyes were fixed on his face, looking fearfully now for signs of illness. There were none. He was noticeably thinner but that was all. His fair hair was longer and he was dressed in a shabby velvet suit of mole grey. There were several men with him, now looking up with interest. One of them had been sketching the scene round him, she saw. Now Victor leaned across to them and said, 'Au revoir. We shall meet later. But first I must escort my friend back to her hotel.' Grasping her arm none too gently, he led her away. 'Look here, Hester, what are you about? Don't you know that in France of all places a young woman must not walk the streets alone? Are you with your aunt and Wilfred?'

'No, I am alone.' She shifted her heavy basket to her other arm and he quickly took it from her.

'What on earth have you in here?'

'Medicines – for you.'

He lifted the checked cover and inspected the contents. When he looked up his eyes had softened. 'You brought these for me? All the way from London? But, dearest girl, my illness is not the sort that can be nursed with – with these

371

things. It is a disease of the blood and it will kill me eventually. Nothing can be done.'

'Oh, I can't believe it!' she cried in protest. 'You don't look ill, Victor. How can it be killing you? Doctors can be wrong – I know they can. . . .' Tired tears began to run down her cheeks, and he took her arm and squeezed it to his side.

'Don't, darling,' he said in a low voice. 'I can't bear it. I wish you hadn't come, Hester. It somehow makes it harder to bear when I remember – that we have no future.'

'We have the present,' she said, controlling her tears. 'I have come to be with you, Victor, for as long as there is left.'

'Dearest girl – darling idiot. You can't stay with me. It will ruin you.'

'We love each other.'

They stopped walking and he looked at her deeply. 'Yes,' he said softly. 'We love each other. I know that now.' Glancing round, he chose a café and led her to a secluded table where he ordered coffee for her and absinthe for himself. 'We must be sensible. I have no money and no future. We cannot marry and you cannot stay.'

She had regained her strength of purpose. 'No, I don't want to marry you. Knowing how your family feels about me, nothing would persuade me to marry you behind their back. I have come to be your mistress.' Her voice had trembled on the last word, but it was out now and she felt better.

'I could so easily be persuaded,' he said in a low voice. 'But because I love you I must be strong. You must go home, back to the Gaiety and to your own life.'

'Dearest Victor, you are all I want in life. I've left the Gaiety and the Guv'nor will never take me back now. So you see, I have nowhere to go but here with you.'

He took her hand, holding it tightly in both of his. 'I haven't a penny except for a tiny income from my grandmother's trust . . . there isn't enough for the two of us to live on. . . .'

'Would you believe me if I told you that money was no problem? That I have so much I hardly know what to do with it? I'm rich, Victor, for Uncle Joe left everything between me and Wilfred. So you see we don't have to think about money any more and you mustn't be silly and proud because that would only waste time.' Her smile faded as she met his eyes, the haunted eyes of a doomed man. 'I love you so much. Please let me stay with you, let us be happy while we can.'

He hastily turned his head away and she felt him trembling. It was her turn now to grasp his hand. It felt thin and dry in her warm clasp. There might be no future, but the present could be made to compensate for all the years that could never be. After a bit his hand relaxed and grasped hers again. There was no need for words now.

The Villa Dahlia stood on the edge of a wood above the sea, two kilometres from Dieppe. A sandy path led down from the terrace across a band of grass to the pebbled beach. From its verandah they could lie back in basket chairs and amuse themselves watching through binoculars the steamers and fishing boats sailing into port. The house belonged to an English family called Ducan who had visited Dieppe every summer until this one, when Mr Ducan's business had taken the family to South Africa for five years and the house was for letting. With the house went Suzanne Treport and her large silent husband Albert. Between them they kept the house and garden neat, and Suzanne cooked meals lavish with cream and butter, for the monsieur needed feeding up in her opinion. Yet all the time she pined for the Ducans, for Miss Victoria and Master Willy and the baby. Before a week was out, Hester felt she knew the family well.

'Ah, madame, the baby!' Suzanne lamented as she laid the table for lunch on the verandah. She wiped away a tear. 'That beautiful baby Eugénie – named after the Empress who came here so often, you understand. That beautiful child

373

will not remember me – she will be six years of age when next they come to Dieppe.'

Lying back on the wicker chaise longue, Hester would listen with lazy enjoyment to Suzanne's tales of the wonderful Ducans which she recounted to Victor in bed, making them both laugh. Her life seemed to be a dream. The days passed slowly in this little house that looked out on the sea in all its moods. The sound of the sea echoed through the dream, through the times when they lay together in the Ducan double bed, surfeited with love and joy. No two people had ever been so happy, she was convinced. 'You are the most beautiful woman I have ever known,' Victor told her. She knew now about the others; about Rosie Locke who had killed herself and about the young woman who was the daughter of his Oxford landlady. That had been a shock; it was such a recent affair, only last winter. But she realized now that he had never been celibate. A physical relationship with a woman was essential to him and she supposed most men were like this. Her father and Uncle Joe and the Guv'nor – they had all had women with whom they slept and whom their wives pretended not to know about. She lived through each day, now knowing that at the end of it was their private world of bed. Cradled in each other's arms, their voices a murmur, they talked long into the night. Neither put it into words; but each knew that time wasted in sleep was time lost for ever. He had a year left, perhaps less. Yet within a week of their relationship, hope had sprung up in him like fresh clear water. He was better. He felt and looked fitter than he had done for months. He even had an appetite again for Suzanne's food and he began to talk of the future, of marriage perhaps.

But Hester refused to consider it. 'Someday, perhaps, if your family can accept me and be happy about it, it will be time enough to talk of marriage.' For she too had begun to hope the doctors were wrong and there was a future for him. He was so well and happy, there was such a light in his eyes.

'What if you become pregnant?' he asked her.

She laughed aloud in his arms. 'That would be wonderful. We would have to get married then of course.'

'We would have to return to England then,' he reminded her. 'You need such a mass of papers before you can get married in France, that it would be considerably easier to have a bastard – no, I don't mean that, darling. But to marry in France would be truly *formidable*.'

One day they went into Dieppe to shop. They had avoided going in case they should run into someone who knew Hester. It was Victor who was nervous of chance encounters and who feared for her reputation and tried to shield her. Hester herself was too happy to bother about it. To Suzanne and Albert she was Madame Cockayne and it was as Madame Cockayne that she gave orders in the shops for goods to be delivered to the villa. They strolled over the cobblestones of the Grande Rue and loitered in the little shops, buying each other small keepsakes: a gold pin for Victor's cravat and a heart of ivory and silver on a fine chain for Hester. They sat on a seat on the Plage and watched the bathers emerging from the machines on the pebbles, listened to the shrill voices of the children riding donkeys.

'Call that a beach,' Hester said scornfully. 'Why, you can't dig *stones*! At Sewerston we had fine brown sand that sometimes dried out to bright yellow. I used to take my bucket and spade and Mama used to sit and watch me . . . ' Her voice trailed away as she looked back into her early childhood; when life had seemed so safe because she had a caring and clever mother who made the best of things. I wish she hadn't died, she thought. I wish Victor could have met her.

'At Sewerston you didn't have this nice warm breeze, I daresay,' Victor said lazily. He had tipped his hat over his eyes and was letting the warmth settle on him like a blessing.

She peeped under the brim of his hat and saw that he was dozing. How much better he looked, she thought exultantly. There was a lift to the corners of his mouth that had settled there in the last month. She took his hand, holding it gently, willing her own strength into him.

He roused at last, blinking at her in the bright sunlight. 'Come on, let's go to the Café Suisse for a cup of coffee.'

His friends, Jacques-Emile Blanche and Walter Sickert, were already there and sprang to their feet to meet Hester. She had a suspicion that they had been at the Café des Tribuneaux the day she found Victor and that they knew all about her; but it was obviously not an unusual occurrence for one of their number to be living with a woman, and they accepted her into the circle more easily for that reason.

'How do you think Victor is looking?' she asked Sickert, a handsome fair man with a gentle manner. 'Do you not see an improvement? He is so well that I'm beginning to think the doctors have made a mistake!' and she laughed happily.

'He certainly looks very bright,' Sickert said cautiously. He forebore to tell her that it was not unknown for someone with Victor's disease to have a recession. She looked so happy and trusting, this beautiful girl who had followed young Cockayne to France, he thought with pity.

She was about to enlarge on her theory when a young man, a thin wraithe of a boy, beautifully dressed and very correct in his manner, stopped, greeted Sickert and was asked to sit down. He was introduced as Aubrey Beardsley and he and Victor fell into eager conversation, for it appeared they had met once at the Rhymers' Club.

'Poor Beardsley – he is dying too, you know,' Sickert said sadly and then flushed painfully under her anguished glance. 'I mean,' he faltered, 'he has consumption and there is nothing to be done for him. . . .'

'I know what you mean,' she said with a heavy sigh. 'It is just that sometimes I want to believe we have a long future.'

He touched her hand gently. 'Maybe you have, my dear. We have all got to have hope of one sort or another or life would be unliveable.'

But only two days later Victor came to her and said that

he had just been weighed by his doctor. He had lost another seven pounds.

Her mouth went dry with fear, for she knew that this was the only outward sign of his illness: a relentless loss of weight and tiredness. She could now see the sharp new line to his jaw, the hollows round his eyes. Slowly but surely the disease was wasting him away. When he had taken his sleeping pill and was heavily asleep that night, she slid out of bed and sat in the chair by the window, wrapping herself in a shawl. Moonlight glanced off the waves on the shore below and along the coast she could see the lights of Dieppe. She could hear the gentle grind of the pebbles being dragged by the receding tide. If he could go out of life like that sea – without strain or pain – but rocked gently and comforted by loving hands – ah, if only he could! Tears blinded her as she looked into a cold future without her lover. I want his child, she told herself. I must have his child.

Not long after this, Ernest Dowson came to stay. He had received an advance from his publisher and had come to Normandy to live cheaply and write. At first Hester resented the intrusion of a third person in their lives, but when she saw them deep in talk on the verandah together and saw the new eager light in Victor's eyes when Dowson read Victor's poem and praised it, she was suddenly very glad.

'Dowson thinks it's the best thing I've done so far,' Victor told her. He was sitting up in bed, his writing block on his knees watching her brush her hair at the dressing table. 'If I can manage to write another I shall at least leave two good poems behind me. It's because you've made me so happy, darling,' he said and held out his hand to her. 'You know how much I love you, don't you?' he said softly against her hair.

It was on the tip of her tongue to tell him about the baby then. For she was almost certain that she was pregnant, had indeed been pregnant for six weeks. But she wanted to be sure, to have a medical opinion and a firm date. Then they could begin to make plans. So she turned towards him silently and he drew her into bed beside him. They made love with the sound of the sea coming clearly through the window and it had never been so good.

She was quite happy now for him to go into Dieppe with Dowson, to meet friends in the cafés and sit for hours talking. They were invariably late for meals and Suzanne would scold Monsieur Dowson for not taking more care of his friend, Monsieur Cockayne. This made Victor smile for of the two, Dowson certainly looked the frailer. But there was some reason for Suzanne's anxiety for when at last Ernest Dowson departed, Victor retired to bed with nausea and headache, lying there looking spent and tired. He refused to have Doctor Lefevre brought out from Dieppe and said it was a germ he had picked up. Hester found it was a relief to put her own nausea down to the same cause; for days she had been attempting to hide it. 'It must be a germ we have picked up,' she agreed. It was becoming urgent that she know for certain about the child, for if she really was pregnant she would have to tell him, and they would go back to England and get married as they had agreed. 'Darling, would you mind if I went back to London for a couple of nights? I need some warmer clothes now that autumn is almost here. These sea breezes are rather penetrating, you know.'

He looked up quickly, and to her surprise, she saw naked relief in his eyes. Taking her hand he kissed it. 'Of course you must go!'

'But not until you are better,' she assured him.

'There's nothing wrong with me. Suzanne will coddle me to death in your absence. Yes, do go – go this week and stay a few days and bring me back all the news. You must go in to Dieppe and book your cabin at once. It will be crowded at the end of the season.'

'There is no great hurry,' she assured him. After all, if she couldn't get home, there was always Dr Lefevre. She didn't like the sharp-eyed little man whom she suspected of knowing that she was not married to Victor. He was icily polite on the rare occasions that they met, polite but not friendly. Madame Lefevre, according to Suzanne, was the biggest gossip in Dieppe.

'I want you to go next week,' he told her firmly. 'I shall be out of bed and you can go with an easy mind. I'll make up a list of books you can ask the London Library to send me. And do bring back some decent soap that doesn't smell of attar of roses.' She was relieved to see that he was now set on her going, so she wrote to Sarah giving her the time of her arrival. But when the time came for them to part she clung to him. How thin he felt in her arms! Despite the happy smiles he was giving her, she sensed his emotion at parting and now she suddenly didn't want to go. She had an uneasy feeling that he was very weak and hiding it from her, that he had only got up to see her off because she would have worried if she had left him in bed.

'Dearest, are you sure you're feeling better?'

'Hester darling, what a fuss about two days! Of course I'm all right and I'm only waiting for you to go so that I can work on my poem.' He kissed her lightly. 'It's going to be good and I'll read it to you on Thursday when you return – so don't be late, darling, or I shall have to use Suzanne as my audience and translate the whole thing into French.' He was talking lightly as he led her to the cab that waited on the sandy road outside. He bent his head and kissed her lingeringly on the mouth. She smiled into his eyes. 'Don't – you'll make me wish more than ever that I wasn't going.'

'Goodbye, my dearest girl,' he said in a low voice and saw her into the cab. Then as it moved away, he moved with it. 'Hester,' he said in an urgent voice.

She leaned out and they clung together and Suzanne smiled proudly at the cabby: it was good to see young love on this perfect September day!

'Look after him, Suzanne!'

'I will, Madame, I will!'

Then the villa and Victor's tall figure (one hand raised in farewell) disappeared from view and she mopped her eyes.

How stupidly she was behaving. After all, England was only sixty miles away . . . She would soon be back.

It was delicious to breathe the crisp air of London again and she found she had missed it very much.

'I'm that glad to see you back, miss,' Sarah cried. 'Sir Wilfred is round every week to see if we've heard from you. He won't be put off, won't Sir Wilfred. He's like a terrier with a rat,' Sarah complained, setting her mistress's valise down in the bedroom. 'Then Miss Crook – Mrs Trumper I should say – has been round twice. Will you be staying this time, miss?'

Only two days, Hester told her. What a pest Wilfred was being. Why couldn't he let her have a private life of her own? She ordered a bath to be brought and lay soaking in it before the fire, her thoughts with her lover. They would each lie alone tonight. Then her mind took an abrupt turn and she stared down at her stomach. Was she pregnant? How long would it take to show? Tomorrow she had an appointment in Harley Street. Tomorrow she would know for certain. . . .

Sarah was tapping at the door. 'It's Sir Wilfred, Miss Kelsey. He's here again.'

She took her time dressing, maliciously keeping him waiting. What an old woman her cousin was! She greeted him coolly and then saw that he was barely keeping his temper under control.

'So this is the way you treat your family, Hester? Going off – God knows where – for months without a word to me or my mother. After all, we feel responsible for you. . . .'

'I'm sorry, Wilfred.' She had decided to be meek and pliable. 'It was bad of me, I know. I had no idea you would worry. After all, Sarah knew I was all right because I was sending them money every month. . . .'

'Sarah's a half wit! For all I knew she and Annie could have murdered you and buried you in the garden!'

She burst out laughing. 'A clear case for Inspector Trumper you thought! Really, Wilfred, you cannot be serious. I suppose I shall have to tell you where I've been all the summer. In Dieppe with Victor Cockayne.'

He nodding, spreading the tail of his coat as he at last sat down. 'I had guessed as much. One didn't know where that was all, and of course I did not tell my mother what I feared.' He frowned, his plump cheeks puffing up so that he looked like an offended hamster, she thought.

He was thinking that it was a blessing she hadn't been in Paris. It had been damned awkward not knowing where she was and dreading coming across her in Paris when he was with – certain people. Paris was his usual haunt, but Paris was as intimate as a village in many ways. One was always bumping into or avoiding people one knew. Thank God, he had never been to Dieppe on one of his weekend trips. 'Does he intend marrying you?'

'Why don't you ask whether I intend marrying him?' she asked dryly. 'He is very ill, you know.'

He nodded. 'So I have heard. Well, he'll leave a trail of bastards behind him when he goes.'

She felt her face stiffen. 'What can you mean?'

'His Oxford landlady's daughter has had a fine son – the image of Victor too,' he added maliciously, his eyes sharp, 'You're not pregnant too, I hope?'

'Don't be a fool,' she said angrily. 'You shouldn't repeat such gossip about Victor – it's probably quite untrue.' But in her heart she knew it was true. He had confessed as much to her. Was she to join the melancholy list of his discarded mistresses? That he was licentious she had guessed some time ago. It was part of his nature but only a small part, she thought with fierce loyalty. With an effort she smiled. 'Don't give me away, Wilfred, please. I'm going back in two days. I intend staying with Victor – until the end.'

Somehow she got rid of him at last and then she went to bed. Sarah brought her a light supper but she could eat little of it. A deep depression gripped her.

Next day the doctor confirmed her suspicions. She would

have a baby about the middle of April, and he advised her to return to London so that he could look after her. She shopped listlessly, the reality of the baby coming between her and the goods in the shops. She would have to tell him now and they would have to get married. She stopped as a thought struck her and another shopper ran into her. Muttering an apology, she turned aside to pretend to inspect a display of winter hats. *But would he marry her?* He hadn't offered to marry Rosie Locke or the landlady's daughter. . . .

The uneasiness remained with her all that day. If only she could run into his arms *now* – blurt it all out and be re-assured, hear him tell her that they would be married at once. Perhaps the English chaplain could marry them at All Saints Church in Dieppe – but no, he had said they would have to return to England. His father would be furious but none of that mattered now.

Next day, as the *Sussex* ploughed across the rough chan-nel and rain and salt spray spattered her face, she stood braced against the rails and waited for the first sight of Dieppe. She could not face the stuffy saloon and dining room. She suddenly felt unfamiliar nausea grip her stomach, leaned precariously over a rail and was violently sick. A hand gripped her and a red-faced old gentleman firmly escorted her to the saloon. 'It is dangerous for a lady on deck, madam,' he informed her and took his leave, firmly convinced he had done her a good turn. It was only with the help of smelling salts that she completed the journey, and by the time they reached harbour she looked decidedly the worse for wear. The wind had subsided now and a pale sunlight glanced off the waves. She went quickly through the customs and secured a cab. Never had she felt such an eagerness to be *home*, for the house she shared with Victor was home now.

In the sandy road she descended with difficulty and counted out the cab fare, wondering where everyone was. Surely they hadn't forgotten she was returning on the after-noon boat?

She left the luggage in the road and climbed the steps to

the Villa Dahlia. Why were all the blinds drawn? The sun was not fierce enough for that surely, but Suzanne always guarded the Ducan carpets and furniture quite fanatically.

Suddenly the lace curtains across the glass front door quivered and the door slowly opened revealing Suzanne's troubled face. 'Madame – oh, *ce pauvre m'sieur!*'

Then Hester understood. Terror froze her and she could not utter a sound. Putting out a hand, she felt Suzanne support her, drawing her inside.

'Madame, m'sieur died this morning – about dawn.'

The shock was like a fierce blow on the face. She bent double and her knees gave way. When she came to, she was lying on the hard horsehair sofa inside the hall and Suzanne was holding a bunch of burning feathers to her nostrils. She pushed them away and struggled to her feet, putting a trembling hand to her icy face. God, how sick she felt – the urgent need to vomit seized her and she stumbled down the steps to the rosebed below where she was ignominiously sick in full view of the road.

Suzanne ran for a damp cloth and then supported her into the house to the sofa again. 'Lie back, madame. You will feel better presently and I shall bring you the brandy. . . .'

'Where is he? How did it happen?'

'He was very quiet all yesterday. He sat looking out to the sea and he slept sometimes. He would eat nothing. Then this morning I took him in his tea – and I saw at once what had happened. He looks so at peace, madame. Will you come and see him?'

'No. *No.*'

'Monsieur le docteur will be here again at six tonight. Perhaps, madame, you will see monsieur then. I have done everything for him that is necessary.'

Hester looked at her dully. Poor Suzanne. She wanted her mistress to conform to the proprieties and view the dead body. But it wouldn't be Victor any more. Just a man's shrunken carcase on their bed – the bed where they had made

383

love so often. No, she wouldn't look at him. She would remember him as she had seen him last, standing on the road watching her drive away. She rose stiffly. 'Please tell Albert that I shall need him to take telegrams in to Dieppe. In about five minutes.'

In the shaded little drawing room, there were roses from the garden in a bowl on the desk. She sat down, looking at the flowers he had had put there for her only yesterday. She felt tears rising hotly to her eyes and fought them back. Not yet. There was much to do for after the telegrams had been sent, she would go back to England on the midnight packet.

Dr Lefevre drove up to the villa at six precisely, to find the woman he had guessed was not really Madame Cockayne dressed for a journey, with her valises being strapped up by the servant.

Hester motioned him to sit down. 'Do not be surprised to see me leaving so soon, Doctor Lefevre. I am not Monsieur Cockayne's wife, you see, and since his family will be arriving tomorrow morning, I have decided to leave tonight.'

The doctor bowed. 'Monsieur Cockayne knew his time had come, mademoiselle. I told him last week that he had only a week or so left. He had become very weak.'

She turned her white face to him. 'He knew last week?'

'He insisted on knowing, for he did not wish you to be here at the end. I was to ask you to journey to Paris to obtain a special medicine for him . . . instead you yourself suggested returning to England for two or three days. He wrote and told me this himself. He was very tranquil.'

Tears had frozen on the surface of her eyes and she could not speak. So that was why he had looked relieved when she suggested leaving him for a short time. He wanted to die alone. She knew why that was: he loved her and could not bear to see how she would suffer at the parting. Lifting her travelling veil, she carefully wiped away the moisture round her eyes. 'Thank you for telling me this.' She picked up a piece of paper and handed it to him. 'This is my London address if it should be necessary to contact me again. The servants are paid. Tomorrow Lord Bridlington and Lord Hornsea will arrive to take the body back to England. They have replied to my telegram to that effect.'

The last he saw of her was a shadowed face in the cab that took her away, and he noticed that she didn't look back even though Suzanne stood and waved with tears running down her face.

When she had stopped weeping she sent for Wilfred.

'Hester, for God's sake!' There was no mistaking the horror in his tone when she told him. He was standing with his back to the window in the Markham Square drawing room so she could not see his expression; but his tone of voice was enough.

'April, the doctor says.'

He walked jerkily up and down, his hands under his coat tails, sucking his underlip in puzzled anger. How could Hester have been such a fool, he wondered. Living with Cockayne all those months and not getting a ring on her finger. Good God, she was going to have a bastard! If it got out she would be done for! 'You will have to get rid of it,' he said distastefully. 'We have enough money to have the whole thing hushed up. . . .'

'No,' Hester said stubbornly.

He stared at her angrily. 'Don't be a fool! There is nothing else for it.'

'I am not going to kill this child because Society says I must. I'll find someone to marry me – pay them well; for after all we have enough money, haven't we?' she mocked him.

'Buy a husband? Preposterous! Only a scallywag would consent to such a thing. Think of the implications. He would have a hand in running the Prickard Line and no doubt his hand would never be out of the till. . . .' He stopped and his face was frozen in consternation suddenly. 'The press. My God, you haven't thought of that! If this leaks into the press we're finished. The Americans set a very high moral value on a business like ours. The slightest whiff of scandal and our ships will be empty. You, a joint-owner of the Line having an illegitimate child . . . ' His voice shuddered into silence. 'We're ruined,' he added after a bit. Then he came and sat down by the silent form of his cousin. 'You will have to go abroad, have the child there and get it farmed out. We can put it about that you're doing a grand tour of Europe. . . . '

'I'm keeping the child. This is Victor's child and I want it.'

'You are mad,' Wilfred said gloomily. 'Stark staring mad.' He stared silently ahead, his brain working fast. 'There is only one thing to do,' he said at last. 'You will have to marry me.'

He saw by her amazement that Cockayne had told her about him. It was just as well, for it made it easier to put into words his feelings about women, his repugnance at the idea of marriage. Even as he talked it became clearer to him every minute that this was an ideal solution for them both. A complete cover for him, a father for the child, status for Hester. Above all, the Line would remain in their joint owner-ship.

'And even better,' he ended, 'the child will inherit it all some day. It's what my father intended. I shall never have a child of my own but this infant will inherit the title which would otherwise die out. . . . '

'It could be a girl,' Hester interposed dryly. She felt too spent to argue with him any longer. She was trembling with weakness and her throat was dry. Grief lay like a pall on her spirit. Oh, God, what am I to do? she wondered. This is a way out. The child will have a place in life. I can bring it up at Stanhope. I can keep Victor's child.

'We shall have to act quickly,' Wilfed was saying briskly as if she had already consented. 'We can get married by special licence this week and let Mama know later.' She would make a terrible fuss, he thought gloomily, for she wasn't fond of Hester.

'She will hate the idea,' Hester said. 'Especially as she doesn't know about you – about you and women, I mean.' She put her head down to hide the sudden tears. The baby had trapped her for good, she realized with a feeling of despair. Perhaps she should agree to have it adopted – no, no, she couldn't consent to that, not Victor's child. Putting her hands to her face she wept and Wilfred patted her shoulder and said she was to leave everything to him.

She couldn't tell him that she was crying now because all her future was being held to ransom.

Ellen wasted no time in showing her feelings by telegram and letter. *Do not proceed* said her last telegram, but by that time they had been married in a Chelsea church. Hester had insisted that her aunt should know about the wedding beforehand, and Wilfred agreed when he realized that his mother would not be able to get to London in time for the ceremony. Her nagging he could not stand, he told himself.

The Blands acted as witnesses. Cissie tried hard to conceal her amazement, but at last burst out when they were alone, 'Why your *cousin* of all people? You could have had anyone, Hester. You could have had that Russian count. . . . '

'No, Cissie, dear, I couldn't. I know and like Wilfred – it's as good a basis for marriage as any,' Hester said, smiling brightly. They were packing her valise and trunk for the journey north to Stanhope ('Not even a honeymoon journey!' Cissie lamented). In the bedroom, a brisk fire leaped up the chimney and a huge bowl of chrysanthemums gave off a peppery smell. Hester felt her throat contract as she went through the charade of being a happily married young woman for the sake of Cissie; who could only stare at her with a bemused expression, as she helped unbutton the biscuit-coloured two piece in which Hester had been married. Watching her step into a travelling dress of bronze velvet that would go under a broadtail coat for the journey, she said wistfully, 'You ought to have had a proper wedding at St Margaret's. I don't understand the hurry.'

Hester was adjusting the velvet toque with egret feathers

on her dark hair. Avoiding Cissie's eyes in the mirror, she said, 'Oh, Wilfred is going to America next week for two months. We're opening an office in Boston – didn't I tell you? No, I'm not going with him just yet; there's a lot to see to at Stanhope, you know.'

'I've known you long enough to talk to you like a sister, Hester.'

Heavens, what's coming now? Hester thought with a suppressed gurgle of rather hysterical laughter.

'Marriage is *forever*, you know. People like us can't divorce. It ruins us.'

Hester nodded. *Forever*. The words closed round her like handcuffs.

'If you have a love affair you must keep it out of the public gaze.'

Hester went across to her friend and hugged her. 'Dear Cissie, please don't worry. I know the rules and I'll be good.'

'You!' Cissie said scornfully – but she patted her friend approvingly.

PART THREE
Hester Prickard

CHAPTER ONE

Stanhope seemed to be afloat like a great ship on a sea that was November mist. Although only midday, lamplight showed through several of the long Georgian windows. The last frail yellow leaves were dropping slowly off the trees in the park. In the chestnut avenue lay great heaps of these rusty leaves, and a pair of gardeners were energetically clearing away the last of them.

The whole place seemed a hive of activity. A man was standing on a ladder mending a window, two boys in green aprons were forming a small procession carrying pot plants from the hothouses to the house and a maid was shaking a duster from one of the spare rooms in the east wing. The young Prickards were about to hold one of their shooting house parties.

Moisture dripped dismally over everything, running like crystal beads along the wire fences in the park. When a thin sunlight broke through for ten minutes, it made the spiders' webs sparkle like gold chains. Sounds fell heavily in the utter stillness and the sad peep of a robin in a hedge sounded as clear as a bell. Through the meadows glided the great green snake that was the river in winter and Hester, who could see it from her sitting room on the ground floor, gave a shiver of distaste. Ugh, November! A month to dormouse in when in the country. The old longing returned like an ache as she stared out – London at Christmas with the Gaiety filled with voices, laughter and music. She could smell again the hothouse flowers waiting for the Girls in Jupp's office. Sometimes they contained a present of jewellery. She could hear again the hansoms' bells jingling as they drove up to the stage door to carry them off to supper at Rules . . . She sighed sharply. It seemed a lifetime away. She was no longer Hetty Kelly, one of the Big Eight, but Lady Prickard, wife of that sobersided baronet Sir Wilfred Prickard, landowner and magistrate. And the mother of a son. Victor Cockayne's child whom they had christened Joseph Patrick.

Her face fell easily into slack lines of boredom nowadays and, as she looked through the window, she was seeing nothing of the park under winter's siege. Instead she saw a row of prancing, dancing legs as the Girls went through their routine. Oh, those gay rippling catchy tunes of Meyer Lutz's! Sharp longing possessed her. If only – if only she could go back! But no one could ever do that.

Wilfred made the most easygoing of husbands, going abroad a lot both on business and pleasure. She didn't dare question him about his life, but the full horror of the risks he ran had become plain to her last May, when Oscar Wilde had been sentenced to two years hard labour (and consequent ruin) for sodomy. She had tried to hint to him that he stood to lose much, but he had shrugged and told her that he always went on the Continent with his friends. There were no vice laws in France. . . .

Perhaps it was better not to know much more than that, she told herself. They each knew where they stood in this odd alliance. He laid no claims to her privacy nor she to his. They met chiefly at weekends either at home or at other people's houses. He loved little Patrick as if the boy were his own and was an indulgent companion when they rode out together. But she was bored and dissatisfied. More and more lately, the longing for a real husband possessed her. Sometimes, in the dark stretches of the nights, she would wake and expect to find Victor lying beside her in the big four poster bed. Then stark reality would deal hammer blows to her heart. He was dead and she had to pretend to be her cousin's wife.

No use repining.

She turned from the window yawning, until her eyes watered. Going across to the fire, she poked the logs into new life with the toe of her slipper. Then she returned to the little walnut bureau set between the windows and applied herself once more to writing out the place cards (and cards for bedroom doors) needed for the weekend. Not many this time. Lord and Lady Lomon, Lord and Lady Amroth (Sylvia Amroth was Lomon's sister), Mr and Mrs Henry Cherry, Miss Nolan and Arthur Dalbeity, the young Scots M.P. who was already being tipped as a future Prime Minister. The Cherrys were a dull pair: he was a shipping colleague of Wilfred's. Miss Nolan was American, a young and lively girl with an outspoken tongue. Hester smiled to herself as she wrote out the name for the Pink Room. Clarice Nolan could be guaranteed to stir some life into this weekend. She also had money and would make Dalbeity an excellent wife – that anyway was the view of old Lady Dalbeity, who had begged Hester to invite the railway heiress to meet her son.

Coming to the Amroths' names she laid down her pen. They would be in separate rooms – Sylvia had made sure of that. Her health, she said, was so wretched and she slept so atrociously. Hester could barely tolerate Sylvia Amroth, a fading beauty who had been the Prince of Wales's mistress before Daisy Brooke came on the scene.

Then there was Amroth. She felt a quiver of inward excitement at the thought of him. She realized that they were on the brink of a love affair. He had pursued her relentlessly all last summer. Well, she liked him – indeed she was greatly attracted to him. Not that she would ever love anyone again after Victor. She was sure of that. Indeed Amroth attracted her almost against her will. He had dark good looks, a fine vigorous body and daring eyes. He rode a dashing course across country in rather the same way he attacked life. He was lonely. So was she. *Perhaps this weekend,* she thought and felt her breath quicken at the thought.

'Miss Bentley's here, m'lady,' said Sarah at the door. Sarah had come with her from the Markham Square house and was now established as head parlourmaid at Stanhope. After two years she still hated the country and was always planning to return to London but never going.

Hester swung round to smile at the red cheerful face. 'I quite forgot it was Thursday! Show her in, Sarah.'

Every Thursday, Agnes trudged across the park from the new dower house that Wilfred had built for his mother. It was visible from the sitting-room windows now that the trees were bare: a redbrick pile with towers, cupolas, fancy tiling and stained glass. It had been built to Ellen's taste and was hideous. Inside, behind the thick Nottingham lace curtains, lay hot rooms stuffed with furniture. Enormous fires burned in the grates all the year round, and a small band of servants kept Ellen moderately satisfied with her lot. She rarely went out herself, so every Thursday Agnes was despatched to the big house to glean news. Agnes always went gladly, as she took a proprietory interest in the baby. His upbringing gave her misgivings. She didn't think Miss Hester (as she still called her) had much idea or she wouldn't have engaged that starched nurse to bring up the heir. Agnes's own niece, Rose Umpleby (who was laundry maid at Stanhope), was the perfect nurse for the child. Rose had helped to bring up ten little brothers and sisters. There was nothing you could teach young Rose when it came to babies and she could sing lullabies in her soft warm Yorkshire dialect until Kingdom come.

But Hester, frightened by her own ignorance of babies, had taken refuge in Nurse, a formidable woman who was hospital trained and able to deal with those puzzling illnesses babies so often got. Rose was only twenty and Hester couldn't see herself leaning on Rose as she leaned confidently on Nurse.

'Tush, a few germs don't matter,' Agnes said comfortably. 'That one you've got with her collar and cuffs doesn't know how to cuddle a young 'un. They need cuddling, Miss Hester.' She had returned to the attack now, warming her feet at the fire and untying her bonnet strings. 'Well, now, I'll say no more but if I had my way. . . .'

'Yes, yes, Agnes,' Hester said hurriedly. 'How is my aunt?'

394

'She'd be better for a good brisk walk every day as I tell her.' In old age Agnes had become devastatingly frank with all the Prickards and they shrank from her tongue. Her eyes rested critically now on young Lady Prickard. 'An' you're looking right peaky yourself. All these late nights and running about. You mark my words, you'll lose your beauty if you're not careful.'

'Goodness, Agnes, do you think I'm pretty?' Hester asked innocently. 'You never used to do. And how you scolded me when I preened before the glass!'

'Well, you're not bad,' conceded the old woman, busy putting on her spectacles. 'I've brought you this.' Out of a capacious covered basket she produced a folded newspaper, the Sewerston Gazette. 'Thought you'd be interested in seeing about young Hoggarth,' and she tapped a news item with a finger.

'Tommy Hoggarth?' Hester reached for the paper and eagerly pored over the smudged photograph of a soldier. It was difficult to see freckled-faced Tommy in this man posing with a fixed stare into the camera. *Local man wins medal* said the caption, and it went on to relate how Sergeant Thomas Hoggarth had led a small party from the 2nd battalion of the 60th Rifles against the Pathans on the North West Frontier. Their officer had been killed and Sergeant Hoggarth had rallied the men and pressed home the attack, putting the tribesmen to flight. For his leadership and courage he had received the Indian Service Medal with clasp.

Looking at Agnes with shining eyes, Hester said, 'I always knew Tommy was brave! Doesn't he look splendid?'

'Well, he takes more after his mother, I will say that. Willy Hoggarth was a plain man. You know he's dead? Some time last year and he's left a pile of money by all accounts. Mrs Hoggarth's sold the shop and built a villa near that Mrs Weston's. What d'you think of that?'

'I'll call on Mrs Hoggarth next time I'm in Sewerston,' Hester said. 'I shall have to go and see the aunts before long.' The Miss Kelseys had been receiving a regular income from their niece ever since Agatha had her stroke two years ago. Up till then she had refused all offers of help from Hester. Now she no longer had a say in the matter. Mary and Martha had closed the shop and turned it into a living room. They could now afford to employ a young servant and had taken their place in Sewerston's social life as Lady Prickard's aunts. They were able to give generously to the church, to sit on committees and organize bazaars. They had never been so happy. Agatha sat in her chair looking on at the changes round her with indifferent eyes.

'I should do that, Miss Hester. Now are you going to show me the little man? His granny's very anxious for a report on him.'

'Yes, Agnes,' Hester sighed and led the way to the west wing, knowing she was in for a bad ten minutes; for Nurse openly resented these visits and outspoken comments from Miss Agnes Bentley.

Today she stood up stiffly and faced her employer, pretending that Agnes was not present. There was not a vestige of welcome in her mein.

Avoiding meeting those angry eyes, Hester knelt on the rug with her son. It was a constant disappointment to her that Patrick was not in the least like his father. She always hoped wistfully for a change in his looks, but as he grew he looked more and more like Will Kelsey with his black curls, dancing eyes and red cheeks. Like his grandfather he had a strong will and violent temper. Of the gentle fair-haired Victor Cockayne he showed not a sign. He still wore lawn petticoats and today he wore a scarlet Zoave jacket over them, while his fat little legs were encased in striped socks and there were red kid shoes with rosettes on his feet. He scrambled up, flinging his arms round his mother's neck and pointing to the impressive tower of wooden bricks he was building. 'Mamma help Pat?' he coaxed. 'High – high – ' and he threw his arm into the air.

'It's lovely, darling. You are a clever boy.' Hester buried her face in his soft little neck. It was at times like these she was utterly thankful that she had made the decision to keep her child. He smelt delightfully of violet powder and his lawn dress was starched and goffered – Nurse certainly kept him beautifully clean. His little body was reassuringly sturdy in his mother's arms.

Agnes bent down to kiss him. 'Poor little love, he's looking a bit peaky I'd say.'

'He's had a cold,' Nurse said in a detached voice, looking over Agnes's head.

'Well, this is a nasty draughty floor. . . . '

'Aggie, look, look!' Patrick tugged at her skirt, pointing proudly at his brick tower.

Bending down, Nurse destroyed it with a swift movement. 'Now it's time for your dinner. Say goodbye to Mama.'

For a moment he looked stunned with disappointment, then he opened his mouth and roared with rage, throwing himself backwards on to the floor and kicking out with his legs. With an effort Nurse heaved him up and dumped him in his high chair, her face red with annoyance. 'No pudding for you today, Patrick. I told you what would happen next time you were naughty.'

'Oh, Nurse, I don't think you ought to take away his food,' Hester demurred nervously.

'Of course she shouldn't!' Agnes exclaimed. 'Yon lad needs his food. Better a sharp slap than that. But it's her own fault the little un's lost his temper . . . knocking his bricks on purpose. She's spoiling his temper. . . . '

'Kindly stop interfering in my nursery, Miss Bentley! My lady, I'd be obliged if you would take Miss Bentley away before there's more trouble. She's bad for the child. . . . '

'Ho, I like that!' Agnes retorted with spirit. 'The idea! You can't do with a bit of plain speaking. . . . '

'Yes, yes, Agnes, but do come away,' Hester urged, leading the old woman out of the room.

'One moment, my lady,' Nurse had followed her to the door. 'While you're here I'd like to know about the nursery maid. Lottie's been gone a week now. When can I expect her back? I'm not able to manage on my own – it's too much.'

'Lottie's mother is ill – you know that. I don't want to sack her, she's a good girl. . . . '

'I can't manage on my own and that's flat,' Nurse said shortly. 'So you had better find someone quickly.'

Hester stared at her. There was no mistaking the insolent tone. 'I understand how you feel but we must give Lottie a chance to return before engaging someone in her place. I'll find out if Wiston can spare someone to wait on the nursery.'

'You're frightened to death of yon besom,' Agnes said annoyingly when they had got back to the sitting room. 'She's a bad sort. Did you see her eyes? Cold as glass. She hurt the baby. I saw the pinch she gave him. The heartless hussy. Now what d'you say to getting rid of her, Miss Hester, and putting Rose in her place?' There was silence and she tied on her bonnet. 'Well, I'll say no more. I hope I know my place. I'm having a bite with Mrs Gaskell over at the stables. We meet at the sewing circle – she's a nice body but can't somehow get her health. Well, I thank the Lord daily for my good health – I haven't lost me teeth yet,' and she bared them for Hester's benefit.

'We all know you're a wonderful woman, Agnes,' Hester said weakly. Agnes's visits usually had that effect.

'And there's another thing, t'little lad's not talking enough. You ought to have had Rose like I said. She's a rare one with children.'

She went away at last, leaving Hester to finish writing the cards in a rush. She went upstairs to put them in the slots in each door and, ringing for Sarah to accompany her, inspected each room carefully. Fresh blotting paper on a desk and more writing paper. A new waste paper basket needed here. An extra blanket in this room. 'Lady Amroth will want a fresh supply of Malvern water by her bed each day, so don't forget that. Have the gardeners brought in plenty of apple logs for the fires? They smell so sweetly in a bedroom. Is Wiston still busy with the silver? Then I won't bother him yet. I'll get Sir Wilfred to give him my list later when they are doing the wine together.'

There was just time for a walk before lunch. Her maid, Julie, fetched her a fur cape and a soft velvet cap and changed her bronze shoes for sturdy outdoor ones. 'You should not be going out, milady, it is not fit,' she said with a shudder of distaste.

'When you've spent a little more time in England, you'll call this "a fine day"!' Hester laughed and ran downstairs.

She went in the direction she preferred above all others, down through the rose garden and out on to the broad stretch of land that went down to the lake. She remembered how, when Stanhope first became her home, she had held its soil in her palm and had known then that she loved it. Returning as its mistress had seemed perfectly natural. It was her money that ran Stanhope, she who paid its servants. Wilfred took little interest in a place he saw only at weekends. Wilfred was its titular master, but those who worked there knew to whom they owed their daily bread.

The bare branches dripped moisture on her head as she walked briskly across the spongy ground, holding her skirt clear of the rank grass. Soon there was colour in her cheeks again. She looked round cautiously. There was no one about. She started to run down the slope, laughing under her breath and nearly losing her velvet cap in the process. Suddenly it was good to be alive and young, with lovely Stanhope to roam in and a baby in the nursery. It was only at nights, alone in that huge four poster bed, that her spirits sank into depression and she remembered that she was married to a man who could never be a husband to her and whom she could not love.

That night she woke with a jerk. She had dreamed that Patrick was screaming at the top of his voice, calling to her. She sat up, shivering in the cold air. Fumbling for matches she lit the candle by her bed. She found herself straining her ears for the child's voice again. It had been so vivid. . . .

I'm uneasy about Nurse, that's what it is, she thought, blaming Agnes for unsettling her.

Getting out of bed, she closed the big window and stood for a moment or two looking out on to the park. The weather had changed overnight and a sharp frost had coated every tree with white. In the dim light just before dawn she could just make out the shapes of the park fence and the roof of the dower house. She drew the damask curtains with a jerk and then climbed back into bed and pulled the sheet up to her chin. She often woke at this soul-destroying hour before dawn when life seemed hopeless and she was the loneliest person in it. She rebelled fiercely against the celibacy of her life. Was it to be so always? Must she wake at this hour for years and years and find herself alone in this bed? There were those in their circle who took lovers and were very discreet about it. None of their friends seemed to know about Wilfred . . . Even if her cousin had been capable of a normal relationship she could not have slept with him. To her he was like a brother, and on that basis they dealt amiably enough with each other. He had a genuine love for Patrick and was proud to call him his son. No, she must never grumble about Wilfred for he had been good to her and kept her secret. Indeed he was glad that people thought Patrick was his son. But I need a lover, she thought. Tears trickled out of her closed eyes as she remembered Victor and those few short months they had spent together.

Sorrow filled her. Although there was no one to hear her sobs, she tried to bury them in her pillow. It was a long time before she slept again.

CHAPTER TWO

On Friday afternoon Wilfred came home. He always arrived at the last moment because he knew Hester would have seen to every detail, only leaving the selection of wines to him.

Wiston had elected to stay with the young Prickards much to Ellen's annoyance, and life had become busy and full for him because the young people entertained lavishly. Between them, he and Wilfred brought in wine from shippers and studied their cellar book gravely.

'Last time he was here, Lord Lomon enjoyed the claret very much, if you remember, sir? There are several bottles of that year left and the younger wine is coming along nicely, I believe.' Wiston held the lamp aloft for them to peer at the labels. 'Then I thought you might like some of the German wine. . . .'

'No, champagne, Wiston. And the sweet sherry for dessert.' Wilfred looked at the menus he held in his hand, his eyes lighting up suddenly. 'Oh, good, Mrs McAndrew's giving us a Bombe Glacé tomorrow night.' He still adored sweet puddings, and his interest in them was greater than in the wines that went with them.

They had started to retrace their steps, when Wilfred suddenly stopped and said rather hesitantly, 'Tell me the truth, Wiston. What do you think of Nurse? Is she good for Patrick?'

Wiston hesitated in his turn. 'I think she looks after Master Patrick quite well, sir. A bit too strict, I fear.' He chewed his lower lip for a moment then added, 'They say she's become very friendly with Gaskell, sir.'

401

'But he's married!'

'I think Nurse knows that. She visits him at the cottage when Mrs Gaskell is out – so Sarah says.'

Gaskell was the rather smart coachman who had been with them for only a year. Wilfred looked harassed. 'There is likely to be trouble there. Mrs Gaskell is not a woman to tolerate any goings-on.'

'Indeed not, sir. But Nurse is a very determined woman. She has made no friends in the servants' hall, so of course the women are only too ready to speak. They don't like her.'

'It won't do, Wiston. Her ladyship will have to speak to her.'

But he found Hester reluctant to interfere. 'It's just servants' tales, Wilfred. I wish you and Agnes wouldn't be so suspicious of the woman. She looks after Patrick very well.'

'Wiston thinks she's too strict. . . .'

'Agnes has been gossiping with him! Anyway there's no time to discuss it now. The carriages have gone to the junction and they'll all be here presently.'

Soon the hall was filled with their guests, who sat down to tea in their travelling clothes. There was a huge log fire, and hot crumpets dripping with butter were being handed round by Arthur, the footman. Sarah stood by her mistress waiting to hand round the teacups; she loved these weekend parties, when she could glimpse the very people who filled the gossip columns of that paper Mr Wiston took. She watched Lady Lomon who had thrown back her furs and was declaring that she was thawing nicely. Now *she* was a duke's daughter, but you never would have guessed it. She looked just like the baker's wife in the village. But it was Lady Amroth whom Sarah really wanted to see. They said she had been the Prince of Wales's lovebird – you could see she had been pretty once. Down in the kitchen later that evening she gave a graphic account of the professional beauty. 'Ever so thin she is. Looks cantankerous too. I don't thinks she's so nice as they make out in the papers.'

'They never are,' Mrs McAndrew said scornfully. 'Hussies the lot of 'em.'

'She looks like a lady fox – sharp, you know.'

It was an apt description. There was something foxy about Lady Amroth's sharp features and hazel eyes under the mass of bright red hair.

Hester was listening to Sylvia's thin drawl as she talked across the room to her host. She was telling him in no uncertain terms that he ought to have put Patrick down for Eton at birth. 'I fear you will never get him in now. I'll see what I can do for you. . . . '

'Please don't bother,' Wilfred said. He smiled at her. 'The boy will be going to his father's old school.'

Hester hastily concealed a smile. Sylvia would not have seen the *double entendre* of course. His father's old school.

'Why are you smiling?'

She looked up and found Amroth looking down quizzically at her. 'Like the Sphinx, you are allowing a small and knowing smile to play round your beautiful mouth. Very secretive. Or do I mean like Mona Lisa?' He sat down on a chair next to hers. 'Dearest Hester, I've been thirsty for a glimpse of you.'

'You're becoming very flowery all of a sudden,' she teased him. 'That's not your style at all.'

His dark eyes looked intently into hers. 'I mean it. I've been counting the hours to today. You know how I feel about you.'

She threw him an eager, smiling glance and, then saw Mrs Cherry peering blandly in their direction. The old pussy, she thought and trod warningly on his toe. But excitement filtered through her veins at this game they were beginning to play – he pursuing, she retreating . . . but not too far. For she had several weeks to consider whether she would take him as a lover. It helped that she disliked Sylvia so heartily, she thought as she began to refill cups.

403

'Amroth's in love with Hester Prickard,' Dolly Lomon called out to her husband who was in his dressing room. 'Did you see how he pricked up his ears at the sight of her?'

Lomon shrugged into his coat quickly. What an indiscreet creature Dolly was. Didn't she remember he had his man with him? 'That will do, Joseph. I'll come back after I have had a word with her ladyship.' Closing the door behind him he said, 'Careful, my dear. Joseph's out there and you know what servants are like.'

'Oh, darling, I'm sorry.' She smiled at him carelessly from her seat before the fire, where she was putting a few stitches in her embroidery while she waited to go downstairs. Plump and greying, they looked like a pair of well-fed pigeons as they sat side by side on the sofa. 'The fact is I'm worried about Robert and Sylvia. Have you noticed anything? After all, she is your sister.'

'That doesn't mean a thing. We were never close. There's eight years between us.'

'Alaric! She's not thirty-nine? I still think of her as a young thing. She was so lovely when she first came out. Everyone raved about her. That affair with Bertie was bad for her. She hasn't been the same since. I think she was deeply humiliated when he dropped her.'

Her husband grunted. 'Well, then, she was a fool. The Prince is a capricious admirer. No woman should forget that.'

'She feels she made a fool of herself. Everyone knew that he was calling in the afternoons. Then suddenly he had turned to Daisy Brooke and you know how long that has lasted.'

'I hear it's coming to an end now. She's turned Socialist and is running a sewing workshop or some such thing.' He chuckled. 'What a character!'

'Yes, you've always had a soft spot for her,' Dolly agreed tranquilly. 'But I'm sure that a lot of Sylvia's bad health is to do with hurt pride – it's become a refuge from the world. It is no wonder Amroth is looking elsewhere. Her bloom has quite gone,' Dolly Lomon said with a sigh.

'Well, it's really nothing to do with us,' Lomon pointed out. 'However, Amroth should remember that it's Sylvia's money that keeps him. He hasn't a penny of his own. His old father went bankrupt in the depression of twenty years ago. Rents were at rock bottom, but the old chap didn't alter his life style by a tittle. He died still believing that the world owed him a comfortable living. There wasn't anything much to inherit. That cotton millionaire bought Copstead if you remember. I was against Sylvia marrying Amroth, and I told him so when he came to ask my permission. Still, she had the worse fellows in love with her. All that beauty and yet she never seemed to get the right offers.'

Dolly said nothing. That Sylvia had never been popular had been her own fault. She had always had a whining and selfish nature, Dolly thought as she put in three vigorous stitches, and if Robert was going to look in lovely Hester's direction, who could blame him?

'There's the gong. Come along, my dear,' Lomon said, offering her his hand.

In her room dressing for dinner, Hester's thoughts had also been with Amroth – or Robert as he had begged her to call him. As she sat in front of the mirror watching Julie at work on her hair, it was Amroth's face she saw reflected: daring eyes, that thin rather hard mouth and the cock of his head were what she saw; not her own image with Julie pinning the ruby butterflies in her hair. . . .

Dinner was a great success that night. Hester felt it and saw that she had got the mixture right. Miss Nolan was talking animatedly to the rather languid Arthur Dalbeity, Hester noted. She hoped the vivacious American girl would give the young MP a chance to talk back. At the moment he was looking at her rather in the manner of a rabbit fascinated by a stoat.

It was Amroth who, when the gentlemen came up to the drawing room, suggested Hide and Seek and claimed Hester as his partner. Mrs Cherry and Lord Lomon, Dolly Lomon and Wilfred, Henry Cherry and Sylvia Amroth and Clarice Nolan and Dalbeity went off in pairs to hide, leaving them alone by the fire.

It proved to be twenty minutes of temptation. A temptation to let him see how much he attracted her; a temptation to allow him to hold her and tell her that he was in love with her . . .

'Sylvia and I haven't got on for years,' he said moodily. 'Now that the children are almost grown-up we tend to go our separate ways. She is absorbed in her health – and isn't strong I admit, but surely she doesn't need to remind me twenty-four hours a day! You're so alive and vivid, Hester dearest.' He took her hand and kissed it roughly, pulling her towards him.

She resisted. 'Don't, Robert – someone might come in. . . . ' She turned her face from his exploring lips. 'Look, the twenty minutes is up. . . . '

'Don't sound so relieved, my dear,' he said sulkily and dropped her hand.

'Don't be an idiot,' she said crisply. 'I can't be found in your arms in my own drawing room. Come on,' she smiled at him and held out her hand, 'let's go and find them all.'

His face cleared and he grinned at her. Secretly she sighed with relief; for his change in mood often lasted a whole evening and was apparent to everyone.

It took a good hour to find all the Hiders who had chosen ingenious hiding places all over the house (only the servants' quarters and the nursery were barred). True, the Seekers didn't hurry, often pausing to smile at each other in the lamplight, to press close to each other on dark stairways and to stop for one long daring kiss in a dim corner of the landing.

When they at last found Dalbeity and Miss Nolan sitting close to each other on the floor of the airing cupboard, Hester

406

thought with secret amusement that the conventions were very odd: they allowed this unmarried young pair complete immunity from censure because they were playing a game. They would never be allowed alone together under any other circumstance.

'We must play this again,' Dalbeity said with a satisfied air, taking Miss Nolan's arm to help her downstairs. He had just learned over the port and cigars after dinner that she was the daughter of J. J. Nolan of Philadelphia. . . .

Lying in bed waiting for her breakfast tray, Hester was aware of such a lift in her spirits that she wanted to shout aloud. She had at last found a man who attracted her enough to want to sleep with him. For two years after Victor's death she had thought she could never find anyone again. He had taken her first fresh young love. With Robert it would be a more mature relationship. Tonight, she thought, he will come to me tonight. For too long she had been buried at Stanhope. Now a whole new life was suddenly opening before her.

'The shooters they go,' Julie said, planting the wicker tray on her mistress's lap. 'And it is raining. Not comfortable.'

'They won't mind that,' Hester smiled. She poured coffee with a new zest. 'I think I'll wear my new green tweeds today and the hat with the feather – yes, I know I was going to save them for Easton Lodge next week, but I've changed my mind.' The green suited her, and today she wanted Amroth to see her at her best. The invitation to Easton Lodge had been marked *To meet the Prince of Wales*; but it was suddenly more important that Amroth should find her beautiful than that the Prince should glance her way. 'And my sables,' she added, pouring out coffee.

The ladies were driven out to the warm clean barn on the Home Farm where lunch had been laid. The guns could still be heard across the wet stubble, as they sat on canvas seats and watched Sarah heating soup and Arthur preparing drinks.

'I hope this is the last drive,' Sylvia said in her discontented voice. 'My feet are frozen. This is not a very good spot for lunch on a day like this.'

Dolly Lomon shot her sister-in-law an angry glance. How infuriating Sylvia could be! So spoilt and rude and uncaring for the feelings of her young hostess who was now looking worried. But, Dolly thought, she was probably doing it on purpose. No doubt she was aware of her husband's interest in Hester Prickard.

'Why don't you walk about a little?' Mrs Cherry suggested.

'She should have joined Lady Prickard and me earlier,' Clarice Nolan said with a laugh. 'When the rain left off for an hour this morning we bicycled to the dower house and back – it was glorious. . . . '

Sylvia turned and gave her a cool stare. 'You must be – indeed you *look* very strong, Miss Nolan. But all Americans seem to be made of cast iron.'

There was silence. The implication of *railroad king* was plain for everyone to hear. Then Miss Nolan laughed.

'You make me sound like a cooking pot, Lady Amroth. Be careful I don't boil over!'

At that moment the sound of men's voices and the yelp of dogs was heard approaching the barn. With relief, Hester gave Sarah the signal to serve the soup.

'I shot badly,' Amroth informed her. He had asked permission to sit on the bale of straw next to Hester. The rain had whipped more colour than ever into his face. As his sleeve deliberately brushed hers, she felt a quiver of excitement. 'I was thinking of you, you see.'

'I'm sorry. Perhaps I had better go and sit next to Alaric Lomon. . . . '

'Don't you dare,' he whispered fiercely, adding loudly, 'I say, what an excellent game pie.' And Hester saw that Mrs Cherry was watching them again.

When he next looked at her it was with suppressed

408

laughter. 'I nearly peppered poor Cherry! Mrs C. would never have forgiven me if I'd brought him home full of shot! All your fault m'dear, although I do think Cherry should keep up better. You swing round to get a nice shot behind you and there's the fellow still yards behind.' He finished the cold pie and gave his plate to Arthur for more. Being in love hadn't affected his appetite, Hester found herself thinking with amusement.

When the men moved off again, the women were driven home, each going up to her room to relax with a novel before the fire or to have a short nap, before changing into fluttering tea gowns and descending to the hall to welcome back the guns.

When they were joined by the men, a long inquest on the shoot took place and Wilfred entered the day's bag in his shooting book amid a great deal of banter and crosstalk.

Seeing Amroth making his way towards her, Hester rose and joined Miss Nolan on a sofa. She saw his baffled eyes as she smiled at him in passing. Really, it was bad of him to make it so obvious, she thought as she talked to Miss Nolan of mutual friends in New England.

She dressed carefully for dinner in one of her new winter gowns: an irridescent green satin with huge sleeves. While Julie carried her used clothes away, Hester stood and looked at her image in the soft light of the many tall candles she liked in her bedroom. Am I still beautiful? she wondered. First youth had gone, but a growing maturity had its compensations. Her breasts were fuller, her shoulders more rounded. Would Victor have found her very changed?'

But I mustn't think of the past, she thought, because it shows in my eyes and tonight I want to be carefree and happy.

Picking up a light wrap for her shoulders, she went to visit the nursery.

It was warm and quiet here and Nurse was sewing by lamplight.

'Is he asleep?'

'Oh, yes, my lady, he went off straight away like he usually does,' the woman said brightly. She led the way into the night nursery and, holding the lamp aloft, allowed her mistress to view her child. Patrick lay on his back, his long lashes a dark smudge on his pink skin, his arms tucked under the blankets.

'Are you sure the blankets aren't tucked too tightly, Nurse? It doesn't look as if he can move. . . .'

'Oh, he is perfectly comfortable, my lady. It's best to keep the little limbs straight.'

'You've managed to break him of that habit of sucking his thumb,' Hester whispered. 'I can't think how you've done it.'

'Just firmness, my lady, that's all.' She had lowered the lamp and was pointedly holding open the door. Hester bestowed a soft kiss on the child's head. In the nursery she smiled at Nurse. 'You'll leave him a nightlight later on, won't you? I remember how frightened I always was of the dark.'

The woman bowed her head and Hester glanced at her again. There was something about the woman tonight – some suppressed feeling. She could feel it loud on the air . . . 'Is there anything else, Nurse?'

The woman looked up. There were spots of colour on her cheeks. 'No, thank you, my lady. May I say how nice you look, my lady? Quite a picture.'

Sarah and Arthur were putting the finishing touches to the dinner table. Silver gilt candelabra held tapering white candles and heavy cut glass (four to each place) glinted in the light. Hester nodded approvingly at Wiston. 'Very nice indeed, but I'm not sure about the epergnes. Two seems too much.'

Wiston stared doubtfully at the epergnes filled with pink and white carnations with maidenhair trailing in between. 'You've always had two epergnes, m'lady.'

'Yes, I know, but tastes change and now they seem, well, too much. Don't you agree, Wiston?' she added quickly.

'Very good, m'lady. Sarah, remove that epergne.' In a low

410

voice he added, 'Can I speak with you a moment, m'lady? I was wondering if you have yet spoken to Nurse?'

'I haven't an idea what you are referring to, Wiston. Why should I speak to Nurse?'

'I asked Sir Wilfred to have a word with you, m'lady. It's about Nurse and Gaskell. Mrs Gaskell has been making quite a scene in the kitchen....'

'Nurse and Gaskell? That's absurd! Mrs Gaskell must be mistaken. Why, Nurse isn't even very young. . . . ' And she was extremely plain, Hester thought. 'Well, I have no time now. I must go to my guests but I'll look into it tomorrow before church.'

She hurried away. Really, what a ridiculous situation! Nurse and Gaskell indeed!

As she entered the drawing-room she looked quickly round to see that all was in order: a good log fire, masses of flowers everywhere, chairs in twos and threes. How lovely her room looked, she thought with pleasure. She had recently had it painted a pale biscuit, with the cornice picked out in white and eau-de-nil. All the sofas and chairs had new velvet covers in delicate colours and black-edged curtains were in biscuit satin with wool interlining to make them hang in thick folds. Ebony cabinets between the windows and the Aubusson carpet created a delicate echo of all these colours. Hester's drawing room was now well-known, and she was envied for having the courage to break away from the traditional heavy furnishings in other houses.

Wilfred came in and she chivied him about the set of his white tie. There was also tobacco on his waistcoat. 'I don't think Dixon looks after you at all well, he's getting lazy. I wish you wouldn't smoke Turkish cigarettes before dinner, you reek of them.'

'Don't nag,' said Wilfred lazily, 'or you'll be sounding like my mother in a minute. By the way, have you been over to see her lately?'

'Wilfred, she is *your* mother; why don't you go? I'm only a poor substitute....'

'*Cave*,' Wilfred murmured as the first of their guests came in.

The worst of their sort of partnership, Hester thought as she went to meet them, was that they never met in the privacy of their bedroom at the end of each day like normal married people. She never had the opportunity of a curtain lecture. Messages didn't get passed on – what *was* this about Nurse?

After a day in the open the men were all pleasantly tired. So, after a slow twelve-course dinner from which they rose at eleven, no one wanted to play games. When the women went up to bed at twelve-thirty some of the men would repair to the billiard room to play and smoke and drink a last glass of whisky. Now they sat and flirted with other men's wives. Miss Nolan and Mr Dalbeity seemed to have a lot to say to each other on a distant sofa and no one disturbed them.

'I think it's going to come off,' Dolly Lomon said to Hester. 'Don't look surprised. I saw Lady Dalbeity last week. Arthur needs someone like her. She's very chic in her way and will be all the rage in London, you'll see. And all that money too – Arthur is a lucky man.' She looked in a kind way at her hostess. 'Did your mama arrange your marriage, my child? You and Wilfred are cousins, I believe?'

Hester had flushed. 'I don't think many marriages are *not* arranged these days, Dolly! Wilfred and I had the Line to consider. Our son will carry on the family tradition, I hope.'

'You are lucky to be free of money worries,' Lady Lomon sighed. 'Few of us are nowadays . . . still we all have comfortable lives and I do so enjoy myself!'

If the woman only knew what being poor really meant, Hester thought. The gap is too great and I'm sure she has little idea that people actually starve. Moving away presently to pour coffee at one of the tables, she found Amroth at her side.

'You've been avoiding me.'

She offered him his cup and laughingly shook her head. 'I've been busy seeing to the cogs of this household. Then

412

I've been bicycling with Clarice Nolan – it's a splendid form of exercise, I assure you. You should try it.'

He was barely listening to her. Fixing his eyes on her, he said: 'I do believe I've fallen in love with you.'

She hurriedly bent over the coffee warmer, fiddling with the methylated flame. 'Please . . . your wife . . . just over there. . . .'

'Sylvia doesn't give a fig for me.'

A fig for constancy. Where had that phrase come from to pop into her mind like that? For a swift moment she was back in the Villa Dahlia and Dowson was reading one of his poems aloud. She had repeated it to herself often. *Life is a masque that changes. A fig for constancy!* 'That is sad,' she said in a preoccupied voice, 'for I believe you are a very lovable man.'

'And you are not happy are you, Hester darling?'

'You cannot know that. . . .'

'You're trapped, my beautiful butterfly,' he said in her ear. 'Do you think I'm blind?'

Her eyes were alarmed. 'What do you mean?'

But he only shook his head very slightly. *You can trust me,* he seemed to be saying. In a low voice he added: 'Let me come to you tonight. Please Hester. I've wanted you for so long.'

There was a burst of laughter from across the room where Lomon was telling a story to the others. Mrs Cherry was bent over her embroidery, gold-rimmed glasses on the end of her nose, a placid expression on her face. Now and again she glanced across at the couple who were standing so close to each other.

'Dearest Hester, I love you.'

'Oh, Robert . . . I don't know.'

'Let me come tonight.'

'Very well.' Her lips were stiff, the words barely audible but he heard. A gleam came into his eyes. 'You darling,' he whispered.

Presently they moved across to join the main group. Mrs

413

Cherry looked up and smiled at Hester, and Hester felt her returning smile was a hypocritical one. *The old pussy,* she thought.

'I won't get into bed just yet,' she said as Julie placed the footstool for her. 'I think I'll read in front of the fire for a while. I don't feel sleepy.'

'Very well, milady. Do you wish that I return later?'

'No, go to bed. It's been a long day.'

Julie went through into the boudoir with the discarded clothes, and Hester could hear the rattle of hangers as she carefully hung everything up. Knotting her fingers tightly, she waited impatiently for the woman to depart for good.

Now she was framed in the doorway again. 'Shall I warm a little cup of milk for you, milady? It will help you sleep.'

'No, I need nothing. Go to bed, Julie. Don't bring my tea before nine tomorrow.' Breakfast was at ten on Sundays, and the carriages would be at the door at a quarter to eleven for the whole party to proceed to church. A good many of them would leave at teatime for there were now good trains from the junction up to London.

The door closed at last. She waited to hear the click of the second door . . . then she sprang up and walked about the room. What had made her say yes? She now felt that she hardly knew Amroth. He was very attractive though. She stared at the bed. It was more than two years since she had lain in a man's arms and a terrible apprehension seized her. She felt she wasn't ready – there was no urgent desire in her body. Simply a wistful need to be comforted and kissed and made to forget. There had been great tenderness in her love for Victor. He had been a gentle considerate lover. With Amroth it would be very different.

She went to the door to open it a chink: by this sign he would guess she was waiting.

What was that?

Somewhere a child was screaming. Screaming at the top

of his voice with terror and rage. *Patrick.* Without pausing for thought, she gathered her robe and ran with bare feet up the stairs and across the landing to the nursery.

In the pitch dark room the child's screams had reached a crescendo of fear and rage.

'Nurse, what is the matter? Where are you, Nurse?' She fumbled for the woman's bed. It was empty and unslept in. 'Patrick, Mama's here – hush, darling – hush!' She ran her hands over the table and found the candlestick and matches. She lit it with trembling fingers and, holding it aloft, let down the side of the cot. As she put her hand on the little boy he shrieked louder, throwing his body about like a small hooked fish. For a moment she wondered if he were having a dreaded attack of convulsions.

Putting the candle back on the table she attempted to lift him – and found that he was tied to the cot by cruel tapes that were twisted about his wrists and across his body. They had cut into his flesh as he turned and twisted in an effort to free himself. Even as she searched frantically for scissors in Nurse's basket she was remembering the exchange of words earlier that evening: 'You've managed to break him of that habit of sucking his thumb.'

'Just firmness, my lady, that's all.'

She had noticed then that his arms were tucked under the blanket very neatly. *Tied down* after he had fallen asleep.

Rage reddened her face, as she bent down and tried to cut the child free of the tapes. He had obviously been biting at the tape for it was wet – like a small trapped animal, she thought. Now at last he was free. She lifted him in her arms and tried to soothe him, but he was incoherent and unable to stop crying. She walked up and down holding him close to her body and talking soothingly, but she was trembling so much she thought she would fall. Taking a deep breath, she tried to stop the trembling and be sensible, rocking the child until he subsided into hiccups against her neck. How dared Nurse do this? The tapes might have strangled him. What if no one had heard him and he had lain there all night, the blankets kicked off, helplessly trussed up like a parcel? How often had the woman done this and gone off to spend the night elsewhere? And with whom?

'Patrick, we're going down to Mama's bedroom. You shall sleep there for a treat. You'll like that won't you? There's a lovely fire in Mama's room.'

He stared at her doubtfully, his lips trembling, his eyes still anxious. She held him close, kissing him again and again. 'Darling, I'll never leave you with that woman – never, never again.'

She carried him back to her room, her arms aching for he was heavy. Closing the door behind her with a foot, she dumped him on the bed and went to find a damp sponge with which, very gently, she removed all trace of tears.

'Pat hurt,' he informed her, holding out his fat little wrists which were cruelly marked by the tapes. So she sponged those too, talking cheerfully all the time, until at last he began to take an interest in his surroundings and forget his troubles. When he was allowed to handle the little silver clock in the blue velvet case he was happy again, talking to himself as he worked hard to remove every silver nut at the back.

She had completely forgotten her tryst and was busy making a nest for her son on one side of the big bed when there was a faint knock at the door, it opened a chink and Amroth's voice said, 'Can I come in?' He blinked, staring at the domesticated scene in her bedroom. The child rolled over on the bed and shouted at him, 'Man, look at this!' His face radiant, he held out two silver screws. With a smothered laugh, Amroth swept him high in his arms. 'Well, you are a fine fellow! What are you doing in Mama's bed?'

'Naughty Nurse,' said Patrick happily and scrambled down to shake the clock against his ear.

'What happened?' he asked quietly.

She pushed her hair back from her hot face. 'That damned woman – sorry, but I'm half mad with anger! She actually tied him to his bed and has gone off somewhere. Come on,

Patrick, I've made a lovely bed for you.' She reached out but the boy wanted to go on playing with the clock and he rolled away from her, protesting loudly. 'Robert, help me . . . he's too strong for me . . .'

He obeyed, a comical expression on his face. 'So not to-night then?' He rolled the child towards her. Together they tucked him in. 'I should let him keep that clock. It will keep him quiet and he'll drop off to sleep in a moment.'

She looked at him apologetically as they moved towards the fire. 'Oh, Robert, I'm sorry. But I couldn't leave him alone in that dark nursery.' She put her hands up and rested them on his shoulders. 'You've been so kind, so understand-ing. I do believe you are a kind man really.'

He pulled her swiftly towards him and they stood in a tight embrace. 'Oh, Hester, if you only knew how much I love you,' he whispered against her hair.

'There's still tomorrow night. . . .'

'No. Sylvia insists we return after luncheon tomorrow.' Kissing her once more he released her and walked to the door. She watched him leave with real regret. When she got into bed, it was to lie sleepless, thinking about him. At last after so long, she was going to fall in love again.

CHAPTER THREE

By ten on Monday the last guest had gone. To Hester's sitting-room came Mrs McAndrew with her list of provisions needed from the town. 'But who is to drive you, m'lady, with Gaskell gone?'

Hester sighed. 'He really has gone then? I must go and see his wife this afternoon. Meanwhile I think Rickaby will do very well. I shall have to see Sir Wilfred about it.' Really, Wilfred was the limit, she fumed hurrying down to the study; it was his job to see to such things. As she expected, he was lounging in front of the fire with a French novel. 'Wilfred, who is to drive the carriage today? I suggest Rickaby. In fact I don't see why he shouldn't have it permanently – Wilfred, are you listening to me?'

'My dear Hester, you rush in here like a blast of cold air and expect me to answer your questions in a trice.' Wilfred yawned and sat up lazily. 'I suppose Rickaby will do for a short time. He hasn't Gaskell's skill or experience – he's just a carter and not fit to drive a gentleman's carriage. Gaskell has been in good service.'

'Don't compare them,' Hester said crisply. 'Rickaby is an honest fellow. I think he should succeed Gaskell at once – after all, he has driven the second carriage often – and draw Gaskell's wages.'

Wilfred looked at her distastefully. How she revelled in a crisis, he thought irritably. He would return to Liverpool with some relief tomorrow. 'Very well, I'll see to it.' He took up his novel again and she plucked it out of his hand. '*Now,*

Wilfred. I have to go into Sewerston. Really, how indolent you are!' She went out into the hall and stood thinking – what next? She· had put Rose in the nursery in Nurse's place and the child had taken to her at once. I was a fool not to listen to Agnes before this happened, she told herself, running up the stairs to take one more peep round the nursery door.

Patrick came running to her, a happy little boy again. Rose had been encouraging him to play with a big ball and his face was flushed with pleasure. 'Everything's all right, m'lady, don't you worry,' she said in her warm voice. 'Mrs McAndrew's sending us up some nice hash for our lunch and a baked apple.' In her clean apron, her round freckled arms bare and her face so smiling and pink, she gave Hester the greatest comfort.

At eleven, a proud Rickaby brought the carriage round. He was wearing the green livery belonging to the errant Gaskell. Both the greatcoat and billycock were too big for him, but his red face was beaming with satisfaction. On hearing from his master of his elevation to coachman, he had rushed down to his cottage to break the news to his wife. Melia had once been a pert, pretty housemaid at Stanhope. Now she was a thin, worn woman with three tiny children clinging to her skirts.

Her delight turned her pale. 'Oh, Joe, an extra fifteen shillings a week? And what about the cottage?'

'Well, not t'cottage, lass,' Rickaby said awkwardly. 'I told master we were snug enough here for time being.'

'Eh, you great fool!' Melia cried. 'This place is tumbling round our heads and is nigh as damp as t'river!'

'I know, love, but I couldn't see Mrs Gaskell and young 'uns turned out wi' nowhere to go but workhouse,' Rickaby pleaded. 'And I told master yon Gaskell needs horsewhipping, and I'd a mind to do it meself if he ever shows his face agin.'

'Oh, Joe, you didn't ought to have talked so to the master!'

'I've known master since he were a lad,' Rickaby pointed

out sturdily. 'He agreed wi' me. Here, help me on wi' the rascal's coat, luv. 'Tis a bit big, but reckon won't show much when I'm on box.'

And now he was on the box and unable to mask his pride. He'd show Miss Hester how well he could drive the fine pair of carriage horses, he told himself as they set off for Sewerston.

They stopped in the square outside Mr Newland's Farm Produce Shop and leaning down, Rickaby put two fingers to his mouth and emitted a shrill whistle to summon the proprietor to wait on his mistress. 'No, no, Rickaby, don't do that!' Hester called, trying to conceal her amusement. How scandalized Mr Newlands looked as he stood bowing on the pavement! Behind him hung every sort of edible fur and feather. The product of their own shoot would be sent over later in the day and 'Fresh from Stanhope,' Mr Newlands would tell his customers, hooking down a fat brace of pheasants. 'Please help me down, Mr Newlands. I'm coming in this morning. I'm afraid Cook has a complaint to make about the beef you sent up.' Over her shoulder, she said, 'Walk the horses, please, and be back here in ten minutes.' After dealing with Mr Newlands and receiving his profuse apologies, she left her order to be made up while she visited some of the other shops in the square. Mr Beddow's eldest son owned the large and well-stocked Grocery Emporium, and here she was bowed to a seat and her order taken by Mr Herbert Beddows himself. It was as she was leaving this establishment – one hesitated to call it a mere shop – that she saw a tall figure in a red and blue uniform striding past.

'Sergeant Hoggarth, m'lady,' Herbert Beddows murmured. 'Done very well by all accounts. Quite the local hero.'

But Lady Prickard had already left his side and was hurrying across the square, holding her skirt out of the mud and urgently calling 'Tommy! Tommy Hoggarth!'

The soldier turned and snapped a salute, his face showing no sign of recognition.

420

'Tommy . . . it's me . . . Hester!' she said breathlessly, throwing back her veil.

His face reddened with shock. 'Hester . . . I mean Lady Prickard. . . .'

'No, of course you don't mean Lady Prickard, you fool!' Hester had burst out laughing. 'Oh, Tommy, how lovely to see you again after all these years! I read about your medal and must congratulate you. You have done so well.'

'Thank you.' He glanced about him. There was Herbert Beddows, his hands under his white apron, watching with the greatest interest, while Mrs Beddows was craning her head over a mountain of cheese in the window. Just behind them, two old women had stopped to watch their local hero being greeted by a beautiful woman who seemed on the friendliest terms with him.

She saw his glance. 'Oh, dear, we're being watched – but I must talk to you after all these years. Come, there's my carriage,' and she beckoned Rickaby who was approaching the square. 'Please come up with me. Where were you going? Perhaps I could take you there?'

'I was going back to my mother's. She lives on the hill, next to Mrs Weston.' Hesitating only a moment, he climbed in beside her.

'Well, we've given the town something to talk about,' Hester murmured, bowing to Mrs Beddows just to show her she had seen her staring open-mouthed.

'I'm afraid so,' he agreed, smiling down at her. 'You always were impulsive, Hes.'

'Oh, how good it is to hear you call me that! No one else has ever done so. Look, it was just here that we saw each other last. I was going off to live with Uncle Joe and you ran beside the carriage and called "Good luck, Hes!"' They looked at each other as memory came flooding back. 'Is your wife at home too?' she asked after a pause.

'She's back in England, but not up here with me.' His face was suddenly lifeless. 'Violet's not – strong. She lost two babies in India and it affected her. We've got a little

421

house near Aldershot. She likes it there. I'm going out to the garrison at the Cape shortly so she'll stay here with my mother.' He didn't tell her that the army authorities had told him he couldn't take her with him until she was cured of her addiction to the bottle. There had been several scandals from which he had had to extricate her, and it wasn't doing his career any good.

'How sad to lose your children. Have you no others? I have a boy and I've called him Patrick.'

'I'm glad to hear that you have someone of your own, Hes.' What a beautiful woman she had become, he thought, his eyes hungrily studying her. And the essential Hes was still there, he could see. If she had changed so that he could no longer care for her – become grand and silly – what a disappointment that would have been. He flushed as he saw her smiling under his scrutiny. 'It's good to see you again, Hes. You're still the girl I remember – only more beautiful,' he added shyly.

'Am I?' she asked delightedly. 'I've thought of you so often, Tommy, and wondered how you were faring. I haven't seen your mother for years, I'm afraid. She must be so proud you've done so well in the army.'

'They've offered me a commission,' he blurted out suddenly. He hadn't told another soul yet – not even his mother. But he couldn't resist telling Hester.

'Oh, Tommy, that's not to be wondered at!' she exclaimed. She looked out of the window. 'We must be there. Shall I tell Rickaby to stop? But this is Farmer Berriman's field – has your mother built her house on that?' Apparently she had, for she could now see a tall red brick house, an exact copy of Aunt Ellen's dower house, she thought with a gasp of amusement. The local architect had obviously used the same drawings for both clients. How furious Aunt Ellen would be when she knew! Only this one was called *Braeside,* the name picked out in white pebbles on the five-barred gate that had been painted a shining black. It opened on to a pebbled drive bordered by young laurel bushes.

'Matty still lives at home,' Tom Hoggarth explained as he helped her down. 'He's articled to Mr Cuthbert Oliphant, the architect. He designed Ma's house. Do you like it?'

'It looks very comfortable. Walk the horses, Rickaby, please. I shall be about quarter of an hour here. I hope your mother won't mind me calling on her like this?'

'Ma will be delighted to see you again,' he promised. He held open the gate, but instead of proceeding up the drive, she turned sharply left and to his puzzled amazement, stooped down and began to dig the turf with her gloved hands. Tearing away a small square, she held aloft some very muddy coins darkened by years underground.

'All the treasure I had in the world when I was fifteen! This is a Jubilee shilling of 1887. Mrs Weston gave it to me for carrying her bonnet to her. Oh, I did get into trouble that day! I can remember it all so clearly. I got *cow dung* on the bonnet box and Aunt Agatha slapped me and wouldn't let me have any supper!' She laughed, a loud clear laugh, looking up at him and inviting him to laugh too.

But he couldn't. He felt his heart give a jolt of loving pity, just as it had done all those years ago when she went hungry so often. Seeing her face so close to his, he felt the old longing again. So he wasn't cured. Years in India, the life of a soldier, a wife and two dead children hadn't cured him of his feeling for Hester Kelsey, his first love.

'I'm going to give you part of my treasure as a keepsake.' She took his hand and put the shilling in his palm. 'There. Polish it up and wear it on your watch chain. It will remind you of me, won't it?'

He stared down at it. 'I'll keep it always,' he said hoarsely.

Hester dusted her gloved hands. 'Now take me to your mother,' she said and led the way up the drive. But the little maid who came to the door informed them that Mrs Hoggarth had gone out shopping.

'What a pity I've missed her. Never mind, I'll call another time and perhaps I'll meet your wife too,' Hester said as they waited for Rickaby to come down the road. 'Will you call on

423

me before you leave for Africa? I'd like to see you again.'

He promised, holding her hand tightly as he helped her in to the carriage.

'Goodbye, Tommy. Remember my shilling!'

He saluted, standing in the road until the carriage disappeared. Yes, she was still the girl he remembered: impulsive, warm-hearted, unconventional. Life hadn't spoiled her yet. She doesn't think of me as I think of her, he thought. I love her. What's the use of pretending? I've always loved her – always will, I suppose.

As he reached the house he was astonished to see his mother peeping out, clad in a large check apron and with a duster in her hand. 'Why, Ma, Martha told us you were out. Hester Kelsey called to see you.'

'I told the girl to say that,' his mother said, impatient with his male stupidity. 'I was helping her turn out a room for your Violet. I couldn't have received her like *this*. She's Lady Prickard now – a great lady in the district. They say she knows the Prince of Wales.'

'Ma, she's just Hester – hardly changed at all. Pinafores and dusters wouldn't have bothered her a bit.'

'I daresay, but they would have bothered *me*,' his mother retorted with some tartness. Beckoning him in, she closed the door with a small slam.

The message that Ellen Lady Prickard wished to see her niece on urgent business reached Hester at lunchtime next day. Wilfred had gone to Liverpool and Hester wondered what awaited her at the dower house. She put on her tweed bicycling bloomers under a short skirt and cycled across the park. The wind was still sending the remaining leaves in eddies across the drive and whipping colour into her cheeks. How much better this was than the mist and rain, she thought. It would soon be Christmas and she had been going to write her cards this afternoon; but now she was glad she had been summoned and had braved the storm.

As she entered the drawing room, Ellen gave a little shriek. 'What on earth have you got on? I hope no one has seen you? Really, Hester, you're a wife and mother now and should not have to be told by me how to behave.'

'Dear Aunt Ellen, how right you are! You really shouldn't be telling me,' Hester agreed mischievously.

'Young people today seem to like to shock. In my day, the very idea of wearing those . . . those articles of apparel would not have been dreamed of. . . .'.

'I don't believe there were bicycles in your youth, were there? Tweed bloomers are really much better than showing lace drawers.'

'Hester, for goodness sake, do give up this undesirable wish to shock all the time.'

'Do you realize, Aunt Ellen we are almost in a new century? The twentieth century?'

Ellen shuddered and drew nearer to the large fire that warmed the room so powerfully. 'I sent for you because I have had a call from a Sewerston friend. She tells me she distinctly saw you taking up a soldier into your husband's carriage yesterday. How could you do such a thing, Hester? Will you never learn? A common soldier!'

'Oh, I did,' Hester agreed blithely. 'How quickly gossip travels when people have nothing else to do! He was Sergeant Thomas Hoggarth of the 60th Rifles, one of my oldest friends. We went to the National School together.'

'The newsagent's son!' Ellen said with distaste.

'Mr Hoggarth is dead and has left quite a fortune. Tommy's mother has built herself a new house next to Mrs Weston's. It's a replica of this one – I suppose Mr Oliphant decided to get two houses out of the same pattern. Or perhaps he copied Mrs Hoggarth's house for *you*?' Hester looked innocently at her aunt.

Ellen gave a start. 'Hoggarth's widow in a house like mine? I don't believe it! He would never dare! Why, I shall sue Oliphant if he has done such a thing. I shall send for Alfred Bracegirdle and find out if it's true.'

'I should go and see for yourself. You don't go out enough, Aunt Ellen. Why don't you keep a carriage of your own and take the air every day?'

'Because one extravagant woman in this family is enough,' Ellen retorted. 'You forget that your uncle left me badly off, I suppose?'

Hester sighed as she got up to leave. Her aunt had a bee in her bonnet about her poverty, she told herself. Ten thousand a year and her own home could hardly be called *badly off*.

'And I suppose that Hoggarth woman will be cutting a dash as a rich woman now? Well, well, what is the world coming to?' Ellen wondered sorrowfully.

'Isn't it wonderful how people can rise in Yorkshire?' Hester asked with a laugh as she dabbed a kiss on the resisting face. 'Just like dough out of a tin! Just like we did!'

Ten days before Christmas they went to Easton Lodge to stay with Daisy Warwick for a shoot. About twenty guests stood about in the hall talking and awaiting the arrival of the Prince of Wales and his entourage.

The Countess of Warwick had been brought up at Easton for she had – as Frances Maynard – inherited it at the age of three. She appeared to like it better than Warwick Castle, which her husband had recently inherited from the old earl. Easton was certainly a charming place, Hester had thought as she and Wilfred were driven along the two-mile drive through a park where deer moved under the trees. The house itself had been burned down almost entirely in the 16th century and had only been rebuilt some fifty years ago by Hopper, the architect, whose imagination had been given free rein over many country houses of the time with not very happy results.

It's not as pretty as Stanhope, Hester thought loyally. But the park was finer. Perhaps Wilfred would consent to introducing deer in the spring.

She glanced across at her cousin (whom she could never think of as her husband) and wondered what was making him frown so. Since the Wilde case, it was her great dread that Wilfred would be found out, compromised perhaps by some discarded friend. It would be awful if she had to change her name and Patrick's and go and live abroad like poor Mrs Wilde.

But now they were here and being ushered in to join the other guests from whom conversation rose, reminding Hester of the noisy starlings that gathered on the bird table at home. She looked round her and said again: *not as pretty as Stanhope*. Eight huge columns supported the roof and the hall reminded one of an echoing museum, stuffed as it was with heavy portraits of past Maynards. Finding herself being looked at by a man with a pointed moustache and very black hair, she smiled at him.

'Have we met before?'

'You are Lady Prickard,' he said in perfect English with just the hint of a foreign inflection. 'Soveral,' he said with a bow.

She had heard of the Portuguese Marquis de Soveral who was an intimate of the Prince's. No doubt this house party would be formed of people he wanted to meet. As she chatted, she found herself wondering why she and Wilfred had been asked. Perhaps because they were rich. The Prince was said to like the company of the rich. I hope he won't want us to entertain him at Stanhope, she thought worriedly. Across the hall she could see the Amroths; Robert was elaborately pretending not to know she was there.

There was a little stir as Lady Warwick came in with the Prince of Wales. They were followed by the Prince's private secretary, Sir Francis Knollys, and two younger men who seemed to be in attendance. She learned later that the Prince had been on an official visit to a new hospital in the neighbourhood, and had taken in this visit to Easton before going to Sandringham where he always spent Christmas.

Hester's first sight of the heir to the throne was something of a disappointment. She had heard so much about this prince who had a winning way with women and here he was, a podgy middle-aged man with a brindled beard and thinning hair, old enough to be her father and Daisy Warwick's too. But as he approached her she saw that his eyes were large and full and very blue, that when he spoke to someone he gave them his full attention. He seemed very affable with his deep resonant voice. Yes, she could sense he had charm. He also had an extraordinary presence, as if he stood apart from all the others round him. This, then, must be the royal aura.

When he reached the Prickards, he seemed to know all about them. He chatted to Wilfred of the Prickard Line and told him he must interest himself in smaller vessels – he must take up sailing and come to Cowes. 'I promise you, Sir Wilfred that it will become a mania with you – I know it myself!' He turned to Hester and she curtseyed over his proffered hand. 'You will know well my old friend George Edwardes at the Gaiety, Lady Prickard. Yes, the Guv'nor as you call him. Tell me, were you there with Miss Lily May?'

She found he knew the names of all the artistes who had trodden the boards of the Gaiety, and quite lost her shyness in talking of mutual acquaintances.

'How did he know I had been at the Gaiety?' she asked Wilfred as they were taken up to their rooms.

'Daisy Warwick will have submitted her list to him for vetting,' Wilfred said shortly. He was annoyed that Hester's association with the Gaiety had cropped up. Like his mother, he only wanted to forget it. But as he went into his room to find his man unpacking, he found his mind lingering on the idea the Prince had put into it. Yes, he might build himself a yacht and compete at Cowes.

That night, the gold and white drawing-room was full of colour as the women in their lovely gowns moved to and fro, forming patterns like a kaleidoscope. When the men came upstairs to join them in a very short time (for the Prince never lingered over port and cigars) Amroth came across to her. 'Hester.'

She smiled at him. 'I am sorry about what happened last weekend.'

Something flared in his eyes. 'Does that mean. . . . '

'Perhaps,' she said hurriedly. 'Not tonight though.'

'You owe it me.'

'I owe nothing.' Her eyes met his and a silent struggle took place. Looking across his shoulder, she saw that Sylvia Amroth was watching them. With a smile and a nod, she moved away.

It was a fine clear day for the shoot next morning. She heard the dogcarts moving off after breakfast as Julie prepared her bath. 'The green tweeds, Julie,' she called, swinging her legs out of bed.

Carriages drove the women out to join the guns for lunch, which had been laid out in a large stone barn with a swept floor and braziers to warm it. A table loaded with cold food occupied one side and footmen stood waiting to serve them. She could now see why Sylvia Amroth had been discontented with the arrangements at the Stanhope weekend. This was luxury in comparison.

When the shooting party arrived it was towards Hester that His Royal Highness made his way, and soon they were laughing together over an anecdote about the Guv'nor. The Prince had great charm and it was difficult to resist those admiring bright blue eyes looking so deeply into hers. Then over his shoulder, she saw Sylvia Amroth's face. It looked nakedly furious. The Prince had not spent much time with his past love, Hester thought. Poor woman, she must feel humiliated. But why had she been asked with him? What Hester did not guess was that Sylvia had begged Daisy Warwick to include her in the house party. Perhaps she had hopes of interesting the Prince again. If so those hopes were now dashed.

'You've scored a big success with him,' Amroth's voice said in her ear when the Prince of Wales had moved on. 'He's

429

a rascal, you know. Don't let him impress you too much.'

'I think he's charming,' Hester protested. She knew that much of her success was due to being young and pretty, a new face on the horizon. It was difficult not to feel sorry for poor Sylvia who had lost youth, beauty and her husband, as well as her royal lover. 'Is it painful for your wife, I wonder? She does not look happy.'

'She insisted on being present,' he said shortly. Then lowering his voice he said, 'Are you going to be hard with me tonight? You know it is inevitable.'

'Very well,' she agreed. 'One o'clock. . . . '

His face lit up for all the world to see. 'Hester darling. . . . '

'For God's sake, Robert, don't . . . she will see. . . . '

With an effort he controlled his expression and began to talk in an ordinary voice about the morning's drive. They must have shot one hundred and fifty brace already. The Prince was a first-class shot and used two loaders . . .

'Tonight,' he whispered as they moved off again.

The die was cast. But she remained uneasily uncertain for the rest of the day, so that she felt very tired by the time she got to her room at midnight. 'Not that nightgown,' she directed as Julie opened a fine lawn one to slip over her head. 'The Jap silk one with the lace. And put some verbena on my hair when you brush it.'

'I have seen the Prince, milady,' Julie said excitedly, brushing the dark hair until it shone. 'I looked from the landing. Smith, Lady Amroth's maid, showed me. He is very fine, I think.'

'He is indeed,' Hester agreed with a smile. Heavens, does she perhaps think I am wearing my best nightgown for him? she wondered.

'Will that be all, milady?'

'Yes, go to bed, Julie. I shan't need anything more tonight.'

Lying waiting in bed, she began to have dreadful misgivings. Did she like Amroth well enough to take him as a lover? *Yes*, she told herself sturdily. She did not love him, and

430

that was just as well because she would not be hurt when he left her. She stared at the firelight, the only light left in the room, and it was not of Victor that she was thinking. He had become a shadowy figure in the past. It was of Tom Hoggarth that she thought. If it had been Tom coming to share her bed tonight . . . She sat up and shivered in the warm room. What had she done? Robert Amroth was a stranger – she hardly knew him. Oh, Tommy, she thought with sudden longing. But what was the use of longing for him when he was going away again for years?

There was a light tap on the door. Very quietly he came in and locked it behind him. He looked very handsome in his striped silk dressing gown. She saw his teeth gleam in a smile as he bent over her. The danger of this assignation was obviously adding spice to the situation, she thought. She was glad that he did not smell of spirits but of a fresh cologne.

Sitting on the bed he drew her up to him, encircling her with his arms. 'Are you sure, dearest?'

'It's a bit late to say that now!' she retorted and he laughed under his breath. A sudden silence fell and she realized he was unsure. Then tenderness replaced apprehension and she touched his cheek with a gentle hand. After that she had no time for regret. She was aware only that he needed her and that she was responding to his need.

Lieutenant Thomas Hoggarth, newly commissioned and due to leave for South Africa at the end of January, called to see her in the new year.

Coming into the sitting room, she found him standing by the window and exclaimed, 'Oh, how well it suits you!' as she took his hand.

In his well-cut uniform with the medal ribbon sewn on his left breast, his hair longer and his cap under his arm, he did indeed look well. Gesturing towards the scene outside the window he said, 'I had no idea it was like this, Hes. It's a beautiful place.'

431

'When I saw it first at fifteen I fell in love with it,' she replied, joining him at the window.

His eyes examined her eagerly. How lovely she was in that soft blue dress which clung seductively to her waist and hips. But if Hes were a plain girl I think I should still love her, he thought.

'Has your wife come to Sewerston yet? Why didn't you bring her? I should like to meet her.'

'She is not – very well,' he tried to explain.

Her clear eyes looked straight at him. 'What exactly is wrong with her, Tommy?'

Taking a sudden decision, he began to tell her the sorry tale of his marriage. 'We were young and hasty. India is a lonely place for white people. Her father was sergeant-major of my regiment and I was a raw young private. When he wouldn't consent to the marriage it made me more determined than ever.' He smiled at her sadly. 'You know how it is when you're young? So we married at last and I thought I was the happiest man on earth . . . until Violet . . . You see, Violet. . . . ' He stopped and stared down at his tightly clasped hands. 'Violet wanted other men. One after another. I was only the poor fool who had to stand by and watch it all. When the first child came I thought she would change. I wasn't even sure he was mine and then he died at four months. She lost another one later. Then she took to gin. You tend to drink a bit more in the tropics, but with Violet it became a disease. There – there was a scandal involving one of the young officers. He shot himself. They – my colonel that is – got me posted back to England. They wanted her out of the way, you see. But before we left we had this frontier action and I got this medal. It made the return easier then. Now I've got a commission, but I'm not to return to India.'

She had sat very still listening to him. When tea was brought in, she poured it out in silence. She said in a low voice, 'I had a feeling something was wrong. Just a feeling. Nothing more. You've been very honest with me, Tommy. After all, we are old friends, aren't we? So I must be honest with you too. Wilfred and I are not really husband and wife – I mean we are legally – only he did it to oblige me. Patrick would have been a bastard.'

He stared at her over his cup. 'The boy is not Wilfred's?'

She shook her head. 'No. His father was Victor Cockayne who was Wilfred's friend. I loved him and chose to live with him during the last year of his life. He knew he had not long to live.' Strange how the soreness had left her and she could talk quite normally about him. They said everything died in time: love as well as grief. 'You see, Wilfred needs a wife for other reasons – perhaps I should call it respectability. He – he has a vice. He will never want to marry.'

He stared at her with undisguised horror. 'Hes, how could you do it?' Putting his cup down he said with repressed loathing, 'To lock yourself away in a marriage like this . . . you who are so lovely, who deserve to be happy . . . Oh, Hes, how could you do it?'

'I did it in order to keep my child. Everyone would have suffered if Patrick had been born without a father. He as much as the rest of us,' she added with a sigh. 'One cannot regret being in love,' she reminded him, 'and I was in love with Victor and cared nothing for the consequences. He would have married me, I think, only he died before he knew about the child.'

They were silent in the dimly lit room. 'Then what happens now?' he asked her gently.

'I go on as before.' Should she blurt out about Amroth? She thought not. He would be shocked and she could not bear to see him look at her with disillusioned eyes. 'I am really quite happy,' she tried to reassure him. 'There are many compensations in my life. Now if you won't have more tea I shall take you to see my baby.'

He caught her hand. 'Hes, there are others, aren't there?'

She nodded. 'There are liaisons of a sort.'

He dropped her hand. 'I'd like to see Patrick,' he said and she saw the spell had been broken. He will think I am like his wife – and am I different? she wondered as she led him to the nursery.

But when it came for them to say goodbye, he bent and kissed her. 'I sail at the end of the week. Look after yourself, Hes. Can I write to you sometimes?'

A homesickness for him swept her. She longed suddenly to cling to him, to beg him not to go. Three long years. Anything might happen in that time. Tears filled her eyes. 'I'll write to you every month,' she promised him.

She stood at the window and watched him getting in to his hired fly. Sensing her there, he looked back once; a long deep look as if he could never look away again. Then he was gone.

CHAPTER FOUR

At the end of January, Wilfred went on a prolonged visit to the United States. The manager of his Boston office had decamped with a large sum of money and Wilfred was taking Munro out with him to look into things.

A week later Lord Amroth, his manservant, groom and four hunters moved into the inn in Stanhope village. He was here for the hunting, he told the landlord as he engaged all the rooms in the house.

Hester thought it was a mad plan of his, but she was lonely and easily persuaded by him. Each night she was to unlock the side door in the east wing and he would come in that way to spend the night with her. What could be easier? he asked, sending her passionate letters.

She had thought his plan too risky; things were bound to go wrong and he would be seen. Yet it succeeded like a charm for several weeks. Lying in Amroth's arms that winter made a new woman of Hester – or so he assured her. 'You look like a woman who is loved,' he told her often. 'Your beauty is blossoming as never before. Darling Hester, you weren't made for lonely old maidhood! What a fool you've been!'

She had to admit there was the added spice of living with Amroth under Ellen's nose – she seemed to know nothing about his presence in the village. Unknown to Hester, a vast and silent conspiracy was taking place. She was both popular and pitied, and so she was left alone and lips that usually enjoyed gossip were silent.

Now Hester had someone to appreciate her lovely hand-sewn be-ribboned nightgowns, she told him, even though he insisted on removing them. At first, this desire to see her naked had astonished and upset her. No decent woman surely would allow even a lover to see her *without anything on.*

But she protested in vain. His strong hands grasped the folds of silk and lawn and **drew** them relentlessly over her head. 'It's a sin to clothe such beauty,' he told her. 'My God, you're perfect!'

She had an uneasy feeling that his admiration was similar to that which he felt for his hunters. They, too, were perfect and he was proud of them, running his hand over their bodies as he ran his hand over hers. She told him so, snatching her nightgown back tearfully. 'Not even Victor *saw* me naked. He wouldn't have dreamed of asking me. . . . '

'My dear girl, he was a poet. What d'you expect?' he retorted and tore the nightgown in half.

'You brute! My favourite gown. . . . '

But he had already smothered her protests and she was amazed to find that she liked it.

Much as she enjoyed him making love to her, she preferred the times when they lay quietly talking in the big four poster. He supplied the gap that had been hitherto missing in her life: someone to pour out all her troubles to, to discuss the small problems that cropped up from time to time. He filled the place of the husband she had never had, and proved a much more practical adviser than Victor.

In return, she lent him money. At least, the many sums that found their way into his bank account were described by him as 'loans'. True, he showed no signs of repaying her; but she did not expect it for now she knew exactly how he was placed. Sylvia owned their home and everything else; he only received a quarterly allowance from her. 'And she hasn't increased it since our marriage,' he told Hester bitterly. 'I even have to send my tailor's bills to her now. It's humiliating!'

Hester listened with interest, wondering that he didn't find work of some sort.

'Don't be a fool. Gentlemen don't work,' he told her

436

angrily. 'If you could see your way to paying for my new hunter, darling, I would be eternally grateful. Ladybird's past her prime and the others are long in the tooth too. A pretty fool I shall look when I go into Leicestershire at the end of the month.'

'Oh, darling, must you go? Of course you shall have the hunter but. . . . '

'Don't be an idiot, dearest. I can't stay on here when your husband returns. Do you really mean that about a hunter? You are sweet!' and he kissed her lingeringly. It was dawn. In ten minutes he must rise and dress and make his way back through the snow to the inn. 'I'll go up to Tatts tomorrw.'

'I'll come with you,' she said eagerly.

'Darling, *no!* We mustn't be seen together. Tattersalls is worse than my club for bumping into people one doesn't want to see. It would soon get back to Sylvia.'

She propped herself on one elbow, watching him throw his clothes on. 'Would it matter if Sylvia found out? Why don't we get a divorce and marry? I've enough money for us both as you know. . . . ' Her voice faltered to nothing as he turned a face of real fear to her.

'My God, are you mad? Divorce? We'd be ruined socially for ever. We would have to go abroad to live – we'd be finished here. Think of that! France or worse for the rest of our lives. . . . '

'France is a lovely country. *I* would like it there.'

His eyes were cold with uneasy displeasure. 'I didn't know you could be such a fool. France – any place abroad would be bloody awful. Can you see me trying to hunt in *France?*' He laughed without humour. 'If you're going to talk like that, then we had better stop seeing each other like this.'

His farewell kiss was a mere gesture and she wept after he had gone. In her heart she had always known that their love affair could never end in marriage. It had been stupid of her to ask for more. But she did so long for a stable relationship, one that hadn't to be hidden from the world. Her tears turned to anger when he did not come to her that night.

437

'I hate him! It's over. I won't allow him to use me like this. I'll lock the door and then he can't come back.'

But she did nothing and when he returned the next night and she heard his soft 'Hester?' she burst into tears and held him close, promising never to make such a suggestion again. He was right; she saw that now. He mustn't leave her. She couldn't bear it if he left her. . . .

'Darling, I've got to go tomorrow. The hunting season will be over soon and I've promised to join these friends near Melton Mowbray. I'll go to Tattersalls and find a new hunter – it's sweet of you, dearest, to give him to me – and then on to Melton.' He kissed her tenderly, but suspicion ached in her. There would be another woman in Melton Mowbray, she told herself.

'Besides,' he added casually, 'I've had a letter from Sylvia. You'd better read it while I undress.'

She turned up the lamp and, with a dry mouth, read Sylvia Amroth's letter. Her writing was flamboyantly large and filled three sheets of thick cream writing paper. Her message was simple: she had learned that his sojourn in the North Riding was not for hunting the *fox* but for pursuing a certain lady. After receiving the report from her private investigator she had put the matter in the hands of her solicitors from whom he would be hearing soon. Meanwhile she would be grateful if he would not try to see his children. If he insisted, then she would have to send them home to her mother.

'But she means to divorce you, Robert!'

He shrugged lazily, sitting on the foot of the bed. 'Sylvia's always threatening me. It's her way of getting me home. Her threats never amount to much. We've been through this before. She doesn't mean a word of it.'

'You have had other – lovers?'

He raised his brows. 'Don't be naïve, dearest.'

She bit her lip. Yes, she was being naïve to think that she was his great love; that they had a future together,

He got up, bent over her. 'Move over, my sweet. If it's to be our last night together, let's make it one to remember.'

Amroth's confidence that his wife's threats 'did not amount to much' was misplaced. Two weeks after his departure to Leicestershire, Hester received a letter from Sylvia's solicitors in London – she was to be named as co-respondent in the Amroth divorce case. Messrs Hemlock and Withers requested that her solicitors get in touch with them forthwith.

The thought of seeking Alfred Bracegirdle's advice made her shudder. Every detail would find its way back to Ellen. Besides, she must keep her trouble to herself as long as possible, in the hope that Sylvia Amroth would change her mind. The hope was not a strong one; for she had a shrewd idea that Sylvia detested her and wanted her social downfall.

I've been a fool, Hester told herself miserably. Even Uncle Joe's money couldn't rescue her now. Nothing could.

She walked up and down her sitting room, re-reading the letter from Sylvia Amroth and wondering what she ought to do. Outside, it was a March day with the cold winds blowing through the trees with a shrill whistling sound. Scudding clouds chased across a pale blue sky and she knew there would be the smell of growing things, of a world re-born after the hard winter. She couldn't stay indoors a moment longer, she decided, going upstairs to change her shoes. Soon she was walking briskly across the spongy ground towards the pink dogwood near the lake. Catkins were full out and the bright spasms of sunlight dazzled in the wide pools left by the melting snow. She breathed deeply. As always, Stanhope worked its magic and her cares fell away from her. What did it matter? What did anything matter while she was young and vigorous and could run against the wind which poured an icy draught down her throat, until she was breathless and laughing and had to subside on a fallen tree trunk? Resting on it, she looked at Stanhope, *her* Stanhope, and loved it. Even if Sylvia Amroth carried out her threat and ruined her, she wouldn't leave here. She would live at Stanhope and be content, she thought confidently.

Then, as she was smiling round on her domain, she came to earth again. Stanhope belonged to Wilfred and Wilfred was sensitive to Society's censorship. He went to great lengths to hide his way of life, never risking discovery in England. If she were named in this divorce case Wilfred would divorce her and Society would sympathize with him. She would be forced to leave Stanhope. Worse, he would keep Patrick and would have the law on his side. She had said the child was his; everyone believed the child was his. She stood to lose everything.

Her buoyant mood evaporated. She felt quite sick. 'Oh, God, what a fool I've been!' she said aloud and hid her face in her hands. Her legs were trembling as she rose and began to walk back to the house. She would be an outcast, she who had learned to love the ordered round of their social lives. House parties at great houses. Chats with the Prince of Wales. Cowes next year. The Season beginning in May and this year she intended taking a house in London for two months. All – all that would be over if Sylvia Amroth went ahead with the divorce.

As she came in by a side door she was met by Sarah in a state of excitement. 'Oh, m'lady, you'll never guess who's here!' she blurted.

'Don't be silly, Sarah. Of course I shan't play guessing games,' Hester said sharply.

'I had ever such a shock when I opened the door. Mr Wiston was having his rest and I was to answer the front door bell. And how it clanged! "Sounds like the fire brigade," I said to Cook – joking like – and then I opens it and there was this mite. "I want to see Lady Prickard," she says, walking in and looking all round her. I nearly dropped in my tracks ... I really did. ... '

Hester sighed. She could see now how it was that Wiston still regarded Sarah as an apology for a parlourmaid. Sarah

440

was garrulous and didn't take her duties seriously, he would say, shaking his head. 'Well, who was it?'

'Posy Collins, m'lady. Eight years old and a proper little lady. I put her in the room off the hall.'

Posy. An image of a fair, delicate four-year-old child crying for her kitten flashed across Hester's mind. She went rapidly across the hall, throwing her cloak to Sarah as she went. How on earth had Posy found her way to Stanhope?

As she opened the door, a little girl slid off a chair too high for her and curtseyed. Under the sailor hat the small pinched face was unmistakeably Posy Collins. She was small for her age, and the blue sailor suit was far too thin for early March. In her gloved hands, she clutched a miniature handbag and a letter.

'Why, Posy Collins! Do you remember me, Hetty Kelly? Is it me you want to see?' She bent and kissed the little composed face.

'I don't really remember you,' the child said seriously. Her large unblinking eyes stared up at Hester. 'No, not really,' she added, shaking her head. 'But Mama talked about you and said I was to come to you and what train I was to take.'

'Where have you come from? Why isn't Mama with you? Where is Mama now?'

Under the battery of questions, the child seemed to shrink. Hester saw at once her mistake. Putting an arm round Posy, she led her to the fire that Sarah had lighted. 'Come and get warm, Posy.' Taking the small hands in hers, she drew off the darned cotton gloves and chafed the icy fingers. 'You must be hungry after your journey. I'll get Sarah to bring you chicken sandwiches and a glass of milk.' After she had rung the bell she returned to the hearthrug, talking about the walk she had taken and the lambs in the Home Farm fields. When Sarah brought in a tray, the child fell to eating with a will, but she didn't gobble the sandwiches and eat and drink at the same time. Belle had brought up her child well. She had loved her dearly – Hester felt a shiver when she realized she was thinking of Belle in the past tense. 'What was that letter you were holding?' she asked with a smile. 'Was it for me from Mama?'

Posy said, 'Yes,' in her small voice and pushed the white envelope across the table towards her. Hester slit it open. It was written feebly in a pencilled scrawl that was faint in parts.

> By the time you get this I shall be dead. My one anxiety is for Posy. When I die they will put her in an orphanage and I cannot bear the thought of that. I have only one friend in the world and that is you. I never appreciated what you did for me and Posy but I know you care for the child. Keep her and love her, Hetty. I see you are a great lady now – Here the letter trailed off but below in a stronger hand, Belle wrote: The luck has always been bad. Now I have a growth and not long to go. Don't let me down, Hetty. You were an orphan too, remember? The luck has always been bad.

Poor Belle, she had never seen that she was always her own worst enemy, pushing those who would have helped away from her.

There was no address. Hester looked up at Posy. 'Where were you last with Mama? In London?'

'Oh, no. Mama was in the chorus at the Grand Theatre, Leeds,' Posy said eagerly. 'I went to see her. She looked lovely. But she had this bad pain here – ' She touched her chest. 'So she stayed in bed at Mrs Fisher's and I got the doctor for her. Will she be better soon? She said they were going to take her away to make her better and I was to stay with you until she came back.'

'I think she'll be better before long,' Hester said gently. 'I'm so glad you've come to stay, Posy. There's such a lot to show you here, such a lot to do. I'll get you a little pony and teach you to ride. . . .'

'Will it be long? Before Mama comes?'

'Can you remember the address? Then I'll write and ask

her. Meanwhile, you shall have a little bed in the night nursery with my little boy, Patrick. He's only a baby still, you know, but he'll love to have someone to play with. And Rose, his nurse, is such a kind person. Come and see her with me now you've finished.' She held her hand out and Posy, with growing confidence, took it and walked out into the hall with her. 'It's – it's very big,' she whispered as they went upstairs.

'It only seems so because you're very small,' Hester smiled down at her.

Sarah, hovering in and out of the baize door leading to the kitchens, smiled and nodded up at the child. Posy waved at her. 'Where is the other one?'

Hester stopped. 'You *do* remember! Annie went to another place when I moved here.'

'What became of Blackie?'

'He went with Annie. He loved Annie, you know. Cats always like the cook because there's always plenty of food about. And Blackie was a greedy kitten. He grew enormous. Would you like another kitten, Posy? For your own?'

'No, thank you,' the child said very politely but firmly. 'You see, I shan't be here long enough and when Mama and I are travelling about, we can't take a cat with us. Landladies don't like cats, you know.'

'No. How silly of me. Well, here we are, Rose, a visitor to stay with us. Her name is Primrose Collins but we can call her Posy.'

Rose, asking no questions, came forward smiling her broad smile. Patrick was having tea sitting in his high chair. Dipping a finger of toast in his mug of milk he offered it generously to the visitor. As the milk dripped on to the carpet, Posy laughed. Smiling at the two adults she took the soggy toast and pretended to nibble at it, making ferocious, hungry noises. Patrick burst into chuckles and was just prevented from dipping the rest of the toast in and making what Rose termed 'a horrid mess, the bad boy'.

'Well, I'll leave you to manage, Rose,' Hester said. 'I'll

come up and see you later about arrangements. We shall have to put another bed in here. By the way, Posy, did you bring any luggage?'

'Oh, yes, I forgot,' Posy said absently as she examined the nursery. 'It's on the steps outside.'

'But how did you get here from Sewerston Junction?' Hester asked as the thought suddenly struck her.

'The nice man at the station said he knew Stanhope and he would send me up by the carrier. That's how I came,' Posy explained.

Hester wrote at once to Mrs Fisher at the Leeds address Posy had given her, but she heard nothing. It was puzzling. Meanwhile there was much to do, for Wilfred was due home at the end of the week after an absence of two months. On one thing Hester was determined – she would conceal the Amroths' divorce from him as long as she could. But as she went about Stanhope, she was very aware that her future here rested on a knife's edge.

Wilfred came home late one night. He had brought presents for Hester and Patrick but was, as always, after these trips, slightly irritable and apt to grumble. 'How is my mother? I hope you haven't been neglecting your visits to her, Hester.'

'No,' Hester said shortly. She wanted to tell him about Posy and this was obviously not a good time. She determined to do it after breakfast next morning and got up to join him in the dining-room at nine o'clock.

She found him looking perturbed.

'I just went into the drawing-room to have a look round,' he said, 'when I thought I saw a child. A little girl, pale and fair. She was humming a tune and wandering about touching things.' He poured himself coffee and stared at Hester. 'Is she real? She looks like a little ghost – didn't take any notice of me at all.'

Hester concealed a smile. Rose had told her of Posy's

444

love of wandering over the rooms at Stanhope, staring at and touching things. ('She's a queer little dear,' sighed Rose. 'Lovable, but dreamy. She tells Patrick nonsense tales by the hour. Then, just when I want her, she's gone and Sarah finds her in Sir Wilfred's room or the east wing. I've told her and told her but she doesn't listen.')

'Does the ghost wear a blue dress with blue ribbons in her hair?'

Wilfred looked at her suspiciously. 'Who is she?'

'Why, Wilfred, you're privileged! You've seen – actually seen the ghost of Stanhope! And in daylight too,' Hester mused, stirring her coffee. 'You are lucky.'

'A ghost? Don't be a fool, Hester. Come on, out with it – you've brought in another child. Is that it?'

'Not brought in. She arrived on her own account. Posy Collins. Do you remember Belle Collins, who was in the Gaiety chorus with me? She appears to have been taken ill at Leeds and sent the child to me. For all I know, Belle is dead now. I've written to her landlady but there's no answer yet.'

'Oh, that woman. I remember you were very good to her and now she dumps the child on you. Typical. She's probably gone off with a man and the child is merely an encumbrance,' Wilfred said. He got up to serve himself a second helping of kidneys and bacon.

Watching him, Hester thought that he had put on a great deal of weight. He had also bought himself New York clothes and they were terrible: yellow boots, a checked suit and – horror of horrors – a close-cropped haircut that did not suit him at all. 'I don't think Belle would do that. She loved Posy. But until I find out more, I'm keeping the child.'

He turned to look at her; a sour look of dislike. 'Up to now, Hester, I've let you run away with the idea that you can do as you like here. Let me remind you that Stanhope is mine. I shall say who lives here, not you.'

She flushed angrily. 'Then it is time you took on the financial burden of running this place if you feel that. And giving the orders to the servants. You even leave the outdoor staff to me, Wilfred. While I stay here, Posy will stay.'

'What do you mean? *While* you stay here?'

'Has it never occurred to you?' she said in a quiet voice, keeping her emotions under control with an effort. 'That I might go? That I might need a real husband?'

He turned a face of naked fear towards her. 'My God, you couldn't do that to me? It would ruin me – the Line – everything!'

She got up, looking at him with contempt. 'Don't worry. I shan't reveal the truth about our so-called marriage. If I go it will be up to you to divorce me, won't it?'

She felt him staring after her as she went out of the room.

CHAPTER FIVE

When at last a letter came from Leeds it was uncompromisingly plain.

> Dear Madam,
>
> Yours to hand. Mrs Collins died and buried Leeds City Cemetery last week. Glad to hear Posy all right.
>
> Yours truly,
> M. Fisher.

Hester put it in her desk, her face troubled. How could she tell the child? She was so happy at the moment. Wilfred had raised no further objection to her presence in the house. He had been sulky when he went off to the Liverpool office, but they had not crossed swords again and Hester intended to leave it like that. Time enough when the Amroth case came into the open and she faced ruin. How Aunt Ellen would be justified, she thought bitterly. She had always predicted that Hester would bring disgrace to the Prickards one day.

Meanwhile there was Posy.

With an effort, Hester brought her thoughts back to the child. It really would be best to say nothing for the time being. Posy would probably not ask . . . no, she would say nothing.

Having come to that decision she looked through the rest of her post. Among the invitations and bills was another envelope written in an uneducated hand to *Lady Pricard*.

447

She opened it, read it quickly then read it again. It was the most extraordinary missive she had ever received. It was from one Hilda Smith, personal maid to Lady Amroth until recently dismissed.

> *. . . She said I took her gold watch but that I never did. I have a letter which would interest your ladyship. It is for sale.*

Hester wrinkled her nose in distaste. It was obvious that the wretched woman was hitting back at her former employer. *It is for sale.* She looked at the address. Islington. Well, she would have to go up to London sooner or later to consult a solicitor. It would be as well to see what Hilda Smith had for sale. If it was one of her letters to Amroth, she could keep it. Buying her letters back was not going to save the day, of that she was certain. Sylvia Amroth meant to have her pound of flesh.

Miss Hilda Smith sat looking very genteel in Lady Prickard's private sitting-room in Brown's Hotel, Dover Street. Clad in a black jacket and skirt with a jet-trimmed bonnet, she sat bolt upright on the edge of her chair clasping a handbag with both hands. She had a sharp-featured thin face with restless black eyes and a whiskery chin. She was plain and lonely, yet a veiled air of excited triumph seemed to leak out of her eyes. *I'm someone to reckon with* those dark eyes seemed to proclaim.

Julie had let her in, greeting her affably. 'Why, 'allo, Heelda! I hear you have left Lady Amroth. Where do you work now?'

'Nowhere, dear. I'm hoping I shan't have to work no more,' Miss Smith said with a thin smile. 'My fortunes have changed for the better lately. I'm getting on, you know. Fifty-five last birthday. I could do with a little place of my own now. I'm fed up with serving helpless women like that one of mine – she was a bitch, I can tell you. Not like the countess, her mother. Now *she* was a great lady but you don't get them like that any more. Most of 'em are no better than they should be . . . why, I could tell you. . . . ' She broke off as Hester, dressed for the street, came in and motioned Julie to leave them.

Miss Smith got up and curtseyed. 'Very good of your ladyship to see me. I'm sure.'

'What is this letter you have, Miss Smith?' Hester asked without preamble. She had not asked the woman to sit down again. 'Is it one of mine?'

'Oh, dear no, your ladyship! What an idea!' tittered Miss Smith. She opened her large handbag and brought out a letter written on thick creamy writing paper. Holding it close to her chest, she said carefully, 'It is for sale, your ladyship.'

Hester took it and saw with quickening interest that it was embossed with the royal cipher under the heading *Windsor Castle*. It was from the Prince of Wales to Sylvia Amroth during the short time she had been his mistress.

My own dear little Sylvia it began and ended *Ever Yours Bertie.*

'How did you get hold of this?' she asked sharply.

The woman looked defiant. 'Lady Amroth is not a very careful lady. I've plenty more like this one.'

'Why were you dismissed? Did you steal that gold watch?'

A dull colour crept over the yellow face. 'It wasn't true! I never took what I shouldn't have been given in the first place. The old countess meant me to have it. She always said I was to have it when she went. After she died, Lady Amroth took me on as a personal maid. She could never keep any of us long. I never got the watch . . . the watch that was really mine! So I took it – why, she never used it herself. Old-fashioned, she called it.' The woman dabbed her mouth with her handkerchief. 'She dismissed me without a charac-ter. Now where can I get a job after that? She's taken the bread out of my mouth, she has.' She leaned forward. 'Now that letter is worth something I reckon. I know how you are placed, your ladyship – there's not much I don't know! It will come in real useful will that letter. Would you say a a thousand pounds?'

'A thousand pounds? You must be mad!' Hester threw the letter back. 'Get out.'

'Are you sure you want me to go? Think, your ladyship, just think what this letter means! If the Prince of Wales knew that this letter could be shown in court as evidence against Lady Amroth – why, he'd do anything to prevent it, I'm sure. Don't you think he would stop Lady Amroth trying to divorce her husband? Think of the scandal! The old Queen would be so vexed to see it in the newspapers.'

Hester took the letter again. She read it rapidly and shivered. It would be horrible if this letter were used to prove Sylvia Amroth's adultery with her august lover – and yet it could be used. 'Very well. If you call later – say six o'clock – I'll have the money ready for you.'

'Very sensible of your ladyship.' The woman held out her hand. 'And I'll keep the letter until then if you please. I wasn't born yesterday,' she added, insolent now that her fish was hooked.

As soon as the door shut behind the black-garbed figure, Hester flew to the writing table. Hardly pausing to think, she wrote to Sir Francis Knollys, the Prince's private secretary, asking him to call on her at Brown's Hotel on a matter of urgent business that concerned the Prince of Wales.

She sent Julie in a cab to deliver it by hand at Marlborough House. She herself hurried into Piccadilly to visit her bank, and to ask them to deliver a thousand sovereigns in two small bags at her hotel that evening at a quarter to six.

At six o'clock exactly Miss Hilda Smith was shown into the sitting-room by Julie. Smiling ingratiatingly, she delivered up the letter which Hester at once locked in her writing case. With a disdainful finger she indicated the bags of sovereigns. 'Count them if you must but not in my presence. I shall go into the bedroom and give you ten minutes. Don't do this again or you might find yourself in serious trouble.'

Going into the adjoining room, she washed her hands vigorously. She felt ashamed, unclean. Yet she must be staunch and carry through her plans. Such a lot depended now on their success: Patrick and Posy, Stanhope, her reputation.

Feeling suddenly sick and faint, she lay down on the bed, trying in vain to compose herself.

Julie came in and found her there. 'Milady, are you ill? Wait, I shall bring you the smelling salts and then a little cologne to bathe your face. It is very refreshing.' A shrewd woman, she suspected that her mistress was in some sort of trouble.

Hester smiled at her, blinking away tears. 'Oh, Julie, what fools we women are!' she sighed.

'*Oui, madame.* How I agree! I have the reply for you from the gentleman at the Prince's house. Wait, I will fetch it.'

Breaking it open, she found a formal reply in the third person: Sir Francis Knollys would call upon her tomorrow at eleven o'clock.

He was announced by Julie at three minutes past that hour. He took her proffered hand and released it quickly. She was aware at once that he was ill-at-ease and wary.

'Won't you sit down, Sir Francis?' She indicated a chair by the bright fire and she took one opposite. There was something in his demeanour and appearance that unnerved her. He sat quite silent, looking at her with aloof intelligent eyes under heavy lids. His thick grey moustache hung over a receding chin that the stiffness of his shining white collar sheltered. He alarmed her far more than the Prince of Wales had done at their first meeting, and she tried in vain to warm the atmosphere by referring to the weekend at Easton.

'Delightful' he agreed. Then he waited.

Clearing her throat, Hester wondered how on earth to begin.

'You wished to see me on an urgent matter, I believe?' he began rather impatiently.

'Yes, I did. If you will give me five minutes I will explain.' Then frankly and simply, she did explain, glossing over nothing. 'I am fighting for my very life, Sir Francis. The last thing I want is a divorce.' She went across to her writing case and unlocked it. 'A former servant of Lady Amroth's brought me this yesterday. Believe me, I do not wish to use it in court as evidence of Lady Amroth's own adultery with the Prince. I simply want His Royal Highness to dissuade Lady Amroth from taking any action against me. The whole case must be dropped before any of it becomes public. I am sure His Royal Highness would agree with that.'

There was silence while Sir Francis read the letter. Then he looked up at her with contempt. 'This is a form of blackmail, Lady Prickard.'

'Is it? Well, if it is, it's in a good cause. I have a child I must protect. As you see, I am still young. Would it not be tragic if my whole life were ruined by this one piece of folly on my part? It is all over between me and Lord Amroth – I give you my word.'

Sir Francis sighed. In his heart he could not blame this beautiful young woman for fighting back. Divorce was unthinkable; social suicide for both her and Amroth. He found himself wishing once more that his august master would think twice before sending his women friends such incriminating letters. He rose, handed back the letter. 'I will do all in my power to persuade His Royal Highness,' he said in a low tone. Bowing over her hand, he left swiftly.

She sat where he had left her, feeling weak with relief. With trembling hands she reached for the writing case and locked the letter away again. Tears began to trickle down her face and somehow she could not stem them. She had won; her future was secure again. But what now?

A great emptiness stretched ahead like a desert. She was not yet twenty-five. God knows, she told herself with a sob, she had committed many mistakes in her life, but none worse than marrying her homosexual cousin. Money and position and Stanhope could not compensate for the aridness of her life. She had done it for Patrick, because she wanted to keep her baby. Did she have to pay for this for the rest of her life?

She was feeling so ill and depressed by the time she returned to Stanhope that she retired to bed and Dr Mayne was summoned. He fussed into her bedroom and after examination gravely told her that she was suffering from exhaustion of the nervous system.

'You see, Lady Prickard, the social life of today imposes great strain on the – ah – delicate system of ladies. You need a long rest, free of all worry. And you must adhere strictly to my diet – I will leave details with your maid. And one of my young men shall come up at once with a mixture of mine that you will find immediately efficacious. An iron tonic – yes, I have thought for some time that I should put it on the market. It has remarkable results.'

So remarkable that Hester ordered Julie to throw it away after two doses had left her trembling and sick. 'If it's meant to take away my appetite, it's succeeded. It's poisonous stuff,' she declared.

'But, milady, perhaps it only makes you ill at first?' Julie's thrifty soul disliked the idea of wasting any of the expensive tonic.

'Throw it away and ask Wiston to send me up champagne with my lunch. My uncle was a great believer in champagne,' Hester remembered.

But even after champagne, a great depression clouded her spirits. She cried into her pillow and wondered whether it was worth while ever getting up again. Then Julie came in with her post and there was a thin foreign envelope: a letter from Tom Hoggarth at the Cape. She sat up with a cashmere shawl round her shoulders and devoured it eagerly, reading it again and again. He had sent her his love. Tears blotted the letter. Tom cared for her, and now at last she had to admit

453

he meant a great deal to her. He was married to another woman and they could never be more than friends. Tommy, her oldest friend who had grown into the only man who could ever bring her happiness.

She kept the letter under her pillow like any schoolgirl. That night, she slept well for the first time for several weeks.

She was in bed for two weeks. Outside it was spring at last. The sun shone warmly and leaves began to unfurl. She hated her pale face reflected in the mirror and gave up looking at herself.

Every morning, Rose brought Patrick and Posy in to see her. 'I think the little girl's worrying about something, m'lady,' she whispered one morning. 'Off her food and crying a great deal.'

That made two of them, Hester thought wearily as she kept Posy back when the noisier Patrick was carried away by Rose. 'Climb up here beside me, Posy.'

The child obeyed with Hester's help. How thin and light she felt! Like a little bird. 'What's wrong, Posy darling? Can't you tell me?'

Dumbly, the child shook her head, plucking at the silk eiderdown. Her huge eyes had blue rings under them, and were full of unshed tears.

Hester braced herself. 'How would you like to stay here always, Posy?'

She felt the child catch her breath, then her heart racing. 'Mama?' she asked in a low voice.

'Mama is dead.'

With one swift movement Posy threw herself face down on the bed. 'I knew she was! I *knew* she was! Only you didn't say anything . . . no one said anything. . . . '

'Oh, my poor little Posy!' Hester cried remorsefully. She had shirked telling the child at first, and then her own troubles had obscured Belle's death. How could she have been so thoughtless? Posy was not a baby but nearly nine years old. She had spent several weeks wondering if her mother had recovered and was coming to fetch her. 'Oh, forgive me, darling. It was stupid – so stupid of me. Mama was very brave, Posy – but then you know that. She knew she had not long to live so she sent you away to live with me – to be my little girl.'

Posy raised a flushed, tear-stained face. 'But now you're ill!' she cried desperately. 'Are you going to die too?'

Hester rocked her in her arms, reassuring her as best she could. No wonder the child was worried! Her second mother had now taken to her bed. 'I'm getting up tomorrow,' she announced. 'And I'm going out into the sun – that's the best medicine, you know. So then you'll see for yourself that I'm not going to die – of course I'm not! I'm going to get you a small bicycle and teach you to ride it and then we can go all over the park together!'

Posy blinked, scrubbing at her eyes. Sorrow would lie on her spirits for a time but she would recover now that she knew the truth, Hester assured herself. And next day she got out of bed and made herself go out. Her spirits rose at once with renewed hope, and that evening she began what was to be a regular monthly letter to Tom Hoggarth.

CHAPTER SIX

Tom Hoggarth didn't come home in 1899 as everyone had expected.

There was trouble in the Transvaal, he wrote to Hester, and home leave was cancelled.

Over the intervening years the letters they wrote each other had become those of lovers. On paper they had slipped into a relationship from which there was no going back.

When I think of coming home, Tom wrote, *I think only of you. Is that wrong? What I once felt for Violet was a boy's love. It has gone for good.*

Simply and truthfully, he laid bare his love and she responded with swift passion. *Oh, Tom, how I long for you! There can be no future without you. What are we to do?*

The future did not hold promise of fulfilment. Violet was mentally ill and would have to be cared for all her life. Tom could not love her, but his compassion for her was unchanged. And Wilfred would never let Hester go free because she shielded him from the world's gaze. To outsiders he was a model husband and father of a son – who could suspect such a man of pederasty?

Through the seasons Hester wrote to Tom Hoggarth; he was the rock to which she clung in her loneliness. She longed for his homecoming, feeling that with his arrival all difficulties would be resolved. So when she learned that he was not returning that summer after all, it was like a blow to her heart.

Many times during those years she tried to make contact

with Violet, but without success. Dorrie Hoggarth stood between her and the sick daughter-in-law who was never seen downstairs. Violet would be said to be 'resting as she's not strong' or 'not well enough for visitors today' whenever Hester enquired after her.

Meeting Matty Hoggarth in Sewerston one morning, Hester asked him bluntly if his sister-in-law was avoiding her. 'I'd like to see her, for you know that Tom and I are old friends.'

The young man shot her a guarded look. 'Yes,' he agreed. He twirled his bowler hat in nervous hands and then blurted out, 'You see, Hester, Violet's alcoholic so Ma just pretends it's something else.' He fell into step beside her, a well-set-up young man at whom she looked approvingly. 'I don't know what Tom's going to do. He's due home next year, you know, and Violet's just – well, a mess.' He shuddered. 'She looks twice her real age. She doesn't bother to dress. She gets up and starts on the gin right away. We've tried cancelling her order, but she ran out into the street in her nightdress. Ma had such a fright. She might have had to move right away, you know.' Matty Hoggarth turned his serious eyes on Hester. 'We've come on in the world and can't afford a scandal. It's all right if you're a belted earl but for Ma – the newsagent's widow living in that refined district – no, it wouldn't do.'

Hester looked again at Tom's brother; what a precise, old-fashioned youth, she thought. He's going to rise in the world and poor Violet will have to be kept under control or there won't be any clients for Mr Matthew Hoggarth, architect. The cloth of his jacket was excellent, his black bowler hat well-brushed and the ribbon ironed. He wore dove grey gloves and carried an umbrella and looked as if he had never seen a joke in his life. It was obvious that the potential danger of Violet Hoggarth loomed large in his well-ordered life.

'Tom's a captain now,' he told Hester proudly and she pretended surprised pleasure. 'He's better off without Violet and that's the truth, but how is Ma to carry on looking after her? She does it for Tom's sake, but she's going to have to think of me before long,' he added resentfully.

457

His words remained with her and one day she went to *Braeside* to call on Mrs Hoggarth. 'I wonder if I can see Violet,' she asked. 'No, don't look like that, dear Mrs Hoggarth. You see, I know.'

Dorrie Hoggarth put her silver teapot down with a bang. 'Matty hasn't learned to keep his mouth shut yet,' she said tartly. 'He's for ever on at me about how bad Violet is for his career, but who's the one doing the talking, I'd like to know?'

'Tom told me nearly two years ago,' Hester said.

They stared at each other.

'And he writes to me regularly,' Hester added.

'He's a married man! He's got no business to be writing to you! You'll excuse me, Hester, but I'm going to speak my mind. . . .'

'No, please don't. It will do no good. Tom and I are adults, and we're both married. I just want you to know we're great friends. Tom has told me everything.'

His mother put her handkerchief to her mouth. 'You and he – you're not lovers?'

Hester laughed. 'He is in Africa and I am here! No, we're not lovers but very close friends.' She tried to control the colour that was flooding her face under Dorrie's suspicious scrutiny. 'Just friends,' she repeated firmly.

'Then why are you looking like that? You would never steal that poor girl's husband?'

Hester opened her mouth to reply and then stopped. The door had opened softly and a woman had come in. She had once been very fair and pretty. Now in her white lawn negligée with her hair tumbling limply round her narrow face, she looked like a lost soul. Her vacant eyes circled the room. 'Where's the gin? You did promise me,' she added accusingly.

Dorrie had risen, her hand to her mouth. 'Violet, you mustn't come down like this!' Her eyes flew to Hester's face.

Hester too had risen. She had gone very pale. So this was Tom's wife. Not the drunken harridan of her imagination, but a thin woman with bewildered blue eyes. The firmness of her skin had gone and it sagged round the mouth and eyes – but she had been lovely once! Hester thought with a sharp stab of pity. Impulsively she reached out and took Violet's cold hand in hers. 'I'm Hester Prickard. I've known Tom for years.'

'Pleased to meet you,' Violet murmured vaguely, then returned to her complaining voice. 'You promised I should have the new bottle today – you promised.'

'Go back to bed, dear,' Dorrie said hurriedly as she led the unresisting figure to the door. Closing it with a snap she turned to Hester and said accusingly, 'Well?'

Hester was gathering her furs and gloves. 'Don't worry. She's quite safe. I'll never do her any harm,' she said in a low voice. She felt sick with misery, hating herself and Tom. Violet was as helpless as a child and needed as much care and love as one. What they contemplated was unthinkable.

She wrote to Tom that night. *How can we harm this help-less creature?* her letter ended. *She needs our protection – but Tom, I do still need your love. Help me to bear it, but while Violet lives there can be no future for us.* She wept as she closed the envelope, for she was deliberately destroying any hopes they had harboured about sharing a life together.

After the letter had been despatched, she felt exalted for a time. It had been the right thing to do, she assured herself. But later she felt depressed – especially when no more letters came from Tom. It seemed that she had killed the one good thing in her life.

Tom's prediction of trouble in the Transvaal proved correct.

Hester uneasily read of the mounting tension in Africa, all through that hot and stormy autumn, when the leaves were whipped prematurely off the trees by the strong winds. By October 7 the Boers had handed their ultimatum to Sir Alfred Milner, and that day mobilization was ordered in Britain.

To Wilfred's annoyance he lost Arthur, the footman, and

the new head gardener who were both reservists with the local Yeomanry.

'Good heavens, haven't we enough regular troops to deal with a pack of Dutch farmers?' he asked disgustedly. 'Of course this will be disastrous for business – just when we have branched out with new vessels on the African route.'

Hester looked at him impatiently – was that all he could think about? Her own heart was heavy with foreboding. Tom was out there. Tom who had so recently been promoted to captain.

One wet, stormy evening, a message came from the dower house. Miss Bentley urgently requested Lady Prickard's presence.

Hester went down into the hall to speak to Ellen's footman herself. Rain ran off his waterproofs as he stood holding his soaking cap and dripping all over the rug to Wiston's annoyance. 'If you please, my lady, it's her ladyship. Miss Bentley is worried.'

'Lady Prickard is ill?'

'Been in bed these last two days and won't have a doctor.'

'I'll come immediately. Wiston, please send to the stables for the dogcart to come round at once.'

Agnes was waiting in the lamplit hall of the dower house and, as Hester entered the house, she pounced on her with relief. 'Miss Hester, I'm right glad to see you! M'lady won't have me send for the young doctor what's taking our doctor's place while he's in Scotland. She says she'll wait until he comes home – but I can see she's bad. Happen you can persuade her. I don't like the look of her at all.'

Ellen tried feebly to be cross when Hester was brought in, but a fit of coughing made her inarticulate. Hester took the plump dry hand in hers. 'Dear aunt, why haven't you had Doctor Knowles to see you? I assure you he is most sympathetic and very up-to-date in his methods. Shall I have him brought? William can take the message, for I have got the dogcart outside.'

'Very well,' Ellen whispered. There was lurking fear in her

eyes. 'I don't seem able to breathe – perhaps he can give me something?'

'Of course he can. Now lie back and don't try and talk.'

Doctor Knowles arrived within half an hour; Hester noticed how grave he looked after he had examined the patient and had re-joined her on the landing. 'She is very ill. Her heart and lungs are badly affected. If Sir Wilfred is in England he had better be sent for.'

'She isn't going to die?' Hester said, startled.

'I don't know. She is near the crisis. It will be tonight, I fear. I should have been sent for some days ago. There is nothing I can do now. Her temperature is still rising.'

Crouched over the drawing-room fire, Hester waited throughout the night while the doctor came and went and Ellen struggled for breath, her cheeks bright with colour. Once or twice, Hester crept into the bedroom to sit by the bed and hold her aunt's limp hand. Across the bed, Agnes went on mopping the flushed face.

'Wil-fred?' Ellen gasped pleadingly.

'He's on his way. He'll be here by morning.'

'Too . . . late,' muttered Ellen.

Above her head in the drawing-room, the old mahogany clock ticked the seconds away. The autumn gales battered the windows and Hester drew her chair closer to the fire, hearing overhead the soft sounds from her aunt's room. A servant came in and built up the fire, brought her tea and exchanged a few words. Dawn came. She went across to the window and drew back the curtains. As the sun rose, thin ribbons of pink and green streamed over the tops of the rocking trees.

Some day, she thought sombrely, I shall be lying up there. Alone. Just as alone as I am now. Patrick and his wife will be down here waiting for me to die. I shall have been alone since Victor died in '93. Were those few short months with him all I shall ever know of marriage? Real marriage? For we were man and wife as surely as if we had been married. Is that all it will be? A few short months and then over for good.

461

She turned back into the room, the tears wet on her cheeks. Oh, Tom, come back safely, she prayed within herself. Don't leave me to the long empty years that will bring me to the hour of my death without knowing your love. . . .'

There were footsteps coming down the stairs, pausing outside the door. She knew before it opened, that the doctor had come to tell her Ellen was dead.

Wilfred did not reach Stanhope until the late afternoon. If he felt grief he concealed it admirably. He looked pasty and dissipated, sounding as irritable as he looked. His mother's death had come at a highly inopportune moment it seemed. Didn't Hester realize that the war in Africa had really broken out at last? 'Those blasted Boers have put their foot in it this time.'

They were in her sitting-room, a place he seldom entered. He sat by the fire, a file of papers on his knees; for he had wasted no time in going into Ellen's affairs. 'Her ten thousand a year comes to me and afterwards to Patrick,' he was pointing out.

Hester stared at him. There was nothing about Wilfred that she cared for these days. Was she really to be handcuffed for life to this man who, by his own admission, feared and disliked women? On an impulse she got up from the sofa and came to stand in front of him, her hands clasped before her, her head high. 'Wilfred, I don't want to go on with this farce of a marriage. Now that your mother is dead and there is no one to be hurt, couldn't we get a divorce?'

His head jerked up. There was real malevolence in his eyes as he jumped to his feet and she shrank from him. He thrust his face in hers. 'Are you out of your mind, you little fool? Divorce? Us? Don't you realize it would mean business *and* social ruin for us both?'

'I don't care. All I want is to be free – just to have some life of my own. Why should I be tied hand and foot while you are free to lead a strange life of your own? Yes, you can

462

even venture outside the law because you feel safe married to me . . . *oh!*' His hand had come up and landed with a resounding smack on the side of her face. 'How dare you?' she gasped, taking a step back. But he followed her, taking her arms in an iron grip that made her squirm.

'Don't let's have any wild talk, my dear,' he said softly in her ear. 'You wouldn't like anything – rough to happen to you, now would you?'

She stared at him, mesmerized. This was no longer plump, easy-going Wilfred but a dark, menacing stranger who was actually threatening her. 'Don't touch me,' she said with a shudder. 'Take your hands off me!'

But he took not the slightest notice. Tightening his grip, he shook her violently. Her hair tumbled down, but if he hoped to cow her he didn't succeed, for she landed a kick on his shin that made him loosen his grip. She wrenched herself free and retreated to the window to stand beside the bell pull. 'Get out or I shall summon Wiston,' she said from a dry throat.

'You take one false step,' he said with slow emphasis, 'and I shall make certain you never see Patrick again.'

'Patrick is my son. You can't take him from me.'

'You think not? Then you had better consult a lawyer. The children of a marriage are always the husband's property. You are an ignorant woman if you think you have any rights in this house at all. Patrick is *my* son, the heir to the title, to Stanhope and the Prickard Line.'

'He's not yours, he's not!' she cried hoarsely. 'He is Victor Cockayne's son and you know it!'

'Don't be a fool.' He shot his cuffs with a curious complacency. 'Strange that he is registered as my legal son, isn't it? I have a copy of his birth certificate in my desk. Go ahead and try to get a divorce. I'll be well rid of you if all I hear is true. But the boy stays here with me.'

After he had left the room, she threw herself on the sofa and wept bitter tears. What a fool she had been. Anything – anything would have been better than this gilded prison she found herself in. If she left, Wilfred would be as good as his word and she would never see Patrick again. The child was useful to Wilfred, showing the world that he was a normal husband and father. Any allegations she could bring against him would be dismissed as a woman's desperate attempt to win freedom from her marriage. She was very neatly tied to Stanhope and Patrick, and of course to Wilfred Prickard, second baronet and co-owner of the great Prickard Shipping Line. Against such a man there could be no breath of scandal.

Ellen's death, unlike Joseph's, made no stir. She had taken no further part in the life of the village since that date. First at Stanhope and then at her new dower house, she had woven herself a warm cocoon that protected her from a harsh outside world. Now she was dead and the flag of the church was at half-mast, and a small black-gowned procession filed out of the church to the reopened grave. With no emotion on his face, Wilfred sprinkled the ritual handful of earth on his mother's coffin. The vicar read the final prayers; the doctor blew his nose loudly and they were turning away and back into life. The sexton and his mate hardly waited until the last mourner had gone through the lychgate, before they were there with their long-handled shovels, replacing the small mound of brown earth.

Hester, looking round, could see them. Poor Aunt Ellen, she thought, suddenly moved. She enjoyed warm fires and rich food and a soft bed . . . and now they were leaving her alone in the cold damp churchyard, with the rain and leaves falling off the trees.

The dower house had to be emptied of Ellen's possessions. Like a squirrel, she had hoarded everything against that chance evil day when she would be poor again. As Hester and Agnes opened cupboards, pillows, feather boas, old-fashioned dancing shoes, fans and sashes, family albums and broken false teeth fell out in showers. On shelves lay chipped crockery and glass (the missing pieces carefully wrapped in paper and labelled), dusty Bibles, boxes of odd buttons.

The gardener's boy stoked a fire and the pantry boy carted out boxes of rubbish to be burned in the open. Glancing out of a window, Hester smiled as she saw the fun the two boys were having as they threw a motheaten boa across the flames, shaking sparks into the air like a display of fireworks. Then the butler came out and boxed their ears, and the scene became decorous again.

Agnes came in examining a fine linen sheet which she held close to her eyes. 'I've found one of Miss Ellen's trousseau sheets,' she announced. 'Did you see anything so fine?'

'What shall we do with it?' Hester asked. It didn't escape her notice that her aunt had become 'Miss Ellen' again to the old servant, who had come from her mother's house with her as a bride.

'Do with it?' Agnes looked affronted. 'Why, nothing, Miss Hester. Just put it away with a nice bag of lavender. . . . '

'No, Agnes,' Hester demurred. 'We must clear the house completely Sir Wilfred says. Nothing makes a house smell more than cupboards full of damp articles growing green mould. The house is to be closed, you know. Now wouldn't you like that sheet to add to the others you are taking to your new home?' For Agnes was retiring at last to a cottage next to Rickaby's in the village. Hester adjusted a number on the sheet of paper she held, stretched her arms and groaned 'Oh, Agnes, I'm too tired to do any more. Let's have a cup of tea.'

Agnes was clasping the trousseau sheet to her bosom. 'Eh, I never thought I'd outlive Miss Ellen and sleep between her sheets,' she said and there were tears in her eyes. 'Not that I'll ever sleep between them,' she added, 'they're far too good.' As she went out of the room again she paused in the doorway and said, 'It's funny to think this place will be empty till you come to live here one day, Miss Hester.'

The bottom seemed to fall out of Hester's stomach as the door shut. A kind of despair gripped her, and she looked round wildly, as if for a way of escape. She was Lady Prickard, rich and fortunate in the eyes of the world; yet here she stood shivering with sick fear at the thought that life held nothing more for her than long years of *ennui* and a final home (if she outlived Sir Wilfred) in this terrible, ugly house. *I can't . . . I won't stay* – But she knew she would; there was nowhere a decent woman could go to except to her own home. Besides, she would lose Patrick. She was trapped as surely as one of the rabbits in the Stanhope woods.

CHAPTER SEVEN

That terrible week in December, the week before Christmas, was dubbed Black Week in Britain. During an eight-day period, three major battles were fought and lost by the British troops. The names of those far-off places had an ominous ring to British ears: Colenso, Stormberg and Mogersfontein. The Highland Division, routed at Mogersfontein, suffered the most grievous loss and there was universal mourning in Scotland. At Colenso, the newly appointed Commander-in-Chief, Field-Marshal Lord Roberts of Kandahar, lost his only son, who, with three others, was awarded the Victoria Cross. Now, the popular 'Bobs' was on his way to the Cape with the new chief of staff, Lord Kitchener, and Sir Redvers Buller (caustically called 'Sir Reverse') was stepping down. Now at last, thought the nation from the Queen downwards, now at last our fortunes will change. . . .

An increasing anxiety about Tom (from whom she had not heard for three months) drove Hester one day to call on Mrs Hoggarth. As she walked up the drive of *Braeside* she was astonished to hear screams and shouts from inside the house. As no one answered the bell and the noise increased, she opened the front door herself on an astonishing scene.

A struggle was taking place on the stairs. Matt, his mother and a servant were trying to force a distraught Violet back up the stairs to her room. At the foot stood the frightened cook holding her apron up to her mouth and uttering moans of despair. 'Oh dear, mum, oh dear! Eh . . . take care of the

pictures! Well, I never did . . . never in all me born days.'
She caught sight of Hester, uttered a little scream and bolted
through the baize door like a rabbit to its warren.

'Leave . . . me . . . alone! I will go . . . I will!' Violet
screamed.

'You bloody won't!' Matt Hoggarth shouted. 'I'll strap
you down before I . . . let . . . you . . . ' His voice gave out as
he tugged at his sister-in-law. She seemed to be possessed of
demonic strength and the concerted effort of the three of
them seemed unable to budge her. She lashed out with hands
and feet and teeth, her nightdress half over her head, screaming abuse in the language of the gutter.

'Oh, what is it?' Hester cried.

Catching sight of her, Dorrie Hoggarth (her face scarlet,
her hair tumbling out of its combs) cried, 'She's trying to
run out in her nightgown – can you help us get her to her
room?'

Once laid on her bed, Violet subsided into a strange silence.
Her narrow face was still pale, but she had bitten her tongue
and a dribble of blood was leaving its traces down the side of
her mouth and on to the pillow.

'See to her, Martha, there's a good girl,' Mrs Hoggarth
directed, pushing her hair into place. The buttons on the
front of her blouse had burst open and she fumbled with them
tiredly. Matt had gone out of the room like a tornado and
somewhere a door banged. She beckoned Hester silently into
her own neat bedroom. Standing in the middle of the room,
she burst into silent tears.

Hester, very shaken herself, came and put her arm round
the ample shoulders. 'Don't,' she said in a low voice.

Dorrie made an effort to wipe her eyes. 'Our Tommy's
wife,' she said sorrowfully. 'Poor Matt. He's at his wit's end
and so am I. Where's it going to end? We've had complaints
from the neighbours already. She screams and breaks the
windows and runs half-naked in the garden if we don't watch
her. I tell you, Hester, I'm fair distracted. We shall have to

move and this address is so good for Matt's work. But I can't stand it much longer,' and she sobbed again, her face suddenly old.

There were answering tears in Hester's eyes. It was terrible to think that Tom was tied for life to this half-mad creature who existed only for gin. Poor Dorrie Hoggarth too. She was too old to be expected to cope much longer. 'Tom will be back home in a few months when this war ends. It can't go on long.'

'She's no longer sane,' Dorrie sobbed. 'It's the gin. It's softened her brain. She's only twenty-eight and she's ruined. Such a pretty girl she was too.'

'You will have to get a nurse for her. I'm sure Tom would say so.'

But Dorrie was beyond making decisions at the moment. 'I'll have to see,' she said dully. Her eyes anxious, she added, 'You won't tell anyone, Hester, will you?'

Hester put an arm round her. 'Of course not. Now let's go downstairs and sit by the fire. It's a beastly day,' she added, glancing through the window at the grey, heaving German Ocean which seemed to merge with the grey sky. 'Do you realize,' she said when they were settled in the neat over-furnished drawing-room that was Dorrie's pride and joy, 'that in two days time we shall be in a new century? There's going to be a bonfire and fireworks at Stanhope and Patrick and Posy can't talk of anything else. 1900! Doesn't it sound strange?'

Dorrie had recovered her composure. As she rang for tea, she sighed. 'It's all right if you're young, but I'm too old to care much. All I know is I'm going to be fifty-three in May.'

'Have you any news of Tom?' Hester asked casually.

'We've heard nothing since the beginning of November. Then it was only a note and a cheque for Violet's keep. He's got no need to send me anything but that's Tom all over. Matty thinks he's in the thick of the fighting. I tell you, Hester, sometimes I think it would be better for him to be killed and out of this mess. What life is there for him with *her*? It seems her mother went the same way.' The tears began to flow again and she reached frantically for her handkerchief.

'You're shocked and depressed,' Hester comforted her. 'You must get someone to look after her and keep her off drink. Shall I look round for you? There's an agency in Harrogate, although it would be best to ask your doctor. Please try not to worry.'

She couldn't take her own advice and, as she was driven back to Stanhope, agonizing anxiety for Tom's safety made her feel sick and exhausted. The concealment was the worst part, she thought wretchedly. She knew she had no rights where Tom was concerned. She simply had to wait and endure the misery of not knowing where he was or whether he was alive or dead.

Although they were in mourning for Ellen, Wilfred seemed to be holding weekend parties in his own wing, she noticed. She learned of this from Julie who was obviously disapproving. 'I think Sir Wilfred is only entertaining business colleagues,' Hester said quickly. But she doubted very much whether this was true. She avoided all contact with him now, and pretended to know nothing of what was going on. But that there was something vicious in these parties was almost certain. The guests arrived very late at night; few people saw them apart from his own manservant, none of the staff entered the east wing until the guests had departed.

All through that winter Hester's uneasiness grew. Now that his mother was dead, it was obvious that Wilfred had grown reckless and was bringing his rakish friends to stay. Julie had assured her that there were no women at these gatherings, hoping to comfort her mistress. Hester feared that her information was correct. She knew very little of sexual deviation, only what she had gleaned from the reports of the Oscar Wilde trial, and she wondered sometimes what possible form these parties could take.

Huge mahogany doors had been built across a landing to close the east wing away from the rest of the house. It even had its own outside entrance, that same door by which Amroth had entered the house all one winter when Wilfred was away. Then the east wing had contained only Wilfred's set of rooms. Now she understood it was as gorgeous as Aladdin's Cave. Or so Julie said the servants had told her. Pride forbade her trying to see inside herself. But if, as she suspected, the parties were of a dubious nature, didn't Wilfred realize that he might run foul of the law?

As usual it was Agnes, that avid reader of the local paper, who brought her the news: Captain Thomas Hoggarth had been badly wounded at a place called Paardeberg on the Modder River on February 18.

Three weeks ago – and Dorrie Hoggarth had never let her know, Hester thought with pain. She saw Agnes's eyes on her and tried to give an imitation of a woman concerned for an old friend; concerned but no more. When Agnes left, she fled to her bedroom and walked up and down in agony of spirit that would not be comforted.

Perhaps he was already dead . . . oh, God, not Tom, not Tom too! she prayed incoherently. 'I'll do anything . . . anything if You'll only let him recover . . . if You'll only let me see him once more. Oh, God, *please*,' she prayed dry-eyed, her nails digging into the palms of her hands. 'I promise I'll never see him again . . . I'll never tell him I love him . . . I'll do anything, God, if only You'll let him live!'

So she bargained with God, terror burning in her heart.

Presently she grew calmer. She must find out more. Now. Today. She would go to *Braeside* to enquire.

She sent a message to the schoolroom that she was going into Sewerston and would like Miss Peasegood and Posy to accompany her. Posy was in need of walking boots and there were several other things needed, she told Julie who was

471

helping her into a green velvet coat and skirt with a sable hat and scarf.

'But it is very cold, milady. I will fetch footwarmers,' Julie said disapprovingly. She shuddered as she looked out of the window at the snow still lying on the ground with no sign of spring after a hard winter.

Yes, it was a bitter day, Hester thought, looking out of the carriage windows at the unthawed snow in drifts beneath the hedges, at the leafless trees and the low grey sky. And it's bitter weather in my soul too, she thought despairingly. I no longer feel young. Happiness has eluded me. I've lost the hopefulness of youth. . . . She felt the sting of tears under her lids. Behind her back, Posy bounced on the seat with excitement at the unexpected treat of a visit to Sewerston.

'Oh, Aunt Hester, can we have tea at Owen's like last time? And can I buy chocolate to take back to Patrick? Then can I have twopence, please?'

Hester turned to smile at Mary Peasegood, Posy's young freshfaced governess who was engaged to the curate at Sewerston. 'You had both better have tea while I am calling on friends. Miss Peasegood, will you take Posy to be fitted for her boots? And if you would like to call and see Mr Foster, do so.' Let the girl enjoy her happiness while she could, she told herself, feeling the rush of grief in her breast. Youth – hopeful youth went so soon.

'Oh, thank you, Lady Prickard,' Mary Peasegood gasped, her cheeks flushing happily. 'And shall we wait at Owen's for you to pick us up afterwards?'

'Be ready by five and don't keep the horses waiting, will you?'

By the time the horses were climbing the hill to *Braeside* her anxious impatience had turned to dread. What would she find at that house? What fearful news awaited her? News that she must receive with just the right amount of sympathy and concern and no more.

Her whole body felt icy as she was shown into the drawing-room. A small fire burned in the grate, the sort that thrifty

Dorrie kept in case visitors called. On the mantelpiece was a photograph of Tom in uniform. It hadn't been there last time. She stared at it, repeating his name silently to herself . . . the door opening made her turn swiftly. 'I came as soon as I heard. Have you more news of Tom?'

Dorrie motioned her to a chair and sat down opposite her. 'We had a first letter yesterday. A scribbled note really, written from the hospital at Cape Town.'

Hester held her breath. 'Is . . . is it a bad wound?'

'It's his shoulder. Part of it has been blown off. He's got a wound in his neck too and part of one lung is affected. He wasn't able to give me much detail. You could see he was weak the way he wrote. Hasn't the letter reached us quickly?' Dorrie marvelled, ringing for tea. 'I saw in the paper that the *Dunottar Castle* got in on Wednesday. That's not one of yours, is it, Hester? It must have brought the mail.'

Hester shook her head. 'Is . . . is his face all right?'

Dorrie looked at her. 'He said nothing about his face.'

The servant came in bearing a huge tray loaded with food. Dorrie inspected it. 'Tut, Martha, you've forgotten the hot water as usual.' As the woman went out, she added, 'Aren't servants a trial? I give up hope of trying to train Martha.'

'Yes,' Hester said dully. She realized that Dorrie was deliberately trying to make her a casual visitor calling to enquire after her son. With an effort she tried to make the sort of conversation a casual friend of Dorrie's would make: servants, the weather, the war. Then she burst out. 'I must know – you must tell me! How bad is Tom?'

Dorrie frowned. 'You'll forgive me asking, Hester, but something Tom said in his letter. . . .'

'Yes?' Hester asked eagerly. 'What did he say? Did he send me a message?'

'What are you to Tom and what is he to you?' Dorrie asked sternly.

'We love each other.' She met Dorrie's eyes without flinching guiltily. The time for guilt was past. In the silence they could hear the small noises of the house: a door shutting, feet coming and going, the clock ticking loudly.

'It's wrong – it's very wrong!' Mrs Hoggarth's voice was harsher than Hester had ever heard it. 'You have a husband and child and Tom has a terrible responsibility in Violet. You've no business to carry on . . . what will people say?'

'We haven't "carried on", Mrs Hoggarth. It's nothing like that. Nothing so trivial. It's a deep love that has gone on growing since we were children. We've each married some-one else – and regretted it,' she added in a low voice. She suddenly longed to tell Tom's mother about Wilfred – about Victor and his child. It was on the tip of her tongue to blurt it all out, but she bit it back. Wilfred's secret must not be revealed to anyone; it could ruin him.

'When Tom comes back he will have to make a home for Violet,' Dorrie went on. 'She is better. She's not drinking so much and she eats a little now. I haven't bothered to get a nurse, she's so much improved. I can tell you, Hester, I'm not having any scandal in this family, so you can just go home and forget our Tom.'

Hester rose. 'We shall go on loving each other. No one can stop us.'

Dorrie rose too. There was an angry flush on her cheeks. 'I've suspected this for a long time. When you think what the Prickards have done for you, Hester! Why, you came from nothing and your uncle gave you a position and money and now you've got the title and that lovely place – well, it's base ingratitude, that's what I say.'

'Your ambitions are not mine,' Hester said, gathering up her furs. 'I only want a little happiness. Is that too much to ask of life?'

They parted stiffly, all the warmth that had grown between them quite gone.

On reaching home, Hester went with Posy and her gover-ness up to the nursery to see Patrick who was in his bath.

'Mama!' he shouted, jumping up and down while Rose tried to dry him. 'Why didn't you take me? Naughty Posy!' he said threateningly. He was a sturdy boy with rosy cheeks and sparkling eyes, and Hester privately thought that he was beginning to prove too much for Rose, his nurse.

'Well, that's an unkind thing to say to Posy when she's brought you chocolate,' she reproved him. 'Miss Peasegood, I think it's time Patrick started lessons with you. What about tomorrow morning?'

'I'm busy tomorrow morning,' Patrick said, hurriedly emerging from his towel. 'Can I start next week, Mama? Please?'

'Tomorrow,' his mother said firmly as she kissed him goodnight. The trouble with Patrick was that he was getting spoilt. In two or three years he would have to go to school, but already she quailed at the thought. The little boy was at his most engaging and, although Wilfred's threat of taking the child from her terrified her, she knew that when the choice had to be made – if it ever had to be made – she would not let the boy go. She was as firmly held to this unnatural marriage as if real steel chains held her.

She slept badly and woke with a jerk. A light was flickering across the ceiling – and it came from outside.

She got out of bed and cautiously peered out of the window which was over the terrace. In the dark, the park stood out as a white mass for there had been another late frost, but the moon was obscured by cloud. She stretched sleepy eyes, trying to focus on the point in the garden where the light had seemed to come from. She waited and presently saw a lantern's flicker and then a man emerging with care, the lantern now obscured by his cape. She saw his silhouette clearly: it was a policeman. Breathing a sigh of relief, she was turning back to her bed when the thought struck her – what was a policeman doing at Stanhope in the early hours of the morning? Who could have sent for him . . . but would he be acting so stealthily if someone had sent for him?

She opened the window at the bottom very carefully and poked her head through. She could now see the east wing of the house. Lights were streaming from its windows and, as she listened holding her breath, she could hear voices and music. So Wilfred was back and had brought his strange friends with him.

She lit a candle and saw that it was two o'clock in the morning. Throwing a Shetland shawl round her shoulders, she made her way across the landing and down one flight of stairs. The east wing jutted out into the garden at the back and now she could plainly see its brilliantly lighted windows. No curtains had been drawn and heads moved to and fro. She stared. Surely there were women present? She could make out elaborately arranged heads with diamonds twinkling in the hair. The sight astounded her, for Wilfred positively disliked women. The double doors, she realized at once, were ajar and that was why she could hear voices and laughter so clearly. A bar of light filtered out and she cautiously edged nearer, shivering a little yet determined to see into the forbidden wing at all costs. With a trembling hand she pushed open one of the doors and stared openmouthed. *Aladdin's Cave* had said rumour, and rumour had not been wrong. All the scents and sounds of the gorgeous east were here behind the double mahogany doors. Vivid wall hangings, brilliant lights and a strange sweet smell rushed at her as she stared.

She was about to take further steps into the corridor when two women came out of a room giggling together. They gaped at her in surprise. But their surprise was nothing compared to hers, when she realized that one of them appeared to have a shorn head and held a golden wig under one arm. And then the truth dawned. They were not women, but boys dressed in women's clothes.

'And what do you think you're doing?' said a voice behind her and a familiar chubby hand came down on her shoulder. With two bottles of champagne under one arm, Wilfred had just returned from a visit to his cellar.

She stared mutely, a rabbit in the power of a stoat.

'Spying, eh?'

'I didn't know you were home,' she said and was annoyed to find that her voice was a terrified thread of sound.

'Yes, I'm home and I've brought a few friends with me. Go back to bed, Hester, and never come here again.' He pushed her unceremoniously through the doors.

'There is a policeman outside,' she said just as the doors were about to shut on her.

Very slowly, they reopened. Wilfred's eyes glittered at her. 'What did you say?'

'I saw a policeman on the terrace.'

'You're lying!'

'No, I'm not. He has a lantern. I saw the light.'

She heard him mutter, 'The fools. They haven't drawn the curtains because of the moon. . . . ' Then he was hurrying down the corridor, forgetting after all to close the doors. She stared her fill. At the boy-women who were still gaping at her, and at the lights and the colour. What an extraordinary place Wilfred had created for himself! She turned towards the boys. 'Go home,' she said harshly. 'Go back to your families and never come here again, no matter how much you are paid.'

By the time she regained her own room she felt exhausted. Creeping into her cold bed, she lay shivering with shock. So that was what went on into the early hours. A party – no, a travesty of a party with boys to take the place of women. Here, under the very roof of her beloved Stanhope with her children asleep in the west wing. She sat up and in the darkness said violently, 'I won't stand for it.'

Wilfred came to her sitting-room at lunchtime. She noticed that his complexion was yellow and that he refused to meet her eyes.

'Look here, Hester,' he blustered, 'I realize you have a fevered imagination, but your story of a *policeman* out on the terrace last night is too much to swallow.'

She could see that he was uneasy. Frightened even. 'I wasn't pretending. I looked out of my window and saw him. I saw his helmet and cape. He held a lantern. Then I saw your uncurtained windows and realized he was trying to see in. People aren't fools, Wilfred, and without doubt the servants have carried tales to the village of your Arabian Nights in the east wing. The *east* wing – how aptly named. And you must know it is against the law to procure boys for your own vicious purposes.'

'You're talking nonsense – it was a fancy-dress party last night. The police have no right to come on private property.'

'Perhaps it's the opium smoking that goes on?' It was a shot in the dark that struck home. He blinked at her, his bluster evaporating.

'What do you mean?'

'You were using drugs last night. I smelled them and of course it all fits in with the Eastern background. Good God, how bored you must be to have recourse to such a way of life!' she said contemptuously. 'I always suspected you never did any real work in Liverpool and that Munro really runs the Line –'

He had recovered himself. Taking a menacing step towards her he said in a low hard voice, 'If you try to make trouble for me, I'll break every bone in your body.'

With an effort she concealed her fear of his twitching hands. 'Wild talk, my dear cousin. What a weakling you are, Wilfred. You've got into appalling company because you are a very rich and idle man. Some of your friends are using you. You'll ruin yourself in no time.'

'You'd like that, wouldn't you?' He gestured wildly. 'All this would be yours then. Let me tell you something: if I suspect trouble, I shall leave England and go and live in

Paris. And of course I shall sell Stanhope and naturally take my son with me. You'll never see him again. Remember that, Hester, before you do anything rash.'

CHAPTER EIGHT

She was shopping in Sewerston on the last day of March when Matty Hoggarth came running out of his office in the square and stood before her, his face full of suppressed excitement.

'Tom's home. Got here two days ago. He's only fairish. His left shoulder's been shot away and he's in pain. But he said I was to let you have this if I saw you.'

She took the envelope in a shaking hand. 'Oh, Matty . . . oh, Matt. . . . '

'Hey, don't cry here!' He looked round frantically, and then guided her down a quiet side street. 'Look, Hester, I'm on your side. The sooner our Tom's free of that woman the better I say.' His face had hardened. 'He's had a raw deal has poor Tom. He's a decent bloke and deserves better. He's told me what he had to put up with long before she went funny. He's never been happy with her, you know.'

'But your mother told me that Violet is improving. . . . '

He was shaking his head vigorously. 'That's only Ma trying to patch over the cracks. Give Vi more than a bottle of gin a day and she'll be over the top again. When she's sober she's still not sane, you know. She thinks the postman is her enemy now and she throws things at him – I can't help being sorry for Ma, new in the neighbourhood and all that.'

Hester dabbed at her eyes. 'It's – just that I'm so thankful he's safe home again. I love him, you know, but I don't want to harm his wife. She's to be pitied. . . . '

'I'm not going to let Tom throw his life away on *her*,'

Matt said sternly. Abruptly, he raised his hat and turned away. She watched him walking with a firm purposeful step back towards his office and smiled tremulously. Matty was so young, so certain about everything. She envied him. Once back in her carriage, she tore open the envelope and devoured Tom's letter. Joy brimmed over and she wept again. He loved her still. Nothing else mattered. The way ahead was dark, but already hope was flowering in her. Looking out of the carriage window it seemed to her that spring had come suddenly. The whole familiar landscape had changed in an hour.

She called at *Braeside* two days later carrying grapes and port for Tom. She saw only Dorrie Hoggarth.

'Tom is confined to bed and the doctor says he mustn't have visitors. Sit down, Hester. When we heard the hospital ship had docked Matty went down to Southampton with a nurse and brought him back here.'

'You must be so thankful to have him home at last.'

'That I am.' Dorrie fussed with the cameo brooch at her throat. 'And of course Violet's beside herself with joy. Can't do enough for him. I never thought she had the makings of a nurse in her!' Dorrie lied with a smile. 'She's proving a real little helper.'

Hester looked at her with misery in her eyes. 'I . . . I don't suppose I could see him . . . just for a minute? Just from the door?'

'Out of the question, my dear. Doctor's orders. He's very weak you know, and can only see the family. But I'll tell him you called. Thank you very much for these. How are your husband and little boy – Patrick, isn't it? He must be growing up fast,' Dorrie rattled on relentlessly.

Hester shook her head dumbly, holding back tears with difficulty as she stumbled to the door. He was so near. Only upstairs. And it was four long years since they had seen each other. She turned at the foot of the stairs. 'Please, please,

31   481

Mrs Hoggarth, let me see him for just a minute.'

But she had humiliated herself in vain. 'Go away, Hester, and stop being a nuisance,' Dorrie said angrily. 'This may be the way you carry on in your station in life but it's not ours! Tom is Violet's husband. Leave him alone and go back to your own.'

When the front door shut behind her unwanted visitor, she gathered her skirts and mounted the stairs to the best spare room where she had settled her wounded son. He was lying on his back in the big bed, his bandaged side supported by rubber pillows. Although he was still tanned, there was a drawn look on his face. A little frown was the only sign he gave of being in pain. A thin sunlight filled the pleasant room and flowers stood beside the bed.

'Go down, Nurse, and get your tea,' Dorrie said briskly to the white-starched figure who was taking her patient's temperature. 'Anything you want, dear?' she asked, her voice soft with love. 'Just tell Mother and she'll get it.'

Tom valiantly concealed his impatience. If only she wouldn't treat him like a child! Raising heavy eyes to her face, he tried out a grateful smile. 'Nothing, Ma. You're doing too much for me as it is.'

She fussed over him fondly, unconsciously hurting him as she tucked in bedclothes. 'It's a grand day and we'll soon have you outside for an airing.'

In a baby carriage, he told himself wryly. 'I thought I heard a visitor. Who called?'

'Just Mrs Weston. She's a wonderful old lady, you know.'

'I thought. . . . ' A spasm of coughing seized him and she hovered over him anxiously. That would be his left lung. Pray God it would heal. They had taken a huge piece of metal out of it. How bloodless he looked. Much older, too.

'Eh, Tom love, I hate to see you like this!' she exclaimed, helplessly. 'I'm really vexed this should have happened when you were doing so well too. Yon's a stupid war. It should have finished at Christmas.' She went towards the door.

482

'Now I'm going to send Violet to sit with you a while.'

'No, for God's sake, Ma, don't. I can't take it!'

'No, Tom. . . .'

'Oh, stop pretending!' he shouted feebly. 'Can't you see what the rest of us see? She's not sane. She thinks someone's after her all the time. First the postman, now you. . . .'

'Me? Why, Violet has no better friend than me in the whole world!'

'Don't you notice how she watches you? Like a cat with a mouse. She comes in to tell me how cruel you are to her — you're stalking her, she says. The only person she seems to care about is Matt. God knows why, for he can't stand her. She's queer about men though and it wouldn't surprise me if she tried to get in his bed.'

'Don't talk so coarse,' Dorrie said indignantly. 'Matty indeed. All he can suggest is that we put her in the county asylum.'

'He's right.' Tom shifted wearily. 'She's unpredictable. But you watch. When Matt comes home she gets as excited as a two year old.'

That evening, Dorrie watched carefully and saw that Tom was right. As soon as Matt came home, Violet came running downstairs. She heard their voices, low and urgent. Opening the door suddenly, she looked narrowly at them. Startled, they stared at her. 'Why, hullo, Ma,' Matt said quickly. 'Run upstairs like a good girl, Vi. I'll see you later.'

That night Dorrie couldn't sleep. Her brain seemed on fire. Was ever a woman so beset with difficulties as she was? If it wasn't one thing, it was another. What was Violet doing overhead? she wondered irritably. She seemed to be moving about restlessly. Bless me, if she isn't singing now! Dorrie thought indignantly. She struck a match and peered at Willy's silver watch hanging from the bedpost. One o'clock. Well, if that racket continued, she would go up and be firm with her.

But presently silence fell on the house and she composed herself for sleep once more. Her mind roamed back over the years and she was drifting into unconsciousness when a new sound made her sit up, her heart beating hard. Someone was carefully opening her door. 'Yes, who is it? Is that you, Nurse?'

Out of the darkness a pair of thin, steel-strong hands fastened round her throat. She managed one loud shriek before she lost her breath and clawed and choked at her assailant in vain. She knew now who it was, for a stale smell of gin poured in a hot stream into her face, as her daughter-in-law tried to choke the life out of her.

'Dearest Hester, it's been far too long since I saw you!' Mrs Trumper said, holding her former pupil in front of her. What deep rings there were beneath those turquoise eyes! And little lines that hadn't existed before now showed at the corners of her mouth. 'My dear child, you look in need of a rest. You've been playing too hard.'

'Playing!' Hester laughed. 'Don't you realize what a sober matron I've become?' She looked round the pretty little sitting room of the small house in Surrey where Alice Trumper lived so happily with her policeman. 'How pretty this is! Oh, I'm so glad I came. When you wired that you could have me at such short notice, I just packed a bag and set off. Oh, I've needed your advice so much, dear Alice. That's why I haven't brought Julie. . . . '

'Thank goodness for that! Can you see Julie happily occupying the box-room?' She poured tea into rose-decorated cups. 'Is that chair comfortable? Have another cushion.'

'It's perfect. Everything's perfect. How clever it was of me to think of coming!'

'Why did you, Hester?' Mrs Trumper asked in her quiet voice.

Hester put down her cup and inspected her hands. With her head down she said, 'If you knew – if only you knew how unhappy I've been. Even now I can hardly speak of it.' She stopped, looking up suddenly. 'The Inspector won't be home yet, will he? Of course I look forward to meeting him again, but there's so much I have to say to you alone first. Do you realize you are the only person in the world I can talk to?'

'Can't you talk to Wilfred? He is your husband after all.' Mrs Trumper's eyes were very direct.

'Least of all Wilfred. I know you've wondered why I married him. Well, I can tell you now.' And in that quiet sitting-room Hester finally found the courage to pour out the story of the last few years. She omitted nothing, not even her affair with Amroth. When she came to her love for Tom Hoggarth, her voice broke and she lifted the cup of cooling tea to her lips. 'So now you know,' she said wearily.

Mrs Trumper had remained completely silent. Now she said gently, 'Dearest child, did you think I hadn't puzzled over your marriage many times? But as it was obviously due to something you could not confide in me, I didn't question you. I knew that something very strange had happened, especially when your baby was born seven months later. I have known about Wilfred for years, even before the day I caught him with the pantry boy at Stanhope. So you see I wondered. From what you tell me, Wilfred has now thrown discretion to the wind. Decadence is very fashionable in some quarters still, you know. Wilfred was always weak, but I think his dislike of women stems from the way he was brought up by a mother who dominated him. Your uncle tried so hard to "make a man of him" but without success. He liked being protected by his mother. Now it seems he has taken to drugs as well and this explains the change in him. He was always an amiable youth,' she added. 'Come, I want to show you my garden. When you're rested you shall tell the other half of your story.'

In her bedroom that night, she talked things over with her husband while she brushed her hair. The inspector was sitting up in bed in a green and white nightshirt with a book in his hands and glasses on the tip of his nose. He hardly seemed to be listening, but Alice knew that this was an old habit of his. Under his indifferent air, his brain was alert. He showed this by one or two pertinent questions and, when at last she turned the light out and lay beside him, she felt comforted. Leonard would know what to do.

Hester spent four days at the Trumpers. From here, she wrote a long letter to Tom and hoped it wouldn't be kept from him by his mother. In it she told him she had come to the end – she could no longer go on living at Stanhope. She intended looking for another house in the neighbourhood, but must take care not to let Wilfred know her plans because he had threatened to take Patrick from her.

When the letter had gone, she felt a deep relief; for she had seen in black and white the plans she had vaguely framed for her future. For the rest of her time in Surrey, she enjoyed herself in the company of Alice Trumper, going up to town to the theatre and calling on Cissie Bland whom she hadn't seen for two years. It was remarkable how her difficulties seemed to shrink to nothing in four days. Perhaps her courage began to ebb back then.

'You look so rested. I'm delighted,' Alice told her, seeing her off at the station. 'Come again before too long, Hester.'

'I feel renewed,' Hester told her tranquilly. 'I think I can face anything now.' Only now was she realizing what a strain the last four years had been. Four years when she had been unable to confide in a living soul.

Little did she guess that she had been the subject of several vital conversations between the Trumpers.

'I've been in touch with the North Riding police,' her husband told Alice as they dressed for the theatre on the second night of Hester's visit. 'Superintendent Beeton is an old colleague of mine. It was one of his men she saw on the terrace. He says they had heard rumours and now have confirmed everything.' He held out his cuffs for her to fasten the gold links. 'So you've no need to worry any more, my love.'

'So what will happen?'

'They'll probably issue a warrant for his arrest.'

She covered her eyes. 'I've hated doing this, but I can't see her life ruined. My poor Hester! Her beauty and money have not saved her from many bitter experiences. This time Fate needs a little push.'

As she alighted at Sewerston junction and Rickaby's face welcomed her, Hester waited for the old fear and dread to flood back. She had come home to take up the burden of her life again. But her courage held, and so did her determination not to allow Wilfred to bully her into submission.

She went straight up to the west wing, to the sane atmosphere of the nursery. Patrick scrambled on to her lap and Posy sat at her feet while they both tore open the parcels she had brought them from London: a pair of silver doves revolving on an ebony musical box for Posy and a scarlet fire engine for Patrick. Even Rose had a present of a dress length to make her a best outfit for summer, and there was a book for Mary Peasegood. When she at last went to her own room she found that Julie had unpacked her trunk and was carrying away her outdoor clothes to be brushed and pressed.

'Wiston has brought you a glass of madeira and a sandwich, milady. Your letters are on the table.'

Hester sat down in her favourite chair before the bright fire and looked with pleasure round her pretty room. It was no use pretending: she loved comfort like a cat, she told herself ruefully as she turned over the letters on the salver. She saw at once there was one from Tom. He was still only able to write with difficulty and his erratic scrawl was hard to decipher; but she rapidly got the gist of it as she read with horror of Violet's manic attack on Mrs Hoggarth. She had, it seemed, nearly succeeded in throttling Tom's mother, but Matty had heard her screams and arrived only just in time.

We cannot think where she has been getting the gin, Tom wrote. *The shrubbery beneath her window is full of empty bottles. We have tried to get her into that nice Home in Harrogate but there are no vacancies at present. I won't let her go to the County Asylum which is a terrifying and hopeless place. Dearest girl, my mother has told me she behaved badly to you when you called. Come soon. She will welcome you, I promise, and I am thirsty for a sight of you after all these years. I'm not giving up hope nor must you.*

She read it again. *We can't think where she has been getting the gin.* Now what had Matty said when she met him last in Sewerston? *Give Vi more than a bottle of gin a day and she'll be over the top . . . I'm not going to let Tom throw his life away on her.*

So it had been Matty. He had secretly carried extra bottles of the gin she craved to his sister-in-law, in the hope of destroying her. It hadn't worked that way. Instead Violet had nearly destroyed his mother. Hester shuddered. How close to disaster the Hoggarths had been! But it was a measure of their desperation that even quiet Matty had been driven to take steps to get rid of Violet.

She got up, letting the other letters fall to the floor. She could think of nothing but her meeting with Tom tomorrow. She knew she wouldn't be able to sleep tonight for excited happiness. At last . . . after all these years . . . they were going to see each other again!

Dorrie Hoggarth came to the door herself. Kissing Hester, she humbly said, 'Will you forgive me?'

Hester took her hand, her eyes on the purple marks still showing on Dorrie's throat. 'Of course. I'm so sorry about everything.'

Dorrie nodded. She couldn't speak of it yet. Taking her visitor upstairs she pointed to a door. 'In there. He's waiting.'

Now that the moment had come, the moment she had longed for for years, her feet felt leaden. Instead of joy, dread filled her. Would they be strangers? Would they be so strange to each other? . . .

'Hes! Is that you, Hes?'

'Yes!' She opened the door wide and they looked at each other with strained eyes. With a swift gesture she snatched off her huge hat and threw it on a chair. Then she ran to the bed and pressed her face to his, their hands clasped tightly. . . . 'Oh, Tom, oh, darling. . . .'

He was equally incoherent. 'Hes, is it really you at last?'

She lay on the bed beside him, holding him tenderly. She could feel their hearts racing against each other. He held her close to him with his good arm. Neither spoke now, for they were savouring a moment neither had thought would ever come.

'I'm never going to let you go again,' he whispered.

'Nor I you. We can't . . . we can't . . . it would be too cruel!'

'You must leave him, Hes. For God's sake, leave him and come away with me. I shall always have the burden of Violet because I shall never be able to get my freedom while she lives. But you can get free of him and you must. The army won't want me back. I'm finished as far as that's concerned. You'll be taking on someone with nothing to offer – not even a whole body. . . .'

'Stop.' She kissed him. 'I would take you if you only had half a body. You can't get rid of me now, I warn you! Those letters we wrote each other – those four long years – they've brought us together in such a strange way. I know you better now than I did. Don't you feel that?'

He nodded, smiling into her eyes. 'Yes, I do. They made up for all the lost years when we married the wrong people.'

'There's only Patrick. Wilfred insists I can't have him.' She sat up, her face troubled, but he pulled her down again.

'I'll find a way once I'm fit. We'll run away and take the children with us. You won't have to give up Patrick. I promise you that.'

She sighed happily, believing him utterly.

489

That fellow was not going to destroy Hes, Tom told himself as he held her close, not if he had any say in the matter. And now he had.

'He's due home today,' she said. 'He usually comes on Fridays.'

'Don't let him suspect anything,' Tom warned her. 'I know his sort. He'll retaliate in the most spiteful way he can think of. So don't give him the chance, Hes. Promise me you won't?'

'I promise.' Sitting up, she looked for her hat. 'I hate leaving you but I must go home. I've kept Rickaby waiting long enough.' They exchanged a last lingering kiss. 'Some day,' she whispered and he whispered back, 'Some day soon.'

To her surprise Wilfred had already arrived, Wiston informed her as he opened the door. 'Sir Wilfred has to go abroad. I believe he is catching the evening boat from Hull. Shall I serve lunch, my lady?'

'No, wait. I want to see Sir Wilfred first. Is he in the east wing?'

'Yes, my lady. Shall I inform him you are home?'

'No. I shall go there myself.'

Wiston stared after her. Never to his knowledge had her ladyship gone into the east wing.

She went through the huge double doors and called out. 'Wilfred, I want to see you. Where are you?'

She heard a movement and turned into a room to the left of the passage: he was on his knees at the grate burning papers. He looked up sharply. 'Well, Hester, so you've achieved your ambition at last,' he said jeeringly.

She stared at him, her heart missing a beat. 'What do you mean?'

He got off his knees, dusting them fastidiously. Through an open door to the right she could see his man bundling clothes into open trunks. 'Well, haven't you always longed to see my private apartments? You nearly succeeded the other night – remember? Now, look your fill. Don't let me stop you,' and he bowed mockingly. 'After today I shall have no need of them.'

'Where are you going, Wilfred? And why so hurriedly?'

'I'm going to Holland tonight and then to France. I shan't be coming back.'

She stared at him uncomprehendingly.

'Don't look so innocently amazed, Hester. This is your doing – as if I didn't know that!'

'I have no idea what you mean! Are you leaving because of something I've done? For some special reason?'

'A very special reason.' He kicked the dying embers in the grate. 'There's a warrant out for my arrest.'

The colour drained from her face. 'For God's sake, why?'

'Very well done, m'dear,' he said approvingly. 'You're becoming quite an actress.' Suddenly he had grasped her wrist and was pulling her towards him. 'You've been away, haven't you, to the Trumpers? Well, your policeman friend hasn't let the grass grow under his feet. You told them about me, didn't you? So Mr Interfering Trumper has set his heavy-footed friends on to me. But they're not going to get the chance – they're not going to put a finger on me. I've known what might happen – look what happened to poor Oscar – and I've had my plans made for a long time.' He released her and shouted through the door. 'Dixon, haven't you finished yet, man? Get a move on, for God's sake.' Turning back to Hester he went on in a normal voice: 'I'm not sorry to shake the dust of this country off my feet. I shall enjoy living in France – a far more civilized country, my dear Hester. I intend selling this place and buying a chateau near Paris. The boy will grow up bilingual.'

She clutched the back of a chair. 'You're not taking Patrick with you. I won't allow it. He's my son. . . .'

'*No*. He is my son. Remember? We've had this out before. But of course you must join us in France! I shall look forward to seeing you as the chatelaine of my new home. Really, you have quite a talent for housekeeping. . . .'

She made for the door. 'Patrick isn't going with you! Nor am I.' In one swift movement he reached her and turned her back into the room. She saw the man, Dixon, look up with remote curiosity. 'Let go of me, Wilfred!' She struggled to control her panic.

Through his teeth he said, 'You will remain here. Rose has my instructions to pack the boy's clothes and prepare herself for a journey tonight. She thinks you are coming with us – funny, isn't it how people will insist on thinking us an ideal couple?' He grinned and Hester, looking into his eyes for the first time, saw the stranger who now lived there. She shivered.

'Patrick will not be going with you, Wilfred. If you take the boy out of this house, I shall inform the police and all ports will be closed to you. Yes, I know all about what's happened,' she lied. 'The police have agreed to let you get away. But one word from me that you are taking the child with you and they will be waiting at Hull – or Newhaven – at all the ports. You see, Inspector Trumper told me exactly what I should do.' Now, she thought, now he will kill me. Leave me locked up in this horrible room and go free himself. I have burned my boats now. Keeping her eyes level with his, she waited.

For a moment he faltered. She saw his mouth open a little. Then he whirled round and shouting, 'Bring the stuff down, Dixon,' he snatched up the Gladstone bag that had been his father's and pushed her away from the door. 'You bitch. I'm well rid of you. I hope to God I never set eyes on you again.'

'Hurry, Wilfred,' she goaded him. 'There's not much time. Sell Stanhope by all means. I have no intention of staying here any longer. I'm going away too.'

He paused, turned back slowly, his blazing eyes full of hatred. 'With one of your lovers, I suppose? You think I haven't known of your little adventures, don't you? You'll never find happiness, Hester, however hard you try. You're legally tied to me and I shall enjoy never letting you go. I'd say it was a small price to pay for all my father gave you, wouldn't you?' The door slammed and she heard his footsteps going down the stairs.

She sank to the ground and kept very still, her hands tightly clasped in front of her mouth. A huge silence seemed to fill the room and press down on her. Presently she heard the sound of the carriage being turned on the gravelled drive before the house. Then silence again.

It was over. He was gone. Stanhope would not see him again.

Stiffly, as if she were suddenly stricken by old age, she got up and stumbled to the window. From it she could see the rose garden, bare now in April, and the long vista to the lake. She stared out, the scene blurring before her overflowing eyes. *A small price to pay,* he had said.

CHAPTER NINE

Tom took out Hester's note from under the pillow and said tersely, 'Shut the door, Ma, I've something to tell you.'

She came over and sat on the chair beside the bed. 'What is it, love?' she asked anxiously, noting the spots of colour on his cheekbones.

'I got this from Hester this morning. Her husband has left England for good. I have told you his strange nature, so you will understand why he has had to leave. The threat of prosecution is hanging over him.'

Dorrie listened in silence, her worn hand fingering the purple bruises on her throat. If Tom had looked up, he would have seen the naked misery in her eyes. He would be going away again. With her – with Hester Prickard and her children. For a moment or two, jealous possessiveness gripped her and she had difficulty in keeping back hasty words. Then she looked at her son's face and her anger died. It was only right that Tom should have some happiness at last. He had done his best by that poor creature upstairs; but Hester was the only woman who could bring him happiness – had been the only woman really throughout these bitter years. They had both been young and blind and had made terrible mistakes. Perhaps now – with a little courage – this could be put right.

'We're going away, Ma, as soon as I'm fit.' He thought he saw her wince and added quickly, 'I'm sorry if this hurts you. Hester can only be my common law wife because we're both tied to other people. I hope you'll understand, Ma.'

494

'Yes, love, I do,' Dorrie assured him quietly. 'Where will you go?'

He was surprised at her brisk acquiescence when he had braced himself for reproaches. 'As far away from here as possible; to another country. Australia or America — somewhere we can make a fresh start. But I don't want to leave Violet here being a burden to you and Matt. There must be another mental home in Yorkshire where she will be well looked after. We've got to face the fact that she's never going to get better. The doctor told me this last week after her attack on you. The gin seems to have altered her brain. It's eating her away but she can't do without it — my God, what a situation for any human being! And there's one thing you must know, Ma. Violet had been unfaithful to me many times before she became an alcoholic. Our marriage was over a long time ago and I never believed that the last child was mine.'

'I guessed that, Tom. I can see how the gin is slowly killing her and there's nowt to do but wait.' A long sigh filled her, her eyes never leaving his face. It was a pity, she told herself, that she loved this elder son of hers so much more than the younger, for he was going to tear the heart out of her time and again. He had already spent most of his life away from her in outlandish places and now he was leaving her again. For good perhaps this time. She could still remember the anguish she had felt all those years ago, when he had come in late to tea and blurted out that he had joined the army. That had been because of Hester too. Perhaps the anguish she felt now wasn't quite so keen because she was getting old, and she had learned by now that life was full of partings. She said this aloud and he grasped her hand.

'Mother, you aren't old — only fifty-three!'

She smiled, shaking her head. 'Tell me this, Tom, and tell me truly: will I ever see you again when you go away this time?'

He nodded. 'I promise I will come back as often as possible.

It will be just as if I'm posted abroad in the army.'

'And you'll live on her money?'

He flushed, moving restlessly in the bed. 'I've thought of all that. You know how I shall hate it, but it would be folly to let the Prickard money stand between our happiness now. When you've been through what Hester and I have been through, money is the least of our troubles. Oh, yes, I'm still stiff with pride,' he added ruefully, 'for no man likes to take so much from a woman and I have only my army pension. But I shall find work to do – any sort of work that's open to me, and there's no room for pride in real love, Ma. I shall have to live with the soreness of not being the provider all my life; but we're not going to let the best years of our lives slip away because she's got too much money.'

She could see the new serenity in his face and she pressed his hand lovingly. 'God bless you, Tom, you deserve your happiness.'

She went thoughtfully downstairs to her drawing-room, the room that was her pride and joy in the house she had built with Willy's money. It was so stuffed with furniture and bric-à-brac that no one was allowed to dust it but herself. Going to a drawer she took out a clean checked duster, shook it open and began her daily task with her usual thoroughness. All the time she worked, her brain was in a ferment. She was frightened of Violet – no use denying it – and she avoided going to see her on her own. But she also felt pity – the pity one felt for a sick animal. If Violet was a cat or dog lying up there, they would call in a vet to put her out of her misery. So wasn't it time that someone had the courage to do for Violet what they would do for a sick animal? It would mean that Tom would be freed of the intolerable burden of worry that he had carried for so long.

'And I'm the one who must do it,' Dorrie said aloud, carefully dusting the brass elephant Tom had brought home from India.

Her mind seemed to be working like clockwork as she dusted the overmantel, brushing the dark green velvet with a small brush. It was really very simple. She would dispose (for that was a better word than *kill*) of Violet in such a way that it would look like suicide.

She shook the duster out of the window, folded it neatly and put it away in its drawer again. Then she stood in the centre of the room, her eyes far away, her brain busy. What she proposed doing would be her gift to Tom, her adored son whose suffering was her suffering. It would be a mortal sin, but the burden of this on her conscience would be a small price to pay for his happiness. He would be free. A smile lit up her face and she turned and left the room, walking with a firm step up the two flights to Violet's room.

The servants had already cleaned it for the day. A bright fire was gathering strength in the steel grate. Pretty plants and ornaments had once adorned the shelves and tables, but they had all had to be removed – those that Violet had not already smashed in a drunken frenzy. The fire was covered by a heavy guard, the windows were locked.

We're protecting her as if she were the most precious object in the house, Dorrie thought, as she made her way over to the chair by the fire where Tom's wife sat inert and silent. Picking up a silver-backed brush she said timidly, 'Let me tidy you, Vi.'

Violet's eyelids lifted with an effort and she stared dully at her mother-in-law. Her once-pretty face was gaunt and grey; black smudges surrounded her eyes and her mouth was agape. With a tired gesture she pushed the brush away.

'Now come, Vi. . . .'

'Leave me alone, dam' you!' Violet suddenly hit out viciously with her hand.

Dorrie shrank back, all her old fear rushing into her. Violet's hand had hit her painfully on the nose and she hastily retreated, vividly remembering the feel of those prehensile fingers closing round her throat. Those same fingers were now shakily pouring out more gin from the green bottle she kept beside her.

Dorrie watched helplessly. What was the use of trying to

cut down the gin as the doctor instructed when Violet became demented and flew into a dangerous rage without it? The servants had strict instructions not to bring her more than one bottle a day and in the evenings she now got a strong sleeping draught, so that the scene of the other night would not be repeated. But giving her an overdose was not the answer; it would be too easily found out.

There were two windows to this room: one looked down on the garden and the other was placed on the side of the house overlooking the shrubbery. The room was on the second floor, and from the main window one could see the moors that lay north of Sewerston. There was also a glimpse of the bay full of dark tempestuous water. The April sun had only been fitful, and now a swift shower of hailstones was buffeting the window panes. Pulling aside the heavy lace curtains, Dorrie unlocked the main window and cautiously opened it. It moved easily and cold air rushed in, blowing out the curtains.

'Whad y'doin'?' Violet's slurred voice rose peevishly from the chair. 'I'm bloody cold. Shu'it, ol' woman.'

'Just letting a little air in,' Dorrie said over her shoulder. 'It's very stuffy in here.' She closed it and moved to the side window. The side window would be best. This was more difficult to raise, but when she did, she found that the wind was much less powerful on the side of the house. It hardly ruffled the curtains at all. The outside sill – like all the sills on *Braeside* – were of best Westmorland slate. Putting her hands outside the window, Dorrie felt how straight and smooth the slate sill was. A bottle of gin would sit here snugly without toppling over. This afternoon, after lunch, she would creep up here and put Violet's bottle of gin outside on this ledge, leaving the lace curtain drawn back so that she could see it from her chair. . . . Violet ate very little of the food that was brought up to her but she drank deeply from her bottle at this time and usually fell into a heavy sleep on her bed. She would wake and look for the bottle, and see it outside the window that faced the bed. She would lurch over to get it; go

498

further and further through the open window and fall head-long into the shrubbery far below, where in the past so many empty bottles had been hurled. It would be quick and merci-ful, Dorrie thought as she closed the window and smoothed her hair.

She went quickly down to her bedroom, closing the door behind her. Her fast-beating heart was making her dizzy. Taking up a clean linen handkerchief she sprinkled eau de cologne on it with a trembling hand. She pressed it to her lips and nose, waiting for composure to return to her.

I'm going to do it. This very day. It will be for Tom.

That afternoon, Hester had herself driven over in the carriage.

Wearing a brown velvet dress under her long sable coat she clutched a sable muff to her body. From under her huge brown velvet hat, her shadowed face looked pale and drawn and she came across the room to him saying his name like a talisman. 'Tom ... oh, Tom.... '

As he caressed her, he could feel how her body trembled. His concerned eyes could see how ill she looked. 'Take off your hat, dearest,' he ordered gently and she obeyed, pulling out the pearl-headed pins with clumsy fingers. Then she pressed her face close to his and they remained like this, quite silent, for a minute or so.

'He's never going to free me,' she said in a low voice. 'He says he enjoys having me tied to him . . that it's a small price to p-pay. . . . ' Tears shook her and she was incoherent.

He twisted round to look down into her face. 'I could kill him,' he said with restrained violence, feeling himself utterly helpless.

'Oh, Tom, what fools we were! What utter fools! We could have been happy years ago. . . . ' Her tears were hot against his skin and he kissed her comfortingly.

'Life is seldom cut and dried, Hes, or only for a few lucky ones. We have come slowly and late to this love, but it will be all the better for that, you will see. And we are still young, darling.'

She nodded, drying her tears. She could not tell him this yet, but she was dreading leaving Stanhope and the kindly people who served her, and setting out to make a new home in a land that was strange to her. But they would be together, she reminded herself as she put her handkerchief away, and some day they would come back to Stanhope and live there peacefully if she could buy it from Wilfred.

He watched her expressive face, shrewdly guessing at her thoughts. 'Are you strong enough to come away with me?' he asked her bluntly. 'There will be talk, Hes. We are married to other people and there are few who know the true nature of our marriages. You'll lose many friends, perhaps never see some of them again, and you'll lose your social position as Wilfred Prickard's wife.'

She held up her head proudly. 'You should know that I do not give a fig for that! As long as I have you and Patrick I shall be happy. And, Tom, there is Posy, Belle Collins's daughter. I have adopted her, you know.'

'I promise you they will be like my own, darling. Some day, we shall have children too.'

'Yes,' she said softly. 'I want a large family.'

'I've been wondering where we should go,' he went on. 'Lying here thinking it over I believe we should go to Australia – or one of the colonies.'

'I've been thinking too. Tom, would you hate to go to America – to New England? You see, Wilfred will not be taking an active part in the business any longer, simply drawing an income from it. The running of the Prickard Line will now be my concern with the help of Mr Munro. I don't know if I can do it – at least not without your advice.' He returned her look in silence. For the first time he was being made aware of the great wealth and power this girl possessed. Hester could go to America and live the same sort of life she had been used to in England. One of her own boats would carry her there. She could place him in her shipping office in

Boston – fear jerked his heart, as he remembered how powerful she was now that Wilfred had gone for good.

'Oh, you'll love New England! In the fall the woods look on fire . . . the trees are like flames running through them. There is a crispness in the air that is so different from England. . . .' She stopped. 'Tom?'

With an effort he smiled at her. 'Yes, it's a splendid idea,' he agreed. 'I like the idea of working in the shipping office and I'll do my best to master the job. I'm only a plain soldier, Hes, so don't expect wonderful things of me.'

'Rubbish!' She bent and kissed him lingeringly. 'You'll be splendid I know.' Their lips met in a long kiss for she was no fool – she had guessed what his pride was having to swallow in order that they might be together. She didn't deserve him, she told herself humbly, and she would spend the rest of her life giving thanks to him for his love.

He held her close, his eyes serious. He had always been his own man and now he would have to learn to be her man. There was a certain bitterness in his happiness but not for worlds would he let her guess his feelings.

There was silence between them and into this silence fell a sharp sound – a door banging overhead. Feet came running down the stairs and the door suddenly flew open to admit Dorrie Hoggarth. Her face was ashen. 'Tom, – Tom, she's dead! Vi's dead!' She put out a hand blindly and Hester ran forward and guided her to a chair. They waited while she took one sobbing breath after another.

'Tom, she's dead – Vi's dead,' she repeated over and over again.

'Are you sure? She could be sleeping deeply.' Tom reached over and patted Dorrie's arm.

'She's dead, I tell you!' she shouted suddenly, 'and I'm glad . . . thankful. . . .' Burying her face in her hands, she wept convulsively.

'Where's Nurse?' Tom demanded. 'Fetch her, Hester, and go with her and see for yourselves. . . .'

'No!' Dorrie said. She got to her feet. 'I'll take you, Hester, come with me.'

Violet was still sitting in her chair before the fire. Beside her on a silver tray was her luncheon, still untouched and cold now. The dark green bottle of gin was two-thirds empty and the glass was on the hearthrug where it had fallen from Violet's lifeless hand. Her eyes were open, her lips drawn back across her teeth as if life had left her in a spasm of agony. For she was dead, Hester realized as she lifted one cold hand and felt for a non-existent pulse.

Dorrie still stood by the door, her shoulders drooping. 'She's dead, isn't she? I knew she was as soon as I came in. She wasn't snoring, you see. I meant to kill her,' she said in a dry little voice. 'I came up here not ten minutes ago to put her gin bottle on that ledge outside this window. I thought – I hoped she'd lean out – fall to her death. That's what I wanted, you see. Then he wouldn't be worried any more, my poor Tom.' Her voice trembled to a stop.

Hester approached her impulsively, putting an arm round the ample shoulders. 'You must forget that,' she said in a firm voice. 'Don't tell Tom – don't tell anyone. Promise me? You had come to the end of your tether and I'm not surprised. I think we'll find that Violet's heart just gave out at last. She ate nothing and drank only that poison. You see how thin she had become? It was inevitable and you haven't anything to reproach yourself with.' Leading her to the door, Hester added, 'You're free now as well as Tom. When we go to America and settle in New England I want you to come out to us for at least six months. Matt has the servants to look after him, so don't say it's impossible. Will you come, Mrs Hoggarth, even though we may not be married for some time?'

Tears poured down Dorrie's cheeks. She nodded, unable to speak. She wasn't crying for Violet – at least she didn't think she was – she was crying for a wasted life, and because she knew that hers would be the only tears shed.

Hester stood beside her, her face pale and thoughtful as she remembered all that Tom's wife had rejected in life. A little shiver went through her, a little shiver of thankfulness that she was being given this chance to make a new life for them both.

'Let's go down to Tom,' she said and led the way.

EPILOGUE

One Friday evening in July 1900, the S.S. *Golden Jubilee* edged out of the Mersey, giving three triumphant hoots on her siren as she did so. In nine days she would dock in New York, for she was still one of the fastest boats on the Atlantic route.

'We've started!' Posy cried, her face ecstatic. 'Oh, Aunt Hester, please let us go up and wave goodbye to England!'

They were in the owner's stateroom, part of the suite always occupied by Joseph Prickard on his many crossings to America. Hester had attended many parties in this pleasant room and she was looking round it now with reminiscent pleasure. There was the silver vase given him by a delighted passenger on the maiden voyage – and there was the burn on that oak table which one of Uncle Joe's cigars had made – how he had cursed!

'Is that my grandfather?' Patrick asked, gazing up at the portrait of Joe that occupied a third of one wall. 'He looks cross.'

'He was never as stern as that in real life,' Hester said softly.'He was the kindest man on earth. I loved him dearly.'

'Please, please, dear Aunt Hester, can we go up?' Posy pleaded. 'Uncle Tom is up there, I know, and I'll hold Patrick's hand and not let him fall overboard. . . . '

'Mama would tell the captain to stop at once,' Patrick said serenely. 'It's her boat, you know.'

'The captain would be very cross with us both!' Hester

505

assured him. 'He would say, "Stopping for a little boy? Not likely!" '

Patrick looked anxious. 'But, Mama, you would *make* him stop, wouldn't you? Promise?'

'Just take care not to fall overboard,' his mother told him. 'Hold his hand, Posy, and find Uncle Tom. I'll be up in a few minutes when I've opened these telegrams.'

Tom Hoggarth was leaning on the rails, watching the widening gap of green water opening out between them and England. He turned to the children as they joined him. 'Are we going to wave goodbye?' for Posy was carefully unfolding a diminutive lawn handkerchief.

'Have you got one, Uncle Tom?' she asked anxiously.

'*I* haven't a handkerchief!' Patrick shouted in frustration. '*I* want to wave too – I know, I'll wave my hat!' He tugged the large panama hat that was held by elastic under his chin and waved it gleefully above his head. The next moment the hat was spinning out across the water. They all stared after it in consternation.

'Oh, Patrick, your best sailor hat!' Posy wailed. 'What will Aunt Hester say?'

'Better the hat than the boy,' said a laughing voice behind them. Hester had taken the precaution to tie a chiffon veil round her own hat, for there was a stiff sea breeze. She wore her favourite turquoise blue and Tom thought he had never seen her look so beautiful or so happy. Reaching for her hand, he drew her close.

'Darling, I'm a duffer at looking after the children,' he said in her ear. 'I'm still shy with them. You'll have to teach me.'

'When we get to the farm,' she said and stopped, so filled with happiness that she was speechless. Their farm. Their new home waiting for them in Vermont. A long rambling house of painted board. A porch covered in red Virginia creeper. Post and rail fencing to keep the livestock out of the garden and a river with a creek. 'We shall be happy there,' she said with conviction. There they could begin to live at last. All the pain and bitterness would be in the past.

'And no regrets?' he asked quizzically.

'No regrets.' Her eyes met his with an expression of trust and content he found moving. Once settled in Vermont she would take on his name. Mrs Thomas Hoggarth. It had a good solid sound to it. Their union would not be legal but, until the day came when they could make it so, she was content to be his common law wife. 'I shall have to return here every year or so,' she reminded him. 'Munro says I must continue to take an interest in the English side of the business now that Wilfred has left it. And you've got to learn all about the American side, don't forget.'

'It scares me,' he admitted. 'I've never been anything but a soldier. The business world is a mystery to me. Learning the shipping business will be something of a challenge. But I mean to do my best. I owe you so much, Hes.'

She put her hand on his wrist. 'Don't. Never say that. You see, I know my uncle would be pleased if he knew that I was sharing his business with a local boy – and also that I was happy. He always wanted me to be happy. You are the sort of man he would admire – a man of action who has done well in his career. Besides, what use is his money if we can't use it together for the family?'

'And you're not too upset that Wilfred has sold Stanhope? I know how much you loved it.'

Her eyes sparkled suddenly. Then she lowered her lashes and said demurely, 'As a matter of fact – I'm delighted he sold out.'

He tried to see her expression behind the veil. 'Hes! You loved the place!'

'Yes, darling, I did. I *do*. Tom, would you be angry. . . .' She stopped, watching him carefully.

'You didn't put in a bid for Stanhope?' he demanded in disbelief.

'Worse than that.' She took a telegraph form out of her pocket. 'I made an offer for the whole place and the furniture.

The agents could not very well refuse. Look: this tells us that Stanhope is still in the family. *Our* family.'

When they heard their laughter, the children came running to join them.

'Look!' Hester cried, pointing to the east. 'The last of England!'